The Completion

Chris Marsh

BACKWATER PUBLISHING

BackWater Publishing
4 Brynford Close, Woking, Surrey GU21 4DW

Illustrations by Felicity Marsh.

ISBN 0 9525289 0 8

British Library Cataloguing-in-Publication Data.
A catalogue record for this book is available from the
British Library.

Printed by Biddles Ltd. Guildford and King's Lynn.

For Fizz

Pattern and Permaculture

The theoretical basis of this new-science-fiction story is called 'pattern'. This is my own development of Rupert Sheldrake's 'Hypothesis of Formative Causation' (*The Presence of the Past.* Collins 1988) about the power of habits in nature, which also accounts for human society being stuck in destructive paths. I am deeply grateful for the insights Rupert Sheldrake gave me. Recognising harmful habits is the first step to breaking them, but we also need to develop different ones. In my story, humankind moves on to a set of alternative patterns which was inspired by the 'earth care and people care' philosophy of permaculture - an increasingly well-known system of land use design. My debt for these ideas is due to Bill Mollison (*Permaculture, A Practical Guide for a Sustainable Future.* Island Press 1990) and his many followers. The extreme form of permaculture described in this book is my own invention.

The Completion would never have been completed without the involvement of
> Rebecca Smith of Praxis Books,
> 'Sheridan', Broomers Hill Lane,
> Pulborough, West Sussex RH20 2DU

I am grateful for support and criticism from
> David Gearing, Barbara Halliburton and
> - especially - Felicity Marsh.

Chris Marsh

Contents

Illustrations

v

Part One – The Technological Ages

⋘ ⋘ ⋘

–Justin? It's Bea.

–Hi! Nice surprise. How are you? I've been meaning to ring you. How's the baby? Still enjoying motherhood?

–I'm fine, and so's Poppy. But she's not such a baby now – two next month. She's a little love, most of the time – and life seems so fascinating when you see it through her eyes.

–It's still strange one of our crowd being a parent – makes me feel old – doesn't it you?

–I know what you mean. Being with a baby makes me think of sheep and lambs, just eating and breeding. Actually it was that got me writing again. I haven't found one small baby a full time job – I suppose I'm fairly organised and she sleeps quite a lot – and she seems to take the clatter of the keyboard as a signal she's to play by herself.

–You've actually moved on from pen and manual typewriter! What are you writing?

–Science fiction – a whole book – my first novel, even! I've just finished it.

–Have you got a publisher?

–Not yet. I've never done anything like this before, so ...

–I didn't know you liked sci-fi.

–It's not empires-in-space or bug-eyed-monsters kind of science fiction. It's about the future here on earth.

–*1984* or *Brave New World* dire warnings stuff, eh? Yes I can see you going for that.

–No, it's not dire warnings. You can only get away with that these days if you can be seriously funny – like Ben Elton. My book comes up with questions rather than threats – it's kind of allegorical, I think.

1

–Four 'M's.

–What?

–I had a girlfriend once – before ... you know. She was doing English Lit. at college. I remember her saying – it stuck in my mind – I suppose that's the idea – allegory is four 'M's. The first M's a bit of a fiddle: M for the Made-up story; but then you have the Mirror held up to society, the Moral message, and – er – the Mystical layer.

–Mmm, I like that. That's just what I need. That's what I rang you about actually.

–You want me to read it?

–Would you? There's a big chunk about virtual reality and I need someone to check it out. And I'd like your view of it generally.

–I'm not an expert ...

–Thanks Justin, you're a pal, I love you to pieces! That reminds me, I should have asked, how's Lionel?

–We split up. A couple of months ago now. He still comes round now and again.

–Oh, Justin, I am sorry.

–I'll survive. Do you want me to read the whole thing and then comment, or a bit at a time? What's your timescale?

–It's up to you. I'll post you the whole lot anyway. But bit at a time would be best for me I think – I don't think I could cope with a whole book's worth all at once. How about after each chapter, there are fifteen altogether.

–OK, I'll do that. Are you on Internet?

–Come off it, Justin, I'm not interested in computer dating – or browsing academic papers from the University of Nebraska. I haven't got an anorak, either.

–Oh very funny! Internet users aren't all computer nerds. I use it mainly for electronic mail.

–Why not post me your comments?

–Because I wouldn't get round to it. Snail mail, snail mind, they say. I'll ring you.

–I can't wait! Bye for now, then.

–Bye, Bea.

Dear reader from necrotech,

My name is Pool. I live in the completion age and I am going to take you on a journey through the future of humankind on earth, from your time on, to the completion. How long a journey it is in linear time as you conceive it I cannot tell you, because my people do not see time as you do, but it is an enormously long time; longer than the time from the evolutionary origins of the human species to where you are. I will tell you in due course who we are, and what we are waiting for as the cycles of human destiny turn.

On our journey you will not be seeing everything that happened, because obviously that would be too much for me to tell in any detail. Nor will you get just a superficial view of the main stages, because that would leave out the real experience. What I shall do is share with you a few episodes from the many journeys that I have taken into the consciousness of actual people, who exist in my past but long before my personal lifetime; again, as you understand the person and the lifetime, which is different from how we perceive these things. The episodes are stepping stones through the main plot, which is the story of humanity. The fragments of plot in each episode are glimpses of lives lived: some of which are mini-stories with their own bit of completeness; others, like the one which follows, have no resolution; are little more than a face passed in the street with a life behind it that you scarcely know. The first fragment is part of the life of a woman called Bony Bailey. I experienced it from inside Bony's skin and her consciousness, by what we call a 'shift'. I did not travel piggy-back in her mind; I *was* her, and her alone, but I remembered the experience when I returned, and then wrote it down. Why people of the completion age have been taking such journeys I will tell you in due course.

1

Pattern Mathematics

Bony heaved her guts out over the lavatory bowl and spat and spat, 'Tche, tche' – dry biscuit and bile slime, shuddering, clutching her shrunken stomach. 'Oh God!' She leant sideways to rest her shoulder against the wall, and wiped dribbles of spit from her clammy mouth with a hand that was not part of her and which flopped to the floor while she explored her mouth with her tongue and found it disgusting.

She looked up, her eyes rolling round the pale green walls to the wrought iron frame of the wash basin. Water! She crawled up on rubbery limbs and aimed a floppy hand in the direction of the tap and, pushing at it, released a noisy jet of water. Balancing her lower half carefully, she bent over and sucked in the cold, clean liquid, rolled it around her teeth and spat, 'Tche, tche'. She looked up, wiping her forehead with a damp hand. 'Better now, Bony?' she asked the face in the mirror.

The face in the mirror was far from bony. Chubby from childhood, the teasers in the playground had made 'Bonny' into 'Bony', which had stuck to her for the rest of her life. It was a nickname after all, made her feel she had friends. She had slimmed down a bit in her teens and twenties, but had spread steadily since – now not actually obese, but definitely very plump. Her mousy hair was turning an even duller grey. She cut it herself, really short, and cultivated a bit of an image with big dangly earrings and ethnic smock over a long black skirt.

When Trish had been there she'd made a real effort to be healthy, done the wholefood and lentils thing, made bread, the lot. But Trish had gone off to college. So Bony cycled to the supermarket, almost every day, stuffed herself in the Coffee Shop, picked up a trolley full of packet food, wobbled back with the carrier bags over the handlebars, then ate it all – and drank – red wine by the big, cheery glassful, slurping the blues away, slumped in front of the telly.

Not all the time; there was her work, and sometimes she really got into it. Since being made 'redundant' two years ago – actually displaced by a younger teacher with a smart suit and personal organiser – she'd been doing some research. But it was damned hard keeping to it and putting in the hours when there was no one else involved. No one had asked her to do it, no one was paying her, probably no one would be impressed by it when it was done, if it ever was. And she was so lonely!

She was feeling better, a bit. 'Cup of tea and a nice hot bath?' she offered herself. 'Sorry, no bath, can't afford it, blasted water meter – I hate showers.' She shivered, looked around and snatched up the shawl she'd dropped earlier, wrapped it round her shoulders, pushed her feet into her old mules and shuffled to the kitchen.

Putting the kettle on, she glanced at the clock. 'Twenty past one, past bed time. Who cares when's bedtime? Going to do some work, haven't done a thing all day, too sorry for myself.' She nibbled at a dry biscuit in case she was going to be sick again, even worse on an empty stomach. She grimaced at the remains of the 'Cod Provençal', and scraped it into the over-full waste bin, on top of the packet with its tempting picture. 'No more fish, all diseased I expect, all that shit in the sea, planet'll sick us up next, probably already is.' The kettle clicked itself off.

'Peppermint, I think, refreshing.' She fished out a bag on a string, into a mug from the drainer, sploshed on the boiling water, then shuffled around the partition into the dining area, also her study. Putting the mug down, she rolled out the swivel chair, eased into it, switched on the PC, put down the dry biscuit, 'Crumbs not good for the keyboard,' she said aloud as the thing hummed into action.

There was always this difficult transition from her lonely, lazy world – full of self pity, little treats and distractions, into her Important Work, that she loved, and could, on a good day, really get into. The freedom of it was wonderful. None of the interference and frustration of her years as a maths teacher. She had wanted to bring out the 'natural mathematician' in each of her pupils. The system said 'No. You teach this syllabus, to this timetable, from these books, and assess your pupils this way, so they get good grades in the public exams, and enhance the School's Reputation.'

She opened a document containing an early chapter of what she thought of as her 'book', although she had only daydreams of getting it published. 'Polish, polish,' she said gleefully, jabbing on the 'insert'

5

key to make sure she did not over-write any of her wonderful words. Taking a slurp of the peppermint tea, she read the familiar yellow-on-blue type.

'Mathematics is the study of patterns. Human survival, indeed most animal survival, depends on recognising patterns: distinguishing food from foe, mate from rival, self from surroundings. Human animals were late evolutionary arrivals, with no central role in the ecosystems they emerged in, so they made a living as opportunistic scavengers. Our major evolutionary strength was being capable of recognising a wide range of interesting patterns, in an environment full of uninteresting ones.'

Bony changed 'ones' to 'patterns' and back again, as she had done many times before. 'Not quite happy with that bit,' she muttered. And yawned. Her tummy rumbled. 'That's good, settling down. Think I'll go to bed. No, must do a little bit.' She tapped the 'PgDn' key a few times. 'Ah, yes.'

'The conventional scientific paradigm focuses on a few relatively simple patterns, such as atoms and genes, virtually ignoring the vast majority of complex patterns in nature, at the same time making the huge assumption that the rest are all accumulations of the special few. The patterns studied are seen as geometrical forms in the spatial dimension, but are believed to change over time as a result of mechanical and electrical forces acting upon them, in obedience to a set of laws, which are expressed in mathematical language. This, of course, is a human mental conception. However, over the past two hundred years especially, the mental conception has been externalised in the construction of machines, and in uniform plantation agriculture, which between them are rapidly displacing the diversity of complex patterns on this living planet.

'There have been a number of scientists in recent years who have begun to question the mechanistic model, and its effects. Only one has come anywhere near recognising the peculiarity, and sheer unlikeliness, of the conventional model of how change occurs: the biologist Rupert Sheldrake. Sheldrake's alternative hypothesis conceives the agents of change as being memories of past forms, whereby new forms occur in the present time by tending to follow the forms closest to them in the library of memories. Everything from subatomic particles, atoms and molecules to cells, organisms, ecosystems and human cultures behaves, develops and persists by

6

resonance with similar forms in the past.'

'Need to give some examples here, I suppose,' Bony said to herself, 'Always a bore that. What was that bit I thought of in the Coffee Shop – about rabbits and acorns? I wrote it down on the cover of my cheque book.'

With a grunt of irritation she got out of the chair and went into the kitchen area to where she usually dumped her shoulder bag. Rummaging in its depths she extracted the cheque book and peered at the scribble in blunt pencil which was barely legible over the pale grey cover. Reading it as she made her way back to the computer she bumped her head on the edge of the partition. 'Bugger! That hurt.' She amplified the jottings as she inserted the new passage.

'The patterns of oak trees and rabbits in the past determine the germination or embryonic formation of new oak trees and rabbits, and their growth and behaviour. The same kind of influence holds human attitudes and conduct in their path. A human child becomes a social creature primarily through the presence of the cultural patterns which have accumulated, and are still present, in his past, and only secondarily by deliberate upbringing and education. Understanding the power and persistence of past influences is vital at a time in human history when radical changes are needed. It is almost as difficult for human society to undergo profound change as it is for an acorn to give birth to a rabbit. A cultural reincarnation is required, and the circumstances for that fresh gestation can only emerge out of the breakdown of the existing forms.'

2

A Journey through the Ages

That was the first of the shifts.
                                        I felt it was important to begin with
someone recognisably of your own time, which was towards the end of
what came to be called the 'necrotech age', or just 'necrotech'

Bony Bailey suffered from a deprivation sickness which was common
in the materially over-burdened sections of society in necrotech. The
main symptom in her case was dependence on food and drink containing
substances which provide intense sensations of pleasure or comfort. She
was typical of a necrotech individual in that she lived enclosed in her
mind. She also – and this was less common but not unusual – held the
whole world in her mind. This was an attitude called 'globalism' by the
few who warned of its dangers, and it caused a person's conception of
the world to shrink. Phrases such as 'the global village' and 'one world'
reflected this attitude, as did images of the planet hanging in space.
Globalism was encouraged by those with power over the economy,
which was increasingly global and unrestrained, and brought about
cultural and ecological homogenisation. It was accentuated by global
threats such as nuclear war and disruption of the biosphere. People like
Bony often felt personal guilt over the problems of the world, and saw
saving the world as their own responsibility. The 'Pattern Mathematics'
Bony was developing is a marvellous conception. It does indeed have
saving potential. But not for people still enclosed in their mind space.
Now we shall leave Bony and move on.

I am going to have to take you over some giant strides forward in time
between the shifts. To help you across I am including as much
superficial account of what happened in the meantime as I think you will
need to land safely.

During your lifetime, and that of Bony Bailey, the necrotech age was drawing to a close. That age is the entire period from the emergence of the human species from their hominid forebears to your present. The name means 'death-based technology', and refers to the dependence of mankind on energy derived from the combustion of dead organic materials; from wood-burning cooking fires through to the fossil fuel based technology of your times. It also refers to the use and abuse of materials and processes – whether they are obviously living like trees and chickens, or apparently non-living like water and rock – as if they are unaware and disposable.

We shall be moving on into the age called 'bionecrotech', and after that to the biotech age. The biotech age proper is the period when combustion had been replaced by the technological equivalent of respiration and decomposition, and many other processes, materials and structures which life makes possible: the technologies of life instead of those of death. The bionecrotech age is the transitional period between necrotech and biotech, when fossil fuels were replaced by newly-grown biofuels, which were then still burnt to produce energy in order to power similar machinery to that in use during necrotech, and when biotechnology had not progressed beyond the crude tampering called 'genetic engineering'. Just to complete this simple division of humanity's story into ages: after the biotech age came the pattern age, which was oceanic in its extent, and after that the completion age, which is my time. I shall tell you of those as we near them.

I shall now tell you something of what happened between necrotech and bionecrotech: the time of the next subject, whose name is Fred Drakely.

From the perspective of Fred and his contemporaries, what happened was the collapse of human society, locally and globally. Viewed on a large scale the collapse involved wars, famines, disease epidemics and a devastating environmental crisis, brought about by the prevailing economic model, which, like a fire, was spreading its devastation, consuming life on earth, but still failing to grow fast enough to provide new jobs for workers replaced by automation, or by their industries moving to parts of the world where there was cheap and compliant labour to exploit.

The signs of the collapse visible on a large scale, and occasionally generating some people's sympathy via the news media, were symptoms of a deeper malaise. The globalism of the economic system caused local communities to break down. Consumerism was promoted, and diverse local sources of provision were replaced by world markets favouring transnational corporations. The effects locally were competition, shortages, poverty, corruption, oppression, and killing – sometimes outright war. Most of the cruelty and suffering was invisible, and the prevailing attitude to what *did* show its sad and ugly face was: 'It's not my problem'. It was the ignorance and denial of responsibility which earned the disapproval of the people of bionecrotech, and which they took great pride in having addressed.

I cannot tell you if this picture of what took place is a true one; firstly because the world is so much bigger and more complicated than anyone's mind can take in, so how could we know for sure what happened to the world? Secondly, how people view the past depends so much on their own present, on what they are told and on what they let themselves know, which in turn contribute to how they picture their present as well. The same applies to you, of course, in your time. You are affected by the accidents of what life puts in your way, and you are subject to socialisation, even if you call it by names like 'indoctrination' and 'propaganda' and believe that only other people are taken in by such deceptions. In Fred Drakely's time they did not regard socialisation negatively: they called it 'public education'.

So, depending on the influences on you, you may believe that 'the collapse of human society' is just around the corner, you may feel you are in the midst of it already, or you may believe that the world is working pretty well, and that any problems are exaggerated and not fundamental. Strange as it may seem, the 'truth' of what took place to bring about the transition is unimportant: call it a recovery after a collapse, call it a revolution, call it the result of social evolution or technological innovation: it does not matter; but the transition did take place from necrotech to bionecrotech.

From the episode in the life of Fred Drakely, you will see that bionecrotech was an optimistic age. The people of that time were very proud of their advanced society, in which some of the most serious problems of your age: poverty and injustice, speculation and corruption, waste and pollution, were solved. But if we had Bony Bailey with us to make her comments, she would point out to you how much had not changed: how the patterns of society: people's attitudes and expectations, and the roles they played, had scarcely changed at all. Indeed, some of the reforms which appeared to have been won in your time proved short-lived and dissolved away, and the older patterns returned.

I have had several shifts to Fred's time, and I picked out this one to tell you about because Fred's circumstances on that day filled his mind with material which is useful for the story I am telling to you, which is not Fred's story, remember, but humanity's.

–Hello! Hello! Bea, you there?

–Da-da.

–Hello, Poppy. Where's Mummy?

–Give the telephone to Mummy, pet. Ta-a. Hello! Sorry, who is it?

–Bea. Hi! It's Justin. Is this not a good time?

–It's fine. Poppy, go away and play sweetheart, Mummy's busy.

–Are perfect mothers allowed to say things like that to their children?

–Sure. Teach her she's not the centre of the universe like some American brat. No, really, she's toddled off quite happily. So, are you reporting back on my book?

–Give me a chance, Bea! It only arrived yesterday. I've made a start: the first few pages. But I was actually ringing to say I'm thinking of organising a get-together. Go for a pizza first and the Bell afterwards – this Saturday or the next. I thought I'd try you first – because of getting a baby-sitter.

–Oh great! Not this coming Saturday, though – I've promised to take Poppy to see my grandparents. The following one should be OK.

–Good! I'll see who else I can rustle up.

–You said you made a start on the book. The beginning's so important. What did you think? Spotted any allegorical 'M's yet?

–Yes, there's heaps of M for mirror and morals – the Bony woman and the part about the Ages: it's all about current world problems. That's all become a bit of a bore, so I was glad you solved them all in one sweep, before the story's really got going.

–I did that so I could show up the problems underneath that no one notices!

–Oh, I'm expecting more messages – since you say it's allegorical.

–It's *questions* more than messages, really.

–Right. On the M for made-it-up, I like the term 'necrotech' – that could catch on with the green brigade. And 'shift of consciousness' time travel avoids the dreaded paradox perfectly because the time traveller can't change anything. But the main thing is it isn't really made up, is it? I mean, I've always thought the past is all still here, so why not *shift* to it; that's probably what we do in dreams. That's M for mystical, I suppose.

–The past *is* all still here – that's the basis of pattern theory, and that's

12

serious science.

–I know it is: I've read Sheldrake's book *The Presence of the Past*. It's a bit confusing that you use *pattern* as if it were a scientific term, but I suppose that links it with common sense, in a way that *morphic fields* and all that wouldn't. Tell you what the presence of the past reminds me of: that New Year we spent together in the Lake District – remember?

–I'm not sure *remember's* the right world. I got really drunk and insensible that night.

–It was the next day I was thinking of – January the first. We didn't get up 'til about three, we were all hungover and miserable, and we had parsnip soup – again.

–Ugh! I can taste it now. That was before you invented that roast with mashed parsnips and salted cashews, and sage and rosemary we found in the cottage garden. Delicious! I still make that. Who was it bought all those parsnips anyway?

–Jeff, I think – a job lot from the market. Anyway, the soup was disgusting and it was pouring with rain, and we couldn't go to the pub because we'd disgraced ourselves in front of the natives the night before. Then someone said something melancholy about the old year, and time slipping away, and then you said that if time didn't slip away the universe would get terribly overcrowded.

–Yes, I remember that. Then Joe, wasn't it, said we'd bump into ourselves in the past going backwards and forwards to get the beers from the kitchen, and he demonstrated, and we all started trying to be where we'd been as well as where we were ...

–... and ended up doing the okey-cokey to the pub. That's the patterns of the past idea, isn't it?

–Definitely!

–Those were the days! Now we're the older generation.

–We're also still what we were before, remember.

–Don't you think you'd better get back to your poor neglected daughter?

–Humph! Yes, I suppose I should. Thanks ever so much for the feedback, Justin. I'm so pleased you liked my beginning.

–I'm looking forward to the next bit about Fred, the optimist. 'Bye for now then.

–'Bye.

13

3

Vanity Frames

The book stopped reading. They had arrived at the Centre. A final gust of wind had knocked the car slightly off its course as it entered the storm lock, and the bump diverted Fred's attention from the story, so it stopped reading.

The car glided gently now along the underground tracks for about a hundred metres. It stopped at an ascent ramp and opened its door for Fred to step out. He watched as it slid into a nearby bay and plugged in its solar re-charge plug and connected up to the alcohol supply to be ready for Fred's journey home. He cocked his head at it, making a clicking sound of approval and admiration. The wonders of modern clean technology gave him constant gratification. It was a great time to be alive, he sincerely believed, and was always telling his children so.

Fred strode up the ramp which spiralled towards the subterranean ceiling and emerged in a corridor above ground level. A small, smiling female figure was hurrying along the corridor towards him, her progress impeded by the tight skirt of her plum-coloured suit and her absurdly high-heeled shoes.

'Dr Drakely, hello there. Excuse me.' And she stopped in front of him breathless, and patted her panting chest before holding out her hand.

Fred cringed inwardly at the 'Dr' title. Academic achievement was not something one wanted acknowledged. Its prestige had vanished now that intuitive innovation had made nonsense of any search for theoretical truths. Fred had collected his two degrees on the leisure learning credits system, aquaculture for his first degree, then algal mutagenics for his PhD. He had once had hopes of gaining advancement in his job from these qualifications, but not now. Now they were an embarrassment. Should he suggest she call him 'Fred'? But that could sound over-familiar at a first meeting; he had no idea who this woman was. Better say nothing about it.

'I am a little early,' he apologised, shaking her extended hand. 'I was worried there'd be a hold up on the motorway train – with the storm alert, you know. Actually I was surprised not to be re-scheduled for a leisure day.'

'Obviously you are needed here,' she smiled. 'The others haven't arrived yet. I'll show you to your office and you can relax for a bit. Oh, yes, sorry, I didn't say did I, my name's Anne. I'm secretary to your jot.' Her smiling face still fixed on Fred, she turned her body and started to teeter back the way she had come. She lost her balance and he caught her by the elbow. Safely side by side they walked along the softly carpeted corridor. Fred looked down at her neat cap of red hair and smiled: *secretary*, what a quaint job title, he mused, what use could we possibly have for a secretary?

The path of the corridor curved to the right. The left-hand wall arched smoothly from floor level to above their heads and was evidently the exterior wall of the unit, glowing with natural light, which its cells would store to continue glowing if needed after dark and to supply solar-sourced energy to the rest of the building. The right-hand wall was perpendicular, and contained a series of doorways. Fred counted three closed doors before they reached their destination, which was an open door into a short corridor terminating in an opaque daylight panel, and just before that an open doorway on either side.

'Here we are,' said Anne, leading Fred through the right hand doorway. 'Make yourself at home. Would you like some coffee? It's dome-grown, not nova. With or without?'

'Thank you, yes please. No caffeine, thank you,' he said primly. No drugs or stimulants for him; he did not need such things.

With four or five paces Fred reached the recliner, the only piece of furniture in the small room, and climbed into its orthopaedically-contoured, novaskin-covered comfort. 'You'd love this, Tim,' he said inwardly to his young son, to give himself permission to play with the chair's control pad, tipping himself forwards and back, and sliding the chair around the floor. Then he swung it around to survey his new office. 'Nice,' he observed.

In plan, the room was a section of a thick ring. The shorter convex curve was a full height sliding glass door to a domed garden with a ring of citrus trees, bright with shining leaves and yellow, green and orange fruit, and in the centre a pool and a fountain; he could hear the splash and trickle of the water. Between the trees and the pool was a circle of pink marble benches. The garden was surprisingly sunny for an autumn morning, an effect Fred guessed was contrived by the thickness of the glass of the domed roof being graded to bend the sunlight downwards.

Both straight walls of the office contained doors. Through the one he had come in by he could see Anne's cubbyhole beyond, and inside it a portion of her plum coloured back as she bent over the coffee-making things. The opposite door was open, and he could see that it led to a little bedroom, necessary in case one was stranded at work by the storms. Not that it happened very often – only five times in Fred's fifteen years of employment; curiously though, two of those had been in the previous year, and he had quite often been rescheduled due to others doing extra days.

He wondered if someone could be stranded for so many days that he got the rest of the year allocated to leisure. If that happened, people would begin to give up the idea of years like they had weeks and months. Fred remembered his little girl, Louise, saying, 'What's a week, Daddy?' He had got in an amazing maze trying to explain it to her. It had made him recall why there were always seven people in a job-share team: tradition, originally one day's work a week. Now weeks had disappeared, but there were still seven men in a jot – interesting. With less and less travelling, more 'conference' work, 'conference' school and 'conference' shopping, with 'windows' being into the system rather than to the outdoors – and even mirrors were windows these days – all contact with oneself, others and the world would be through the system. So things like months and years, even days – weeks of course had been people's invention anyway – would cease to have any independent reality.

Fred's mind switched back to his survey of the new office. Off the bedroom would be a shower cubical and a chute. Good idea. He struggled out of the recliner's embrace and made for the door. Inside and to the right were two other doors as he had expected. He slid the nearer one open to reveal the chute: a bio-digester device on a flexible, pressure sensitive stem so that it could serve either as a urinal or shitting bowl. Fred dropped his trousers and pulled the chute to his bottom. The stem stiffened as the smart material felt his weight. He had a wee and a crap and smiled as the device released a swirl of warm soapy water to wash his bottom, sucked the water down the chute with the waste and

16

sent warm air to blow him dry.

Fred's daughter, Louise, had been one of the first generation of babies to benefit from portable 'chute-aways', as they were called, which provided nappies for the incontinent of all ages and for menstrual blood disposal. He had heard they were now being used in protective clothing, into which the wearer was locked, so preventing the smuggling of materials in body cavities. On a daily basis, the chute-away was emptied and cleaned by coupling it to a chute, which re-used the same small quantity of water; no paper, or other 'disposable' material was used once and thrown away, and the tiny amount of concentrated solid waste was routed into fertiliser production. Brilliant! It really added to the pleasure of your crap, thought Fred, as he pulled up his trousers. Then he returned to the recliner and turned it to face the longer, concave curved wall opposite the garden.

The wall was one big system screen. As soon as Fred looked at it the screen began to display for him a promotional sequence for the global corporation which owned the Centre and employed Fred. A subtle background of optimistic music accompanied the vision. He sat back in the recliner and watched, his expression indicating a slightly supercilious pride.

A giant algae harvester was steadily steaming over a wide expanse of ocean towards a gorgeous orange and pink sunset. The setting sun was reflected in all its glory in the ocean waves on the left-hand side of the screen, and it illumined to a lurid green the area of algal field yet to be scooped into the vessel's bowels, which stretched to the right-hand wall. As the harvester was about to disappear into the sinking orb, a block of gold letters zoomed out declaring, 'Salt Water Industries – Harvesting the Sun – Unlimited Clean Energy for Sustainable Economic Growth'. Then a composite picture grew from the four corners: a twenty lane motorway with car-trains and truck-trains snaking along, breaking up and re-forming as they passed a junction; a huge de-salinization plant; an equally enormous recycling plant; and a great plantation-scape boasting the latest in landscaping art, fractal geometric patterns produced by a free coloration DNA sequence in the genetically engineered agricultural raw material crop.

'New one,' observed Fred of the promotional sequence. 'Could do with some of those patterned G-ARMs around here,' he mused, recalling the unrelieved green of the prairies he had passed on his way to the Centre. 'No one cares though, they all look inwards.' He pressed

17

the control pad of the recliner to swing himself round and look again at the pretty garden, and wondered when he would meet the people who presumably shared it with him.

'Here we are,' said Anne, coming through the door with his coffee, its delicious fresh aroma wafting towards him. She carried a small cafetiere, a china cup and saucer, cream jug and sugar basin on a novateak tray, which she put on the left arm of his recliner to which it clung.

'Lovely, thanks,' he smiled. He watched her turn and walk out of the room, her plum skirt stretched tantalisingly across her decidedly plum-shaped bottom. He adjusted his underpants to accommodate his uncontrollable response, and mentally sent an apology to his beloved wife, Min, who would be at home consoling little Louise over the cancellation of her first school attendance day. Louise had been so looking forward to going to 'real school', as she called it, dismissing conference school as 'boring'. Her big brother Tim told her she soon would not know the difference, but when Fred left, surprised that his trip was not cancelled too, Louise was clearly all set for a whole day of tantrums.

When he had finished his second cup of coffee, Fred wondered what he should do. Anne had mentioned colleagues being due to arrive. Was a meeting scheduled? he wondered.

'Anne!' he called out. Her smiling face appeared, not in the flesh this time, but in subtle holo-relief in a window on his wall screen. He scowled and tutted audibly at the pale pink vanity frame which surrounded her face.

'What's the matter, Dr Drakely?' she asked, her smile falling away at his obvious disapproval.

'Oh, sorry, Anne. I didn't mean to, er...,' he tailed off. 'It's just that I don't like van-frames – it's to do with the work I've been doing.'

'But everybody uses van-frames. I mean, it's part of people's privacy isn't it. After all you could be doing anything when the phone goes,' she giggled briefly and then put her hurt look back on.

'I don't know why people need privacy. As far as I'm concerned privacy is the same as secrecy and conspiracy and they're against the law, and quite right too. Anyway I'd really appreciate it if you'd take yours off in the office.'

The pink blur cleared, revealing the plum suit again. In her hands in her lap was some craft work, crochet he thought it was. Well no harm

18

in that, no need to hide it.

'Thank you. I really appreciate that,' he said smiling, working hard to put back the friendly smile on her face, but she was looking at him stolidly, her lips slightly pursed.

'I was just wondering,' he went on, 'what I should be doing. Is there a briefing meeting set up, or should I ask for instructions through the system?'

'Oh yes, sorry, I should have told you,' she said, her smile beginning to return. (She did say 'sorry' a lot, Fred thought.) 'There's a big meeting this afternoon. All the jot members for the whole task group are coming. Meanwhile you're to carry on with the work you were doing at Greenwich. You did look at the prep pack?' she asked. 'With your family?' He nodded twice. 'Well, you're to think about that again before the meeting, but you shouldn't look at it from here. Actually it's probably wiped off now. Oh and I was told to tell you that your probe has been cleared for release by the Tech Board. What does it do, your probe?' she asked.

'It traces hidden messages in van-frames,' Fred replied.

'Oh, I see,' she said, and vanished.

Fred was beginning to feel just a little bit uneasy about his new job. There did seem to be some slightly irregular things happening. For a start, having a meeting, actually in the flesh, of all the jot members for the whole task group: that was never done. The whole idea of job-share teams was to divide the work up so that everyone had a job to do, and earned his, and his family's, living. The job share team members were parts of one worker, not seven workers. If they ever worked together the whole system broke down, and there could be unemployment and poverty all over again like back in necrotech. It was not as if there could ever be full-time jobs for everyone now that production was completely automated and financial dealings banned.

Another strange thing was being told to do some work at home, viewing that prep pack. That was time over and above his jot slot, the same thing again really. And then to be told he must not view the prep pack from the office and that it would have been wiped off: it was not supposed to be possible to wipe anything off, it was against the anti-secrecy laws. And as for telling him not to look at something, that was not right either.

Fred was proud of the way things were done, he liked to see everyone conforming to the conventions, so that everything stayed free, fair and

19

open. So he felt uneasy at what he saw as contraventions. But then his usual trust and optimism took over again. After all, starting a new job was perhaps a special situation. This was only his second job in fifteen years so he did not know the drill. Once the regular routine was established, things like this would not happen. Then a happy thought banished his worries: he had permission to use his probe. Wonderful! Curious how quickly it had been passed though. Oh stop it Fred, you're getting paranoid, he rebuked himself. Better get on.

He looked at the screen and it began to show its promotional sequence again. 'Clear!' Fred commanded, and it did. 'This is Fred Drakely checking in to resume Project Seed Security, previously located at SWI Greenwich.'

Two large windows opened on the wall screen showing still holo-images of the faces of two women, frozen in mid-conversation. Both women were of late middle age, grey-haired and unusually weather-beaten for members of an indoor society, and both looked very gloomy, one had tears glistening in her eyes. They were surrounded by the cheap standard van-frames which turned the background into little shimmering squares.

'Confirm release-for-use of my van-frame scanning probe.'

'Release confirmed,' said 'Silver', the system link voice.

'Load and run the probe on these frames here,' Fred commanded. There was a negligible pause before Silver replied, 'Nothing there, Fred.'

'Hmm, pity. Did you scan the whole of the recording sequence?'

'Yes, Fred. Nothing there at all,' the voice responded, Fred imagined a little huffily.

'I'll want to know who else uses the probe and for what, now it's released. Add that to my profile.'

'The probe is released for your use alone,' said Silver.

'My personal use!' Fred exclaimed. 'What about my co-jos?'

'At Greenwich or Taunton?' it asked.

'Oh I see,' said Fred, relieved, 'this is just a transitional situation, then?'

'Perhaps,' said the link voice, which made it sound almost human, but 'perhaps' was one of the standard responses to voice patterns which suggested hypothetical questions.

'May I remind you, Fred, that these two subjects have put in a joint request for information on why you have been tapping their calls,' said

20

Silver.

'Oh right. I'd better deal with that. Run through that last recording for me will you.'

Fred's job at SWI in Greenwich had been to track down seed smuggling rackets. Now that opportunities for smuggling had been virtually eliminated – thanks, in some small part, to Fred's jot's efforts – the work had switched focus slightly to keeping an eye on potential saboteurs. The jot had received a tip-off about an old seeds network still in communication. These two women seemed to be part of it: one, named Nell Dowthwaite, had been Professor of Hydroponics Genetics at the University of East Anglia, before it was closed down; the other, Mildred Phipps, was the wife of a retired DNA matching home worker; the couple lived in Perth in Western Australia. One of Fred's co-jos had intercepted a videphone call between these two subjects.

The two women on the screen were now talking animatedly, not anything directly to do with seeds, they were organising what they called 'The "Farewell to Permaculture" Convergence'. Fred knew about permaculture. The practitioners of this home food growing methodology had been amongst the most tenacious seed smugglers, until hands-on gardening was improved out of existence.

'Silly ideas! self sufficiency and nature worship,' Fred said aloud, as if to the women on the wall. Goodness knows what harm they could do, he thought. Don't know why they didn't realise that, there's no lack of information. The shame of it though, having to have their daft organisation actually de-recognised and its history put in the off-profile archives.

Most people of Fred's generation condemned non-conformity, and they took pride in the human achievements of the century of post-necrotech recovery. A great deal of 'public education' helped to cultivate and reinforce such attitudes. His reaction to the recording reminded Fred of part of the prep pack he had been given to study at home, which was very largely public education material. Anne had said he was to think about the prep pack again before the meeting so he tipped back the recliner, shut his eyes and tried to cast his mind back to two days earlier when he had viewed the very first sequence in the pack, which was about New Way economics. Very little of the pack was new to him, but Fred intended to talk the children through it all carefully to make sure they appreciated the wonderful world they were so fortunate to be growing up in. So both children were with him, at least at the

21

beginning.

Little Louise was immediately fascinated by the huge dark eyes of the female presenter – none other than the brilliant Arabian economist Fatma al-Ankari, peering alluringly over the veil of her traditional Muslim costume as she narrated the first part of the sequence. Al-Ankari's liquid voice intoned, 'The persistent failure of the necrotech economy had several causes including financial speculation, protectionism disguised as free trade, corruption at all levels, but particularly amongst the wealthy, and a general abandonment of morality in business dealings.'

At this point there was an animated cartoon showing a globe turning slowly around; on its surface a crazy mad rush of skinny little ants worked machinery, packed tiny boxes and pushed miniature carts around; and there were various dubious characters: a great spotty toad behind his big desk counting gold coins, a slit-eyed lizard slithering around corners with documents marked 'secret', and a rat gnawing a hole in a money bag; they grew fatter and fatter as the ants rushed faster and faster and got thinner and thinner. Louise giggled and Tim and Fred smiled just a little.

Al-Ankari's voice over the cartoon said, 'Our solution has been to remove the opportunities for cheating. We have banned usury and the hoarding of money.' A fairy appeared, waved her wand, and the toad's desk and coins vanished. 'We have a single global currency, used only to facilitate the exchange of real goods and socially useful labour.' The rat's money bag vanished. 'We have established a completely open global information system which now accommodates all business dealings, records, accounts and transactions.' The lizard's documents vanished. 'We have introduced job sharing, so that everyone has a source of income to exchange for, at the very least, their basic needs.' The ants stopped rushing and got fatter, the other creatures shrunk smaller and started to join in the work.

Then Al-Ankari's veiled face re-appeared. 'But our greatest achievement is our new agriculture,' she went on. 'By replacing fossil fuels with new solar energy captured by growing plants, we have averted the threat of "Global Warming" from the build-up of carbon dioxide due to the combustion of fossil fuels, and helped to eliminate the pollution and waste from industries based on petroleum-derived chemicals.' Behind Al-Ankari's head appeared old film sequences of smoking industrial stacks, waste dumps, victims of pollution-caused

22

diseases, power stations, dead trees and crumbling stonework. Then she waved a wand just like the fairy's in the cartoon – 'Look Daddy, the fairy's wand,' said Louise – and the grim pictures vanished, to be replaced by a glorious dawn sequence and Al-Ankari spread her arms in welcome. 'Here is Tim Harbright to tell us all about the new agriculture', and a handsome middle-aged man strode in from the side and bowed to her as she bowed off.

Fred had named his son after this famous man, one of the foremost trailblazers in the quest for clean technology. It was Harbright who had 'done the sums' which showed that fossil fuels could be superseded by new solar, without any curtailment of economic growth, material prosperity, or loss of mobility for people or goods. And here was the great man himself elucidating his theory, with charts and diagrams and illustrative film sequences.

'Necrotech agriculture,' said Harbright, 'was highly mechanised and chemical-dependent. It required, simply for the raw material "at the farm gate", let alone transportation and processing, something like ten times as many calories of fossil fuel-generated energy as the calories of solar energy taken up in the crop.'

Young Tim, Fred saw approvingly, was full of attention, leaning forward, his head propped on his hands, his elbows on his knees.

Harbright explained that the same level of automation, or better, could be employed without fossil fuels, but that since the agriculture had to provide for its own, and industry's, energy needs as well as food and petrochemical substitutes, about twenty times the previous global cultivation area was required, which meant that all dry land, plus ocean and lake surfaces, had to be used. Dramatic land-clearance shots were shown at this point in his talk, and the subsequent installation of irrigation and agrochemical treatment systems. Fossil fuels had been used for the last time in the years of preparation for the new agricultural revolution. An old news item was shown of Harbright himself ceremonially closing the last oil well.

'Pause,' ordered Tim, and turned to his father. 'Are they still alive, that woman and Tim Harbright?' he asked.

'Oh I don't think they can be,' said Fred.

'So was all that stuff recordings of what they really said, or were they just puppets?' Tim asked. 'I mean, apart from that last bit about him closing the oil well.'

'Don't ask me, you're the expert on virtual reality,' Fred said, rather proud of his son's perceptive question. 'Talking of which, is Mummy still in the cubicle?'

The family had recently acquired a system cubicle, which allowed the user to experience being inside the system world without putting on headgear which Min had never liked. Min had promptly given up going on real shopping expeditions or using the catalogue system, and was spending a lot of time going 'conference' shopping. She had already worn out or broken several touch-pads feeling her way around dozens of different hypermarkets, shops and street stalls. Young Tim had pointed out to his father that Mummy was now quite happy with no touch-pad, just rubbing her fingers, with no tactile input from the system: as Tim said, for most people sight and sound were so dominant they imagined or disregarded the minor senses.

As the sole income earner in the family, Fred was permitted to scan Min's shopping orders before they were processed, otherwise they would have been put on compulsory budget control, and they would have been ashamed to look anyone they knew in the face. Everyone who looked them up would know, of course, because there would be a 'don't trade' brand shown on all their foreheads.

'We can look,' said Tim. 'Where's Mummy?' he demanded of the system. The prep pack was replaced by an image of his mother examining melons piled on a barrow. As if the system would send along unripe ones, Fred thought. Funny how old habits persisted.

'Oh well,' said Fred, 'supper'll be a while then. Time to play a game. Load the *Life Energy Game*,' Fred ordered the system. The start screen appeared, a picture of the earth in space, one side bathed in sunlight. The game was a clever simulation of how solar energy was distributed in New Way agriculture, production and transportation. It provided interesting exercises in mathematics, as well as helping children to see how cleverly the New Way worked.

'Oh not one of those!' groaned Tim. 'We do that sort of stuff all day in conference school.'

'All right then, let's look at the next section of my pack. It's about G-ARMs I think.'

'Oh that's really boring! You look at it. I'm going to my room to look up Tim Harbright.'

The system does isolate people, Fred thought, watching Tim's retreating back, even though it brings the whole world and its history into your home.

'Oh well, it's just you and me, baby,' said Fred to Louise, patting his lap. She climbed on and made herself comfortable. 'Resume prep pack,' he ordered the system.

In the next sequence, an anonymous background voice talked over film sequences. There was no veiled woman or cartoons to hold Louise's attention, and she dozed off, leaving Fred watching on his own. But that was all wrong. He had been explicitly told to have the family watch it too.

'Tim, come back here!' he called. 'This is for my new job now. It's really important, they said, that my family should see it too. Mum's in the cubicle, Louise is asleep. Come and help me out, there's a pal.'

'Okay, I'll watch it from here,' said Tim, his face appearing on the screen.

'All right then,' Fred sighed. 'Resume,' he ordered the system.

'Most plants growing on the planet are now genetically engineered agricultural raw materials, commonly called "G-ARMs"', said the presenter. 'They are produced on an industrial scale for biofuels and biochemicals as well as for the food industry. Conditions "in the field" have to be as close as possible to the experimental conditions in which the G-ARMs were developed. Any uncontrolled garden plot or wild patch nearby could pass across weeds, pests and diseases, with unpredictable, even disastrous, results.'

Now, lying back in the recliner in his new office remembering it all, it occurred to Fred that this was just what the two permaculture women and their friends needed to be told. When he talked to them, he would be able to have the facts and arguments fresh in his mind. So he sat up and addressed the system.

'See if you can get these two women on for me,' he ordered. 'I'll talk to them together.' Then he lay back to remember the rest of that G-ARM section.

'All the wild areas and plots of traditional crops, which we call "biodiversity reserves", are now confined inside novaglass domes,' said the presenter. He then suggested the donning of headgear – Fred complied – and took the viewer on a tour through reserves around the world: tropical rainforests and deserts; temperate woodland, meadows and wetlands; and gardens and little fields from various regions in different climate zones; all of them under novaglass in controlled conditions. Then the viewer was led into the basket of a hot air balloon, and lifted high in the sky to look down on the patterns of G-ARM plantations, with the occasional dome or cluster of domes, and lines connecting them which from that height could not be identified, but which would either be surface roads or the new infrastructure channels.

'This system of protection is proving particularly valuable,' said the presenter, 'because, as well as preventing biocontamination on the plantations, the domes protect the reserves from the damaging high winds people call "the flatteners". Trees and bushes for fruits and nuts are now being grown under domes because the flatteners can tear out any plant more than a metre high.' Fred was surprised and a little disapproving to hear the presenter using the popular slang for the high winds. He was one of those who preferred to call the winds 'storms' because it made them sound transient, and did not emphasise their damaging effects.

At this point Tim interrupted the sequence to put himself on Fred's screen. 'Dad,' he said, 'Miss Jakes, my conference school teacher, says the flatteners are getting worse, and that's why there's now more conference school and hardly any attendance school. She says it's because they cut down all the trees in the world for the new farming.' Tim threw this last remark at his father as a challenge.

'That's nonsense. They don't know what's causing the *storms*,' Fred replied, emphasising his preferred word. Some people say it's the left-over effect of fossil fuels combustion, and that it'll settle down once the G-ARMs have mopped up the excess CO_2. Some say it's part of a natural climate change. And anyway, most of the trees were cut down long before the new farming.'

'Why doesn't the system know?' Tim demanded.

'Well, weather is terribly complicated – "chaotic" it's sometimes called: little things you can't measure accurately enough can have big effects later on. There are old models on the system from necrotech which were supposed to show how the climate works, but their predictions have been wrong as often as not; it's just too complicated to model.'

'Why not use intuitive innovation?' asked Louise, who was wide awake, now that something interesting was going on.

Fred was surprised at this coming from his six-year-old daughter. 'Do they teach you intuitive innovation at school?' he asked.

'Don't be silly!' she said, with her child's scorn. 'You can't *teach*

26

intuitive innovation. You just switch off your working-out mind and let in your dreaming mind.'

'Is that what they told you at school?' Fred persisted.

'No. I just know that,' she boasted, with her small snub nose in the air. 'Obviously if you don't try so hard it's easier.'

'Hmm, you could be right about dreams,' said Fred. 'I seem to remember hearing somewhere that many of the old scientists made their discoveries in their dreams; or anyway, when they weren't really thinking about whatever it was they were trying to understand.'

'Miss Jakes says that scientists didn't discover anything; they made it all up,' said Tim. 'It only got to be real when things were made which worked like they said.'

'That's right,' said Louise. 'Only things people make have *works* in them. Everything else in the whole universe does what it does because it knows what it does. And your dream mind knows too. Anyway, I'm going to make myself a van-frame like Fatma's,' she said, and she wriggled off Fred's lap and went to her room. Fred grimaced.

'She is a funny old mixture, your sister,' he said. 'She comes out with something that really makes you think, and then goes all silly and feminine over van-frames.'

'What did she say that made you think?' asked Tim.

'Well, about intuitive innovation being able to predict climate change when even the biggest computer models couldn't do it.'

'Nothing very clever about that,' Tim scoffed. 'That's the whole point of intuitive innovation: you don't get very far by analysing life and looking at the bits as if they're some machine someone built – all you get is G-ARMs and stuff. You have to forget about the laws of science, use your imagination, and help the impossible to happen, and it will, or it might. Anyway, I don't know why you go on about van-frames. I think that's what it's about for everyone: the system's one big van-frame kit.'

Fred frowned. 'What an awful thought! Well anyway, fancy van-frames take a lot of system time and that has to be paid for, so I have to think about my new job and this prep pack. It's cultured materials next – are you interested?'

Tim shrugged and said, 'Maybe.'

Fred had to be content with that, so he said, 'Resume,' and it was off again.

27

First there was an old film of a necrotech yeast factory. The narrator took the viewer around and pointed out all the gleaming steel pipes everywhere, the huge containers of molasses the yeast fed on, the computer room from which the valves to let in trace chemicals were controlled, the robots wrapping and packing the blocks of yeast.

The voice then explained that similar methods were now used to make a vast range of cultured materials, such as novateak and other timber substitutes, novasteel and other metal substitutes and, of course novaglass; all the factories being powered by biofuel energy.

Fred noted that the cultured production of animal product substitutes, such as meat, leather and wool, was not described. Some people were squeamish about the idea; that was probably why.

At this point he was interrupted by Louise dashing in to complain that the system would not accept her new van-frame. Fred went to her room to look at the image in her 'mirror'. Louise had painted a black veil all over her face apart from around her eyes, which she had coloured brown. She had then called up a friend from school to show it to, but the system had told her it was an invalid van-frame and could not be sent.

'It's invalid because it covers too much of your face for people to know who you are,' explained Fred.

'Why could Fatma have one like that then?' Louise challenged.

'Well, I suppose because her veils are part of her religion,' Fred answered.

'What's religion?' Louise asked, in a sulky voice which said she did not really want to know, for which Fred was grateful.

'Anyway, the system can probably see through her veil, but not through yours.'

'Like with system surgery?' asked Louise.

'Yes, I suppose so. As long as someone's "face lift" just makes her look younger it's allowed. But I think it's all very silly. Why people can't just be themselves is a mystery to me.'

'Well I expect they're young and beautiful to themselves, so they want to be seen that way,' said Louise.

'Hmm,' said Fred, impressed with her wisdom, in spite of his own opinion. 'Anyway, why do you want to cover over your pretty little face?'

'Well perhaps I'm *really* an eastern princess,' she said.

28

Fred smiled at the little dark creature in the 'mirror'. 'Tell you what,' he said, 'you ask your brother how to copy Fatma Al-Ankari's veil from my prep pack sequence into your van-frame, and lighten it up enough for the system to accept it. It would be prettier anyway if your face showed through a bit, and then your friends could tell it's you being an eastern princess.'

'Ooo, yes! Thanks Daddy. I want to speak to Tim,' she demanded of her system screen. Tim's face duly appeared. 'What d'you want, siss?' it said.

'Why couldn't you just go into the next room,' Fred sighed, but she did not hear him. He went back to the living room, and the cultured materials.

The next part was about in situ cultured production. This was new to Fred, and he was very impressed. The old way was for the component parts of roads, buildings etc. to be made from cultured materials in the factory, then transported, and assembled by robots on site. The new way was for an outline to be traced on site – again by robots, since people no longer worked outside – and then the outline fleshed itself out, drawing the material needed from a piped source. The method was being used for the new infrastructure channels, which would 'grow' for miles along the path it 'knew' to take; and to start it off, all that was needed was the channel outline at the start. The channel would draw its own food with it. The innovators had recently achieved a breakthrough in incorporating photosynthesis and other cell metabolism into the feeding systems: the channel branches were covered with green fins and scales which converted solar energy into sugars. They were calling this new technology 'Intos', which stood for 'intelligent organic structures'.

Always willing to be impressed as Fred was, he was beginning to wonder what on earth the great green channels could be for. Water? Possibly for transporting newly desalinised water to plantations: that might require big pipes. Other water was recycled locally in quite narrow pipes, so that would not be what the Intos channels were for. Then the recording enlightened him: he found himself inside one of the channels, pale green light diffusing through its walls. Throughout the height and width of the channel were moving belts carrying what looked like the makings or the leftovers of a host of grand banquets. Side branches of the belt moved into and out of holes in the channel's sides. Fred was then being carried along one of the main belts – one of those carrying the debris from a feast – and he arrived in an enormous kitchen.

The belts were now passing slowly in front of work benches. The attendant workers, Fred now saw, were disembodied human-like hands on long, flexible arms. The hands were preparing elaborate dishes of food with the concentrated attention of trained chefs. As Fred stared, bemused, at the dedicated culinary creativity, he noticed that the middle fingers of the hands bore eyes at their tips.

'Dr Drakely! Dr Drakely!'

'What? Oh, er, ... Anne. Sorry, I was thinking about the prep pack and I must have dropped off. This recliner's too comfy.'

'No wonder! The prep pack's not exactly a thrill a minute, is it? I've brought you some more coffee.' She put the tray onto the recliner arm. 'Careful, don't knock it,' she said as Fred struggled up.

'*I* thought the pack was really good,' he protested earnestly. 'We all need to be reminded —'

'Oh, I suppose so.'

'And that new Intos stuff, that was interesting surely?'

'Sshh. That's the hush, hush part,' she whispered, and glanced at the screen. 'You mustn't talk about that, not here anyway.' She swung Fred's recliner around to face the garden – he grabbed the coffee pot.

'What do you mean "hush, hush"? I don't hold with secrecy and I'm not going to start now, new job or no new job.'

'Oh, you scientists! You're so naive,' Anne muttered at him. 'Anyway, I don't think they'll be able to hold it up for long; and I don't think anyone's going to buy those creepy kitchen hands, or pay for that food; personally I don't care what I'm eating once I'm in the system.'

'I don't know what you're talking about,' said Fred.

'The Intos, the green dragon. *They*,' she breathed in Fred's ear, nodding in the direction of the domed garden – Fred followed her glance, but there was no one in the garden – 'They,' she whispered again, 'want to stop it, because there's no profits in it – can't be – it's all sunshine, you can't charge people for sunshine, can you? I did economics in leisure learning, I know what I'm talking about. They think they can use Tech Release to hold it up. But they won't stop it for long – you'll see. The green dragon's the only way we'll survive the flatteners.' Fred stared at her, completely bewildered.

'Anyway,' she said, more loudly, 'the reason I woke you up is that there are two ugly old women on my wall. They say you returned their call, and they're insisting on holding. Oh, sorry, they're not friends of yours, are they? They don't sound friendly.'

'Oh, yes, right,' said Fred, relieved at something he could handle. 'You'd better put them on.'

'Switch callers to this screen,' Anne ordered. The two women from the recording were now on Fred's wall. Anne smiled at them. 'We're sorry to have kept you waiting; here is Dr Drakely now.' And she teetered off.

'Good morning, Dr Dowthwaite and Mrs Phipps. Thank you both for returning my call,' Fred smiled ingratiatingly. 'I really do apologise for the delay. Actually, I've just started in a new jot and things are a bit hectic at the moment. So, what can I do for you?'

'You called us,' Nell Dowthwaite snapped. Her friend's approving nod and look at Fred suggested that she was going to be keeping the score.

'In response to a request from you,' said Fred, still smiling.

'Well, we may have complained about being spied on – but we didn't actually expect anyone to get back to us,' Nell said. Mildred reflected disgruntled resignation and looked at Fred.

'We really don't want to upset people, so we're always happy to explain why the surveillance is necessary,' said Fred smoothly.

'What are we supposed to have done to have people like you spying on us?' Nell demanded. Mildred nodded twice this time and her look at Fred was defiant.

Fred was used to this sort of complaint. Some people, especially older ones, had not yet accepted that openness was best for everyone, and that there was no point in openness unless there were jots like his looking in on what people were up to.

'It's the function of my jot to monitor the communications of anyone in this region who might possibly be a threat to bio-security,' Fred replied, trying to sound firm and official but amiable. 'My understanding is that you, Dr Dowthwaite, have been talking to members of a former seed smuggling network. The call we picked up between the two of you involved permaculture, which has also been involved in seed smuggling. So I don't really feel that our interest was unjustified.'

'What do you suppose we're going to smuggle seeds for? Nobody's got any private land any more. You can't even have a window box. As for permaculture, that's been banned. All we were doing was organising

31

a farewell – a *conference* one, since we can't even have a real meeting, in case we swap seeds, I suppose. What's the harm in that?'

'No harm at all, I'm sure,' replied Fred soothingly. 'We just have to keep an eye on former gardeners – for a while, until we're sure they're not finding some way to carry out domestic cultivation.'

Fred had almost forgotten Mildred Phipps, who now spoke for the first time in a keening voice and with tears in her eyes. 'All we ever wanted, Harvey and I, was to work in our little garden. We had a lovely little garden before they moved us to a sector; now we don't even have a balcony, not even a real window to the outside. You've taken away all our pleasure and you still won't leave us alone.'

'You've got a sector!' exclaimed Fred. 'Well I don't know what you've got to complain about then. My family's been on the list for a sector for five years now. We're still in an old-fashioned house and the noise from the storm baffles is terrible. We're hoping that with the new jot being out here ... I suppose you've got a sector too?' he asked Nell Dowthwaite.

'Yes, a single person's sector, nasty little cell with all system walls. Anyway, we're not here to talk about the housing lists. You still haven't said what you think we might do. As I just said, it can't be smuggling seeds, surely?'

'Because you wouldn't or couldn't?' Fred countered in a jovial, bantering tone. 'You, Dr Dowthwaite, used to have access to genetic material in your work. Are you going to tell me that you've severed all links with the facilities at Norwich. There are still biodiversity reserve domes there, I understand.'

'Yes, there are bloody domes at Norwich. Your SWI lot took them over, as you well know – not very intelligent that, Mr Spy.' Fred smiled indulgently at her word play. 'And I've been round them since I left, like any other member of the general public. Togged up in a nappy and space suit. You couldn't put a seed up your bloody nostril!'

Fred disapproved of women using bad language, so he made sure he was extra polite back to her. 'Well you see, Dr Dowthwaite, that's only part of the point of the protective clothing. It's also to protect visitors against biting insects and so on: it works both ways. I prefer to visit via the system myself. I've been into several of the domes: tropical rainforests and all sorts. And even home gardens – from all round the world – you'd be interested in those,' he said, turning to Mildred, who responded with a choked sob.

'You stop upsetting my friend,' said Nell, looking as if she was going to cry too in sympathy.

Fred would have preferred her to stay rude and angry. If there was one thing he could not cope with it was women crying – he never knew what to do or say. 'Oh dear, sorry, really, I didn't mean to upset Mrs Phipps, not at all – or you, Dr Dowthwaite. I just thought she could visit those gardens from her sector, with system walls all round she wouldn't need headgear. She could design her own garden too.' Fred knew he was rambling on, but it seemed to be all he could do. 'There are leisure learning courses on garden design and implementation. My son Tim says that soon people won't know the difference. She could dig the soil and sow seeds and watch them grow, just like in a real garden, without the backache! Well, anyway, you could try it – give it a chance – you never know ...' he tailed off. Both women were now crying noisily.

Nell blew her nose on a grubby handkerchief. Probably does her own laundry, Fred thought. She looked at him soulful and red-eyed, and said in a choked up voice, 'You've turned the whole planet to desert, utterly destroyed nature, and you're actually proud of it. We gardeners, for years, generations even, our mission has been to save a little bit of nature here and there. Do you remember the robins, Mildred?' Her friend nodded and smiled through her tears. Nell went on, 'Sometimes I dream I'm back in our little garden and the robin is on the apple tree chattering away. And my husband Bill and I, we're both planting out seedlings – him on his side of the garden, me on mine – we had different ways of gardening you know – he used to dig the soil two spits deep all over – he loved to dig, my poor Bill did – and he liked everything in neat rows. Then me on my side of the garden with my mulch beds, all in whirly patterns, plants which are best friends next to each other. "Call yourself a scientist!" Bill'd say – but we never tried to work out whose way was the best – we weren't competitive. But we grew so much food! Do you know, I think we could have fed the whole street from our garden – if they'd been content with what could be grown in our climate, that is. If only the world had gone that way instead of all this G-ARM ghastliness.' The two women smiled sadly at each other.

Fred felt a bit more confident now the tears seemed to have stopped. He wondered how someone who rambled on with such nonsense had got to be a professor in a science faculty. 'Oh come on now,' he said, 'you're just not making sense. Let's just consider what you've been saying. One,' he said, holding his hand up with four fingers extended and pointing to his little finger, 'One: the New Way agriculture is highly productive – you can hardly call the plantations *desert* – and it has saved the planet from pollution – as you must know. Two: there have been no species extinctions since the biodiversity domes were constructed – I'm sure you'd find there are robins and all the other garden birds living happily in some dome somewhere – just ask the system. Three: you couldn't feed everyone in the world from home gardens – what about your grains and your sugar and your meat – oh, I suppose you're vegetarian – your dairy produce then; and anyway, most people just don't want to do all that labouring work in their gardens. And it would make their food more expensive, with having to buy seeds and fertiliser and everything —'

Nell interrupted him. 'We never bought seeds; we collected seeds each year and replanted, or swapped with neighbours, or things seeded themselves – on my side especially.'

'And you wonder why your calls are tapped! That's illegal; it's stealing. All genetic material belongs to the corporations.'

'They stole it from the people,' Nell replied.

'I'd say they stole it from the planet; from the plants and animals themselves,' corrected Mildred.

'That's right, you're absolutely right, Mildred,' said Nell. 'Anyway, it's daft to say it's stealing to let plants seed themselves.'

'But the law is the law. Just because it's easily done doesn't make it right. It's like years ago, before the system, when people made illegal copies of computer games and software, and recordings of films and music. It was easy to do, but it was wrong because it put the companies who had the rights to the stuff out of business.'

'So we could put the corporations out of business? The chance would be a fine thing!' said Nell. Her friend laughed.

Fred ignored this. He was still holding his hand up, so he came to his fourth point. 'I was also going to say, number four: if you believed in self-sufficiency, how come you were working in hydroponics?' He put on a 'got you there' expression.

'You think that's inconsistent? No, the way I saw it was this: on a small local scale, the community could produce fresh produce out of season using hydroponics. I was working on tomatoes; we had very good results. I'm not totally against new methods; I just think it's crazy to turn over the whole planet to unnatural species – if you can call these monsters *species* that is.'

'But we have to feed the whole world. Before the New Way people used to starve and many children were stunted.'

'So you take over the whole planet just to feed one species. What about all the other species?'

'I told you, we haven't lost a single species since the domes were constructed.'

'*We haven't lost* – you make it sound as if other species are our property. You wouldn't do that to human beings – say to them, we've got a representative genetic sample, the rest of you can just die.'

'Of course not. People matter as individuals.'

'Well some of us think other species matter for themselves, for their own sake, regardless of what we might use them for, or whether we like them.'

'I'm sure you wouldn't say that about garden pests and disease organisms – moths and fungus and aphids and so on.'

'Yes we would. We'd make sure there were natural controls in the garden, to get a balance so we're not destroying anything.'

'Natural controls are still controls. Nice ladybirds kill nasty aphids. I don't see that it's any different, essentially. But the point is, you couldn't feed everybody in messy ways like that. It's just not productive enough.'

'It depends what you mean by *productive*. Garden production produces more food per acre than industrial food production – ten times as much, it's been proved time and again. But those Ghastly-ARMs, they've taken up every square inch of the planet practically.'

'But it's not just food: we also have to provide energy and raw materials, remember. Tim Harbright —'

'Don't talk to me about Tim Harbright,' snapped Nell. 'When I was a child we lived in a lovely part of the north-west of England called the Lake District. People used to visit from all round the country, the world even, though I don't believe in all that tourism. Anyway, they cleared off all the trees and the sheep and everything, and they planted biofuels everywhere, even on the lakes. It was just solid green everywhere; that awful lurid green that hurts your eyes. They called it "harblighting", didn't they – you heard it called that?'

'I expect people called it something like blight when the sheep were introduced hundreds of years ago,' Fred retorted. 'You talk about the area if it were untouched wilderness. The G-ARMs're just another phase of development.'

'Well there was real wilderness where I lived,' sighed Mildred. 'They harblighted all the heathlands and deserts in Western Australia.'

'Oh come on now, surely that was a good thing in every way. It was useless desert and now it's productive.'

'It wasn't useless to the wildlife. And it was beautiful: a deeply spiritual place. The New Way has destroyed the planet's soul.'

At this point both women suddenly disappeared. Fred stared at the blank screen wall for some moments and it began to display the SWI promotion. 'Anne!' he called. 'What's happened to my callers?'

Anne hurried into the office in person. 'Sorry, Dr Drakely. I had to close you down, the meeting's starting.'

'You interrupted us?' Fred was annoyed. 'Don't you think that was discourteous?'

'Oh, I did switch them to my wall and explain. I don't think you were getting anywhere with them, were you?'

'You were listening?'

'Yes, why not?'

'No, no reason.'

'Anyway, we must go. Come on, follow me.'

Anne walked towards the domed garden and through the open sliding doorway. But then she was not in the garden: the garden still looked and sounded just as before, but Fred could see no sign of the plum suit amongst the trees. How strange! He took some moments to extricate himself from the recliner. He walked towards the garden, but he found the way through blocked by an apparently transparent and non-reflecting surface. It was not glassy hard, but slightly yielding like a firm pillow as Fred's head and hands reached it. Then, as he continued to move towards it, he felt himself drawn through rather suddenly.

On the other side, instead of the garden, was a circular room full of people, and the buzz of conversation. Fred looked back at the surface he had come through. Now it appeared to be a mirror. His own startled face looked back at him. His brown eyes stared, his finely drawn dark eyebrows were raised below a wavy row of wrinkles; and above them – surely further back than usual – was his neatly combed straight dark hair, greying at the receding temples: but surely he wasn't going grey! And his ears stuck out. And that silly moustache which always looked rather dashing. The truth dawned. It's a true mirror, he thought, and all that stuff I've said about system surgery, and I've been doing it too, or the system has for me. Well, well! And then a realisation came: this is not a system wall, the system cannot see in here. We're hidden from the system! Fred's earlier uneasiness returned: what is going on? he wondered.

Fred saw in the mirror that someone had come up behind him: a plump, rather pink man, with a sparse crew cut. 'Hello there. Just got here? *Saul,*' and he offered his hand. Seeing Fred still looking at the mirror wall he remarked, 'Amazing stuff, smart materials.'

Fred turned around, managed a smile, and held out his hand, which Saul squeezed damply. 'Hello Saul, good to meet you, I'm Fred Drakely. Any idea what all this is about?' he waved at the room. 'It's unusual isn't it, getting co-jos all together in a – um – private meeting?' He detected a slightly patronising look from Saul before the man took him by the arm saying, 'Come and get yourself a drink and a few nibbles, Fred. Round this way.'

By weaving this way and that, pushing, and 'Excuse me, sorry,' Saul led Fred between the men standing in the aisle between rows of seats occupying half the room. At one side of the area in front of the seats were tables laid with food and drinks. Behind the tables were several young women, all rather similar to Anne, and Fred spotted her neat red head amongst them and waved.

'Your bird, that one? She worked for me for a while, called Anne isn't she?' asked Saul. 'Come on then.' He squeezed through the crush around the drinks tables until they were opposite Anne. 'Your boss needs a drink, love,' Saul grinned at her.

'Hello, Mr Sarney,' she nodded at Saul, who winked back. 'Dr Drakely, what can I get you?' she smiled at Fred.

Fred looked at the bottles of all shapes and sizes, green, brown and clear. 'A soft drink, please,' he muttered.

Anne looked along the bottles. 'I'm not sure ... Ah, tonic do you?' Fred nodded. 'Ice and lemon?' He nodded again.

'Come on now,' said Saul. 'I think we need a drop of gin in that, don't you?' He clapped Fred on the shoulder, and Fred thought perhaps he did and shrugged acceptance. 'And the same for me, thanks love, and make it a big one, save coming back too quick.'

There was less of a crush around the food table. Fred followed Saul, took a plate, and put on it a few little biscuits with pink or yellow stuff twirled on top. Now fully equipped they mingled. A seemingly endless round ensued of exchanges of names, and pleasantries about previous jots, home localities and families. Saul stayed with Fred throughout like a jovial pink shadow, and kept his tonics topped up.

At last there was a signal that the formal part of the meeting was to start shortly: the young women came round with trays to collect glasses and plates and to wave encouragingly in the direction of the seating. Saul now drifted away from Fred's side, but once everyone was settled, Fred saw him seated on the low plinth facing the audience with a small group of other men, one of whom then stood and walked to a lectern at the front of the plinth. To Fred's astonishment, the man held a sheaf of paper, which he laid on the lectern. Fred had seen paper aplenty on recordings of the old days on the system, but never the real stuff, which he had understood was no longer made. Fred was sitting near the back and he noticed quite a few of the men sharing surprise with their neighbours. Perhaps he was not the only one feeling that there was something strange about this meeting. But presumably they were now to be told what it was all about. And anyway, all the unaccustomed alcohol was making him feel mellow and unconcerned.

The man at the lectern had an air of authority about him. He was quite a bit older than Fred, but still in good shape: slim, well-built, upright, his crinkly grey to white hair cropped short and his clean-shaven face lined but firm, and with strong, regular features. He glanced through the papers, then looked up with a calm expression which commanded attention.

'Welcome, gentlemen, to this briefing meeting. My name is Howard Meredith.' Fred thought he recognised the name, but could not place it. 'I hope that some of you are beginning to get to know each other. We have an interesting bunch in this room today: researchers, tech-release people and bio-security agents. Each one of you has an impeccable track-record in your area of work and some specialist expertise of an innovative nature which is particularly appropriate to the project we are embarking on today.' My van-frame probe, Fred thought.

'First of all, I'm aware there are some worried men in here today, and I must try to reassure you. You all know what an important advance for world society has been achieved by making all dealings and transactions

38

completely open and accessible through the system, and recorded for all time in the archives. Those of you engaged in surveillance work have handled the disquiet this sometimes provokes in certain quarters with admirable courtesy and diplomacy. You all, I know, believe in the value and fairness of the principle of openness.

'But –' He paused and scanned the walls. 'It cannot have escaped your notice that our meeting today is not open: the system is not able to see or record us here. We meet in secret.' A soft hiss of drawn breath rose and then died down. 'Some of the research and tech-release men here today know that very occasionally some work has to be kept under wraps for a while. I have with me on the platform the jot which heads up Secrecy Control, which comes under the World President jot itself. You will have an opportunity afterwards to direct any concerns you are still feeling about secrecy to them. The one thing I will say now is that all of us up here are reassured about any concerns we may have had by the knowledge that all – I emphasise: *all* – such work is initiated and closely supervised by the Prejot. The system is in fact not completely unaware of these few projects – it cannot be if you think about it. It knows we're all here, breaking the jot rules.' He smiled. 'It sees some of us appearing suddenly from the garden when we go to use the chute, and then disappearing again.' There was a titter of amusement. 'It ignores suspicious circumstances like that *only* when they are associated with a Prejot project under Seccon.'

Fred felt his disquiet melt away. He joined the collective sigh of relief from around the room. He smiled and nodded at his neighbours. He felt rather important and sat up straighter in his seat.

Meredith shuffled a page of his notes to the back and continued. 'As you know, you've been brought together for a new job of work. We have about twenty jots here, all members being present because of the off-system briefing this project requires. This is a Tech Release Board project, which again comes directly under the Prejot. Projects like this are part of the process by which the release criteria of the Board are determined. Some of the criteria for deciding whether to release or refuse some development or invention are obvious: things like compatibility, standardisation, avoiding rapid obsolescence and waste. But one lesson we have learnt from the disasters of necrotech is not to assume that clever innovation is bound to be beneficial.

'The project has been set up by the Prejot in order to undertake a global benefits check for the whole class of new developments called "intelligent organic structures" or Intos. You jots here will cover European Region. The official name of the project is "Intos Implications Investigation" or I3, but it has been dubbed the "Green Dragon Task Force".' Fred joined in the ripple of laughter. 'I hope you all managed to look at the prep pack section on Intos?' He looked up and Fred nodded. 'Well, I expect you get the reference to green dragons then – they're actually part plant and part animal in their metabolism. This technology is a long way from tech release, largely because the Prejot is very unclear about what effect it would have on society. But before we get down to that, for the benefit of the people here not involved in the research, we'll give you a short run-down on how Intos came about.' Fred did a little shuffle to attention; some other men did the same, whilst others slumped back. Meredith turned another page, cleared his throat and sipped from a glass of water.

'You've all used smart materials – chute stems, of course, furniture such as the new system cubicle recliners, and now this new method of dividing living space.' Meredith nodded towards the glassy wall. 'As far as the interested public is concerned, the basis is nanotechnology, which means it's designed right down at the molecular level to produce the desired effect at the macro level. But the implementations I've mentioned are not actually nanotechnology at all – because nanotechnology doesn't work.' Meredith raised his eyebrows at the surprised faces, Fred's amongst them. Then he glanced behind him at the group on the platform and nodded. One of the men stepped forward: a tall, thin man in a crumpled grey suit.

'Allow me to introduce Tom Hammond, who can tell you about this better than I can. And of course you can collar him later if you want to know more. Tom.' Meredith passed his sheaf of notes to the other man, who turned to the next page, ran his finger down and nodded.

'Yes, good afternoon, gentlemen. As Meredith's just said, research into nanotech hit serious problems – some time ago now. There were unpredictable effects at the macro level – a phenomenon the lab jots called "wildness". We kept that quiet, of course: no sense in frightening everyone! "Emergent properties" is the official term. Anyway, efforts to stop wildness occurring came to nothing. We spent years trying to figure out what was wrong with the molecular construction to cause this random unreliability. Then intuitive innovation caught on as the best approach to problem solving and invention. We gave that a go, and ended up incorporating the problem into an invention – we harnessed the wildness using intelligence – hence Intos: artificially intelligent artificial life. Like natural life, it's carbon-based. The intuitive innovation people say it taps into a reservoir of memories of organic strategies. But that's not my area at all.

'Oh, yes, I should tell you, we now use the term "holotech" rather than "nanotech", because what this harnessed wildness consists of is a holarchy of holons – a holarchy being a hierarchy without the power from the top. A holon is an entity which is simultaneously a whole, with its particular capabilities, and a part of one or more other holons. Each level of a holarchy gets on with what it knows how to do independently of the levels above or below, and influence flows both ways.

'Anyway, to move on, there is a second side to Intos, something quite unconnected with nanotech and its problems. The other aspect of Intos came out of a refinement of voice recognition by the existing system. It arose spontaneously, out of the system's learning capabilities, and then we spotted it and called it "flicker choice". It's a very interesting feature. The system – the old kind and the Intos-based – can recognise the needs and desires of a user without any vocal command or conversational speech interpretation. We assume it was taking in visual data on user responses during oral exchanges, and discovered various patterns of facial expression which enabled it to anticipate users' oral responses. Now what we see happening is, the system runs a series of choices in front of the user's eyes and interprets the facial responses. Sound and hearing can come into it too, of course. When it's got the preference, it refines that down to a series of choices within that, and so on, and then it delivers what's needed or wanted.

'We've done a controlled trial of Intos interacting with users. In spite of not being connected to the old system, it very quickly cottoned on to flicker choice and, being holotech-based, it then began to acquire emergent properties. At present it's only used in a very restricted way – just for constructing channels. What worries Tech Release is the question of what we'd be releasing if we let Intos loose, because we wouldn't know what it was going to be capable of next. There are economic implications too, I believe, but that's not my area. I'll hand you back now to Meredith.'

'Thanks, Tom,' Meredith said, and took the stand again He scanned the raised faces, some of which, including Fred's, were tense with concentration. 'As I said earlier, if you haven't understood all of that,

41

and I'd be surprised if you did if you haven't met it before, don't worry. You'll have plenty of opportunity to consult Tom, or one of his colleagues, later today, or some other time. I'm coming to the actual job now, you'll be glad to know. The reason we need the Green Dragon Task Force is that the quite astonishing potential benefits of Intos have likely consequences which worry us a great deal. When the Prejot first heard of these developments, they were seen as having great employment generating possibilities. There was talk of bringing job sharing down from seven to four, or even three. But now we've realised that Intos could have the opposite effect. It could eliminate the need for jobs – work – almost entirely.' Meredith nodded to acknowledge the stir that created. 'Because, you see, this new generation of system can identify what people want, learn how to provide that, evolve new ways of providing, and grow as big as necessary to accommodate the needs and desires of an expanding population – all by itself, without *any* human assistance – at least, none of the kind we normally think of as work.' Meredith had evidently reached the end of his notes and, putting them down, he stepped down from the lectern and stepped into the gangway between the two sections of seats. He continued talking as he walked slowly between the rows of men.

'We just do not know what effect the introduction of this new generation of system would have. What will people do without jobs of any kind? They spend more time at leisure than at work now, of course. But many men's identity is tied up with their job, however little time they spend on it. Women have less of a problem, of course, since they have been encouraged to concentrate on home-making. But men, they don't seem to take to that; it doesn't satisfy them. So, before we let this innovation out, we want to try it out on a very special sample of men and their families. That's where you come in.' Meredith had reached the end of the room. All the heads were craned backwards towards him. He walked slowly back to the front.

'The plan is this. You will all be re-housed in sector accommodation at this Centre, with the latest personal system cubicles, which have touch-sensitive exercise recliners, so you can be kept fit. There will be no travelling for your families – no attendance school, for the children. The families will take turns in the small Intos facility we've set up, again on this site. It's pretty similar to the old system, except the cubicles are Intos cells, which feel different: I've tried one myself and

42

you can tell they're alive. There's no physical connection between the system dome and the Intos dome, and you would have to walk from one to the other: I hope it won't be too blowy; the baffles here are pretty good. You men will walk to this office here to report – on paper – and you'll have secretaries to help you with that.

'I am sure you'll take great care that no harm comes to the *subjects* of this experiment! But remember about the holonic approach: the whole as well as the parts. We want you and your families to regard this testing phase in the context of the whole of the New Way, hence the prep pack, which you will have access to in the Intos facility, and which will have more information added about the Intos as and when we're getting to know it. There are some people working on these developments who say that Intos will bring about the *real* Biotechnology Age. Current technology still uses thermal energy, from burning biofuels, what we've had is only bio-*necro*-technology! I don't know about that; we've done our best and achieved a great deal. Anyway, it's possible we'll have to go for Intos sooner rather than later because of communication problems with the existing set-up. Your brief could change at that stage to a wider social surveillance role: what we're calling "Phase 2" of the project. Until that occurs, your families' outgoing system communications will be filtered to ensure they don't let anything out too soon.'

Meredith was now back at the front, and he sipped from his water glass. Then he nodded towards the group on the platform. Saul stood up and came forward to join him.

'Let me introduce you to Saul Sarney now. He's going to talk to you about the sort of problem we want you to look out for once we get to Phase 2'

'Thanks Howard. Right, guys,' Saul grinned down at them. 'Phase 2 proper is when these new developments are out in the public domain, which is going to happen; this is too big for Tech Release to hold on to indefinitely. However, the way I look at it, Phase 2 needs to begin right away. Howard and I don't see eye to eye on this one, so he's very kindly letting me have my say. I'm a surveillance man, so I guess I tend to look at it that way from the start. It seems to me that what's happening is happening, regardless of the technology. It's happening with the existing system anyway – flicker choice is just one example – and we need to keep an eye on the way it's going. I don't propose to tell you how to do this job. Letting your own families have a go with Intos is one thing, but we've got to make sure society doesn't break down with the kind of way of life Intos could bring about. One area that concerns me personally is transport. All through history major economic changes and expansion have been associated with improvements in transportation. We now have a potential technological revolution which could make transport completely unnecessary. Think about it: no one needs to travel; everything you need is piped to you, including all your information, entertainment and human interaction. That's already possible, and increasingly necessary. But what about not being *able* to travel? It's one thing not needing to; it's another being actually locked in. How is that going to affect people? Will they have to be provided with illusions they're still going places? If they need illusions – travel won't be the only area – will they be convincing enough?

'Howard's mentioned the work implications. Leisure is already a vital area, and well provided for. That's fine while people can still see leisure occupations as what they do when they're not working. But when there is no work, entertainment has to become a major source of personal identity. Maybe, again, they'll have to be provided with illusions they've got work to do. Some say we need an extension to the vanity frame idea, so that people can make something of themselves. In fact, providing entertainment through the system, particularly interactive rather than passive entertainment – virtual reality, that sort of thing – is almost certainly going to be the only type of work people can do for each other in the future.' My Tim! Fred thought proudly, trust him to get that right.

'Some of the effects we're concerned about are not new to the Intos generation of system: that's just going to compound problems concerned with a knowledge orientated system by extending it to the physical side. We've had to keep an eye on the existing system which, of course, learns and changes all the time. I'll give you an example of the sort of thing we've had to do. The system has no central intelligence function, as you know, but bits of it "get ideas". A year or so ago it was deciding all over the place that children shouldn't engage in sport any more. It identified sport as the major means by which people, especially the young, are socialised into accepting competition – in the interests of the market system of course. It decided – on the basis that there are no longer any material shortages – that competition was not in the human interest, and set about removing the conditioning. It stopped offering children any information about sport: what sport is, where they can participate, VR simulations involving the experience of sport, the lot. Now one of the Tech Board surveillance teams spotted this and reported it. And it was decided, partly on the basis of the possible introduction of Intos, that sport, and the attitudes and activities of necrotech generally, would be essential material for public amusement. So a system direction flush was circulated to tell the system to drop those ideas. That episode shook us up a fair bit, I can tell you. Soon after that the Prejot began to consider setting up this project to look at the implications of implementing Intos.' Saul glanced at Meredith, who gestured 'Carry on.' 'Right,' said Saul, 'that seems to be enough from us. They'll be a short break, coffee or tea or whatever, and then divide into small groups so that the expertise we've got assembled here today gets spread around a bit. Then we'll gather together to report back. We'll leave questions until then if you don't mind. Thank you, gentlemen, for your attention. And best of luck to you all!' He grinned broadly, waved and walked back to the group on the platform.

Fred got up then a little too suddenly and felt his head spin. He steadied himself on the back of the chair in front and then made for the wall. He pushed through to one of the offices, perhaps the one he had occupied that morning, he could not tell. He made for the recliner, got into it and lay back. He shut his eyes, and he could hear the splash and trickle of the fountain in the garden that wasn't there.

It was not only the gin that had put Fred in a whirl; he felt worried. At one level he was meant to be worried – that was the job, worrying about Intos. But he was also still worried about the secrecy. And what Tim said about the system being one big van-frame kit. And Mildred Phipps crying for her garden and Tim saying we wouldn't know the difference and Min feeling the melons and not knowing she was just rubbing her fingers together and little Louise being really an eastern princess ...

–Hello. Can I speak to Justin Clements, please. It's Beatrice Harper.

–Hi, Bea. How are you?

–Fine. Are you busy?

–Not too busy for you, my sweet. I tried ringing you Sunday evening.

–I wasn't back from seeing my grandparents in Newcastle. I had to stay Saturday night: there's just the two of them in a three bedroomed house, so no excuse to stay somewhere else, and we didn't get away until after tea. I hate it there: so smelly – old people you know. And they've got this disgusting old dog – ought to be put down – and it's such a job keeping Poppy away from it – well, I couldn't really, it'd hurt their feelings. I don't suppose she'd catch anything off it, and it hasn't any teeth left, but ...

–You're not terribly fond of dogs, are you! Remember that ghastly stray that wouldn't go away after Jeff fed it? You practically left home.

–Don't remind me! Haven't heard from Jeff in ages, have you?

–Last I heard he was in Norway – practising conflict resolution trying to understand why people there seem to need to kill whales.

–I think it's just a cultural pattern – there doesn't have to be a 'why'. Have you read more of *The Completion*?

–Yes. I read about Fred Drakely. Can't decide if he's a male chauvinist pig or just a dork.

–You don't like him?

–Was I supposed to?

–He means well.

–Oh, yes, terribly earnest, isn't he. Actually, I suppose I was taken aback by the silly secretary bird. I thought: this is supposed to be in the future – so surely women should be equal to men – not wearing silly clothes and making the coffee – worse than the women in Star Trek with their tight tunics and mini-skirts.

–So you think women are achieving equality nowadays?

–No. I suppose they're not. Not really – it's mostly talk. Lots of women working, of course, but mostly low paid, domestic-type work – cleaning, serving and sewing sort of stuff. So I suppose what you're saying is: even if the world changes, people don't change – and there'll always be men in suits.

–Not always, I think – it's just there's a lag.

–Because of pattern?

–Quite. What did you think of bionecrotech technology?

–There's an awful lot of it – enough for a whole book, let alone one chapter.

–Maybe I could have written a whole book about this period, but the idea is for the chapter to represent a whole era of human history – a few centuries maybe.

–A few hours of story covers a few centuries?

–Yes. It's only time, after all, and people follow patterns so much they're virtually all the same person.

–And they're moulded by the technology, I suppose?

–I think so, but from the past too, not just what's current. Anyway, what did you think of the technology?

–Horrible! – those biofuel monocultures. But I thought the idea was intriguing – taking over the oceans and all the marginal land, and preventing small-scale cultivation for fear of weeds and pests.

–What did you think of the office and home technology?

–I loved the vanity frames, especially system face lifts – that's really being moulded by the technology! Most of what you've described could be done now, I think. Presumably you intended that, and it's connected to the idea of putting innovation on hold until current developments are used to full advantage. Tends not to happen in a free market, of course. And I see that a few centuries on, or whatever, they've finally got the paperless office that was talked about back in the '70s. And the use of VR for shopping and education, that's well on its way. But the stuff at the end of the chapter about the Green Dragon. That's something else!

–Mmm, I think it is. Anyway, any allegorical 'M's?

–M for Morals, definitely. They've wiped out all of nature in the interests of human welfare and sustainability. That can't be right.

–Do you think nature cares? It had a good innings before Homo sapiens came along – four billion years or so. And you could say that our species plus our monocultures is what nature has become.

–Already? In our time?

–Sure. That's what you mean by the allegorical mirror, isn't it?

–Yes, I suppose so. So the green dragon culture – the Biotech Age, is it? – will be another mirror on life today?

–I'm not telling you. Read on, Macduff!

–OK, Bea, I'll do that. See you at the Pizza Express on Saturday – eight o'clock.

Our journey continues.

We move on now from bionecrotech to biotech: from biofuels and G-ARMs to intelligent organic biotechnology, from job share teams and conference shopping to life in the green dragon: a transition which took place over perhaps only two or three generations from Fred Drakely's lifetime.

As we did earlier with necrotech and bionecrotech, we can consider why the change took place from bionecrotech to biotech. Bionecrotech was actually one long change, well intentioned, optimistic, but diabolical in its innocent destructiveness. Again, it is possible to attribute biotech to a crisis, in particular the extreme weather conditions, possibly brought about by the final elimination of natural ecosystems. The storms destroyed rigid man-made structures, rooted out trees, and made travel increasingly difficult and hazardous. The advent of the intos biotechnology, which exploited artificial organic metabolism, grew into the ultimate global city, may have saved humanity from that crisis, or it may just have been the next stage in technological innovation.

Bony Bailey, the pattern mathematician, would probably have pointed out that many human patterns were perpetuated into biotech. The green dragon was a city: like all cities it walled its citizens in, protecting them from needing to know the means of their subsistence, and spinning elaborate fantasies to sustain their beliefs in their importance and worth. Biotech continued a pattern which originated in bionecrotech of strict social equality: there was no longer any need for human labour, so everyone was a citizen, and no one was a slave.

Biotech caused no further harm to the planet. Its metabolism was mainly plant-like: it used energy direct from the sun and it put down roots to get water and minerals; it assembled the chemicals of life to provide food for the inmates and to construct and repair their cells. But it was unlike a plant in having human-like intelligence and memory through which it provided the illusions which saved the inmates from a vegetative state which they would have found intolerable, and probably died from boredom.

Life in the green dragon's city was idyllic. Each individual received a perfectly balanced diet, was kept hygienically clean and physically fit, was mentally stimulated or diverted, and provided with the self-image he or she desired, together with self-determined success and admirers. The dragon was the perfect provider, and expected nothing from her charges but the knowledge that she was needed: indeed, it was only their desire to escape the paradise she assembled that made her begin to die – but that comes much later.

Biotech was the age of abundance and indulgence for everyone. It was a dream come true, but could anyone in necrotech have predicted the form that dream would take? I doubt it. Throughout necrotech, from the stone age to the nuclear age, there have been visionaries, great minds and inventors of all kinds of cleverness, who must have hoped that their grand schemes, brilliant theories or technological breakthroughs would transform the dreary struggle to a world of plenty. Some may have dreamed that the end of scarcity would render unnecessary any injustice, exploitation, and perhaps all forms of cruelty and suffering. Probably cynics commented that such a world would be very dull: what satisfaction could there be in indulgence unless others coveted it?

Biotech satisfied both dreamers and cynics. There was no injustice or exploitation. No one suffered unless they liked to. But everyone who wanted to be exploitative could indulge that, everyone who needed to be envied was, everyone who had to win and be cheered and admired got his fill of adulation. Those who wished to be heroes or commanders of armies or rulers of states, they could do those things, as could would-be tyrants and torturers, murderers and rapists, sexual perverts, cannibals and satanists. On the other hand, there were those who were content to spend their lives exploring the knowledge and artistry humanity had achieved, and to add their own contributions. Biotech rivalled classical antiquity and every subsequent surge of intellectual excellence in its cultivation of the mind. Works of genius poured into the intos dragon's already overflowing libraries and institutions.

Although there was continuing creativity and new thought, the world of biotech was largely retrospective. It was necrotech re-lived in all its phases, with all its pride and shame, over and over again, for generation after generation. In early biotech the period most commonly relived was late necrotech before the collapse occurred, simply because the intos memory, inherited from the bionecrotech 'system', was full of its images. Later on the focus changed, and it proved vital that it did so.

Those who lived during that age paid no attention to the passage of time in the 'real' world, or to anything else in the 'real' world. Indeed, it was a social convention crucial to sustaining the illusions which made life worth living that one did not admit that the 'real' world existed at all. Those from my time who shifted to biotech frequently had some difficulty deciding on their return whether they had been someone in biotech or had travelled right back to necrotech itself.

There was one human activity which was new to biotech, although, like everything else, it drew on the past. Among those who delighted to entertain others through theatricals of one form or another were the providers of 'storyframes'. They worked with the intos dragon to provide interactive stories for people to participate in. Their work required them to break the social convention and face up to the physical circumstances of life in biotech. I experienced a shift to a trainee storyframer, a woman named Amelia. The episode begins as she is demonstrating the storyframe she has created to a group of experienced framing professionals. In her storyframe, Amelia plays a queen named Agnetha. I hope this episode in Amelia's life will provide you with an effective insight into the biotech world.

4

Storyframes

Agnetha carefully examined the intricate patterns on the skirt of her tabard where it draped over her knees, and hoped that no one would notice that she was avoiding looking at the spectacle below. Grunthor could not see her because she was on his blind side. Their dais was too high up for anyone in the crowd to see her eyes clearly. Fortunately, the dignity of her position excused her from cheering the high spots of what was being done to the pathetic scrap of humanity strapped to the torturing frame.

The purpose of the ceremony was to break the spirit of the Terrever. To the audience the screaming of the victims was the sound of the smashing into fragments of what had been an integrated whole: a people bonded to their land, a land now in the possession of Grunthor, a conquering son of the Arklash royal family. This land would now be named Grunthor after him. He was now its king and she was, for now and perhaps for some while, Grunthor's queen.

Agnetha's hands beneath the tabard cradled her swollen belly and felt the movements of their child. Surely a baby son would protect her from the fate of her predecessor, the Lady Delaine. She shuddered at the memory of queuing in the procession of torture victims after her people had been beaten in battle. Grunthor had visited her the night before, and raped her as he had raped several of the prettier girl and boy prisoners. As she was led to the torture table, he had stood up: a signal for the ceremony to freeze in its bloody tracks. For a long moment he stood there, apparently considering her fate and, by implication, that of the Lady Delaine, sitting dignified but surely trembling at his side on the dais. Her fate was sealed, not so much by Grunthor preferring Agnetha, but because it was at the battle against Delaine's people that a spear thrust had crushed his brow and bitten into his eye socket, bursting the eyeball. In vengeance for the loss of his eye and his handsomeness,

52

Grunthor slowly raised his hand and held it out, palm upwards, to Agnetha. She was led up the steps to him. Delaine was disrobed and taken down to her lingering death. Her robe, this tabard, had been placed over Agnetha's head.

And now the people whose art had created the tabard had been overthrown. She wondered if another garment like it would ever be made. It had been taken as peace payment many years previously, when the Arklash collectors had visited Terrever. In return, the Arklash undertook to protect Terrever from foreign invaders. The fact that the Arklash themselves were the most likely invaders was something that the Terrever muttered to themselves, but would not dare utter in protest to the collectors.

The Terrever people had very little worth taking. Their simple life was based on a diet consisting mainly of wild herbs and fruits, concentrated into areas around the thatched huts by a simple gardening: unwanted vegetation was covered with layers of leaf litter, which made a compost on which seeds from preferred plants were scattered. They also ate raw fish from the rivers and sea, and game dried in the sun was stored for food for the winter; certain reeds and grasses provided them fibre and building material.

Each year when the collectors came, the Terrever pretended to cooperate with them in hunting expeditions, but led them well away from the wild herds. The collectors usually went away with a few slaves, and the impression that Terrever was a poor land.

In fact Terrever was a fertile country, with extensive forests and rich soil. Its rocks contained all the minerals that humankind had ever valued. But mining, tilling the soil, cutting trees and burning were taboo – or rather, unthinkable – in the Terrever culture. They were a deeply spiritual people, and they honoured and communed with the conscious web of life. They took seriously the need to keep their numbers stable and, in recognition of this, each spring they sacrificed a newly wed young couple by towing them out into the ocean on a reed fishing raft, and leaving them to starve to death. The sacrificial victims were clothed in tabards made from dyed cloth decorated with tiny fragments of fish bone, shells and fruit pips. They took all year to make. One year the collectors had arrived shortly before the ceremony. They saw the garments and took them as part of the peace payment. Since that year the sacrificial victims had gone to their fate naked; the Terrever would not make the sacred robes again for fear they would be defiled. If they were forced to make them, Agnetha doubted the effect would be so lovely, and she shut her mind to the scene below her and meditated upon the webs and spirals and the detailed pictures of plants and animals, and she imagined the sacrificial victim for whom it was made doing the same during her slow dying.

It had been almost a century since the 'discovery' by the Arklash of Terrever and the five other nations of the lesser continent. Sadly for those peoples, the Arklash royal family had seven sons, and all the territories of the greater continent were occupied by other branches of their family. All but the oldest son had to find a kingdom. Grunthor was the youngest. He was the most skilled at the arts of war and he had won many of the battles for the lesser continent, but the proprieties dictated that each land he won had to be offered first to an older brother, until all were established in a kingdom of their own. At last only Terrever was left. It had been an easy conquest. Two swift raids on the compounds on either side of Terrever Bay had wiped out the nation's pathetic defence forces. A few weeks of tramping around the country, slaughtering, raping and burning, and rounding up prisoners for torture had destroyed Terrever's gentle people. Their spirit was already crushed when the formal spirit-crushing ceremony took place.

As the screaming of the prisoner and the roaring of the crowd rose and fell, Agnetha thought back to the shrieking and thundering of the storm on which they rode the last stage of the long voyage across the Western Ocean to this land, only a few weeks before. The fleet had waited many days just beyond the horizon, until the stormy weather that Grunthor needed had moved over them from the north. He paced the decks in a fury at the delay, having depended on a suitable storm descending, as they were wont to do at this time of year. At last the storm had come, a howling fury of a storm as if to make up for keeping him waiting.

Grunthor had left her with her women attendants in the great sailing ship as he was rowed ashore. It was early morning, not yet dawn. The heavy wooden ship, its sails furled, dropped and staggered up again in the deep trenches which were sucked open and re-filled as the towering walls of water collapsed from above. She huddled below the deck in the hellish damp dark and imagined the spirits of the storm crying above the roaring water.

Grunthor had described to her with triumphant relish a few hours later how he and his men had crept from the beach to the Terrever compound, surprising the inhabitants in their sleep. Because of the storm, the few lookouts on the cliff tops had seen them too late to sound the alarm shells. The Terrever people had fought as best they could, grabbing their stone clubs and leather shields as they awoke to the sound of smashing and screaming. It was a total massacre; no time to take prisoners. Grunthor and his men ran swiftly and quietly to the compound on the opposite arm of the bay and slaughtered everyone there also. This bay was vital to the Terrever for fishing, but it was also their weak point and the most obviously in need of defence. Grunthor believed that most of the Terrever defenders would be in the two cliff-top compounds, and that if these were captured, the whole country would be his. He was right; it was a victory unworthy of his skills as a warrior and a leader of armies.

He told her the tale of the two battles, with much embroidery, as they feasted on the beach later that day, beneath the shelter of the hollowed cliffs. Dozens of carcasses tied up on spears were already dripping fat into the fires. Before they were ready to eat, great bowls of offal: hearts, livers and brains, were passed around. The conquerors dipped in their knives and either sucked the juicy morsels raw or held them to the fire to toast. As they guzzled and boasted, they relished the physical and spiritual nourishment from their fallen enemies. The battle feast initiated the process of rebirth into this new land.

At the coronation a few weeks later, when all of Terrever was vanquished, the rebirthing continued. This time the Arklash warriors had live victims to first torture slowly to death and then eat. The greater the torment the more total the drawing out of the Terrever spirit, so that the Terrever ancestors would hear and know and wither away, and never haunt the new-born people. Through the agony of this birth, the Terrever would die and the Grunthor would be born.

Agnetha felt her child move. Soon he too would be born into this new land, out of her agony. Perhaps her lord would grow to be gentle then. She thought of him lying by her side the night before, his henchmen crouched in the corners of the tent. Grunthor needed no privacy for his rutting, and he took no risks with his safety whilst asleep. These henchmen belonged to the Arklash family, were cousins of the royal brothers. They had everything to gain by their loyalty to Grunthor. She however could not be trusted, since slave wives had been known to take suicidal vengeance. After he had taken her roughly from behind, into her anus to make her cry out in pain, he had turned onto his back and was instantly asleep. He lay like a fallen warrior laid out on his bier, his legs straight and his arms crossed over his chest. This apparent vulnerability, a reminder of his mortality, made a tenderness rise up in Agnetha's heart.

'Well, that's my storyframe: if I can call it *mine* after all your help. Not much to show for all the work we put into it,' said Amelia, twisting in her pink plush armchair in the viewing room to look at the little audience beside and behind her.

'It's simply terrific, darling!' cried Luke, who sat beside her on the front row. He wiped his shiny bald head with his handkerchief and beamed at Amelia and swept the others into a heap of warm approval.

There were now five people in her audience, all of whom had assisted her with some aspect of the production; someone new had appeared with each stage of her progress. Besides Luke Featherday, her teacher and guide, there was lean and dark Cora Flinch the horror expert, scruffy Oliver Sheridan the frame-playwright, pink and plump Amadine Puleston the costume designer, and gorgeous Dean River the actor. She did not know any of them at all well and, although she had become very absorbed in her first attempt at framing, she did not feel she really belonged in this larger-than-life 'set' of dedicated frame creators.

'Fabulous! wonderful! lovely! lovely!' they all exclaimed.

'Well, do you think,' she asked tentatively, 'it's good enough for release?' She wanted to ask, and was trying to imply: what about me, have I passed?

'Release? Oh definitely! Folks'll love it,' said Luke. The others echoed agreement.

'Well, while we're here, Kiddy-winks,' he went on, 'I've got a couple more new frames we could view. Standard stuff, so they could go out straightaway probably.'

'Not too long, I hope,' said Amadine, restlessly rearranging her plump pink form in the armchair, 'I'm famished!'

'No, not long, darling. These are just little sketches; plenty of flex potential. You should know: one of them's your latest, so we'll keep that 'til last. The other's by a new framer, but nothing very original came out of it. It's a boy's frame. Quite nice. A boy framed it actually – quite a young kid.'

The boy swam back and waved dismissively behind him.

'Look at that old ship. You said we were going to see something good. That must be at least a hundred years old; monsters like those went out with fusion energy. Show us something smooth, why don't you? Let's go home, lads!'

A triangular space vehicle drifted apparently slowly in a void distantly bounded by a solid silver backcloth of stars. Its steely blue exterior was pitted with scars from accelerating to near light speed through gravelly debris.

'Wait a bit. Have you looked where it's going?' the guide grabbed the boy's arm as he reached the pod and pointed it over to the right. 'And don't inhibit your umbilical reeling in; it's not meant to be a skipping rope!' The boy let go of the loops of fine cord connecting him to the pod, and it was sucked in until it was taut. He looked along the guide's arm. The other boys all looked that way too.

As a distant shape moved aside they could just make out a tiny circle of absolute black, barely discernible in the silver curtain. As their minds attuned to the enormous expanse before them, they realised that the old ship was lining up in an attenuated queue forming a spiral arm about the black dot.

'The dustbin of the solar system,' the guide explained. 'The World Federation agreed five years ago now that all nuclear waste and contaminated materials could be dumped in a local black hole. I don't suppose it's the most exciting development as far as you guys are concerned, but we think its rather impressive. We're working on how to take up the disintegration energy that's given off, but we have to find a way of avoiding wholesale transference of anti-particles to Earth. Do you want a closer look?'

Without waiting for a reply, the guide closed the transparent gate of the pod and jumped the tiny vehicle nearer to the 'dustbin'. He left it in resist mode and reopened the gate. He swam out with the boys in tow. They spread out into space around him, their bodies shivering uncontrollably in the turbulent currents which marked the boundary of the hole. Any further and they would be sucked in.

They watched as the old spaceship approached. As it neared the boundary, for all its huge bulk, it went into a spin. An apex of its triangular body crossed the boundary by a tiny margin and was instantly spun out into a filament which spiralled towards the hole, becoming vanishingly fine. Various unconnected parts of the ship followed its trail. The massive body seemed to melt into strands of molten metal, some shot back away from the hole in their direction.

The boys whooped with excitement and tried to catch the fragments as they burst into cascades of light energy. One ball of light persisted for some moments, and they tossed it between them and shivered in the shocks it imparted as they touched it.

'Wowee! Over here, get this one before it blows!' The boy turned a somersault towards a shimmering ball of blue light and gave it a header.

The boy turned freely in the supportive medium. His naked body was suspended in a white space, a globular cell. He turned to face them and waved.

'Well, that was it. Quite good eh? Lots of flex potential, I think.' Luke looked around at the group.

Amelia hastily shut her mouth, conscious that she had been gaping.

Luke smiled at her. 'You liked that one?' he asked.

Her throat felt dry, and her voice came out husky. 'That last shot. What was that? It wasn't ... ?'

'The boy framer himself in his cell? Yes. Oh, dear, the unmentionable! I'm surprised you haven't got over that prudery.' His voice was light and teasing, but Amelia cringed.

She struggled to adjust to actually seeing the level of existence below what she had thought of as the real world, but which framers called 'the basisframe'. She whispered, 'How was he able to float about like that?'

'All kids' cells are like that now,' said Oliver. 'It's the new way the dragon provides. The cell is filled with this jelly mesh you can breathe in. It can go solid as well if that's the sensation you need.'

'I didn't see any hands – or chute, for that matter,' said Cora. 'How do they get fed?'

'You can eat the cell stuff, and wee and crap into it,' Oliver said. 'I don't know what goes on in the medium, but obviously it does what's necessary. Most of the time you're unaware of it, of course.'

'What's the stuff taste like?' asked Amadine.

'Like something you're eating in a story. Hamburger maybe for that kid. Caviar or cream cakes for you, eh? Or you don't know you're eating at all.'

'Does this type of story only appeal to kids?' asked Dean. 'I mean, should we release it recommended for boys only – and girls, of course, if they liked it? Because it might not work without the cell stuff support and mobility.'

'Oh, the old smart recliners are not bad for sensation of movement,' said Luke. 'But I think, yes, it is boy's stuff. I suppose part of it comes from video games. *Space Invaders*, that sort of thing.'

'Do you have boys' frames like that now – you know, zapping the nasties?' asked Amelia.

'We don't create any new ones. Virtual reality grew up on that stuff,' said Luke. 'We do need more of the non-aggressive kind, like that one we've just seen – there's been quite a demand for them lately. It's possible the dragon puts hormones or something into the males' diet to suppress aggression. It might have got the idea from what used to be done to most male domesticated animals – usually by chopping off their you-know-whats.'

Amelia carefully kept her shocked reaction from showing in her face. 'How is it they still need porn frames then?' she asked.

'Oh, I don't think sexuality and aggression have to go together,' said Luke.

His remark made Amelia feel better since it touched on her academic speciality. 'Actually, I looked at that in my research,' she said authoritatively. 'In ancient cultures where there was a lot of affection and cuddling, the men were less aggressive and sexually demanding. I think, with men, sex and fighting can be their only ways of touching and being touched. And the late necrotech economic system needed men to be competitive, which is the same as aggressive, so boy children were deprived of affection to make them competitive, so they'd admire the ruthless and successful, expect social inequalities and so on.'

'Interesting theory. Well, we don't get any actual touching at all, so we must need simulated sex quite badly. Anyway, the dragon can't actually castrate us, it has to collect spunk for us to breed, and so it has to get us excited. Actually, the other new frame is a soft porn one. This is the one Amadine framed. It's very soft porn actually; just a nice masturbation aid. If it's going to bother you, Amelia, would you rather we left it to another time?'

'Oh no, go ahead. I've got to get used to this if I'm going to go on with framing – and I would like to, if you want me.'

'Good girl! Here we go then.'

When Amadine appeared at the top of the marble staircase everyone on the lawn below looked up at her, their faces alight with love and admiration. She was perfectly beautiful. From her white-blonde hair, spun into a sugar confection around her softly sculptured face, to the sparkling slippers on her tiny feet, she shone with loveliness. There was not a shade of envy to mar the onlookers' admiration, because they were beautiful too. Gorgeous male and female creatures, beguilingly attired in pastel silks and satins, paused in their gracious parading to smile up at the new arrival.

Beautiful also was the scene surrounding them: the silvery grey palace with its little turrets and balconies; the intricately carved banisters festooned with pink garlands; the pale lilac carpet down to the lawn; the emerald grass dotted with starry white flowers; the tiers of rose bushes interplanted with palest blue pansies, blossoming trees trailing their branches; bluebirds trilling over the soft harmonies from a quartet of white wigged musicians, elegantly wielding their bows over their gleaming instruments.

Amadine descended a few steps and then paused, scanning the faces below for that one special face. She was teasing him. She knew well where his face was amongst the others; she felt the warmth of his gaze as a physical touch on her body, caressing her cheek, her ears, her throat, the swell of her high round breasts barely covered by soft ruched lace. She felt her large pink nipples spring hard and erect as his remote fingers circled them coaxingly. His examination explored the layers of pearly chiffon around her thighs, tossing them lightly aside until he slithered up between her legs and tickled the sticky lips of her wide open and welcoming love channel. At last she allowed their magnetic attraction for each other to draw their eyes into a locked beam. She stepped down towards him, her body rampant with invisible desire. She paused before him, her eyes locked to his, their surroundings a blur of humming colour. They danced. They danced, engaged in erotic stimulation, by the fingers which knew their bodies best.

The scene on the palace steps faded, and instead of the gyrations of the beautiful couple they could see a naked fat woman slumped on her recliner. She was waving one of her arms in the air in a way which bore some resemblance to the movements of the erotic dancers. With the other hand she was expertly masturbating, her flaccid thighs apart and straining rhythmically. A serving hand took a capsule from a thermos jar and carefully pushed it up her vagina.

A bit optimistic, Amelia thought; she looks too old to conceive. Then she noticed that the cell view had not shocked her at all this time, and felt smugly pleased with herself.

'Lovely, darling, delicious!' said Cora to Amadine. 'Can't wait to have a go at that one myself.'

'Yes, it's great,' said Oliver. 'Maybe the transition from the walk down the steps to the feely bit was a bit abrupt though, don't you think? Too much for user flex, maybe? Might be better worked up a bit there.'

'Would the user always be a woman?' Amelia asked.

Amadine said, 'Well, I thought a woman and a man could take the two main parts, or one or other would be a puppet. With two real participants it could be more of a tease.'

'I agree,' said Oliver. 'If lots of people chose it you could have everyone in the scene real, including those lovely musicians. It could turn into a real orgy. I say we release it, with or without the little tweak I suggested. What do you all think?'

'What I think is that a spot of lunch is called for,' said Amadine, pulling her large pink person out of the plush armchair with surprising agility and waving her outstretched arms in circles to usher the others out of the viewing room. They obediently trooped through the door into the dazzling light of a long narrow conservatory. Beneath the striped shade of a group of palm trees planted in stone sarcophagi a cold buffet was set out on an oval table with a lime green cloth.

'After all Amelia's blood and gore – or was it Cora's – I'm so glad there's no meat,' said Amadine, eyeing the oysters, smoked salmon, prawns and caviar, various cheeses, fresh fruit, thinly-sliced brown bread and chilled white wine. The others laughed loudly and sat down on the cane chairs with pink and lime flowery cushions.

Amelia went with the rest of them and sat down, but she eyed the food dubiously, and thought about cell stuff and serving hands. Nothing seemed real enough any more.

She noticed Luke looking at her. He leaned over and whispered in her ear, 'Don't dwell on it. Let what seems to be, be. It's what life is all about.'

'Nice drop of Sancerre, hopefully,' said Oliver, peering at a bottle. He extracted its cork with practised skill and poured a tasting amount, with a drop-avoiding twist of the wrist, into one of the twinkling glasses. He lifted the glass to his nose and sniffed. 'Mmm, not bad. Help yourselves, children.' He topped up his own glass and passed the bottle on.

Amadine filled her glass clumsily and caught the drop that dribbled from the bottle on one of her pink painted fingernails. Noticing Oliver's slight wince, she sucked in a mouthful noisily, leaving a crescent of pink lipstick on the glass. 'Cheers! Here's to Amelia's deliciously nasty storyframe,' she said. 'Long may it chill the bored hearts of our users, bless them!' They chinked glasses, with chortles of mocking disapproval at their own vulgar manners. There was a lull in the conversation as they passed dishes, loaded plates and started to eat. Then they began to chatter, much as they did at the endless parties. Music came on. Some other people wandered in and were welcomed loudly.

Amelia joined in as best she could, in the food and the gossipy talk, all the while wondering what was going to happen next. Her frame was going to be released, but was that going to be that, or had her career as a framer now been launched? At last she could bear the suspense no longer, and turned to ask Luke, but he had gone, faded out. So she departed too.

Amelia emerged in Celia's library, deep down in the basement where she had researched the Arklash. The passages leading from the spiral staircase were lined with deep shelves stacked high with blocks of stone on which ancient symbols had been carved, also clay tablets of cuneiform writing and scrolls of paper and animal skin bearing characters in long-forgotten languages. She wandered around for a while, peering at the tablets and scrolls, still hoping for a sign that there had been people resembling the Terrever her imagination had created. She found nothing that held echoes of humans who would not use fire or excavate the ground. She sighed and wandered back to the stairs.

Careful not to step off into the void at the core of the spiral, Amelia called up to her friend, 'Celia, where are you?'

A faint voice floated down, 'Seventeenth century. Come on up. Try flying.'

Amelia considered for a second or so attempting to zoom up the centre of the staircase, but could not manage the concentrated intention required. Sighing again, she resigned herself to trudging up the stairs. As she climbed, the crude stone blocks of the lower levels were succeeded by better-shaped steps, later by highly finished and polished stone treads, some of marble. The hand rail also changed from coarse rope to carved stone or wood.

'Nearly here,' Celia's silvery voice called down. 'I've made some tea.'

Amelia craned her neck upwards, and could just see Celia's pale oval face gazing down from high above.

At last she made it to the level where Celia had been dusting and arranging the leather-bound volumes on the shelves, and had pulled out some works of seventeenth century scientists which she had stacked on the floor beside the tea table.

After sitting down, getting her breath back and sipping tea from the delicate china cup Celia handed to her, Amelia peered at the pile of books.

'Galileo, Kepler, Boyle and Newton,' she noted. 'Impressive stuff. Are you reading this?'

'Oh, I dip in here and there.'

'Isn't it all in Latin or something?'

'I suppose I could view it that way. The intos provides. I suspect it reads to me; I don't think anyone can actually understand the written word any more.'

Amelia was surprised at her friend being so relaxed about the illusions. For her it was still uncomfortable knowledge: she would rather she had remained in ignorance, but presumably un-learning unpleasant truths was impossible.

'What happened about your storyframe?' Celia asked. 'Have they accepted it?'

'Well, yes, but I'm not sure it's *my* storyframe. They took out all the good bits. All that was left was a horror story.'

'The users will flex it, won't they? Isn't that the idea?'

'Yes, of course. But the ideas I wanted to get across are so hidden they'd need interact mode to get them out. As it is, any user would identify with the Terrever without understanding what was special about them, and set the Arklash into the enemy role, and never know that all humanity is Arklash and there've never been people like the Terrever.'

'Well if that's what you wanted to tell them, no wonder the *Virtual Stardom* people vetoed it. Quite right too. You don't want your users to get so guilty and depressed that the intos thinks their lives aren't worth living and cuts their supplies off.'

Another of those unpleasant truths; how many more are there? Amelia wondered. Suddenly it was all too much and she burst into tears. 'Oh, Celia,' she blubbed, 'I thought you'd understand; you're supposed to be my friend. I was trying to do something for the future – to give us all hope. My lovely Terrever – to show how people could live when we get out of this horrible dragon thing!'

'Oh, my poor pet, don't cry. You've done so well with all those funny storyframing people. Why don't you tell me all about it. I'll listen, that'll be a start. You've been too busy while it was all going on, and I am interested, really.'

Amelia looked at Celia's sweet angel's face looking so sympathetic.

'Yes, all right. I suppose that would make me feel better,' she said.

Amelia had not been a regular user of the join-in stories produced by *Virtual Stardom*, but in an idle hour following a demanding day of research work into patterns of social evolution she asked for 'something diverting', and was routed into one of their romances. Just after the usual announcements of forthcoming releases which preceded the entry point, there was a call for trainee storyframers. The advertisement's gushing blonde female chat-face said that this was the opportunity of a lifetime, and to be sure to take it up right away. On an impulse, Amelia asked the face to 'tell me more' and was routed to an interact-face.

'Hello there, Amelia,' the face beamed at her. 'I'm Luke Featherday from *Virtual Stardom*, Trainee Framer Development. I do hope you're going to give us a try. Storyframing's great fun, an absolutely marvellous pastime, and you'll meet some of the most creative and interesting people.'

'Well, I wasn't really looking for a major time filler,' said Amelia doubtfully. 'I've got some research work I'm fully absorbed in. I was just going into one of your romances for a bit of relaxation and I saw your chat-face. I'm sorry to have bothered you.'

Amelia felt, rather than saw, the interact-face switch to its owner in real-time. Either her response was not covered by the interact-face repertoire, or she had said something particularly interesting to the owner: she sensed it was the latter.

'You're a researcher,' Luke in person responded. 'That's great! We are particularly interested in drawing in trainee framers with some serious expertise.'

Amelia regarded Luke thoughtfully. He had his own distinctive image such as she associated with the entertainment industry, consisting of a visual challenge and a studied 'look', but he was certainly not one of the world's beautiful people. His most noticeable feature was a large ball of a head, smooth, shiny and bald from his straight black eyebrows right over his skull to the line where a fringe of dark hair curtained his neck and ears. Beneath his eyebrows were deep-set black eyes with long lashes. The rest of his face was vanishingly ordinary and oddly still, in contrast to the animated voice it gave out. He wore a black silky shirt, neatly buttoned to neck and wrists, with a large handkerchief spilling from the breast pocket. During the lengthy period Amelia was to know Luke, the only change to his appearance was the colour and pattern of the big handkerchief, with which he constantly wiped, or as it seemed *polished*, his gleaming brow.

On that first encounter Amelia decided she liked and trusted Luke. Perhaps it was his warmly resonant voice, exuding sincerity. She instantly formed the impression that there was some serious purpose behind the apparently trivial business Luke was part of. She also decided not to insist on having the serious purpose explained before they were ready to tell her.

'All right, Luke,' she said, 'I'll give it a try. What do I have to do?'

'That's great!' he beamed. 'Welcome aboard the fun wagon!' Serious purpose notwithstanding, Amelia began to learn that the 'fun and frolic' thread had to be kept going, almost as if it were a lifeline. She grinned back at him.

'To begin with,' Luke continued coaxingly, 'what we'd like from you is a set of ideas for a new frame: as innovative as possible.'

'That's tricky,' she said, carefully keeping her smile going. 'I'm not a regular user of your stuff; I wouldn't know if my ideas were new.'

'No probs. The dragon'll check them out. You'll get my interact-face telling you whether or not you're duplicating. We wouldn't want to cramp your style by specifying any particular theme, but you could try to bring in something from your research field.'

This was an instruction put tactfully, she could tell. When Luke had faded out and she was alone in her basisframe, her neat little one-room flat, she knew the background for her storyframe would be something to do with contrasting societies.

So Amelia invented the Arklash and the Terrever: archetypal baddies and goodies judged by the values which had emerged from her own analysis of what it was about Homo sapiens which had led to the development of necrotech. The Arklash could be based on any one of various pre-industrial necrotech cultures. The Terrever were simply the opposite of necrotech, which she had decided meant they would not use fire or excavate the ground.

She called Luke and explained the idea to him.

'This is a new concept, you say?' he asked. 'I mean, not just to framing, but to the academic world?'

'Oh, yes,' she replied, and would have said more, but Luke interrupted.

'That's what we're after then,' he nodded, and then polished his head and beamed at her. 'Wonderful, great! Go ahead then, and see what you can do with it.'

'Do what?' she asked.

'Create a virtual world.'

'I wouldn't know where to start. Is there some sort of training course I should do?' she asked.

'Not that I know of, pet,' Luke replied. 'When you've learnt the trade you can set one up; you're a teacher, aren't you?'

'Yes, I suppose I am. I give adult education classes on pattern theory.'

'Sounds fascinating, darling, you must tell me about it some time. Anyway, you have a go putting those Akak-what's-it people of yours into the movies – just go for it and see what comes up. If you get stuck using flicker choice, you might like to try interact mode. You can use my face any time you like.'

What Luke called 'flicker choice' was the normal mode of interaction with the illusion provider, which Celia called 'the intos' and Luke called 'the dragon'. Amelia had used this mode all her life, as did everyone else, but had not until now needed to refer to it by name, although she knew what he meant. In flicker choice mode, the intos offered to the user sequences of options, often with subliminal rapidity, and then selected from and refined the choice by examining the user's facial expression or voice for indications of satisfaction or dissatisfaction.

So Amelia set about creating frame views of her contrasting cultures by sitting in her flat, and thinking about the ideas she had thought up. She expected the Arklash to be easy and to appear before her eyes. She had found plenty of useful details in Celia's library, and decided that the Assyrians from the ancient Near East could be a useful model. They had been suitably ruthless and belligerent, as well as being proficient at technology. She had not found any information about a human culture like the Terrever though, but there would surely be something in the intos archives, they were so vast.

Amelia sat and sat until her eyes were sore from staring, but the expected visions did not come. All she was offered was some late necrotech documentary television features, and photographs from magazine articles, about popular history, archaeology, anthropology and so on – plus several absurdly unrealistic films about Vikings and Egyptians. The only offering for the Terrever was various tribes of hunter-gatherers, some of whom had survived into late necrotech, but even they had used fire. Luke had been right about flicker choice: it was no use. She projected rejection until all the available images were exhausted. After that she was left staring at the wallpaper.

She would have to use an interact-face so that she could make explicit vocal demands. Luke's face was available for her to use, and it had been hovering in the background waiting for her to give up.

'Having trouble?' the Luke face asked cheerily.

'There's nothing coming up on ancient civilisations.'

'Nothing suitable for your frame, you mean,' it corrected her.

'Why is that?' she asked.

The face beamed Luke's calm smile and told her, 'Virtual reality was invented in 1960, television in 1926, cinema in 1895, photography in 1830. Before that just words and drawings. What did you expect, darling, time travel?'

'What can we do then?'

'Use your imagination, pet; there isn't any in here.'

The Arklash first, Amelia thought, and the Terrever will be the opposite. How they use the land: that's the basis.

The dusty urchin tried to lever the rock, which weighed perhaps half his own weight, into the basket. The jagged shape had wedged itself awkwardly in the neck, and the boy heaved on it to shift it deeper inside. Then he squatted with his back to the basket and pulled the leather strap over his head, lining it up across his forehead. He eased the weight of the rock onto his bent back to carry it from the quarry. The great hole in the landscape was crawling with children engaged in the same task. Adult slaves were wielding iron picks and crowbars to separate lumps of rock. A double crocodile of people wound from the quarry lip, down the hill and across the valley to where the great dam was being built. Those going out were bent double carrying baskets of rocks, those returning were running, forced on by drivers with whips.

The child's bare feet dented the springy herbs as she crept along a faint animal track at the edge of the sacred wildwood. She was tempted to enter the mysterious green cavern within, but the rule was that to go in was to stay in. To go to the forest was to end this life to dissolve into the timeless cycles. One day she would go, but not yet. She had accompanied two of the grandmothers here a few days before, and watched them walk in, and marvelled as their awkward frail weight was transformed in the shower of light from the canopy to a fey lissomness. She stared in wonder as the grandmothers ran like squirrels up the mossy trousers clothing the roots of the huge trees, and leapt down onto the soft ferns of the forest floor.

The child peered through at the tumbling sea of undergrowth, but the grandmothers were no longer visible. This time she had come to gather berries from the edge. The fruit glistened in the morning light. She was reluctant to break the necklaces of spider web threaded with dew droplets which hung across the bushes. Stretching on tiptoe she reached out a finger to catch the end of a web and moved it gently and touched it over a branch a little further back. The pretty strings were still intact, and she could ease off the berries, one by one, from the cluster which now protruded beyond the web. She laid the berries in her rush basket and repeated the careful process many times, slowly progressing along the edge of the wood. One time, for all her care, a thread of spider web broke, shedding its dewy beads. She was unconcerned. It was only a game, but a game with the purpose of disturbing the patterns of life as little as possible.

The last tree came crashing down and was stripped of its branches and dragged away by a team of sweating slaves. The tree had been left standing longer than its fellows to provide shelter for the supervisors, but now that all the other trees had gone and the debris had dried sufficiently for burning, it too was felled. A procession of priests and administrators had reached the site, and its dimensions were paced out and noted down by a scribe. One of the priests was handed the fire box. Mouthing some special words for the occasion, the priest lit a taper and set it to one of the oil-soaked torches held by a supervisor who then backed away, bowed low to the priest and marched importantly to the next supervisor, set light to his torch, and returned to his place. One by one the torches were lit, until the great area: once forest, now plantation, was surrounded. At a sign from the priest the dried forest debris was set alight. In a few days, teams of slaves would break up the soil, mixing in the ash, ready for sowing a grain crop to provide bread for the inhabitants of the city.

The children squealed with pleasure as they tumbled in the deep leaves. This part of the wood was in its accessible cycle. Gathering of herbs and fungi was allowed here, and dead leaves and compost could be taken for mulch. When they had had enough of play, the children began to scoop up armfuls of leaves and cram them into the big baskets. When the baskets were full they lifted one each and followed the path out of the wood. They pretended to be weighed down and staggered about, accidentally on purpose barging into each other. The village was not far. When the children arrived they took the baskets to the area where it had been decided they could make a new herb bed, to allow one of the old ones to rest and return to its wild state. They put the baskets down and on hands and knees plucked the wild plants growing on the place for the new bed. They were careful not to disturb the roots or expose the soil. They left the pluckings on the ground. Then they tipped the dead leaves they had collected over the remains of the wild plants. They spread them evenly and weighed them down with rushes. The following spring they would scatter onto the mulch layer the seeds they had gathered earlier from other garden plots and from the forest. They stood around the new bed, pleased with and proud of their achievement. Other villagers came to look and to praise.

Godsfreesonson eased the last cask into the boat. His father, Godsfreeson, looked gloomily at how low the boat now floated. It

70

would not take much of a sea to tip the boat and let the water in over the side. But they dared not send less than the proper tribute: half the year's production of wine. They only had one boat. There would not be time for a second round trip before the trade winds turned. It had been too good a year. The half that was left would not command a good price in the local market. The family could not eat wine, it had to be sold for money to buy food and other necessities. But they were proud and did not complain. They were highly privileged to be a free family. Godsfree had been freed by his high priest owner in return for some mysterious deed he would not tell of, even on his death bed. As a freeman, Godsfree could have his own sons. Slave men did not breed. Slave women produced priests' bastards for the next generation of slaves. Godsfree had been awarded a plot of land with his freedom. It was in a vine growing area, so grapes were all he was permitted to cultivate. If Godsfreeson sent less than half their produce as tribute, and the tax inspectors found out, or some jealous neighbour told them, the whole family would lose their freedom, and probably Godsfreeson would lose his life. The heavily laden boat would have to set sail, and the family would have to sell enough wine to buy a lamb for sacrifice to ask the gods for just enough wind, but not too much, so that Godsfreesonson made the journey to the city harbour swiftly and safely.

The mosaic of Arklash and Terrever life grew slowly, but Amelia was satisfied with her progress; she was getting there, bit by bit. A routine had developed: first she thought of an idea for a fragment, then she ordered the Luke face to find a still image of suitable scenery, then she described the people and selected their exact appearance through flicker choice, then she mimed what they were doing, then she told the Luke face to animate the people accordingly for incorporation into the scene.

She became so absorbed in her two worlds that she was startled when she detected the Luke interact-face transmute into Luke himself. "'Scuse me butting in, Amelia love, but my interact called me in: you've put it in worry mode. I think I've been neglecting my duties towards your development as a framer. My excuse is you were doing so wonderfully well.'

'And I'm not doing so well now?' Amelia asked.

'No criticism, darling, just a spot of advice, okay, based on what we've found over the years.' Luke polished his brow and glowed at Amelia. 'These are little gems you've created, but too detailed just for background. We must leave something for the users' imagination, pet. Must have flexing potential in our frames, okay.'

Amelia reluctantly had to agree. Flexing was what distinguished storyframes from old fashioned non-interactive 'films'. A frame had to be just that: an outline for the users to fill in and modify according to their interests and imagination. A popular frame would acquire through use a complex maze of possible routes and variations, but the original framer had to be restrained about filling in detail, so that the first few users who participated in the story had something left for them to create. The frame releasers, such as *Virtual Stardom*, would ensure that a new frame was picked up by several initial users at once, so that they would give the frame that essential dimension of multiple choice. In theory, the framer could build in several initial choices, but experience had shown that this was best done by users.

'I suggest, pet, that you stand away a bit, and think about the complete frame. You've got more than enough background and social context already; what you need now are characters and plot. A good frame has all its components present, consistent, interesting and credible, but only lightly sketched in. That's the art of framing, Amelia sweety. When you design that course, that'll be the main lesson.'

'I see,' said Amelia glumly. 'What do I do next then?'

'Invent some characters.'

'Well I was working towards that; I've got Godsfreesonson and his family.'

'Hmm. I can't see Godfrey thingy as enough of a baddie for an Arklash character.'

'He's not bad at all. The Arklash are meant to be a bad *society*, not bad people. That's the point I'm trying to get across.'

'Darling, storyframes are for entertainment, not for getting points across. We mustn't confuse the users: you have to give them nasty baddies and nice goodies.'

'But I thought you liked my idea about contrasting cultures,' Amelia said forlornly.

'Oh I do, pet – it's really new. But a storyframe's not meant to be a lesson in social history. It's got to have stars. I can bring someone in to help you if you like. Cora Flinch is available; she's terrific on nasties. I'm having a party at my place tonight. Cora will be there and I could introduce you.'

After the session with Luke, Amelia felt thoroughly confused about what her role was, but she decided to complete what she had started and go along with whatever the professionals wanted.

Amelia had so far declined all the party invitations, to Luke's place and elsewhere, but now she had to go along. When she emerged in Luke's basisframe, she found it just as she would have imagined: a huge room open to a balcony overlooking a moonlit ocean, plush sofas and thick carpets everywhere, lots of people talking loudly over loud music. Luke led her through the crush to meet Cora Flinch, and Amelia almost laughed out loud at her, she was such a caricature of her specialism. She had a pale hollow-cheeked face, thin lips with a smile that revealed slightly prominent canine teeth but did not reach her eyes, black hair in a snood, and red nails on long bony hands. The three of them retreated to the balcony to discuss Amelia's frame and Cora was gleefully enthusiastic about taking on Amelia's Arklash characters.

The next morning Amelia showed Cora the background fragments, and explained her concept. Cora seemed even less interested than Luke had been in the social message.

'The Terrever mustn't use fire or disturb the soil,' Amelia told her.

'Fine by me: they're not very exciting anyway – but the users should be allowed to change that, so you can't get too inflex about it,' Cora said, and then a gleam came in her eyes. 'Couldn't they be building a castle, your slaves lugging rocks around?'

'Well, I thought a dam – for irrigation, you know. How a people produce their food is the basis of their culture. Necrotech food production disturbs nature, hence clearing forests for plantations and damning rivers for irrigation. The Terrever would work with nature: that's how I thought of their gardening.'

'Oh, I think we should have a castle,' said Cora firmly, and the image changed accordingly.

'I'll leave you to it, then, shall I?' said Amelia.

When she next called up the frame, she found that Cora had got a set of shadowy puppets for the Arklash royal family, including a belligerent young son called 'Grunthor'. She had pulled in some war-game material, the routine of enslavement and torture was sketched in, and she had just thought of the slave wives idea.

Amelia called up Luke, wanting to explain that this did not really fit in with her concept, but Luke had seen it and was obviously thrilled.

'Well done, Amelia, pet!' he gushed, as if she had done it herself.

73

The next stage was going to be adding a plot. Luke suggested bringing in further *Virtual Stardom* assistance. Amelia did not feel the frame was really her own any more, and she accepted the new helper resignedly. At the next party, in someone else's basisframe this time, Luke introduced her to Oliver Sheridan, an unremarkable looking plump man in a crumpled linen suit, who seemed to know all about what she was doing already. When Oliver had wandered back to the party, Luke took Amelia to the edge of the balcony: this one had a view of pine trees silhouetted on the horizon and a lot of night sky, and they tried spotting constellations.

'Right up above us, that's the Plough,' Luke said

'I think I can see Orion, the Hunter,' said Amelia. 'Those three bright stars down there are his belt. I wish we could really see the stars – you know, outside the dragon.'

'I don't know that there's any such thing as really seeing them. Who's to say that what you see with the naked eye is real in any absolute sense. And as for telescopes and other devices, you see more, but whether it's more real ...'

Still gazing at the night sky, Luke went on, 'I've been thinking – might be an idea if you have a break while Oli explores your settings and characters, and sketches out a frameplay.'

Am I being moved out of this altogether? Amelia wondered. 'Just what I need, I'm exhausted,' was what she said.

'You could tell those students of yours about that social pattern stuff,' Luke said.

'I'm not sure I've got any students,' Amelia said. 'They're probably just puppets. No one's really interested in my ideas. I was quite excited when you seemed to like them: I did think that framing might be the way some other people might actually get what I'm saying.'

'I get it, honestly I do. It's just that you can't tell anyone; you can only hide it in there somewhere, and maybe they'll find it, and think it's their own.'

Amelia found herself in a women's lavatory with rows of cubicles and washbasins. 'Cloakroom' was what she called it mentally, although there was no provision for hanging cloaks or any other outer garments. She was conscious of aching muscles and panting breath, as after exertion. A bicycle ride and climbing two flights of stairs came to mind.

74

She felt dishevelled and looked for a mirror. There was a full-length one on the far wall and she walked towards it.

'What a mess!' she said, staring at the image of a middle-aged woman with a lot of wavy greying hair, wearing a green lightweight jacket, and with the strap of a large bag diagonally across her chest. Her legs were enclosed in sagging trousers of a dark red colour.

'That's not me,' she declared, 'not what I feel like anyway.'

The mirror image changed. Now she saw a young girl, potentially pretty with perfect, unspotted skin, an eager smile and bright brown curly hair. But she was too plump; her limp, flowered frock was too tight; and she wore owlish glasses and had a brace on her teeth.

'Ahh!' said Amelia, sympathetically, but shook her head.

The girl rippled through stages of maturity, acquiring small breasts and fining down to a pleasing slimness of body and long legs. The image settled on a young woman with wavy hair pulled back into a high chignon. She was wearing slanting winged glasses, a sack-like pink dress well above her knees. She was bony thin. The eager smile had an anxious fixity about it.

'Go on,' Amelia commanded.

The image changed and changed again. The glasses disappeared, replaced perhaps by contact lenses. Hair styles and fashions came and went. At first not ageing noticeable, gradually lines of anxiety betrayed the eager smile and deepened in the softening skin. But then a shift occurred – and the woman had altered at a deeper level. The smile had faded, but so had the anxiousness lines, and a new calmness was apparent.

Amelia pointed eagerly, but then looked again, disappointed. The image had returned to its starting point. Amelia shook her head again.

The image continued changing. The hair greyed further and lightened to white. The body spread and then began to shrink again, and then to crumple – stooped, bow legged, gnarled at the fingers – but charmingly draped with floating mauve chiffon. The image finally halted at an ancient crone in a sprigged night-gown. She was almost bald, her scull draped with mottled translucent skin, a few long brown teeth in a dribbling lipless mouth above a whiskery chin.

Amelia shivered. 'No, not that one – go back, go back.'

The image obediently returned once again to its starting point.

Amelia sighed. 'Well at least smarten me up. I remember all those years when I was younger, always feeling older than I was, and unattractive – what a waste! Let me at least have a bit of style with my new confidence.

The woman's clothes whirled through a myriad of possibilities until Amelia's eyes were dry from staring and her mind was in a whirl.

'Black, all black,' she commanded. 'Long skirt, boots, loose top.' And it was done.

'Ah, that's better! That's me. The hair's still a mess though. But I'll fix that myself.'

The shoulder bag, of tapestry fabric, was still across her chest. Amelia removed it, opened the zip and found on the top a carefully folded black stole, of an open-weave black fabric, subtly patterned in white, which she draped around her shoulders and knotted loosely in front. Then she rummaged in the lower reaches for a comb. Discovering it at last, a brown plastic afro-comb, designed for frizzy or unruly hair, she jabbed at the tangles. The comb did no more than charge the hair with static electricity so she went to one of the washbasins, turned on the tap and, bending down awkwardly, dangled a few hanks in the stream of water. She looked in the mirror above and finger-combed in the dampness. Strands of hair now framed her face unflatteringly; a strong broad face with high cheekbones and firm jaw, the form revealed by her once-firm flesh having fined down into a thinner covering, just beginning to soften and wrinkle. It was an intelligent face, still etched with a few deep lines – permanent scars of her earlier chronic lack of confidence, compensated for by the fixed smile and animated talkativeness.

She licked her finger and attempted to smooth down the few unruly white hairs in her eyebrows. She smiled at the face and it smiled back. She scowled and it looked sternly back at her. She turned away from it with a shrug and a slight shudder and, shouldering the bag, made her way out of the cloakroom, turned right down the corridor, through sets of heavy fire doors, along more corridors, up concrete stairs, past numbered rooms to the one assigned to her evening class.

As she walked in she switched on her role: respected teacher and awarder of grades and helpful criticism. Her students seemed out of place in the classroom, as anything warm and living would clash with the cold grey angles and steel and plastic, inexplicably tatty in spite of the robust utilitarian construction. The early-comers had evidently tried to form a semicircle out of the trapezium-shaped tables, presumably designed for flexible disposition, but defying any arrangement which

76

was not rigidly angular. The floor space having been filled with an irregular horseshoe of tables, the table legs made noisy metallic barriers against any attempt to set chairs behind them, let alone settle bottoms, books and bags ready for the business of the evening. However, her entrance provided the incentive for the group to get their settling done and have all their faces looking expectantly towards her by the time the last two or three had hurried in.

Amelia perched herself on the edge of the table placed for her use. It slid backwards with a jerk, so she moved round it and sat on the chair. They were all there, she noted, and checked by a quick count: twelve would-be storyframers. Never very good at names, she tried to remember some of them.

There was Simone, a very pretty and curvaceous blonde woman, too cartoon-like, Amelia thought, and wondered if she would drop that look if she stuck with the course. Then there were the two tall thin men with very short hair who always sat very close to each other, a gay couple perhaps. She could not remember their names since she had dubbed them Bill and Ben after two puppet characters from an old children's TV programme. The thin bird-like dark one was Philip, and next to him Pippa, a Pappagena to Philip's Pappageno, but they were not a couple, at least not as far as she could tell. There were the four who were usually early, came together and often got in a huddle in discussions. They were Don, Barny, George and Arthur, all youngish and ordinarily good looking, and she was not sure which was which, apart from George, who was the one who always had something to say. Then there were the three quiet ones, two women and one man. Amelia looked at her list. They must be Jane, Hannah and Douglas.

'Good evening, everyone,' she smiled. 'I'm glad you've all managed to come. So, let's get on with it. As I'm sure you're well aware, the next coursework assignment is coming up soon —'

There was a collective groan from the students.

'— so I think we should stick to theory this time. The essay question is on the very important subject of the patterns of late necrotech, which most of us follow in our basisframes, and for a lot of storyframes too. So I thought we'd study a few passages in the *Pattern Mathematics* set book to give you some theoretical structure to base your essays on – just a list of patterns won't get you good marks, I warn you. We haven't talked about this book before, although I expect some of you've had a look at it. What did you think of it?'

The students shuffled uncomfortably, and sneaked little grimaces at each other.

George put his hand up, and Amelia nodded encouragingly, 'Yes, George.'

'I have actually read this book from cover to cover – twice —'

'Oh, George!' said Simone. The others said, 'Wow!' in mock admiration.

'– and I wouldn't say it's an easy read. You have to hang on every word, but it's good stuff when you get into what the woman was getting at.'

'Well I couldn't get into it at all,' Pippa piped up. 'It's just so *theoretical*. I mean, it was just solid words!' She looked around the others, who evidently agreed.

Amelia smiled. 'No pictures or conversation, eh? Yes, I know. But that was the usual style of academic books in late necrotech. There weren't any visuals with the book, not even a picture of the author, Bony Bailey, because she never got the book published; we don't even know how it got into the system. There was a crude knowledge network in those days. I expect she had access to that, and her ideas eventually got caught up in the info-sweep. Lucky for us, if that's what happened.' Most of the class looked as if they wished it never had.

'Actually, I'm not expecting you to understand the whole book. You're already familiar with the central idea, which is that everything that happens, everywhere in the universe, is still present, although we can't see it, and that's what shapes what happens next – it's a process of growth. Everyone happy with that?'

They all nodded and murmured, 'Yes', 'Mmm,' or 'Sure.'

'I've picked out three short passages with a little something extra on top of the basic idea. What we'll do is divide into groups – three, I think – each group can discuss one of the bits I've picked out – and then we'll compare notes, okay?'

There was some scraping and clashing as they rearranged the metal tables and chairs, then Amelia handed out the slips of paper onto which she had copied the three passages.

In view of what Pippa had just said, Amelia gave her group, which included Bill, Ben and Philip the first passage, which she thought was fairly straightforward:

'If we accept that the patterns of the past persist and accumulate, rather than vanishing as each moment passes, not only can we see why the tendency is for human social patterns to continue in the established way, in spite of the damage caused being starkly evident, but we can also see that we, as a species, cannot leave our collective errors behind us and start afresh.'

She left them to discuss it, but managed to listen in.

'This is easy,' said Pippa airily. 'It's just saying human society has bad habits.'

'Who's the one that couldn't get into it!' said Philip. The two of them withdrew from the others for a private discussion of the book itself, which Amelia suspected was a disguised flirtation.

'I wonder if it would have made any difference if people had known about this pattern stuff,' said Ben. 'I mean, if they'd known that it's terribly difficult to get out of habits because it's something physical in the universe.'

'Too late by Bony Bailey's time though, wasn't it?' said Bill.

'She was before bionecrotech,' observed Ben.

They withdrew into a private exchange too, so Amelia moved on to give Jane's group, which included Douglas, Hannah and Simone, the second passage, and hovered a while to see how they got on.

'Every pattern has a life-cycle: it emerges and forms, by resonance with pre-existing patterns; it continues in interaction with other patterns; and it degenerates and dissolves, like other patterns before it. Any pattern which is disrupted prematurely will re-emerge later and continue to its proper completion.'

Simone read the passage quickly, pouted and passed the paper to Douglas, then she examined her long nails. Douglas read the passage and smirked back at Simone. She started to play with a loose strip of laminate at the edge of the table top. Then she leant over and whispered something to Douglas. Amelia heard 'do some storyframing' and gathered Simone thought pattern theory was a waste of time.

Hannah and Jane dutifully read the passage several times, and both fiddled with strands of their hair. They started to speak together. 'No, go on Hannah, you say,' said Jane.

'Oh, I was just going to say it's kind of pretty, you know ... poetic.'

Simone raised her eyebrows at Douglas.

Amelia wished she had mixed the talkative ones around more – and separated the couples or buddies. She was never very good at this sort of thing. She moved nearer to the group and leant between Jane and Hannah.

'Perhaps you could think about what patterns have been disrupted and might come back – if this theory is right, that is.'

'Nature?' said Simone, to Amelia's surprise.

'Yes, good! Go on,' she said.

'Nature got disrupted by necrotech,' Simone said. 'Don't know what it means by "completion" though.'

'I hope necrotech got completed or that would come back too,' said Douglas.

'Perhaps there's no such thing as "completion",' said Hannah. ' I like the idea of patterns all going round and round forever – that's more pattern-like really.'

'Perhaps the forests come back and then people burn them down, then they come back and people burn them down again, then the fo—'

'Yes, Douglas,' said Simone, 'we get the idea.'

'It's got here "degenerates and dissolves", so they all get worn out in the end,' said Jane.

'She might have got that bit wrong,' said Hannah.

That was pretty good for the quiet ones, Amelia thought. It seemed to be all they had to say, and the first group had got going again, so Amelia listened in surreptitiously.

'Trouble with bad habits is you don't know you've got them,' Pippa said. 'Like, I mean, they didn't actually know it was necrotech when it was.'

'Fire and death,' said Philip.

Pippa nodded. She leant over to retrieve the slip of paper which was in front of Bill, raising her eyebrows to ask permission. He nodded. Pippa and Philip looked at the passage again.

'It made us think of all of us still living necrotech in the dragon,' said Bill.

'– even though the real necrotech world is over long ago,' Ben went on.

'We don't depend on fire and death,' remarked Pippa.

'Oh, we do a bit on death,' said Philip. 'Minerals and stuff for babies must come from dead people.'

'Not dead anything else though,' said Pippa.

'That's not what we meant,' said Bill.

'We feel as if we were still in necrotech,' said Ben.

'Well, what else can we do – in here?' Pippa challenged.

'It's escape from boredom – they needed that in necrotech too,' said Ben.

'Fantasies, 'cos there's nothing interesting going on,' said Bill.

'Civilisation,' said Philip.

'Eh?'

'In Greece and all those places, the citizens had nothing to do because the slaves did everything for them, so they invented ... well, maths and philosophy – all that sort of stuff.'

Amelia was intrigued, but George came up to her at that point.

'Can we have our bit?' he asked. She gave his group the third, trickier, passage and moved over to eavesdrop.

'The theory of the persistence of the past leads to an interesting alternative conception of time. If we let go the idea that everything that does not change is perpetually copied from one moment of time to the next, but instead leave it in the time it first appeared, we get a more economical model of the universe . The present time can then be conceived as being discontinuous: full of holes, through which the presence of the past is apparent and influential. Only the tiny fragment of the universe which is different from the past exists in any present moment.'

'I remember that section: there's plenty more on that theme,' said George. 'It's a new geometry of the universe – actually it was the part I liked best.'

Two of the others started to say something at the same time.

'After you, Barny,' said one of them.

'I was only going to say it's mind-boggling stuff,' said Barny. 'Wait a moment,' he said to George, who was probably about to explain it all to them. 'Don?'

'It's easier to understand what it's getting at if you think of just "all people" instead of "everything",' said Don. 'If it says what I think it does, it means we're mostly all the same person. The only part of yourself you could call your *own* self would be whatever tiny little bit no one's ever been like before.'

Amelia nodded and left them to it to go back to the first group.

'You could say the dragon is like the universe and vice versa,' Pippa was saying. 'That bit with "accumulate": that's like the archives always building up.'

'And the bit about not leaving errors behind,' said Philip, 'That's like what Amelia said last class about not being able to wipe out your framing mistakes, so we'd better not make any.'

The others laughed.

'I liked what Pippa said,' remarked Bill. 'The universe is like a library where they keep on adding more and more books.'

'And never throw any out,' said Ben. 'Even the duff ones.'

'Mostly the stuff'd be like boring log books or account books that are almost the same kind of thing,' said Pippa.

'Could be the same *interesting* books over and over again,' said Philip, looking at Pippa as if she were an interesting book.

'I suppose the dragon logs every single one of every single person's choices – in their profile, so it knows what each one likes,' said Bill.

'So there must be billions of choices, all almost the same,' said Ben.

'If the universe's cycles, or library, or database, or however you want to look at it, just keep building up pattern stuff, it's a wonder there's room for it all,' said Pippa. 'I mean, if the universe has to have everything that's ever happened in it: every moment, all squashed up together, it hardly seems possible. That's not what it seems like, anyhow.'

Amelia thought of George's group's passage, and wondered if she should have kept the whole class together. But Jane's group were working it out for themselves, or Philip was.

'The dragon's intelligent organic,' said Philip, 'so it wouldn't work like a silicon computer. Perhaps it merges the profiles into patterns.'

'It would only need one copy of each selection that's the same, and only store anything that's different,' said Pippa. 'Ordinary computers could do that.'

'How would it know which selection was in whose profile then?' asked Bill.

'I don't know.' Philip paused. 'Maybe a particular selection could seem to be in lots of profiles, if you looked at the profiles, but really you'd be looking through the profiles to where the selection was made the very first time.'

'I think you're a secret pattern book reader, after all,' Pippa teased.

'The pattern of the whole dragon itself would be mostly holes,' said Ben.

'So would the universe,' said Ben.

Over the buzz of talking came Simone's shrill voice, 'This is so *boring!*' Amelia cringed, but the buzz carried on. She went back to her table. More fragments of talk reached her.

'There might not be necrotech again if people knew what happened before. ... riddled with guilt when we get out. We'll be nervous of disturbing a fly.'

'... Not our fault.'

'The dragon ... conscience.'

'Anything goes in the dragon. Torture, rape ... boredom – that's the killer.'

'... keep to the values of necrotech more or less ... pattern still working, even when it makes no difference to anything.'

'... all the same person ... was us right through necrotech ... live necrotech frames.'

'If we're all the same person, we're immortal.'

'... my own person, even if that does mean I'll die.'

'You're distorting the concept if you just take the human perspective,' said George. 'I think this is a good geometric model. It's better than having an infinite number of universes – or one universe which keeps vanishing as time passes.'

'Talk about necrotech patterns, George! you've picked up rational science. I'd go for intuition myself. I think it's important to test if a concept feels right by your own experience – what you know. I think someone's done really well if they manage a single original thought or action in a lifetime. All the rest, that you think is yourself, might as well be what someone was like before shining through the holes of time from the past.'

Amelia sighed: So you don't even know what is your own self! Are these students real, or are they all me 'shining through the holes' – saying all the things I believe, so I feel someone's interested? But now even I'm bored with it. I might as well just go.

She stared at a patch of the wall, cracked plaster and flaking cream paint, and wished herself somewhere else. Obedient to her wishes the patch of classroom wall changed to crimson silk.

The formica and steel table in front of her had vanished. Instead of sitting on a steel-framed chair, she was enthroned in a great gold-painted carved wooden armchair with pale tapestry upholstery. Her feet rested on a matching footstool on a gorgeous floral carpet, which extended over the floor of an enormous drawing room, with red silk walls hung with two tiers of oil paintings; landscapes above, portraits below. High overhead was a ceiling painting of gods in conference. A log fire crackled in the grate of the marble and jasper fireplace. The tall windows looked out over a formal garden with a park beyond.

'Gorgeous! This is certainly different,' Amelia said aloud to herself.

For a few moments, the room was empty and quiet. Then a crowd of people and their noise materialised. It turned out to be yet another *Virtual Stardom* party. Cora was obviously the hostess. She glided through the crush, which parted before her passage, wearing a black sequinned gown, and bearing a silver tray of little biscuits with swirls of pink or green stuff.

'Darling, you've come!' she gushed. 'Have a bicky.'

Amelia took one. She looked around the room and remarked, 'This is very grand, but I did think you'd have a castle.'

'Oh, this is the nearest thing I could find. Castles are so draughty and uncomfortable. When this lot has gone, you must let me show you around. It's all here, you know, a complete stately home: it's got dozens of bedrooms, all with four-poster beds, an absolute maze of passages and creaky stairs, a dreadful damp cellar down below, and a huge kitchen with a full-size spit.' Cora's thin mouth spread wide, showing her pointed teeth. 'I think the site was a castle once upon a time, because there is a little dungeon below the west wing. Outside, it's quite fantastic! There's a perfect little Greek temple with an altar, there's a smelly old witch's hovel, and the deepest, darkest wood you've ever seen.' Amelia fancied the down on Cora's pale skin grew almost furry and her eyes gleamed orange.

Oliver Sheridan was there. He took Amelia aside and sketched out for her his almost completed frame-play. She sighed inwardly to learn that her lovely, gentle Terrever were wiped out by the Arklash, who had become such baddies now that they were cannibals, and they ceremonially ate the Terrever – to tear their ancestral spirits away from the land: perhaps that was a tiny trace of her original conception. Amelia thought about pattern theory: of nothing ever being wiped out, but still present in the past. But Amelia had only dreamed up the Terrever, so perhaps it would not apply to them, which made her feel sad, but she kept smiling, as if her survival depended on it.

So when Luke wandered up she told him she was delighted with

Oliver's frame-play and asked him, 'What comes next?'

'Oh, nearly there now. Coming along splendidly!' Luke beamed. 'Next stage is working up Oli's characters a bit. Want another assistant?'

'Yes, fine,' Amelia smiled back.

The next helper was called Dean River. He was the framing equivalent to an actor. Luke found him in the crush and brought him over to introduce him to Amelia. He had a young film star face: good bone structure, wistful eyes, sensuous mouth and soft brown hair which kept falling over his face. His idea of party clothes seemed to be a much-laundered pinkish-brown checked shirt over a faded black T-shirt and washed out jeans.

'Hi, Amelia!' he greeted her. 'We're going to have some fun working this one up.'

'How many people will you need, then?' she asked.

'Oh, just you and me, I think,' he grinned.

'Me?'

'Don't you want to?'

'Well, yes, fine, but I don't know how to do it, and you've got so many more experienced people.' She looked around at the party crowd.

'You'll be fine. It's just like flexing, which everyone does, except that, for an initial frame, you have to go lightly, sketching everything in, but —'

'— leaving plenty of flex potential,' she finished.

He grinned back. 'See you tomorrow, then, at the entrypoint.'

The next morning, Amelia emerged at the frame's entrypoint and found herself on the dais of the great hall of a castle. Dean was already there.

She looked around. 'How come the entry's at the end?' she asked.

'Oh, people quite like that. The frame's mostly flashback. It was often done with films.'

'And novels,' she said.

'Well there you are! – old pattern.'

'What do we do now?' she asked. 'Do you play Grunthor, and me Agnetha? How do the users get to have my memories?'

'It's all your memories the way Oli's done it. The users can make new routes if they want to, and go on from here. But we have to work from what Oli's done, so we have to make your memories real. It's no good having memories in your mind, they have to be in the world. That's where memories have always been – not in anyone's brain: the brain's just a receiver. Where would you like to start?'

'Can we start with the Terrever? The first memory is of the sacred robe being taken as tribute.'

'We should go back further than that, I think. How about doing the sacrifice ceremony, from one of the years before the robe was taken. We'll be the young couple.'

They emerged on the beach of Terrever Bay.

Dean looked around. 'Hmm, I think we need to start in our village, don't we? I mean, wouldn't there be a procession? Have we got a village scene? There isn't one mentioned in the frame-play.'

'I did a fragment about the village gardens. We can build on that.'

They emerged by the children's mulch bed, in the midst of a crowd of children and adult puppets admiring a pile of dead leaves and rushes.

'Oh good,' said Dean, 'you've got some Terrever people. We'll have to deck them all out in appropriate gear. What sort of mood would it be? Solemn or celebration?'

'Celebration, I think. If we're the couple, we'll have to have the sacred robes on. They'd be dyed homespun cloth with a design made from tiny pieces of bone and shell and pips.'

Amelia looked at Dean. His shirt and jeans were gone, and he was wearing one of the robes. She looked down and she was wearing one too. She saw vegetation under her bare feet, and fancied she could feel its cool damp unevenness.

'Aren't the robes lovely!' she exclaimed.

'Hmm, yes, they're pretty good. They're what you just said, certainly, but I think we need something more ... er ... more magical.'

'How do we get that? I can't imagine what that would be like.'

'We need Amadine,' Dean said. 'I thought we would.'

'Another helper?' Amelia felt a little disappointed, she was enjoying being in a twosome with this gorgeous young man.

The other helper arrived, a fat blonde woman in a flowing pink robe who introduced herself as Amadine Puleston. 'Costumes is my line,' she chirruped. 'Ah!' Her eyes lit up at Amelia's sacred tabard. 'I could work that up a bit,' she offered.

'That's what we were hoping,' said Dean.

86

'Fine,' said Amelia cheerily, hiding a tinge of regret at another bit of her creativity getting the red pen.

'Okay, honey. We'll take a break and leave Amadine to it. We need festival clothes for all this lot, while you're at it. Bye!'

The sacred robe did turn out to be a magical garment when Amadine had finished with it. It looked as if it was made from natural materials, but it also had fractal depth: the closer you looked at it the more detail appeared.

'A user could get so absorbed in those patterns that she'd never get on with the story,' Amelia said. 'How come you could get something as wonderful as that out of the dragon with no trouble at all, and I had to struggle for ages to get a pre-industrial culture for the Arklash?'

'Oh, there's loads of computer art in the archives. A lot of it was natural looking patterns. As for your Arklash —'

'Oh, I know about that really. Luke's interact-face told me about there being nothing in the archives before photography.'

'That's not quite true. There was lots of very realistic art. It was all captured in the info-sweep. I'm sure there must be some paintings of barbarians, but maybe only in the off-profile archives, so you had to use inter-act mode.'

'I expect your ideas for the Terrever came from the off-profile archives as well,' said Dean. 'I don't suppose you invented this gardening method.' He pointed at the mulch beds.

'I never found anything in the library on any people like the Terrever,' Amelia said to Celia.

'Perhaps people like that wouldn't leave any writing. They certainly wouldn't have written on stone, from what you've said, and skins and parchment only survive in special conditions – like being sealed up in jars – and they wouldn't have made jars because that means excavating clay and firing in kilns.'

'Where did I get them from then? Where in the archives might they be?'

'You never know, some people in late necrotech might have thought up what the opposite of necrotech would be, and had a try at living that way.'

'They wouldn't have been allowed, would they?'

'That may be why it's in the off-profile archives.'

'How sad more people didn't do it – enough to make a difference.'

'The more of them that did, the more likely that it'd be suppressed.'

'Oh, Celia, how dreadful life is! Sometimes I can understand why people like horror stories: it helps you face up to the real horrors, which are so much worse.'

Agnetha carefully examined the intricate patterns on the skirt of her tabard where it draped over her knees, and hoped that no one would notice that she was avoiding looking at the spectacle below. Grunthor could not see her because she was on his blind side. Their dais was too high up for anyone in the crowd to see her eyes clearly. Fortunately, the dignity of her position excused her from cheering the high spots of what was being done to the pathetic scrap of humanity strapped to the torturing frame.

But she was fascinated in spite of herself. She sneaked a look as one of the spirit doctors applied a hot iron to the girl's nipple. As she screamed and cried out, 'No! Help! Mummy, don't let them!' an attendant wiped her brow with cool water and moistened her lips; she must be kept alive and conscious as long as possible. Next the doctor took a knife and made a fine cut through her skin from neck to crotch, and began to peel the skin away. As the dissection of body and soul proceeded to the cheers of the bloodlusting crowd, Agnetha drew comfort from the primitive certainty that if this ultimate awfulness was happening to someone else, it could not happen to her. Then, ashamed, she looked back at the patterns on her skirt, imagining the breeze rustling the leaves of the two trees which formed the framework of the design. A squirrel rippled down a branch and spiralled the trunk. Another quick look down at the hall: dogs were scrapping for a finger joint which fell to the ground. At last the bloody mess was handed over to the butchers. Who was next? A tall dark woman, thick straight hair hiding her body like a bridal veil. Head held high, she mounted the steps and then turned to face the dais. She raised her hands, holding the corners of a square of cloth: glowing blue with a design of curling ferns. Grunthor rose to his feet and extended his hand towards her, palm upwards.

I hope that Amelia and her friends
have given you some insight into life
in the biotech age. Although it may appear that, as entertainment
providers, they were in the minority and not typical, a higher proportion
of people in biotech created entertainment than did in necrotech, when it
was a commercial business. In biotech there were many similar
alterations from necrotech patterns, such that more or fewer people took
part in the various roles available. In general, people chose to succeed
rather than to fail in the mock necrotech struggles. This continued a
trend from necrotech, when mass entertainment provided similar
opportunities for ordinary people to indulge in fantasies where they
imagined themselves to be the rich and famous.

It is perhaps surprising that the appetite for horror and physical
mutilation, which was a persistent thread in the necrotech psyche,
persisted into biotech. In necrotech itself, this blood-thirsty streak
manifested itself in socially acceptable and disapproved of forms. You,
my reader from necrotech, will be aware – though you may not see it
the way we do – that the ritual observance of one of the most popular
religions of later necrotech involved the torturing to death of its god,
followed by the ritual consumption of his flesh and blood. The same
religion elevated to near divine status those of its holy men who were
mutilated to death by what was called 'martyrdom'. And yet, interest in
similar horrors for entertainment purposes was frowned upon, until it
was brought into the open by the young of necrotech's final years, when
it was readily available in books and films, many of which were
broadcast on universally available television channels. It is not for me to
endeavour to explain this interest, or the contradictory social standard.
It did not disappear, even when the memory of necrotech had faded
away. Our Bony Bailey might say that it was one of humanity's
patterns, and part of who we are.

We come now, after generations had lived and died in the green
dragon's care, to the later period when memories of necrotech were
losing their appeal, and many people were longing to get out, and
imagining what life would be like if they did so. Some of them, like
Jeremy Vetch, the subject of the next shift, hoped to make a gradual
transition, with the intos helping them on the way.

∾ ∾ ∾

–Hi, Bea. It's Justin.

–Hello, how are you? Recovered from last night?

–Just about. Sorry about getting all weepy.

–Poor love! When I saw Lionel there, I thought maybe you were back together. But then I could see you're not.

–It helps to have a good cry now and again, and after one or two drinks ... But you were look a bit woeful yourself, later on.

–Yes, well I started off celebrating – getting the babe off the breast and being back on the booze after all this time—

–I thought Poppy was two years old, nearly.

–She'd still pull my shirt up – in public too! – and nuzzle down. Then, suddenly, she just didn't any more. I was quite sad actually. For a start, that was my excuse for not looking for a job – which is hopeless anyway: environmental science graduates are two a penny these days. Also that's it with the mother and baby stage. I don't see me having another one; I don't fancy marriage. You're more the marrying kind!

–I think that was the problem with Lionel and me – he wasn't ready to settle down.

–But you still see each other – so ... Anyway, he said something to me last night about fancying Dean River from my book, so he's dipped into *Storyframes*. Have you read it yet? What did you think?

–Well, I found it a bit confusing – with so many different scenes.

–Yes, I know. It was almost impossible to write. It's difficult to imagine what it'd be like with absolutely nothing you had to do – you know, everything laid on by the intos, including entertainment.

–That's the allegorical mirror, surely! Lots of people nowadays have an awful lot of leisure, don't they? Major growth area in the economy. Quite a few of the models I do at work are something to do with leisure: I just did a fancy swimming pool for a theme park.

–Yes, but that kind of leisure's very commercial and active. There's also the kind that's sedentary and solitary – that's what I was showing in the chapter. I had two really idle months myself – between my finals and Poppy being born – and I lost myself in books and videos, all the soaps and everything. I switched from one to the other quite happily, so I thought people might be like that in biotech – especially the people who created the entertainment – or imagined they were doing that.

90

–Imagined? Aren't they really creating storyframes through the intos?

–Maybe. But how would they know the difference?

–That's a bit of M for Mysticism, is it? – one of the big questions: what is reality?

–No! There's not meant to be any big question about the reality of living in biotech. Their reality is mostly virtual, but they are actually lying around on recliners, or in cells full of jelly mesh, interacting with the intos.

–Like you lying on the sofa eating chocolate and oven chips?

–Don't remind me!

–Did you watch horror movies when you were pregnant?

–Don't remember. I expect so. Why?

–Well, the torture scenes in the chapter. And I wondered if it'd be bad for the baby.

–Perhaps that's why Poppy's so contented – horror in the womb prepared her for the birth trauma! People need a bit of horror, don't they, even children – Hans Anderson and so on. Do you remember us watching the late night horrors at the flat?

–Yes, I do. You didn't approve at first, and then you just joined in and were completely un-shockable. But your horror scenes break the rules. Horror stories are usually quite moral – the goodies destroy the baddies in the end – but you kill off your goodies.

–So you think the Terrever are my 'goodies'?

–Hmm. No! No, I don't actually. Look – I'll tell you what I think you were saying – and it's important but it got lost a bit in all the other stuff. I marked it – it was when Amelia's trying to imagine the Arklash and the Terrever. They're not really bad/aggressive and good/gentle – they just use the land differently: like the Arklash exploit and distort nature and the Terrever work with nature – they're part of it. That means hard work for the Arklash, hence slavery and war over territory because they keep buggering it up all the time. And the Terrever are gentle because they have an easy life and they don't need to be anything else. But then – where is it – the *Virtual Stardom* people – Luke and Cora Finch – don't get that. They think like most people nowadays – perhaps since the Garden of Eden in Genesis – that there's absolute 'good and evil' and 'right and wrong'. And that's what you're questioning. Am I right?

–You're a genius, that's what you are.

–I am? You wrote it!

–I'm not sure I did. Now *I'm* going to sound mystical. I've found with a word-processor that I can change, cut and re-write like mad. After a while I let go of thinking it out, and things kind of come.

–From the collective unconscious perhaps – another term for pattern!

–Sure. Anyway, I don't know myself what it means until much later. What you just said is new to me.

–Intriguing! One thing I was going to ask you: why do you sometimes call the biotech support system the *intos* and sometimes the *dragon*?

–I don't know really. It just happened. Maybe I sometimes think of it as artificial – you know, very advanced biotechnology combined with IT, AI, VR or whatever – that's the *intos*. But it's also the *dragon* because it's what nature has become – everything's nature – nature being everywhere and always, like pattern.

–Talking of which, I noticed you slipped a bit of pattern theory into this chapter. Is Bony going to save the world after all?

–Well, pattern does, in various ways. You'll see.

–So they do get out of the dragon?

–Not yet. But they begin to want to.

–OK, I'll press on with the book. I hope the next chapter's less confusing.

–Well, it's different. Yes, it is an easier read, I think. It's very helpful to get feedback like this. But I'm not sure what to do with what you've said about that last chapter – how to make it less confusing.

–I wasn't suggesting you change it.

–No, you haven't really been critical of any of it so far.

–From what you said about re-writing it over and over, I guess you're critical enough yourself without me having a go. One thing I would say, though, is that it might be an idea to write something at the start – a Prologue, maybe – to help readers read it in the right way. You know, a bit like books of those *Magic Eye* pictures, which have instructions on how to focus your eyes to make the hidden image spring out.

–That's a good idea. I'll think about how to do it. Oh by the way, you're a bit of an expert in *Word for Windows* aren't you? I'm having problems with page layout and text flow ......

5

Overfleet

Jeremy was the only person in Overfleet who could count and use numbers; no one else could see the sense in it.

Soon after he arrived, Jeremy had gone over to see Bill Fratter, the carpenter, to ask him to make a set of children's building blocks. Bill was working outside in the sunshine assembling drawers for some kitchen furniture. The pieces were stacked up beside him, nicely fashioned shapes in a pale timber with knot holes. A small child worked beside him, collecting each set and leaning the shapes against each other on the ground.

Jeremy nodded a greeting. Bill nodded back but did not stop tapping in his nails. 'Okay if I watch for a while?' There was a gesture of acceptance, and Jeremy sat himself on a stack of timber.

Bill was a study of colour and form. The bright sun picked out red lights in his rough sandy hair. His forehead was permanently creased with concentration above bristling eyebrows with tufted wings. Pale lashes shaded pale blue eyes. His nose emerged abruptly from the dip between his eyes, and extended down to a fleshy tip. It was red and roughened by the outdoors, as were his long cheeks and jutting cleft chin.

Jeremy watched Bill's freckled hands line up the pieces on the small bench between his knees, and hold them as in a vice as he tapped in the nails. Strong calloused hands, but sensitive; an extension of his intelligence.

Jeremy coughed to break the silence, and asked, 'What timber is that?'

'Novateak, same as rest,' Bill said, through the nails parked in his mouth, waving at the pile Jeremy was perched on.

'All cultured, are they?' Jeremy observed. 'How does it get here?'

Bill stopped hammering and spat the nails into his hand. 'These bits

93

here are from what's been broken up. Made things too quick years ago. Doing them again.'

That seemed a good opportunity to ask Bill about the building blocks Jeremy needed. The two of them went into the workshop and rummaged in Bill's box of small pieces. Bill seemed happy to oblige.

As they walked back to the sunny side of the workshop, Jeremy saw a stack of apparently new lengths of various thicknesses and colours, and asked Bill about them.

'We order that up from time to time. Takes a while though to culture. We take a cart over the hill where you came by. No supply channels big enough in the village.'

'Why don't you use the forest?' Jeremy looked up the tree-covered hillside above them.

'Not ready yet, those trees. My father's father planted some of them up yonder. When this young missie's child is grown – he rested his hand on her red-gold hair – he may have a bit of that timber if he wants it.' Then Bill looked at him a little warily. 'Not to burn, mind,' he muttered, recharging his lips with nails.

Bill's helper was scarcely more than a toddler, so Jeremy supposed Bill meant four generations, or about a hundred years, for the trees to grow to maturity. Fair enough. But wouldn't it be easier to say so?

'They have to be a hundred years old before you fell them? That seems a long time. I suppose they are hardwood trees?'

Bill's face darkened. He said nothing and went on with his work. He was making it understood that he had no idea what Jeremy meant by a hundred years, and did not want to know.

Bill was no exception. No one in the village besides Jeremy knew numbers, except perhaps Denis Jarvis. Well, he could recite the numbers up to twenty, and tried to pretend he knew more, but Jeremy doubted if he understood the concept of number, 'Or even the concept of *concept* – now there's a thought!' Jeremy mused smugly.

Denis Jarvis was the headmaster of the village school. It had been his idea that a little knowledge of drawing up plans and working things out – 'mathematics' – would help the village become more self-sufficient. They might be able to make a decent loom for fine woollen cloth. They could construct a mechanical mill, to be powered by the main stream.

They would need someone who had made a proper study of the subject, and no one in the village qualified. So he had put in a request through the intos, and a few insiders with the requisite knowledge, and located near their part of the world, had been suggested. He had spoken to each of them. Only one of those identified was willing to come out – that was Jeremy – but Jarvis thought he would fit in well.

The proposal had divided the village. Some were curious, and willing to give the mathematics teacher a try. Others, Bill among them, warned that it would be the first step back to necrotech: they would be burning down the forest, poisoning the river, and all dying of dreadful diseases. Others said that if this sort of thing was going to happen, they were going to leave Overfleet, and maybe start a village somewhere else. But in the end it was agreed that Jarvis should ask Jeremy to come out: the first new villager since their grandparents had emerged and built the village. Jarvis had suggested that one of the other teachers at the school – perhaps Angela Astbury? – should go with him over the hill to fetch the new arrival.

On the day Jeremy was to come out Mr Jarvis and Angela set off at dawn for the long trek to the nearest main branch of the intos, and the spot where Jeremy would be directed to from the inside. In companionable silence, they hiked up through the new forest, over the top of the hill and up and down the succession of rolling hills down to the plain. Before climbing the last hill, they rested for a while by a stream, and Jarvis told her as much as he knew about the young man.

'He's an academic,' Jarvis said, 'Not one of those game players, acting about all the time. Clever chap. Took up browsing when he was a lad, and got into the old science archives. He's done a bit of storyframing, I believe – old-style science fiction with space rockets and bug-eyed monsters – that sort of thing. But mostly he's been trying to figure out how people used to think in the days of machinery.' He avoided the word 'necrotech', but he noticed Angela's slight frown.

Jeremy was a young adult when Jarvis contacted him. Although he had never ventured outside the intos, he had kept himself physically fit, and was not semi-paralysed from lethargy like so many insiders. He liked learning for its own sake, and had spent most of his time investigating necrotech science and mathematics. His was a solitary exploration – few people shared his interest in the discredited paradigms of past ages – and so Jeremy had no experience as a teacher or communicator. But the intos had found very few candidates for the position, and none of them were any more suitable than Jeremy; and they were all too wrapped up in their stories. Fortunately Jarvis took a liking to Jeremy, and persuaded him to give the Overfleet School a try. What tempted him was the prospect of interesting children in his unusual field; at least, in half of his unusual field: Jarvis had made it clear he wanted no experiments in necrotech science practised in his classrooms, only mathematics.

Angela listened politely as Jarvis spoke, interested but still puzzled about why they needed the new teacher's knowledge. 'Why are you so sure this is a good idea, Mr Jarvis? Why do we need this mathematics? You said it would help us to make more things? But we make such a lot already, and learn as we go along, and show the younger ones how. You know we can't be completely independent of the intos. We couldn't make our own tools, for example – not without digging in the mountains for ...' she waved vaguely at the barren slopes. 'Well, whatever it was they used to use. So does it really matter what we get from the intos: tools and materials, or finished products – things we can't make? And what makes you think we haven't got the balance about right already?'

'What we make is,' he hesitated, 'well – simple and crude. We could make things better if we knew about precise shapes and geometry and measurement. And we could make all sorts of things we can't make now – like nice fine cloth, as I said at the meeting.'

'Yes, but if we made machines, which is what you've been suggesting, there'd be less work, after we'd finished making the machinery that is, and people like to work – it's what real reality is all about, like Hardcastle said. He was right: we like doing spinning and knitting by hand, and grinding our grain between the stones.'

'The grinding stones are cultured,' he observed, and kicked a rock into the stream.

'Exactly! That's what I was saying. Biotech produces all the materials we need without digging up the mountains and all that dreadful burning and poisoning.'

'It's only a bit of mathematics. Can't do any harm. And he's a very nice young man, you'll like him.'

Angela looked at Jarvis and realised he was quite upset. 'Mr Jarvis, I'm sorry. Really I am. It's not for me to criticise when we've decided to give it a try. I expect it will be very exciting, and we'll all learn a lot of useful things.'

When they reached the top of the final rise of the hills they saw the great plain, and the nearest intos loop swooping high above the ground on its molar-like roots. It was one of the oldest parts of the system and erosion had shifted the soil it had originally rested upon. The surrounding hills sheltered that part of the intos from the storms, and so it had never been damaged badly enough to have to regrow nearer to the present soil level.

They carried on walking until they stood looking up at the massive green tube. The sun was at its highest; it should not be long before the mathematics teacher arrived. As yet there was no obvious break in the scaly surface, or in the rippling spiral patterns as the wind curled through the fins. Then, as they watched, they discerned a slight bulge some distance away, travelling along the tube. It stopped almost above them, where the nearest root joined, then bulged out further and formed into a fish-like mouth. The mouth opened briefly, discharging a whitish package which slid to the top of a groove in the root. As the package drew nearer, the groove travelled down, allowing the package to fall and then smoothing itself out above. The package wriggled and rocked for a bit and then broke open to reveal a blinking and slightly stunned young man.

'Jeremy Vetch, I presume,' said Jarvis, holding out his hand to help the young man rise, and to shake hands when he was safely on his feet. 'I am Denis Jarvis, this is Miss Astbury.'

'How do you do, Jeremy, I'm Angela,' she smiled, holding out her hand. Not bad! she thought. He was a little taller than her, slim built and nicely proportioned. He had thick light brown hair, blue eyes, good cheek bones, firm chin, rather full lips and a shy smile. He was dressed in a white tunic which reached his knees, and nothing else. Jarvis was relieved that he had something on, in view of the young woman being present. Recovering from his abrupt descent, he was now shivering in the biting wind. Jarvis threw around him the warm woollen cloak he had brought along, and helped him put on knitted socks and strong leather boots. He was rather proud to be able to provide some things made in the village, and had not requested the intos to culture a suitable outfit for Jeremy's exit to the outside world.

'Where's the village,' Jeremy asked, looking over Jarvis's shoulder at the expanse of green desert, bare apart from a few giant ropes snaking into the distance.

'It's over the hill back that way,' said Angela, pointing behind him to where the land began to rise towards a steep scree slope; an area which, presumably, the early phase of the intos had found unsuitable for putting down its roots. She wondered then where their own newer and narrower supply line joined the main system. There was so much she did not know; perhaps the new arrival was going to help her learn more.

'We have to walk up there?' he asked, looking a little daunted at the prospect.

'Not just up there, I'm afraid,' she replied. 'There are more hills beyond, up and down, up and down. It will take us the rest of the day. I'm sorry, we'll have to get going. Are you going to be okay? I suppose you didn't do much walking in there.' The cloak covered his body, but when she had looked him over before she had thought he looked quite normally built, and fit and strong enough.

'I used to exercise,' he said. 'Simulated walks mostly – around ancient Oxford was my favourite.'

'Oxford?' she queried. 'Oh never mind. We really must go. Where's Mr Jarvis? She looked around, and saw a glimpse of him behind an the intos root, urinating as discreetly as he could. He finished and turned and walked up to them.

'Er, good idea, I think I'll ... Please excuse me.' She ran over to another root, squatted with her legs spread and wee-ed. She rejoined them – they had turned their backs. She giggled, 'Jeremy, do you need to ...?'

He smirked and shook his head. 'No, I'm fine. I suppose this is what real reality is like. No one wees in stories, do they?' They set off in single file, with Jeremy between them, and he kept up perfectly well. But they did not talk, to save their breath and strength. As each hill dropped behind them, the wind lessened, and the air felt warmer. Then they threw their cloaks back to cool down. Jeremy noticed they both wore knee-length tunics, similar to his own, but of somewhat courser cloth.

At last, near the close of day, they reached the top of the last hill. It was a bright dusk and they could see the village. They paused together looking down and Angela pointed out the main features. Clusters of pretty cottages, irregular in shape and thatched, were scattered over the hillsides above a tributary of a river called the Hie, whose broad expanse could just be seen further down the valley. Each group of cottages was surrounded by gardens and orchards. On the lowest slopes were the village fields which provided grains for their staple food. Above the cottages where the hills rose steeply, young trees of a thigh's girth were beginning to touch branches and make a forest.

'Look down by our stretch of the river, Jeremy. There's the upper

98

bridge and the lower bridge, and between them is the jetty for boats. I don't know if you can see – it's getting dark now – but behind the jetty is our market square. Along there are the display stalls. See the thatched roofs to shelter the traders from rain. On market days, everyone comes down the paths from their homes with loads of fruits and veggies from their gardens, and meats and cheeses. And they bring what they've made: cloaks like yours, and knitted things. Some of us make pots and shoes and furniture. And over there, we have tables set, and you can have baked foods and beer and wine and herbal tea – it's like a party – and people play instruments, and dance and sing, and tell stories.'

Jarvis joined in at this point. 'There's the school on the opposite bank from the jetty – the long oval building. Its gardens go down to the river, but we have a strong fence and hedge to stop the youngest children going into the boggy bit by the water, and maybe falling in.'

Angela was going on to tell him where everyone lived; a stream of names and relationships, skills and interests, characters and attitudes. As she burbled away, Jeremy was counting the houses. He counted fifty, and then estimated how many more fifties there were over the valley.

'I make it three hundred, is that right?' He turned to Jarvis.

'Er, yes, that's about it I should think.'

Angela stopped and looked at Jeremy. 'What do you mean "three hundred"?' she said.

'I was counting the houses.'

'What's "counting"?'

Jeremy glanced at Jarvis, who made a gesture for him to answer her. 'One there,' he said, pointing to the nearest cottage and holding up his left thumb. 'Two there,' and he held up his first finger. 'Three there,' and he went on.

'But that's Jay, Morven, Hattie and Archie's place – I was telling you about them just now – they teach in the school, and do spinning and knitting for market. That's Andy, Hannah, Ossie and Dilly – they do potting mostly, and they have baby George now. That's where Linda and Orville live in lambing time. That place is empty now; it was Annie and Old George's before he died. What has that to do with your fingers?' She frowned. 'No, I don't think I want to know. You tell Jamie about counting and fingers, then we'll see.' She ran off down the slope and Jarvis led Jeremy down to his house where he was to stay.

Jamie was the boy who had volunteered to begin having mathematics lessons with the new teacher. Mr Jarvis told all the children at assembly one morning that a new teacher, Mr Vetch, was coming who was going to teach them a very special subject called 'mathematics'. Because the teacher was new and the subject was new, Mr Jarvis and the other teachers thought it might be a good idea if Mr Vetch worked with a single pupil to start with, to see what was the best way to introduce the subject to the others. 'Anyone who is interested, please come to my room after school this afternoon,' he had told them.

After school, Jarvis waited in his room to see if any of the children would turn up. James Sweeting was the only child who did. Probably the others had not liked to put themselves forward and be conspicuous. Maybe the adults had put doubts into their minds.

'Hello, James. Have you come to offer to be our mathematics pupil?'

The boy nodded and smiled, 'Yes Mr Jarvis.'

'Well we don't know for sure if Mr Vetch will think this a good idea. It's the teachers' idea so far. We'll talk to Mr Vetch when he comes. And you can talk to your people at home. Then if everyone is happy, that's what we'll do. Is there anything you want to ask me?'

The question Jarvis feared would come duly did. 'What is mathematics, Mr Jarvis?'

He had prepared an answer. It was the best he could do from his own knowledge. 'It's a way of studying the patterns of things. It's looking at what things are similar to each other and grouping them together and saying how they are similar. A long long time ago, people realised they had copied patterns of similarity into their minds – because that's what minds are for – matching the past from the mind with the present in the world, to help decide what to do – and they decided the patterns in their minds were more important than the patterns in the world, because the patterns in their minds could be exact, and the patterns in the world were only rough. They worked out some rules for the patterns in their minds, and when they made things like buildings they made them with exact patterns. So what was in their minds came out into the world, and made cities and civilisation.'

That was not quite what Jarvis had intended to say, although it had started off all right. Then he got carried away, and was speaking to himself rather than to the boy. When he realised, he looked at him and said, 'Did you understand what I was saying, James?'

'What is *understand*, Mr Jarvis?'

Jarvis thought for a moment. 'It's when you see what I was telling,' he replied.

'No, I didn't really do that,' said the boy.

'Never mind, Mr Vetch will tell it better than I can. That's why he's coming,' Jarvis smiled. 'Do you still want to be our mathematics pupil, James?'

'I think so, Mr Jarvis. I like different things.'

'Yes, good, so do I! Good lad. Thank you for coming forward. Well, off you go now.'

Jarvis explained the idea of a trial pupil on the evening of Jeremy's arrival. 'Sounds fine, whatever you think best,' was his response. He was tired, and somewhat overwhelmed by the sudden change in his life. He went to bed straight after supper, and lay in the dark – even that was a new experience – and tried to collect himself together.

The view from the top of the hill had been Jeremy's first sight of Overfleet. After Jarvis had approached him through the intos, he had found out all he could about the village, and he had expected there to be simulations he could walk through. But there were none. The nearest thing was a storyframe made by Overfleet's founder years before the project was started. It had been a shock to Jeremy to discover that the intos was not omniscient: that all its records were from bionecrotech or necrotech; everything else was story material. There was no record of the world outside the intos, and that included Overfleet, which was the only place where people were living in the outside world. Of course, they were still dependent on the inside, being supplied with many of their necessities from biotech processes, which transformed carbohydrates produced by photosynthesis into cultured materials.

From his initial view of Overfleet with Angela and Jarvis, Jeremy might have thought the village had been nestling in the Hie Valley for centuries. But from his researches he knew that it had been completed only fifty years earlier – or, as the inhabitants would have said, in their fathers' fathers' time.

Overfleet's founder had been a master story writer, Denver Hardcastle, famous for creating some of the most popular scenarios available to the world's players. Hardcastle became dissatisfied with the realities he was creating, and was overwhelmed by the ambition to create real reality in the outside world.

He managed to interest enough people in the venture to be able to organise a physical meeting. They worked out a suitable location for the village, and a route through the intos supply channels for each of the participants. It took several years to order the materials for the construction and to have them grown in culture, and transported outside the intos system near the place Hardcastle had identified. After that, the Overfleet villagers took over and built the village themselves.

As well as timber, bricks and glass, plaster and paints and so on, the villagers had ordered a suitable collection of seeds and cuttings, and small livestock from the stocks of frozen embryos. When they had all the materials assembled they began to build. By the time their youngest children had reached maturity, they had filled the valley with clusters of cottages with extensive communal gardens.

When the main phase of building and planting was complete, Hardcastle himself formally opened the village, and the people who had come out settled down, as if they had been there for generations. Interestingly, Hardcastle went back into the intos and continued to create some of the best stories on offer, and never saw Overfleet again. The intos information about the project went no further than this, apart from vocal records of the villagers' orders for batches of cultured materials. Jeremy had gone through these, studying the faces and the glimpses of rooms in the background.

Jarvis had told him about the history of the school.

The people of Overfleet were a complete mixture of stages in life. A few of the founders had died before the opening, babies had been born, and by the opening there were many children. Hardcastle's initial conception had included a school, and a pleasant oval building intended for the school had been constructed. Since the intos was available in all the homes as a source of information and stories, and all domestic and craft skills could be passed on by those who had them, it was not at all clear what the school would provide.

Nevertheless, Douglas Jarvis, Denis Jarvis's grandfather, had volunteered to be the headmaster, and several villagers offered themselves as teachers.

The staff looked into the history of schools back in necrotech, and found that the reading and writing of symbolic languages had been a major focus. They all agreed that it was pointless teaching such antique means of communication, which the youngsters would have no further use for. They were also very wary of teaching science, because of what it had led to. So they decided to concentrate on arts and crafts and story creation; partly using the intos facilities, but also using real materials – in accordance with Hardcastle's dream. School would be optional, and it

102

would carry on as long as it seemed children liked it and found it useful. So far they had liked it, at least, enough of them had to make it worthwhile.

Jeremy first saw James Sweeting in school assembly, two mornings after his arrival in Overfleet and his first day at the school. He was invited up on the platform beside Mr Jarvis. 'Good Morning, everyone,' Jarvis said. 'Today we welcome Mr Vetch, who has just joined us to teach mathematics.' Jeremy stepped forward and bowed. The children all clapped. Jarvis went on, 'We have a special treat today in honour of Mr Vetch. The music group has prepared a special performance of the Myth of the Dragons.'

At a nod from Jarvis, the doors at the back of the hall opened, and a crocodile of children marched down the gangway, playing a loud and powerful tune on pipes and drums. They wore head-dresses representing blackened trees surrounded by tongues of flame. When they had almost reached the platform, their music changed to an eerie harmony which soared up and down like stormy wind. The children swayed and staggered with the music until they reached the platform, when they all took off their head-dresses and mounted the steps. A drummer and a piper continued the storm tune while the other children disappeared with their instruments into a huge tube of green cloth laid at the side of the platform. From inside the green tube they began to play a variety of lively tunes one after the other. Then the tunes became soft and doleful. The sound dwindled and then, suddenly, the children came out of the tube and looked around them as if in wonder. They played a melody of lightness and pleasure as they skipped around. Then, over the top of the tune came another, sung by a boy soloist with a voice of sweet perfection. The high thread of sound was poignant and sad. The words he sang were: 'Long ago the black dragon burned the forest, the storms came and we hid in the green dragon, we came forth in hope, but there is no forest.' The children stopped playing and sang in chorus, 'There is no forest – no forest.'

There was enthusiastic applause. Jeremy and Jarvis beamed across at the performers and clapped. Then Jarvis waved his hand in dismissal and everyone filed out.

'Come and be introduced to your pupil,' Jarvis said, walking across the platform and putting his arm over the shoulders of the boy soloist.

'James Sweeting and Jeremy Vetch, here you are now, let me introduce you to each other.'

'That was you singing, James. It was wonderful!' The boy nodded, and looked up at him with a steady gaze. His eyes were deepest blue, with long curled lashes. His finely drawn straight dark eyebrows were almost hidden by a fringe of honey-coloured hair. He held out his hand and Jeremy took it with both of his, still thinking of the song, and wondering how long the boy's treble voice would last as he saw the mature shape of his face just emerging from the rounded cheeks of childhood.

'Well, what happens now, Mr Jarvis?' he asked, letting go the boy's hand at last.

'It's up to you. I thought young James might show you round the school – round the village too, if you like. If you want to get down to work, there's a little room out the back – the Small Quiet Room, James. It's got a screen if you need it, though we don't generally use the one in there. There's a table and chairs and a sofa. James knows where to get drinks and snacks. Lunch is up to you – James knows about that too. So that's it really. See you this evening – not expecting a report or anything.' He guided them off the platform and out of the hall, nodded and smiled, and veered off round the corner, leaving them together.

'What shall we do then, James?' Jeremy was feeling overwhelmed by … he knew not what. It was hardly surprising that he felt strange. Until a few days ago, he had spent all his life in a cell, most of the time deep in his studies of ancient thought, albeit with access to simulation systems capable of taking him into any environment, into crowds and parties if he liked. Now he had been thrust into the company of this boy, who had been the star of his first experience of the power of living music, and he was expected to share his life's work with him.

'Whatever you want to do, Mr Vetch.'

'Oh, do call me Jeremy,' he said, then wondered if he should keep their relationship formal. He looked at James, at the garden, the door of the school building, the sky, and back to the boy, and felt quite at a loss.

At this point a rattling noise reached them, followed by a trolley full of small pots, wheeled by someone he knew: Angela Astbury, his other escort to this new life.

'Hello, Jeremy! Hello, Jamie! You look a bit lost. How about helping me put these things in the sun to harden.'

The relief from having to decide what to do was wonderful. Jeremy took the trolley from her and pushed it to the place she indicated, where a long picnic table stood away from the shadows of the school and the trees.

As they unloaded the pots, carefully so as not to smear the intricate designs etched onto them, Jeremy stopped himself counting them, as Angela explained the patterns.

'These are celebration goblets. This one is Anna's, for her sister's menarche party when it comes, soon I should think, she's a well-grown girl. It has goddess images all around, see, each with a tiny sun in the belly and a moon as a crown. Lovely, don't you think? These ones, by the Underwood boys, are for their grandad's burying, not that he's dead yet mind. See the ancient trees and the saplings between, same theme but each quite different, they've put their own characters into the patterns. And see what Gwen has done, a naming goblet for her brother. He has chosen to be called Ray after his father's father, and to have his mother's family name, Reed, and you see those images on the goblet. I think he may decide to change it again, it is a bit odd when you say it, isn't it – too short, I think. Gwen will have to make him another goblet then.'

The account poured on. Jamie was clearly very interested, knowing the people involved, and made comments and asked questions. Jeremy watched them, enclosed as they were in their world. He felt a stranger. He counted the pots after all: fifteen there were, each of them different he could see that, but they were all pots, much too heavy to be called goblets. He thought about his researches into necrotech, when drinking cups were churned out by machinery, many of them intended to be used once and thrown away. At least biotech ones were recycled. What they looked like was imaginary anyway, you fitted them into the story you were in at the time: porcelain cups, pewter tankards, crystal goblets with long delicate stems, not stubby ones like these.

'What happens to these in the sun?' he asked, hardly realising he was interrupting her account which was still going on. 'In the old days clay like this had to be fired in a kiln.'

He saw her hurt look, but she replied, 'They go hard and shiny; really beautiful they are, and strong. The clay is biotech, of course. Look, have you two got things to do, or do you want to come with me to get fish for lunch?'

'Oh please, we'd love to come,' Jeremy replied without consulting the boy, who shrugged when Angela looked at him.

'Fine. We'll go over the upper bridge and see if there's a boat free.

Jamie, go and get me a basket, would you.' He trotted off. She looked at Jeremy quizzically. 'You look bothered, Mr Mathematics Teacher. What's the matter?'

He was fiddling with a little bit of spare clay he had picked off the trolley. He formed it into a neat cube. 'It's like you said just now, I feel lost. Everything's so strange.'

'It must be,' she said sympathetically.

'And I don't know what I'm supposed to do with Jamie.'

'Nothing much at first, I don't suppose. You've only just arrived. Give yourself time,' she smiled.

'When Jarvis contacted me it seemed very clear. I had some knowledge you didn't have in your village – knowledge of mathematics.'

'That's true. I don't think we even know what it is!'

'Yes, but listening to you talking, the day I got here, and you and Jamie just now, made me think that perhaps it was the other way around: that you've got knowledge that I haven't.'

'That sounds fine; we learn from each other.'

'But suppose it isn't like that.' He sat down on the bench. 'Look, let me try to explain. I might get it clearer in my own mind.' She sat down beside him.

'When Mr Jarvis contacted me I thought about it a lot. What he said seemed to make sense. There must be science and technology which you could make good use of, but people are wary, because of the dreadful things that happened in necrotech. But you know about that. You teach the children about it.' He looked at her.

'Yes, we do. I suppose we should do more.'

'Some of you are very wary, Mr Jarvis told me. But that means you're forewarned; you can be selective. But you need mathematics as a basis, which is good because mathematics is just ideas, it's only in the mind, so it can't do any harm, right?' She nodded. 'So Mr Jarvis asked the intos to find someone to teach you mathematics. That seemed okay to me.'

He paused, and fiddled with the piece of clay. 'It was different for people in historic times. Mathematics and science and technology just grew, and were taken on board.' He made a disk with the clay. 'Like the wheel.' She smiled. He made a rectangular block. 'And stone buildings. There's geometry in those.' He rolled the clay into a spike. 'Then smelting, and all the other inventions: they came out of science,

106

and its rules were based on mathematics.'

He made the clay into a disk again and turned it over and over. 'All the technology that came in, it brought about some good and some bad; you can't have good without bad. I'm not sure about the other way. It was good for some people and bad for others, and always bad for the ecology and natural processes.

'The way people thought was based on science and technology, even if they didn't think they knew any. They thought of themselves as small parts in a machine, which had to be kept going, on and on. They accepted and knew the machine, but they didn't even try to control it. And the machine ran on death and burning. Imagine what that did to people's spirits!

'So by the end of necrotech, even the good was dubious. And finally everything went crazy.' He tore the clay into bits. 'There was famine and sickness, and the ethnic wars, then the economy collapsed.'

Jeremy solemnly gathered up the fragments of clay and remade his disc, saying, 'Then bionecrotech sorted out many of the problems – it put the world back together.' He saw Angela start to protest. 'I know what you're going to say: bionecrotech was even worse for the planet. I agree. But it led to biotech, and biotech is wonderful for people. They are secure and provided for; and they are free to live whatever lives they choose. Their lives may be in artificial reality, but people have always lived in dream worlds; and they love it, it's paradise for them. Outside, of course, there's just deserts: green, brown or white deserts, and crazy winds howling around – that's the bad, there's always bad.' He turned the disk over.

'As biotech went on everyone forgot the old ways of thinking: all the mathematics and science – apart from a few oddballs like me. No one needed to know any of it because the intos took care of everything, and anyway the intos's basis was intelligent organic, not machine. Then you people come out, and you have your own way of thinking, and it's lovely to hear you talk. It reminds me of the old ecology: so diverse and detailed and all tangled up.' Then he looked up at Angela. She smiled, but he shook his head and frowned. 'I'm worried for you, you know. I'm afraid that if you start thinking like me, you'll lose those ways; you'll be corrupted.' He fell silent for a moment, looking at her. 'Well that's it.'

She put her hand on his arm. 'We won't be corrupted. Maybe we'll corrupt you!' she smiled.

He opened his mouth to say more.

'No, sorry. I think I understand your concern. We feel it too, some more than others. That's why we suggested you work with a trial pupil just at first. It was our idea, not Mr Jarvis's. We're more involved with the village than he is. He's just absorbed in the school, and he's into the intos a lot. But he's accepted our suggestion. So I think you should give it a try. Share some of your knowledge with Jamie. Then we'll see.' She looked over to the school building. 'There he is with our basket.' She waved and he came over.

'You've been a long time,' she said.

'You were talking. I didn't want to interrupt,' he replied. Jeremy felt the implied reprimand.

They went to the jetty for a boat. Jeremy rowed, awkwardly at first until he got the hang of it. As he pulled back on the oars, he looked at Angela, leaning back on the slatted seat with her fingers dipped in the water. He imagined how she would look in a fine straw bonnet with satin roses and lace, and a sprigged muslin gown; an image from one of his favourite stories. Her face fitted the picture: oval and delicately formed, with soft grey eyes, small straight nose and pink, neatly bowed mouth. He imagined her straight fair hair looped up into coils under the bonnet. He smiled at her. She smiled back. He glanced at the boy sitting in the bottom of the boat with the basket, who nodded cheekily in the direction of Jeremy's naked crotch where his tunic had ridden right up his thighs. Hastily he pulled his knees together, thinking he would have to watch himself in this real reality; things could happen he did not intend.

They reached the fish ponds, and held the boat against the railings while they watched the bright orange carp darting about just below the surface.

'Who feeds them?' Jeremy asked.

'They're biotech fed and cleaned,' she replied. 'I suppose there are channels and filters down on the bottom. All that's a mystery to me; I was hoping you'd know something about it.'

'Not me! I'm even more of a pampered citizen that you are; I don't know anything about the plumbing. My knowledge is all in the mind.'

Jamie chipped in, 'Mr Jarvis said civilisation was about building the patterns of the mind in the outside world; at least, I think that's what he said.'

Jeremy looked at him thoughtfully. 'Yes, I think that's right. That's what technology does.' Then he looked at Angela, 'But I haven't got further than looking at the patterns in the mind, the ancient minds, that is.'

'That's what you were saying you're concerned about: putting out some of those patterns here, and what that would do to us.'

Jamie chipped in again, 'Mr Jarvis said that the patterns of the mind are exact and more the same, instead of messy like in the world. So we'd get to be more the same and more tidy.'

'Oh, I shouldn't like that,' said Angela. 'But some of the patterns in the world are tidy. Look at those fish, so neat and just so.'

'They are all different though, if you look carefully,' Jeremy said, surprising himself by the thought. Perhaps Angela was right: he was the one who was going to be changed. He reached for the net. 'How many do you want for lunch?'

'What do you mean "How many?"?' she asked.

'You do it,' he said, handing her the net.

That afternoon, Angela suggested that Jamie might not want to miss music lessons; a new composition was going to be begun. She sent her own class home – none of the children seemed to mind – so that she could show Jeremy around the village.

She showed him one of the communal gardens. It was like a small forest with fruit and nut trees underplanted with bushes and various vegetables. Part was fenced off for chickens and ducks, and there were some sheep, goats and pigs in other enclosures. They met several villagers, out gathering, or working at their crafts. Jeremy sensed a contrast between those who were coolly polite and others who were warm and welcoming.

Later, Angela led him up the hill into the trees. Jeremy felt that there was something artificial about the forest, in spite of the variety of tree species, whose names he did not know, and the irregular spacing. She knew a few of the species: oak, ash, elm and beech. She explained the artificial feel, and it should have been obvious to him: there was a solid carpet of the bionecrotech plant they called 'bigweed', a hybrid chickweed or stellaria, growing strongly in spite of the shade. She told him it soon sprang though the autumn leaf fall, and stayed green all winter. They used to try to clear it away, as they had to do in the gardens, but it was hopeless, and now they left it alone.

She pulled some out and peered at the earth beneath. 'Some people believe that the spirit of the wild will return some day. And mosses and ferns will grow, and grasses and mushrooms.'

'Watch out for the poisonous ones,' he laughed.

They walked on through the dim silence of the trees. She reached for his hand. The feeling that had struck him in the boat, that he was in a reality he was not in control of, had grown as Angela had taken charge of him. He decided he liked it. He moved his fingers to lie between each of hers and felt her squeeze acceptance of the implied intimacy.

'Let's stop for a while,' he said softly. She turned to face him, reached for his other hand and, crouching slowly back, she pulled him down on top of her spread legs. He kissed her soft and firm little mouth, pushing his tongue between her lips and probing for her tongue which darted teasingly at his. Wriggling sideways, he pulled the tassel of her girdle, and carefully lifted her tunic above her breasts. She wriggled out of it and bundled it under her head, pulled his girdle, and he pulled his tunic off.

'Now what, Mr Mathematics Teacher?' she laughed, pointing her finger to stroke the soft hard knob of his penis. He moved over her so he could use it to touch and circle her nipples, first one and then the other, slowly and carefully. She bent forward to lick it with the crimson point of her tongue.

Then he sat back, leaving a silvery thread of juice down her body. He reached out with his fingers and ruffled the soft curls of her pubes, and lightly touched the swollen pink petals which led to her vagina.

She pulled him into her. In only a few eager thrusts they reached a shrill climax. They lay close and still, each suddenly embarrassed to look the other in the face. She wriggled away and slipped into her tunic. He turned his back and put on his.

She darted a half smile up at him. He put an arm over her shoulder and led her back down the hill.

That evening Jeremy was uncertain what to say to Jarvis. But it seemed that the headmaster had a good idea how the day had gone.

'I'm glad you've made friends with our Angela,' he said. 'I've been thinking since this morning that you need to get to know us a bit, not spend all your time with your pupil.'

Jeremy told Jarvis what Jamie had said about civilisation.

'Bright boy that. Bit of a loner though, not really part of the bunch. Not surprised he came forward.'

Jeremy had also been doing some thinking about the lessons he was supposed to give. The clay pots had made him think that perhaps he would need some materials, paper and pencils at least. He mentioned this to Jarvis, not thinking it could be a problem.

'You can't get paper,' was Jarvis's surprising reply. 'They tried when the school was first started, but we can't make it and the intos won't supply it. Seems to be a rule from back in bionecrotech. No paper, none at all, not for any purpose.'

Jeremy said, 'Back in necrotech they churned out masses of the stuff; more and more as time went on, even after they'd invented computers.'

Jarvis nodded, 'I know; they even used to wipe themselves with it after opening their bowels! Biotech sorted that out. Better diet, less obsessive washing and looser clothing, and bacteria do all the cleaning that's necessary. Nasty idea anyway, I wouldn't want to do it. I don't suppose that sort of paper would suit your purposes anyway,' he laughed. 'What I use for writing on is clay tablets. I believe they did the same when writing was first thought of. I'll show you.'

He went to a cupboard and brought out a wooden tray and handed it to Jeremy. It had a narrow rim around it, and inside a layer of clay, of the sort Angela's class had been using.

'It stays soft you see, as long as you don't leave it in the sun. I write on it with this stylus, and when I want to start again I roll it flat with this little roller. Neat, eh! Bill Fratter made them for me. I've got a stack of them in here.'

'You know how to write then – symbolic language?' Jeremy was impressed.

'Can *you* write? Come to that, can you read?' It sounded like a challenge.

Jeremy was puzzled and a little put out. 'Of course I can,' he said.

'I'm sure you think you can. Look, let's see. There's my screen. Call up *The Mill on the Floss* by George Eliott. You'll see why in a minute. Ask for text, or you'll get a story version. Ask for the bit where Tom goes away to school.' Jeremy did as he was told and a passage of text appeared on the screen. 'Now read it.'

'Tom Tulliver's sufferings during the first quarter he was at King's Lorton, under the distinguished care of the Reverend Walter Stelling, were rather severe. At Mister Jacob's academy, life ...'

'That'll do,' Jarvis interrupted. 'Now, the other day I copied that passage down on this tablet here. See if you can read it.'

Jeremy took the tablet. It was covered with symbols which looked familiar. He tried to do what he thought was reading, but no sense came into his mind. He shook his head, and looked at Jarvis.

'The intos reads it to you, you see. You hear the sense. People were already reading less and less at the end of necrotech; they had a lot of visual and vocal information even then. In bionecrotech, after the paper purge I was just talking about, even the academics stopped reading physical books. It was easier to call them up, and have them read. In biotech, when people came to inhabit individual cells, they had no way of knowing if they were reading and saying it in their minds, or listening to a voice the intos produced. You're no different. I could tell just now, you see, because I could hear the voice too. We don't have cells here; we prefer flat screens, everyone in the village does.'

Jeremy sat there, utterly bemused by this revelation. Did he know anything at all? he wondered. Yes, of course he did. There was information in his head. Obviously he had got it from the intos, but he could carry it around and impart it to others. He took the blank tablet and the stylus, and drew a triangle, then a circle. The shapes were wobbly, but recognisable. He tried writing '1 2 3 4', but found he could not do it. He turned to the screen and said, 'Show me the numbers one, two, three and four.' The symbols appeared, and Jeremy carefully copied them onto the clay.

'Yes, that's what I've had to do. I don't think anyone else in the village has tried it. There's no need for them to. It's just a hobby of mine. I go in for useless hobbies.' And he pouted in self-mockery.

'I can see I'm going to have to do quite a bit of preparation.'

'Well, that's what we thought, the other teachers and I. So that's partly why we suggested you work on it with just James.'

Jeremy was silent for a while. He sat fiddling with the tassel of his girdle. As he did so, he came across the lump of clay he had been playing with earlier, which he had slipped into his pocket. He fished it out and absently formed a cube, and this gave him an idea.

'Mr Jarvis, do you think that carpenter you mentioned would make me some children's building blocks? I think they'd be very useful.'

'Bill Fratter? I should think so. Go and ask him. I'll show you where he is in the morning. There are other people besides him who do woodwork if he's too busy.'

After his visit to Bill Fratter, which confirmed the impressions he had gathered from Angela, Jeremy began to understand what he called 'the village philosophy', undefined and unstated though it was. The inhabitants' inability to count was due to their way of life. Everything was done by a form of collective sensing. There was no recording of time; no clock or calendar. Market day, for example, just happened. If it was a pleasant morning and there had not been one for a while, people just turned up, with their produce. There were no anniversaries. Birth dates were not recorded. But when someone made a significant transition in their lives, there was a ceremony or a celebration.

Jeremy decided that Angela was right. He should just go along with Jarvis's project, and not worry about whether or not it would prove useful to the villagers, or, indeed, whether it would disturb them.

A routine developed in Jeremy's life. If Jamie turned up for a lesson, they worked together; if not, he worked alone; or went along to one of the other teachers' classes. Some evenings he spent with Angela, some with Jarvis. Quite often there were parties which someone would take him along to.

To Jeremy's great joy, Jamie was fascinated by what he had to show him on the intos screen. The boy took to mathematics like a duck to water. He romped through arithmetic, algebra and trigonometry, then Euclidean, non-Euclidean and projective geometry. He loved shapes – 'patterns', as he insisted on calling them: simple polygons, conic sections, polyhedra; and he was thrilled when he discovered how to extend geometry into multiple dimensions using the evolutionary progressions the intos provided.

Jamie's progress was astonishing. He worked through sets and functions, group theory, matrices and vectors, linear transformations, calculus, analysis, flows and fractals: it was all fine, as long as it could be presented or illustrated by patterns, and with Jeremy's instructions, the intos provided.

It was as if all the mathematical thought of past ages was pouring into the child's receptive mind. No, Jeremy thought, more as if Jamie's brain was a channel which led him into humanity's mathematical genius, connected and enhanced by the intos artificial intelligence.

Jeremy was tremendously proud of his pupil. 'He's a natural mathematician; more than I am,' he told everyone.

But the difference between Jamie's aptitude and Jeremy's was more a matter of pace than natural ability. Jeremy showed the way, and Jamie followed with an eagerness which fed on his gifted teacher's more methodical years of study. Their love of the subject grew as the leading and showing merged into a shared exploration. The intimacy was enhanced for Jeremy because it was his first, after a lifetime in a solitary cell. Sometimes he wished for a cell to enclose them both, but their imagination and absorption enabled them to disappear into the intos wonderland, without being physically surrounded by it.

One day, after a morning which culminated in a heady ride around powers of complex numbers, they emerged giddy and elated, and staggered into one of Angela's pottery classes. They worked separately, but part way through the session Angela examined their pots and laughingly exclaimed, 'Just look at this, children; these two are twin souls, their designs are exactly the same!' She held up the pots, both incised by a network of intertwining spirals.

The pot-making episode was exceptional, and nothing like it ever happened again. It highlighted a curious difficulty with the mathematics lessons. Apart from that single occasion, Jamie would not bring any of his understanding into the outside world; into the real world of the classroom. He was totally inept with Jarvis's stylus and the clay tablet, and would not – insisted that he could not – even copy down numbers displayed on the screen. He showed no understanding of the simple arithmetic or algebra Jeremy scored on the tablet.

One evening the building blocks Jeremy had ordered from Bill Fratter arrived. Bill brought them himself, in a large box obviously specially made to contain them. He handed the box over without a word. Jeremy thanked him warmly, inviting him in, but he shook his head and turned to go. Feeling a return of his earlier strangeness, Jeremy watched Bill's back disappear into the night.

Next morning, Jeremy turned out the blocks onto the floor between himself and Jamie. He found that, like everything else in Overfleet, no two were alike. They were regular in shape, but they were not all cubes, which was what he thought he had asked for. There were rectangular blocks of various proportions, cylindrical ones, triangular ones, some cones, and a few were rectangular but with semi-circular sections cut out to leave arches. Those of the same shape were stained in different colours.

He watched as Jamie immediately set to and made a castle. Was there a memory of children making castles going way back into history? he wondered. The castle was basically rectangular, Jeremy noted, looking for opportunities for a lesson. It had a gatehouse in one of the longer walls, and towers at each corner. As Jamie worked on it, it became more and more elaborate. A few blocks remained when he had

114

completed the castle to his satisfaction, and knelt back for it to be admired. And Jeremy, of course, duly admired it enthusiastically.

Then Jeremy gathered up the remainder of the blocks. He made the outline of a square with the straight ones. He traced the shape and looked up at the boy. 'See I've made a square,' he said, encouragingly. 'One, two, three, four corners. One, two, three, four sides. Two at the top here, and two at the bottom. Two and two makes four.' He felt ridiculous speaking to this brilliant boy in such a way.

Jamie's response was to crawl over and mess up Jeremy's square. Then he used the blocks to make some little houses outside his castle.

The message was clear: patterns should be inside the castle of the mind, not outside in the village. The village philosophy should not be interfered with. He thought back to his conversation with Angela over the goblets. If his teaching got stuck at this point, the village certainly would not be 'corrupted' by mathematics; but nor would Jarvis's ambition to introduce more sophisticated technology be realised. He would have failed in what he had been brought out to do. This was a bitter blow after his apparent triumph with Jamie using the intos.

Jeremy's relationship with Angela had a touch of village philosophy to it as well. He had assumed, after their love-making in the forest, that something of the kind would become a regular thing. But, although he spent many evenings in her tiny cottage, where she lived alone, she would not allow any love-making there, and he was not allowed to sleep with her, 'Because we are not betrothed,' she said.

'We can be betrothed, if you like, can't we?' he said.

'Not until we know you are going to stay,' she replied.

'I'm going to stay,' he said firmly, putting aside his doubts about his success as a teacher. He would work something out. He would have to if he wanted to stay. 'This is home,' he said.

'When you have really decided to stay, we shall have a party for you, a surprise party perhaps. After that we shall be betrothed, and have another party for that. Until then, we cannot set up house together.'

Not being betrothed did not seem to rule out occasional walks in the forest, during which, if the ground was dry, and the weather was warm, they would make love, much as before, teasing and quick.

On one occasion, they were putting their tunics back on when Jeremy saw something move near a tree. He darted sideways to see what, or who, it was. It was Jamie and he ran off. Angela just laughed. 'He's interested in you. He wants to know what we're up to together. I don't mind, do you?'

'I suppose not,' he said.

Jeremy told Angela about his problem with persuading Jamie to work outside the intos. He did not share with her his theory about why the boy was so resistant.

'Oh, you can easily sort that out. You don't understand children. You said he likes shapes; well then, give him shapes outside the intos. I'll think about it.'

The next day she came to his room. 'I've had an idea about how to make shapes for Jamie. Come to my place this evening, I'll show you.'

Her idea involved willow wands and thatching straws. She had bundles of them on the floor, and some clay, a ball of string, and a wooden block and a small knife. 'There you are,' she said. 'Show me what you can do with that.' She sat back to watch him.

He cut lengths of willow and laid them end to end to make polygons. He bent one around to make a circle. Overlapped on itself it made quite a good shape, and he bound it with string. Then he tried the straw. He made various shapes by bending the straw, and fixing the ends with clay. Then he made a tetrahedron. 'That's good,' she approved. He made an octahedron. 'Even better,' she said.

Then he had a thought. 'Do you make corn dollies in the village,' he asked. She looked puzzled. 'Look, I'll show you.' He went to her screen and called up some pictures of corn dollies, with diagrammed and vocalised instructions. 'You try.' He handed her some straws.

By the time Jeremy had made a stellated dodecahedron, Angela had made a passable corn dolly: a curved rod of twisted plaiting. 'It looks very phallic,' he smiled, reaching over to squeeze her encouragingly.

'That was the idea, wasn't it – fertility and all that.' But she pushed him away. 'Not until we're betrothed,' she said.

'No one would know,' he replied.

'We would,' she said firmly. 'You must go now.'

The next morning Jeremy showed Jamie the willow and straw shapes. He examined Angela's straw dolly with interest, and asked to see and listen to the instructions for making them. But the geometric shapes he would have nothing to do with.

At last, reluctant to admit his failure, Jeremy related his problem to Jarvis.

'Sounds as if that was my fault. Remember what I said to him about putting the patterns of the mind out into the world and bringing about

116

civilisation, and, by implication, necrotech, and all its destruction. The boy has taken it to heart. Look, I've an idea. Why don't you move on to a bigger class? Try out your teaching on some other children.'

Jeremy began to prepare some lessons for the larger class, not using the intos. He tried to interest Jamie in what he was doing, and was dismayed when the boy burst into tears, and rushed out of the room. He followed him, but he ran away. Jeremy went into Angela's room and told her what had happened. 'Just leave him be for a while. I expect he'll come back.'

In a few days, the first larger class took place. Jeremy tried out the lessons he had prepared and all the children accepted what he told them without any resistance. In very little time, they were counting, reading and writing numbers, doing simple arithmetic and basic geometry. They were much slower than Jamie had been, but perfectly willing.

The lessons continued, but Jamie did not come back. He did not come into school at all. And, of course, since all school was optional, no one would force him.

Although Jeremy was pleased with his success, he recalled Jamie's ruling about keeping the patterns of the mind inside, and he could not help feeling anxious. This was all very well in the classroom, but what would these children take of it into their world; what effect would it have on the village?

One morning a sandy-haired boy came up to him. 'Mr Vetch,' he said, 'my father says he can make something more true by eye than you can with measuring. He says the human spirit is more true than any ruler.'

Jeremy looked at the boy solemnly. 'Your father is right, Peter. You must respect the village ways. Mathematics is just something extra which might come in handy sometimes.'

In a lesson a few days later, two of the children started quarrelling over the building blocks.

'You've got five times as many as I have,' said one, exaggerating. He grabbed at the other boy's pile, who surrounded it with his arms.

A third boy joined in. 'Ernie, I'll give you three of my plain ones for one of your cones, okay?' The deal was done. Jeremy found himself comparing the boys' swapping with the 'trading' that happened on market days; where goods were exchanged and exchanged again, with no evaluation. It was a kind of progressive dance, which ended when everyone was satisfied. What had he started? He longed to be back with

117

Jamie, safely exploring the esoteric wonders of human thought.

Then one afternoon Jamie came back. It was a music practice afternoon, and Jeremy was in The Small Quiet Room idly browsing through old mathematics texts on the system. There was a soft knock on the door. Jeremy said, 'Come in,' and there he was: a smiling angel, ready, it seemed, to play mathematics.

He beamed at him with a 'Hello, Jeremy,' shut the door behind him, and went over to fetch the box of blocks.

'Hello, Jamie, it's lovely to see you.'

'Yes,' he said.

'I've missed you.'

'Yes, me too.'

He tipped out the blocks, and sorted them into two piles: one with the cones and cylinders, triangles and arches; the other with all the rectangular blocks. With those he made a precise square. He sat back and looked at Jeremy. Jeremy smiled encouragingly, not sure what the message was, though clearly the boy was telling him something.

Then he fetched the clay board and the stylus. Sitting on the floor he carefully wrote, '1 2 3 4'. Then he pointed at the sides of the square in turn and said, 'One, two, three, four – sides,' and looked at Jeremy.

Jeremy smiled with the approval the boy must be expecting, 'Yes, that's right, good.'

Jamie got up and stood in front of him. Very lightly he touched Jeremy's right cheek and then his left cheek and said, 'One, two,' and touched his own cheeks and said, 'Three, four – cheeks. Two and two makes four,' and smiled his beatific smile.

Jeremy praised him again, 'Yes, Jamie, well done!' But his heart ached with uncertainty, and he reached out and hugged him. 'Dear Jamie, I really have missed you.' He held him close.

Jamie wriggled himself onto Jeremy's lap. He pointed to Jeremy's chest and then his own and said, 'One, two – boys.'

Jeremy frowned, puzzled. 'Boys?' he said.

Jamie lifted his tunic and pointed at his fat pink little penis, which poked up, Jeremy thought, like a small poisonous mushroom. 'Boys,' Jamie said firmly. And he took hold of Jeremy's hand and put it on the poisonous mushroom, and wriggled himself into the bend of Jeremy's lap, where his penis had sprung erect.

Jeremy drew in his breath, 'No!' he whispered, putting his other hand under the boy to push him off, and found himself touching Jamie's bare bottom. Jeremy felt that old feeling of not being in control, and the sense of relief it brought.

'Five, six – cheeks,' Jamie giggled. He peeled off his tunic, and Jeremy ran his hands over the boy's smooth skin and supple young body. Jamie offered his mouth. Jeremy kissed it, so soft, warm and sweet.

He felt his penis hard and thin – yes, thin enough to ... He felt for Jamie's hole and pushed a finger in slightly. It squeezed him encouragingly. He guided himself there and pushed. A few pushes and he was inside – where? – he no longer cared. The feeling was indescribably delightful. He pushed rhythmically and the boy rocked back. He buried his face in Jamie's neck, his soft hair.

'Do you like me?' Jamie whispered.

'Yes, of course I like you, you delicious little creature.' He wiggled Jamie's firm little mushroom. The boy arched his back, displaying it, pink and proud.

He said, 'We need another boy to stick on mine – one, two, three – boys.' He giggled, 'Four, five, six little boys.'

Then he said, 'Do you like me more than Angela?'

'More than anyone in the whole world.'

Jeremy fought off his climax, prolonging sensation such as he'd never imagined. His whole body and mind vibrated with ecstasy. He screwed up his face with the effort, and saw sparkling lights, and music sounded, triumphant, dramatic. And he came, in a last thrust, and a gasp, crushing the boy's body to him.

The music died. He opened his eyes. The door was open. There was Angela, her drum sticks suspended; and Jarvis with a set of bells; behind them faces filled the doorway. She screamed.

Suddenly Jamie was screaming too. 'Help! He hurt me.'

Jarvis rushed forward and tried to lift the boy away, but they were stuck together, until the shrivelled knob emerged, besmeared and foul. Jamie was carried off, sobbing loudly.

Jeremy cried, 'It's not like it looked. He wanted it. He ... corrupted me. Please, listen!'

Hands dragged him outside onto the path. Heavy boots kicked him, there was shouting.

Jeremy glimpsed Bill Fratter run to the lawn, and heave on a sign which said 'Out of bounds.' He yanked out a long barbed spike. The others rolled Jeremy over. He heard Bill's voice, 'This'll teach you to corrupt our children, Mr Mathematics Teacher.' And he thrust the spike into his anus. Pain filled the universe.

Dear Bea,

Behold! An actually letter, by snail mail, from your mate, Justin – all the way from Ireland. I tried to ring you before I left but no reply. I had a bout of the glooms – empty flat, not enough going on at work to keep my mind off things. Decided to take a trip to see me Auntie Mary in Donegal. Went over on the ferry from Holyhead and hired a motor.

She's an old darling – big help to me when my bombshell caused family ructions. She's my mother's aunt. She's tiny, and really crinkly, like one of the Irish 'little people', I always think. She loves our family – even though none of us are left over there – and she came over to England – which she normally only does for funerals – to patch us up. She's hardly a gay lib supporter, but she wouldn't let anything break up the family – even mortal sin.

Anyway, I took your chapter with me to read and the funniest thing happened. I was on the phone – major flap at work about a sales proposal – and all the pages got blown around the garden. Auntie toddled out and gathered them all up. By the time I was off the phone she'd sorted the pages, and had evidently read at least the last part!

'It's wicked, terribly wicked, what they do to the boys,' she said. 'Even the priests in holy orders, you know.'

'This is only a story,' says I.

'Why would anyone write dirty things like that for a story?' she said.

'Well my friend who wrote the story is saying that the really wicked thing is to teach boys mathematics – how to do sums,' says I. 'But people don't even notice the really wicked things.'

'That the silliest thing I ever heard!' she said. Then she looked at me long and hard without saying a word.

But I could tell what she was thinking, so I said, 'Yes, Auntie, men and boys who are homosexual sometimes do that kind of thing together, but it's not wrong if they don't hurt each other.'

'No? ... Well then, I wonder what's wicked about teaching boys to do their sums. Is it that they're not at home to mind the cows and help out saving the hay? – and now they've all gone away.'

'Yes, Auntie, I'm sure it's very much like that.'

Well, Bea, my pet – if my Auntie Mary can get it, anyone can! Now, don't get mad at me. I know you're not actually saying maths is wicked

– I mean, you were a mathematician yourself, weren't you?, before you went 'green' and switched courses. And obviously you're not saying that child sexual abuse is good. But to challenge conventional attitudes, you sometimes have to take the opposite position – like pushing an old fence post too and fro to loosen it. People are always going to assume you think the opposite if you question what they think – it's the adversarial mentality of our culture – pattern stuff again!

Another thing, as I got into it, I quite forgot that the chapter was just a storyframe. It's a funny business the way we identify with what's going on in fiction. And we're quite forgiving, make all sorts of allowances to let it be real. So it's quite disconcerting to remember that this story is another level removed from reality.

I think the reason for the extra level is that the people in biotech aren't ready to emerge yet, and when they do it won't be into somewhere like Overfleet. I also noticed that the village is still attached to the umbilical cord of the intos – that's a comment on people now who try to live a greener lifestyle, but can always still pop to the supermarket or the doctor's.

That's all for now. Taking a trip to the Giant's Causeway tomorrow – more patterns! I'll be back in a week or so.

Lots of love,

Justin

The next shift is to another

late biotech subject. Before she gets into her story, there is a part of the shift that excited me tremendously when I returned from experiencing it. She is having the sort of random thoughts that come to someone waking up in the morning, which are quite unlike part of a biotech storyframe. What was happening to the subject was that she actually experienced a shift – a transfer of consciousness like the ones I have – all the way back to necrotech. No storyframer had taken her there; her own nascent powers of what we call 'eversight' had come into play. This power was fundamental to the new kind of human being who would live during the pattern age. What appears to have happened is that free and random access to the huge store of knowledge of the past held by the intos dragon released in some people the power to know the past without technological assistance. After the little 'shift within a shift' comes a fairly typical late biotech woman's story. In the story, the subject calls herself Bibbie. After Bibbie we'll really get out of biotech into the early pattern age.

6

Dawning Eversight

Grey light coming in. It's morning. Birds outside, shrill little rattles, and bits of piping tune. Gone quiet now. There they go again. Always make most racket this time of the day – seems so anyway – when I'm relaxed and warm in bed – it'll be cold out there in the garden, but they don't care.

Now radio's come on, blasted thing.

'Surgeons in a Los Angeles hospital, in a ten hour operation, have grafted the liver of baboon into a sixty-two year old man who was dying of a fatal liver disease.'

Disgusting! Poor baboon. Do they think of that? Wonder if he got a good breakfast before he died. Don't suppose so; expect he had to be starved to have him all clean and ready. Was it a 'he' baboon? Rich man nearly drinks himself to death, and buys surgeons to play God. Could it happen in this country I wonder? Could write to my MP.

'Dear Mr Conway-Osborne, I am writing to draw your attention to a disturbing news item on the radio this morning about the surgical transplanting of a baboon's liver into a man in America. Such interference with the sanctity of life is an abuse of Nature and a betrayal of Humanity. We are in danger of losing the desire and courage to face death with resignation and at peace with God. I like to think that such a procedure would not be permitted in this country. I hope you will be able to reassure me on this matter or, failing that, inform me of the regulations which relate to the use of animal tissues and organs, and tell me where I can obtain information about activities of this kind, so that I can try to use my influence, and that of others, to sway the consciences of those involved. I intend to raise this matter with the Archbishop of Canterbury. Yours etc.'

Makes me sound like a religious person that, which I'm not, but politicians, especially Tory ones like ours, probably expect you to bring

God into an ethical issue. Never have written to a Church leader. Probably get a two line standard reply or a chunk of propaganda – just like from my MP. Wouldn't necessarily be any stronger than the politicians on moral values anyhow, Christianity having such a history of wars and persecution. Screwed up their credibility, seems to me, ought to shut up shop altogether.

You can't force morality on people. Ten Commandments, right and wrong, good and evil, that kind of thing – it doesn't help. It divides people: some people do what they shouldn't out of cussedness, and the obedient ones feel smug and disapproving. All you need is love, I say – and being in small enough groups so it's all in the family, families are too small these days, of course. Personally, I'd include that baboon in my family – rather than that bloke with liver disease. Why should his life matter more than the baboon's? Because individuals count with humans but not with animals or plants. But maybe it isn't like that at all. Perhaps there's no such thing as the individual, and we're not as separate as we think we are. We're taught to be separate as babies. Who's that in the mirror then? That's you. This is me. That's yours, this is mine. It's the same with souls too – humans have them, other creatures don't – which could be something we're told just because it's part of religion. So if you have baboons in your family, you wouldn't be religious. Perhaps that's why hardly anyone goes to church in Britain nowadays: we're a nation of animal lovers.

Lots of people still go for religion, don't they. Had a holiday in Sicily once at Easter time. Not many animal lovers there, judging by the furs and leather they parade around in. There was a Palm Sunday procession – hoards of people, big families, children, all waving palm leaves. I got one: they weave them into fancy shapes. Then on the following Friday there was a gloomy procession where they carried a stature of Mary weeping and one of the dead Christ: horribly realistic with yellow skin and red wounds. The main ritual in Christianity is eating Christ's flesh and blood. With the Catholics, for some reason, only the priest gets the blood. They really believe the bread and wine turns into flesh and blood. Seems disgusting to an outsider – torture and cannibalism – but there must be something in it – some mystery we can't understand.

I read the Bible now and again – there is something fascinating about it – but you can't get religion just from reading. It's a history book mostly – *his*-story: the story of men; not many women in the Bible. I wonder what happened to *her*-story: the story of women; there must be one. Perhaps women didn't feel the need to write it down, they just lived it. But when writing down became the important thing, women had to adopt men's religion and history because their own was invisible. Personally I'd like a her-story without religion and morality in it: perhaps not even Love, with a big 'L' – just life with a small one.

7

The Apricot Dome

Bibbie was the most beautiful baby you ever saw. She was like a china doll from years gone by. She had fat pink cheeks, solemnly staring big blue eyes, a tiny nose and a neat little dimpled chin. Her soft curls were palest gold. She had a cherub's chubby body with a fat tummy, sturdy legs, pretty pink feet and dear little arms she held up for balance waving her starry hands.

She lived with her mother in a magic cell made by a powerful dragon. From the cell they could be anywhere and everywhere in the world, as it is, as it once was, and as it may come to be. The dragon kept the air in the cell fresh to breathe, it changed the stuff of the cell to make it nourishing and keep it clean. It had brought the seed and put it in Bibbie's mother so that her baby grew.

Bibbie's mother was very happy in the magic cell, being in the wonders of the world. She did not notice Bibbie at all, even when Bibbie cuddled up to her and suckled at her breast.

The dragon brought special children's visions of animals and fairies and nasty things that said 'Boo!', and most of the time Bibbie was perfectly happy. But she was at that difficult stage of babyhood when they are most lovely and fun but also most bother. So sometimes the dragon had to work very hard to keep her amused.

One day the dragon was trying out lots of teasing little bits of the most fascinating visions, and watching Bibbie carefully to see which one caught her eye, ready to conjure a wonderful story for her to be in. But whatever the dragon tried, Bibbie's attention would not be caught.

So what happened was that Bibbie went wandering off through the cell stuff, which she was not supposed to do. The dragon did all it could to stop her. It tried making the cell stuff get in her way; so that it was hard or sticky or too soft so she fell through it with a bump. It made scary visions pop up in front of her. It made coaxing sounds to draw her back. But the dragon's magic was not strong enough to stop her doing something she was determined about. This was one of the rules from when the dragon itself was made.

After wandering for quite a while, until she was almost too tired to resist the dragon, she came to a black hole which was the entrance to a tunnel. It was deepest softest black inside, the kind of black she had never seen before, blacker even than when she shut her eyes to go to sleep. The special blackness caught her attention, as the dragon's colourful pictures had failed to do, and she was drawn in. The tunnel was very narrow, so she had to crawl. Once she had crawled in she was swallowed up in the darkness. She kept on crawling until her eyes and her mind became worried by the unendingness of the darkness, and she wanted to go back. But the tunnel was too narrow for her to turn, and she did not know how to crawl backwards. She felt tired so she just went to sleep, like babies do.

When she woke up the blackness was still there. She was frightened and so she cried. But the dragon could not help her in the tunnel. It was an ancient tunnel, no longer useful, and the dragon's power had withdrawn from that place.

When nothing happened through her crying she stopped doing it, and then, for want of anything else to do, she carried on crawling. Several times she became worried and tired and slept and cried and crawled again; it was a tremendously long tunnel. Bibbie became very thirsty and hungry, but the stuff of the tunnel was old and dried up and not nourishing like the cell stuff.

At long long last Bibbie saw a point of light which grew bigger as she crawled until her head was poking out of the other end of the tunnel.

She was in the strangest place, such as she had never seen in the world she saw from the cell. It was a huge room, white and gleaming all over, with everything moving in lines, backwards and forwards from one end to the other and back again. The moving lines were broad white belts scattered with bits of colour. The colour came from all sorts of objects and stuff on the belts, each belt having just one kind. Beside the belts, arms and hands were busily moving, reaching for and then doing things to the objects and stuff on the belts.

At Bibbie's end of the room the arms were very long. Each of these arms reached over the belts to pick up one of this and some of that and arranged a collection in a pretty bowl which moved on along the belt, and then the arm started another bowl.

From where her head poked out of the tunnel, Bibbie could only see clearly one level of belts. But there were belts above and belts below. At her end, the belts turned over and ran back the other way upside down. Just as they turned, the bowls tipped off, scattering their contents, and everything fell down. Bibbie reached out and caught something. It was a soft and pretty oval object which smelled nice. She put it to her mouth and bit. It tasted delicious and juicy so she ate it all, except for a hard thing in the centre which she dropped. She watched it fall into the great trench below, where everything landed in a mess whose smell rose up to where Bibbie was and caught in her nose and throat and made her feel sicky.

Bibbie caught more things and stuff as they fell. Some were nicer than others, some she spat out. She was soon full and comfortable inside. But she was still in the narrow tunnel, unable to turn. She emptied her bladder and her bowels and there was no cell stuff to clean it away. The smells made it hard for her to breathe and she needed to move around.

The only way she could get any further was to fall out of the tunnel and down. At last that is what she did. She landed in the smelly mess, sank beneath it and scrabbled back up. She found herself near the edge of the trench and managed to crawl out after slipping back in many times because of the sliminess.

Once she was safely on her feet she forgot how frightened she had been. She toddled across the room between the rows of the bottom-most layer of belts. Near the other end there was water dripping down and she was washed clean.

That was the first part of the story, when Bibbie found the food hall in which the kitchen hands with clever nimble fingers kept on sorting, cleaning and arranging bowls of lovely food which no one needed any more because they had the nourishing cell stuff. A long time before Bibbie came there, the dragon had stopped the arms which used to put the bowls in the delivery tunnels and stopped the belts which used to run along the tunnels. Instead, the dragon chewed up the smelly mess in the trench, mixed it in with the sunshine food made in the dragon's coils, and oozed it into the cell stuff.

Bibbie stayed in the food hall for a very long time. There was plenty to eat and water to drink and lots of movement and colour to interest her. The belts were not very far apart, and moved slowly, so she could clamber from one to the other, across the room and up or down. She could not reach the tunnel back to her cell because of the gap above the smelly trench. In any case, she could not have picked out the correct tunnel entrance from all the others.

She might have stayed there forever if she had not got a taste for a particular kind of food. It was the fruit she had first tasted when she was so hungry and thirsty. It was the apricot.

In her wanderings around the food hall, Bibbie came across the belt where the apricots were cleaned and sorted. She recognised the shape and the smell, and she ate lots of the fruit. Then she carried on toddling and clambering around the food hall, but she kept coming back to the apricot belt for her favourite fruit.

One time when she came back she found there were no apricots on the belt. She cried loudly and long but there was no one to hear her. She wandered off again but she kept coming back to the empty belt until, after an enormous length of time for someone who was only a baby – it would have been from one summer round to the next – the apricots were there again.

After a while, the apricot belt was again empty.

Bibbie was only a toddling baby when she first reached the food hall. She had to grow up to a little girl who could think things out before she could try to do something about there being no more apricots.

What she did when she was old enough was to wonder where the apricots came from. She thought that if she could find that place, there would be more apricots, even when there were none on the belt. That was a big bit of thinking out to do, and there was no one there to help her, and she had no words to do her thinking with. But there is a pattern from down the ages of children becoming clever, and her mind tuned into that pattern to get its cleverness.

It was clever of her to think of going back along the apricot belt to where it came out of a tunnel; to do that she had to run quicker than the belt was going. It was even cleverer to think of climbing onto another belt which was taking empty trays into the tunnel, so that she was carried along into it.

Thus began the second of Bibbie's long journeys along a dark tunnel. This time she could have got back where she came from, by turning around and jumping onto the belt going the other way. But she was determined to find some more apricots so she stayed put, although she became thirsty and hungry and frightened of the blackness.

As with her previous journey, eventually she saw a point of light, which grew bigger until it was the tunnel opening. When she arrived, an

131

arm reached for the tray she was sitting in and put it on a pile. She had to scramble off quickly before the arm put another tray on top of her.

She found herself in the most beautiful place. When she saw it, memories flooded over her of when she was a baby in her mother's cell, and they were in the world that used to be. Tears of joy poured down her cheeks. The beautiful place she had discovered was like the places where animals and fairies were, places from the memory stores of how the world was before the dragon was made and grew.

So that was how Bibbie discovered the apricot dome. What she saw was a forest of delicate trees with the real light of day pouring down upon them as the sunshine streamed through the invisible roof. As she looked up she saw the deep blue of the sky. She smelt the fresh scent of leaves, moist from their morning shower from the sprinklers.

She found more apricots; not the fresh juicy ones she had come for, but shrivelled ones drying on trays in the sun. But they were good to eat, which was fortunate because they were all there was to eat until the new apricots ripened on the trees.

Bibbie loved her beautiful place and she stayed there all alone for many years, watching the seasons pass, and the apricot trees changing: in leaf, growing buds, bursting with pink blossom, swelling into fruit, ripening and being stripped by the picking hands.

She had little to play with. She mixed her daylies with the earth to make a clay from which she formed animals, remembered from the visions of long ago in her mother's cell. She smeared her body with her daylies, making patterns of leaves and flowers.

Every night she slept on the bare earth under the stars, and wonderful and terrible dreams came to her of the world as it used to be, more fascinating and awesome than the little glimpses she had as a baby.

One day she began to make patterns of her dreams on the walls of the dome, from the ground to as high as she could reach. Each morning when she awoke she carefully remembered that night's dream. When her daylie was done she took a little on her finger and began to put the dream onto the transparent surface, gradually adding more tiny dabs and delicate smears.

The dome was enormous. It seemed she would be dabbing dream stuff on its walls forever. But eventually she found herself back at the start. It occurred to her to rub off the earliest dreams to make space for new ones, but when she tried she found the patterns would not come off.

The walls of the dome had welcomed them and had allowed them to sink in to the glassy surfaces, where they gleamed golden brown and lovely.

It was then Bibbie decided to go back inside. She felt she must go, and needed to go, but she did not wonder why because she had no words to wonder why with.

Her next journey was long and difficult. The first part was easy, the ride back to the food hall and along one of the belts to the far side. She climbed down to the lowest level. Then she had to brave the stink and the slime of the trench.

When she was the other side of the trench, she reached for one of the tunnels and pulled herself up. Only then did she realise how much she had grown. She would not be able to crawl into the tunnel and along it. So she had to drop back into the trench, go back across it and clamber up its slimy side.

She wondered what to do. Should she stay here? Should she go back to the apricot dome? No, she must go on. But how?

She looked around for something to help her. She watched the kitchen hands washing and sorting. Then she saw one of them chopping some leafy stuff. Chopping! Bibbie went back to the trench and looked back across at the tunnel entrances. Perhaps she could cut her way through, make a passage wide enough. She turned back and climbed over to the hand which was chopping and pulled at its knife. It came free easily.

Then the terrible part of Bibbie's return journey began. The tunnel was too narrow for her to cut big slices from the surface, she had to chip away bit by bit. The material of the surface was tough and difficult to cut. Once she was inside she could not see what she was doing, she could only feel. Her progress was so slow that she had to enlarge the tunnel a little way and then return, backwards, to the food hall for food, water and rest. Many times she went back and forth, each lap getting longer and longer as she progressed. As the effort became greater, her will was torn; the more she wanted to give up, and the more effort she felt she would have wasted if she did not get to the other end.

The tunnel became her life and herself; there was nothing else and never had been, never would be. So she did not notice the point of light. It grew larger and she did not realise its significance.

It was a shock to find she had reached the other end, so much so that she fainted.

When she woke up a face was gazing down at her. It was a soft wrinkled face with pink eyelids drooping around pale grey eyes, a long nose covered with tiny veins and a thin mouth surrounded by wispy whiskers.

'Who are you, little one?' asked the old woman.

Bibbie did not reply, she had never learned to talk.

The old woman made soothing noises and chattered to her encouragingly.

At last Bibbie made a sound, 'Bi-bi.'

'Ah, Bibbie!' said the woman, smiling.

'Bi-bi,' said Bibbie, and that is how she got her name; she did not really have a name before.

Bibbie looked around her. She was in a cell. She could see the world of the old woman's past where she had her being: the places she had been, the happy and sad happenings, the patterns of her dreams. Immediately before Bibbie's eyes was a confused-looking area, where the dragon was trying to offer some world for her. As she looked in that direction, pictures spun crazily around. Something caught her attention and that little bit grew to fill the space and Bibbie felt herself drawn in. It was a forest.

But it was not her forest, the forest of apricot trees. Her eyes flickered away. One of the trees changed rapidly, becoming all sorts of trees. When it became an apricot tree, and Bibbie flickered interest again, the other trees immediately became apricot trees also. Eagerly Bibbie reached for an apricot. She put it in her mouth. The taste and texture were as she remembered them, but not quite. Withdrawing her attention she discovered she was eating some cell stuff. She spat it out.

But Bibbie was thirsty and hungry. She let herself be drawn into the old woman's world, where the old woman became a younger woman and made her tea and sandwiches and cut her a piece of cake. She sipped from the pretty china cup and nibbled a sandwich from the matching plate, knowing with half her mind that she was eating cell stuff.

For some time, Bibbie stayed in the cell with the woman. In quite a short while she learned about talking, and her vocabulary grew rapidly, and she could make sentences.

The woman's name was Sophia. She told Bibbie many wonderful things about the world, and took her on journeys to see them. Bibbie was very excited because she recognised some of the things she had seen in her dreams. Bibbie told Sophia about the apricot dome with the real trees and the real blue sky, and about how she made her dream patterns on the transparent walls of the dome. The dragon tried to take them there, but Bibbie would not go, not in that way.

'You must take me to see them,' Sophia told Bibbie.

Bibbie wanted to take Sophia to the apricot dome, but she was worried. 'It's a very long way, a very difficult journey,' she said, looking at Sophia's thin, bent and delicate body. 'Even if you got there, I don't think you could come all the way back.'

'I don't think I should want to come back,' said Sophia.

The journey was a trial for Sophia, but she had courage to make up for her lack of strength. From the moment she emerged on an empty tray and Bibbie quickly lifted her off and steadied her on her feet, she loved the apricot dome.

Bibbie showed Sophia the dream patterns. Over a long time, she took her slowly all the way round the dome.

Many of the patterns were of Bibbie's wonderful dreams. Sophia could see in them images of the world that used to be; like those she used to see from her cell, but she thought that Bibbie's dreams showed more things than even the dragon knew. There were many kinds of birds, different furry animals, flying and creeping insects, snakes and lizards, and fish and other sea creatures.

There were some awesomely wonderful dreams. Sophia saw violent storms, earthquakes and volcanoes, and the ages when great glaciers ground up the earth, and the times when the planets had crashed into the earth and shaken it off its course.

There were also terrible dreams of what people had done to the world that used to be: the cutting down of forests to plough up the earth, the cold and stark structures of cities, the burning and filth of machinery, the frantic rushing about and slavish activity of the people.

Lastly they came to a dream picture in which Sophia saw a great archway of intricately carved stone, inside of which was a second, simple and graceful archway with a heavy curtain over it. She asked Bibbie if this picture was of a wonderful dream or a terrible dream, but Bibbie did not know; she only knew that it was the most mysterious dream of all.

On that very day Bibbie found blood dripping down inside her leg. This had never happened to her before so she showed Sophia.

Sophia smiled at Bibbie and said, 'You are growing up, my Bibbie. You are blossoming.' And she touched one of Bibbie's swollen pink

135

nipples. 'You are not a bud but a freshly opened flower. You should have a grown up name – perhaps Sylvie, after your beloved trees.'

But Bibbie did not want a new name. 'I cannot be Sylvie, because then there would be no child Bibbie in the apricot dome, and it was Bibbie who discovered it and put her dreams on it.'

'Now that your bleeding has begun you can get another Bibbie,' Sophia said. 'Bibbie grew from a seed in her mother's womb and made her first journey down a dark tunnel to the light. Now you can be a mother, if you get a seed inside you.'

'But how do I get a seed?'

Sophia thought for a while how best to tell her, then she began. 'I have seen you stroking and rubbing the juicy tickly bits between your legs. I have those bits too, though mine are now old and dry. And your mother had them. We who are like that are called "woman", and a woman has a bag inside her called a "womb" in which a baby can grow, and breasts where the baby gets nourishment after it has come out through the baby tunnel into the light.' Sophia looked at Bibbie, who nodded. Then she continued, 'There is another kind of person who, instead of tickly bits likes ours, has a snake growing from between the legs. A person with a snake is called "man". The snake spits out the seed for a baby. That is the only place to get a seed.'

'How do I get a seed from the snake,' said Bibbie, who, as we know, was very brave.

'There are two ways,' said Sophia. 'The first way is to go and live in a cell like your mother did, and wait for the dragon to collect a seed from a man and bring it to you and put it in your baby tunnel.'

'But I don't want to go and live in a cell,' said Bibbie. 'I belong in the apricot dome.'

'The other way is to find a man for a lover. You will have to go back inside, find a cell with a man in it and ask him to come back with you to the apricot dome.' Sophia's voice became dreamy, and her eyes sparkled. 'You will wander together amongst the apricot trees, and talk to each other and smile, and then you will fall in love and kiss each others' lips. Then he will play with your tickly bits and you will play with the snake between his legs. In a little while the snake will grow until it is this wide,' and she held out two fingers together, 'and just as thick, and twice as long, with a soft hard head. Then you have to slide the snake past your lovely juicy tickly bits and into your baby tunnel, and together you will rub it up and down inside until the snake spits out

136

lots of seeds. One of the seeds will then swim up your tunnel and go to start your baby.'

Bibbie listened to this dubiously, not sharing Sophia's excitement. 'Did you have a lover, Sophia?' she asked.

'I think that I did, but it may have been the dragon's stories. But there is truth in what the dragon shows; I am sure that is what people used to do once upon a time.'

'Then that is what I shall have to do,' said Bibbie bravely. 'I shall go and find a lover. When I have found a lover, you may call me Sylvie, and Sylvie I shall be.'

Bibbie's journey to find a lover was her hardest yet.

First of all she went all the way back to the cell that had been Sophia's, through the tunnel that she had widened before. She thought that perhaps there would be a way from there to other cells. But when she got there, it was not empty. There was a little child in it.

She was happy at first to see the child. 'You can be the new Bibbie!' she said, 'And I shall not need to find a lover and get a seed to grow a baby.' And she reached out to take the child.

Then she saw that the child had a little snake between his legs. It was a man child, and Bibbie was a woman child, so this one would not do.

Then Bibbie looked around for another tunnel which might lead to a different cell where there might be a lover for her. But there was no other tunnel besides the one she had come in by. She got her knife and tried to cut a passage through the walls to another cell, but the dragon would not let her. It made the walls very soft so that the knife could go through, and then it immediately joined the cut up again. When Bibbie tried to push through the soft walls, it made them hard. Although the dragon was bound by the rule to let her do what she was determined to do, there was a stronger rule which said it must not let her come to any harm. And the dragon knew that all that was beyond the wall was the Outside.

In the end Bibbie had to go all the way back to the food hall and then cut her way, little by little, through a different tunnel to get to another cell.

When eventually she reached the cell, to her joy she found a man in it: a person with a snake between his legs. She went over to him and tried to tell him about the apricot dome and getting a new Bibbie and how she needed a lover. But the man was so fascinated by the world he and the dragon were creating that he could not tell that Bibbie was real. He worked her into his story and because she was young and pretty his snake grew big the way Sophia had described, but Bibbie could not bring him out of his story to listen to hers.

The dragon tried to tempt Bibbie with a story in which the man was her hero and lover, but she had spent too long in the apricot dome to be taken in.

After trying for a very long time to make him see her and understand what she wanted, Bibbie gave up and returned: back along the tunnel, into the smelly trench, across the food hall, on a tray through the tunnel back to the apricot dome.

Sophia was overjoyed to see her safely returned, but sad that she had not brought back a lover. Bibbie told her what had happened.

'I found a man but he was too busy with the dragon to listen to me. So I could not tell him about the apricot dome and ask him to come back with me and be my lover and give me a seed for a new Bibbie.'

'Perhaps he would have given you a seed without coming back with you. Did you think of that?' Sophia asked.

Bibbie thought about this. 'No, I didn't think of that. Yes, I see that could have happened; I think he would have liked it. But I'm glad he didn't give me a seed, because I don't think I am ready for that yet. I'm tired and I'm just happy to be with you again.'

Their life together resumed. Each night they dreamed more dreams to put on the walls the next day. The apricot trees blossomed and bore fruit, rested and then woke again.

But Bibbie had changed. Each time the moon was full she would wake in the night to find her blood seeping onto the earth beneath her. She gazed up at the moon and stars gleaming and twinkling through the roof. She felt their utter remoteness, beings she could not touch, powerful, immortal, cold as death. In the morning she made patterns of fear and loneliness around the curtained archway. On those days she felt Sophia's aged face as a threat: in a few more cycles of the apricot trees her new womanhood would shrivel up and it would be too late for her lover to adore her body and keep her warmly secure at night.

On other days she felt her need differently: with a rush of joy and desire, making her run about and dance, glorying in her beauty and womanliness. Then she would sit against a tree and daydream about loving and being loved, and then caress the excitable places of her body, discovering and sounding the strings of her passion.

On one of those dancing days she came to Sophia and told her that she would have to resume the journey to find a lover. Sophia had known that this day would come, and she gave Bibbie her blessing. Straightaway, Bibbie set off.

Remembering the awful labour of widening a new tunnel, she first went back to the man she had discovered before. She sat quietly beside him watching him interact with the dragon. His face was very animated and he was talking loudly into the story. He waved his arms a little, but otherwise his body was still, plump and soft, reclining comfortably in the cell stuff.

'Perhaps if I joined in his story I would get a chance to talk to him about the apricot dome,' she said to herself.

The dragon heard her, and opened up a section of cell wall beside her to tell her what had been happening in the story. It soon realised that Bibbie did not know the story at all, or anything about the place and time the story was set in. It had to work very hard to make her understand; taking her forward in time from the world that used to be of her dream pictures, as well as back from the present, the dragon's time.

When the dragon showed her what had been done to the world that used to be she saw all her terrible dreams again: the cutting down of forests to plough up the earth, the cold and stark structures of cities, the burning and filth of machinery, the frantic rushing about and slavish activity of the people.

The dragon quickly moved on to show her the time that came between the terrible time of destruction and their own time. It was a world of great plantations and vast cities. There was nothing living anywhere on earth besides people and a few slave species. There were huge factories full of dead machines which were powered by burning dead materials to process the slave species into food, and to make things out of other dead materials. Other dead machines tore up and down wide channels between the cities, transporting the frantic people and the materials for the machines and the products of the machines. By that time people had invented machines that were clever, and the air hummed with their communications. Then people found out how to introduce cleverness into the slave species, and that was how living machines like the kitchen hands in the food hall were made, and then the dragon itself. The proper name for the dragon was the 'intos' from 'intelligent organic structure'.

The dragon then proudly showed her its own time: how its coils had grown to cover the earth, how the people had stopped frantically buzzing around, and lived inside the dragon in their individual cells, contentedly playing stories all their lives. The dragon provided for them, and the dead machines they had before were no longer needed and had long ago stopped running.

Finally Bibbie came to understand that the story her potential lover was engaged with was from before the dragon, at the time people were changing from dirty burning machines to clean burning machines. People were still frantically busy, and some people were busier and more important than others because of real-life stories called businesses.

In the next stage of her introduction the dragon told her about the part her potential lover was playing. His name was Rick Lardner. He was a top executive in a big business which was mainly concerned with 'oil': one of the dirty materials which were used to power machines. The dragon told her what had been happening in the drama. Bibbie tried hard to pay attention, but she could not understand why anyone would be interested in such a dull and silly story. The dragon reminded her that the story was about how the world used to be. But it was not the world that used to be which she loved; the one with trees and animals. The dragon said that the man was not interested in that world, which made Bibbie very worried; would he want to come back with her to the apricot dome? She almost gave up the whole idea, but she had spent so much time with the dragon having the story introduced to her that she thought she had better give it a try.

The dragon offered Bibbie the choice between two parts in Rick's story. One was a person from 'Earth Champions', which was a group of people who had got together because they were very angry with the dirty businesses like the one Rick belonged to. They wanted to have the dirty processes stopped altogether, and for everyone to plant trees so that there would be forests again. The other part was a person from 'Green the Earth' who wanted to cooperate with Rick's business in bringing in cleaner machinery.

Bibbie asked about the people playing the other characters in the story. But the dragon told her that until she came along there were no real people playing this particular version of the story besides her potential lover: the dragon took all the other parts itself. It almost sounded sad when it told of how, when it was first set growing, many real people, in cells all around the world, had taken parts in each story, but now everyone insisted on being the central character. People used to invent new stories; now everyone just played their personal versions of

140

one of the few favourites. Bibbie wondered why this one was a favourite. The dragon said it was just because it was about business which was an old kind of story with a strong pattern and she would just have to see for herself.

Bibbie decided she would be the 'Green the Earth' person, because she wanted Rick to like her. The dragon suggested the name 'Barbara Newall'.

Suddenly she found herself walking into a room towards the character Rick Lardner; but he was quite unlike the unmoving naked body she had been in the cell with. A tall, good-looking man in a dark suit rose from behind his huge and gleaming hardwood desk, walked briskly around it and stretched out his hand to shake hers.

'How do you do, Miss Newall – may I call you Barbara, do call me Rick. Good to meet you. I enjoyed our chat on the phone the other day. I'm very pleased you got in touch. I am sure your people and my people have important mutual interests. Do please sit down. Would you like some coffee?' He had pressed a button on a device on his desk and said, 'Coffee for two please, Rita,' before she had time to decline.

She sat down in the studded leather armchair he indicated. He sat down in the one next to her, a little closer than felt comfortable. She pushed her shoes against the floor to try to nudge the chair on its castors a little further away from his, but the thick carpet resisted. She leaned her knees away and tugged at her pencil skirt. She fancied he noticed her little manoeuvres and found them flirtatious.

She smiled, she hoped primly, and said, 'It was good of you to see me so soon. We really appreciate your interest in our work. We faxed you our report on biofuels. Have you had time to look at it?'

'Oh, not yet. But I'd like to hear all about it from you.' He leaned towards her, and she wrinkled her nose at the 'nice smell' on his face.

Barbara opened the slim portfolio she had brought with her, drew out a folder and opened it on her lap. She looked down at the page as she spoke. 'We are aware that your division is investigating the commercial viability of diversifying into biofuels. We, of course, have been looking at the environmental impact.'

'Fine, we are confident your investigations will be thorough and unbiased. The industry has everything to gain from the work you have carried out. Do you have milk in your coffee?'

'No, thank you, and no sugar.' And before he had time for some silly remark about her being sweet enough, she continued. 'The production of diesel oil substitutes, such as "rape methyl ester" or RME from oil seed rape, has been criticised on the grounds that, compared with fossil fuels, CO_2 is reduced and SO_2 eliminated, but methane and NO_2 are increased, so that, apart from somewhat cleaner combustion emissions in city streets, the environmental benefits are marginal. The production cost is, as you will be aware, prohibitive. The yield of fuel per hectare is only 23.8 GJ/T at 1.25 T/ha. Forest biofuels are looking better at 136 GJ/ha for willow. Earth Champions have been trying to drum up some popular opposition, with little success so far. On the RME they tried the land degradation angle, but no one's interested in soil erosion or use of agrochemicals. Using surplus agricultural land for crops for industrial uses is popular with farmers and politicians. On the forestfuels, the Champs are now saying that the big oil companies, such as yourselves, are planning to cut down virgin forest in the Amazon Basin to develop forestfuel plantations. Our information is that there is no virgin forest left to clear.' She looked up at him. He smiled conspiratorially.

She turned a page of the report. 'Now the area of research which interests us – and no one has reached anywhere near production stage as yet – is ocean biofuels: specifically algal biomass. Several gen-enged varieties have been patented, so the research results are in the public domain. It already looks as if it is going to be possible for machinery and vehicles – including the harvesters themselves! – to run on the fuel itself, unprocessed, straight from the sea, thus avoiding any use of fossil fuels in the production stage, which was the main problem with the biodiesel. The yield is looking like twenty to thirty grams dry weight per square metre per day – similar to sugar cane on land – the photosynthetic conversion efficiency is two percent – the energy harvest could be 200 gigajoules per hectare per annum or better.'

She was aware he was enjoying the experience of listening to an attractive woman talking business, but she knew he would be disinclined to take her seriously, just because she was a woman. Maddening! She reminded herself to be smart and cool. She decided to get quickly to the point.

'The central aim of "Green the Earth" is to help bring about sustainable economic growth by publicising and promoting advances in clean technology. The Champs, on the other hand, are anti-technology and anti-growth. In spite of their absurdly radical stance, they can be a nuisance and cause a lot of public enquiries, and they get their pet politicians to try to insist on regulations being drafted, and so it goes on. So this is what we would like your agreement on – and I must emphasise that any cooperation between us must be kept strictly under wraps.' She was conscious of his leering at her with a 'Love to share a secret with you m'dear.'

She gritted her teeth and went on, 'If you will agree to provide the necessary resources to complete our research – we are entirely reliant on donations of course – we will go public on a wholehearted endorsement of the Champs' land degradation concern, and then we slip in an affirmation of the environmental benefits of algalfuels – emphasising the need to be constructive. That should take the wind out of the Champs' sails – they're way behind us on ocean research since they had to give up on getting people worked up about oil spills. Meanwhile, you go full steam ahead on getting ocean cropping rights, and harvester development underway, and so on, and we believe there will be not a single scare story or public enquiry nonsense to hold you up.' She sat back and smiled at him triumphantly.

At that moment there was a discreet knock at the door, Rick said 'Come,' and Rita, an absurdly pretty young woman with bright red lips, jutting breasts and long legs, teetered in carrying a tray of coffee things.

'Rick, there's a woman outside from "Earth Champions". She says you're expecting her, but there's nothing in the diary.'

'What's her name?' Rick was clearly anticipating yet another juicy bird.

'Sylvie Wildwood,' Rita almost sneered. Barbara gasped softly at the name.

'Do you know her?' He was obviously looking forward to a nice bit of drama.

'No,' Barbara said. But I think I'd like to, she thought to herself.

Rick patted Barbara on her thigh and smirked. 'Well, she's right on cue, don't you think? You'd better show the lady in,' he said to Rita. 'And fetch another coffee cup, there's a good girl.'

A large woman swept in, her fringed poncho swirling down to her sensible, rather down-at-heel shoes. A knitted hat was crammed over her unruly red hair.

''Scuse me barging in like this but it's the only way I can reach anyone. I'm trying to organise a "Bring Back Reality" conference – regrettably we'll have to use the intos – and I'd like to know if you would be interested. I believe it's about time we stopped playing power games about the ugliest periods of world history, faced up to our responsibilities, and started working out how we can get out of this wretched beast's innards and see the sky again.'

'What a wonderful idea! I'll join in with that. I can tell everyone about the apricot dome,' said Bibbie excitedly.

Rick was shaking with anger, 'That's enough! Get out of my story, both of you.' And he pointed at Sylvie Wildwood and looked regretfully at Bibbie, who found herself suddenly back in the cell. The soft, plump man was still there, reclining in the cell stuff and animatedly directing his solo story, a very important business person in complete control of his simulated bimbos and acolytes, only very gently teased by the puppets invented by the dragon.

But the dragon had been careful to serve Bibbie too, and so Sylvie had come to the cell with her, still dressed in her poncho and woollen hat. Bibbie looked at her and they both burst out laughing.

'Do you know I really believed I was living that nonsense,' Bibbie burst out.

'Yes, it gets to you, doesn't it. I love busting into private games. Gets the old intos jolly confused, but it can't stop me. Doesn't do any good though, just look at him.'

'But the expression on his face!' Bibbie was aching with laughter. 'Thanks for rescuing me, I feel so silly being taken in like that.' She reached forward to hug Sylvie, who responded, but it didn't feel right.

'I'm not here really,' Sylvie told her. 'We're hugging cell stuff. The intos doesn't do feelies very well. It's always concentrated on sight and sound – because people do, I suppose. They fill in the rest quite happily.'

'Where are you then?' Bibbie asked her disappointedly.

'Can't answer that, lovee. Could be the other side of the planet. Have to ask the beast.'

'Do you think it could show you the way to the food hall where the kitchen hands are; then we could meet. And then I'll take you to the apricot dome,' said Bibbie excitedly. 'Don't ask me to tell you about the apricot dome, you'll have to be there and see it.'

'Why don't I ask it to get me to your apricot dome?'

'Oh no!' said Bibbie, much alarmed. 'We don't want the dragon coming there, it's ours, and special.'

'What's this food hall then?'

Bibbie explained about the kitchen hands sorting the fresh food and putting it in bowls, and the smelly trench.

Sylvie was intrigued. 'There could be millions of food halls then, they must have been part of the old system of feeding people, before the cell stuff. But the beast'll know which one I suppose. Okay, your food hall it is, I'll have a go. You go back there and wait for me. Might take a while – no jet planes these days! What a lark! Better than busting into silly twirps' games. Never did find anyone interested in the conference, until you. So glad we met!' Her face vanished from the cell wall. Bibbie was left wondering if she had been dreaming.

She was just about to go back into the tunnel to the food hall when it occurred to her to ask the dragon if Sylvie would be able to get there. Immediately Bibbie felt herself to have been transformed into Sylvie herself in her cell. She could see Sylvie's red hair hanging down over her shoulders. She was wearing the poncho. An opening appeared in the wall, high enough for her to walk into. She walked along it, then she felt herself accelerate so that her feet were whirring along. The corridor zipped past, sometimes changing direction, often opening up from an apparent dead end. Then she found herself stopped and a couch provided for her to sleep. Then she woke up and the walk began again and sped up. Eventually, after many tremendously long dizzy fast walks, she came out of a tunnel opening, but much wider than those she had known, and there was the food hall. Then, suddenly, she was herself again, back in the man's cell. She now knew that Sylvie would get there, but that it would be a long journey and would take her a very long time. Then she wondered why her own journeys had been so arduous. Perhaps because she had not asked for the dragon's help. Perhaps because she was different. She would ask Sylvie about it, and Sophia, of course. And she felt a guilty pang at not having thought about Sophia for so long.

So she left the man's cell and made her way back to the apricot dome. She told Sophia what had happened, and that one day Sylvie would come, and wasn't it amazing that she had that very name? And wouldn't it be wonderful when there was a Bibbie, a Sylvie and a Sophia in the apricot dome?

Every night she dreamed about Sylvie on her long journey and she knew that she would know when to go to the food hall to meet her.

And that happy day did come and Bibbie and Sophia brought Sylvie to the apricot dome and there they were, the three women: the dreamer of dreams, the world changer, and the gentle listener who waits and learns,

145

and they loved each other in all the ways that women can love and they lived happily ever after.

Every so often there would come a time when Sophia would borrow Bibbie's knife and slice the curtain in the archway and slip Outside and lie down there. Sylvie and Bibbie would search for her and then realise where she had gone. Then they would take some fresh apricots to put in her sleeping hands and some earth to scatter over her body. Then Bibbie would go inside to a man in his cell and get a seed for a baby. If she dreamed of a new Bibbie she would become Sylvie and Sylvie would become Sophia and Bibbie would come out of the baby tunnel. If she dreamed of a man baby, she would go inside to wait for the baby and find a Bibbie to exchange it with. Sometimes Sylvie would go inside and barge into a few stories to try to get some other people to go to find trees and the sky. We do not know if she succeeded because that is another story.

That is how they lived for ever after, and that is how the apricot forest grew in the Outside in the shelter of the apricot dome. And the three women and the apricot forest were still there when the dragon died and faded away; but that too is another story.

–Hello, Bea. It's Justin.

–Hello! You're back from Ireland then. Thanks for your letter. I'm glad I didn't shock your Auntie Mary too much. So perhaps it'll work with other people too.

–I'm not sure about that. I wonder if people will see below the surface to the deep questions. Have you thought about that Prologue I suggested.

–Yes, I've had a brilliant idea how to do it.

–What was that?

–I'll show you when it's written.

–OK – but that could be a while. I was ringing to tell you I'm going away again – for six months this time.

–Goodness! Where to.

–India. Lionel's a Quaker and he's got some contacts out there.

–Lionel's going too, then. Ah!

–Yes – but we're not really together again, and that's not the reason I'm going. It was my idea. Sparked off by your book actually.

–How come?

–Well, the shift of consciousness idea – the narrator and now the person in the 'Dawning Eversight' chapter – made me think of another kind of spirituality – an outward mysticism, instead of the Inward Light that Quakers believe in. I think Christianity's lost whatever it had – I'm a lapsed Catholic, and I agree with what you said about the ritual. Anyway I thought Hinduism – with karma and reincarnation and so on – might be closer to the outward kind of spirituality, which would have to be linked to the past – like your patterns are.

–Can't you find out about that from here? There are Hindus in this country; other eastern religions too. Anyway, what about your job?

–They wouldn't have let me have six months off, and in any case I was finding it increasingly artificial and superficial. And of course, it wasn't just your book: I've wanted to go to India for some time. Everyone I know seems to have gone – and been transformed – and I feel I missed out.

–How are you getting there? Flying, I suppose.

–'Fraid so. You don't approve, I suppose – all that pollution.

–Well, there is that. Also it's part of the globalism we were talking

147

about. But I don't believe in flying in another sense. Every time I see a jumbo jet around Heathrow apparently hanging in the sky with no visible means of support, I just don't believe it's possible. It's against nature. Birds and butterflies should fly, not metal elephants.

–I read somewhere that bumble bees shouldn't be able to fly either: it's against the laws of science.

–So much for the laws of science then. When are you off?

–On Thursday.

–So you won't finish reading my book.

–No – I'm really sorry. You should try a few other people. Anyway, I don't need to read the rest – I've worked out what happens.

–Really! Tell me.

–Well, the general idea, I think is: the people come out of the dragon and they've got eversight, so they can see the patterns of the past – and so they know about the consequences of using fire – so they don't use it, or dig the ground – like the Terrever, from *Storyframes*. Remember: Amelia couldn't find a people like that – because there's never been one – this is new. But the old patterns – including the inward kind of spirituality – are still there in the past, so there's some kind of struggle between the inward and the outward consciousness.

–That's amazing! In fact I call the two kinds of consciousness 'firesoul' and 'watersoul'.

–I like 'watersoul' – an ocean of spirituality instead of a flame.

–So what happens in the end?

–Nothing can be ended – with pattern. That's why you had to call it *The Completion*, isn't it? But I hope we get to meet the woman from the future. And I'm intrigued to know how you describe the watersoul – what it would be like to be one.

–Sorry to disappoint you – I tried, but it's impossible – they don't have any sense of inside themselves to get into.

–I suppose spending an age inside the intos would do that to you – all human knowledge at your disposal on the walls of your cell. It's funny to think of all those slobs just tipped out of the dragon and they become this new wise and spiritual tribe. I don't think they'd have any rituals or religious imagery, by the way. All that's our way of trying to reach the outward mystery – they wouldn't need it.

–I don't have them come out as fully watersoul; they still have some working out to do – quite a lot actually.

–You mean a whole chapter's worth. You always cram such a lot into each chapter.

–Did you read about Bibbie?

–Yes. And, like with *Overfleet*, I forgot it was all a storyframe. But that's like life – losing track of what's really going on, and what matters. The intriguing thing with that chapter though is that the imaginary story is about what we usually avoid – you know: the cycle of life and death – the stages of a woman's life: baby, woman and crone: the human equivalent of sheep, lambs and slaughterhouse. That's the significance, of course, of Bibbie making pictures out of shit on the glass of the greenhouse.

–You mean women get to be creative through natural bodily processes?

–Exactly! Men have always envied women for that – and it's why they have to invent and build – trying to get more powerful than women are.

–Mmm. It amazes me what you see in this.

–When you've had a few more people comment on it you must get a publisher. It could be a best-seller! – a new career could open up, you won't need to worry about getting a job, and you could stay at home with Poppy.

–Lovely thought! But I can't imagine it being a best-seller – the best I can hope for is a cult classic.

The subject of the last shift

was living a fantasy of escaping from her intos cell, but she probably, like many others in late biotech, did actually want to get out, and at last some of them did. Get out into what? is an obvious question. What was the world like outside the dragon's coils?

We have some idea what the world of the dragon was like from the outside, although we never saw it until the creature was dying, since there was no living being on the outside we could shift to. The intos was actually more like a tree than a dragon: a tree global in extent, and having branches which ran along the ground, anchored at intervals by great molar-like roots to prevent the winds ripping it out of the ground. Since it functioned like a giant plant, carrying out photosynthesis, transpiration and so on, the dragon would have served to replace the forests destroyed during necrotech and bionecrotech in that it would have had the same function in respect of the climate, rainfall and hydrological processes. Because of that, it is possible that the 'flatteners', the storm force winds, died down, and benign climates re-established themselves, at least in some regions of the world.

If it had not been for bionecrotech, it is possible that diverse natural wilderness would have returned in between the intos coils. However, the monstrous genetically engineered plants released during bionecrotech were so strong and successful that for the entire era of biotech, they excluded any wild plants which might have re-established themselves. So of course when the tree/dragon died, the extreme weather patterns of bionecrotech came back: the world was again the stormy green desert which Fred Drakely was driven through in the motorway train.

An artificial variety of the wild plant chickweed, or stellaria, was particularly abundant, fortunately, as you will see. This plant had been developed as fodder input to the industries of bionecrotech which produced cultured meat and other animal products. Considered in necrotech science's terms, the plant was high in proteins and fats, with a balance of amino acids and essential oils. It fixed nitrogen, and unlike other hybrid plants it produced true seed, as well as spreading vegetatively. Its originally natural habit of rooting lightly in the soil had been encouraged in the hybrid so that it could be harvested by mechanically pulling it out and rolling it up into great bales. The genetically engineered chickweed proved to be a valuable foodstuff during the early years of the pattern age.

150

When the emergence actually took place the dragon was dying. It seems that the 'creature' was profoundly disturbed by the changed mood of many of its charges, who were seeing through and rejecting the illusions, perhaps because of the awakening of their eversight. The dragon did not have an individual self-awareness to get upset: it never had any centre for its intelligence, let alone its emotions, even if it could have been thought of as having emotions. What happened to the dragon was connected with the way the intos dealt with people who had finished with life. It did not wait for people to die and then dispose of the bodies. Anyone who was inactive and bored got their vital supplies cut off, and then the body was decomposed and the material recycled. Quality of life, which it continuously assessed from the person's level of interest in what was going on, was the only criterion it used. It made no judgement about normality as opposed to handicap or unfitness.

By some quirk of its own logic, the dragon interpreted the desire for escape of some of its inmates as a rejection, and a sign that its own life was over, and it began to let itself die. As a result, people discovered the system failing: the stories and illusions did not appear in response to their wishes. The basic processes of life sustenance continued longer than the illusions, but boredom set in, and so the intos disconnected the cells of inmates who had nothing to keep them amused. No one could repair the system: it had evolved far beyond the skills even of its long dead innovators to understand it, and no one had any practical knowledge or manual skill, even if they imagined they did.

Eventually parts of the exterior walls began to lose their toughness and it became possible to break out. The few who had survived, perhaps through having eversight as a substitute for the intos illusions, escaped into the outside world.

My next shift for you then is not an intos story. The people you will meet lived on the earth under the heavens. As you will see, they had none of the material comforts developed during necrotech, and no system dedicated to sustaining them. But the air they breathed was clean, and they could see through the fresh air to more stars than you could even imagine.

The subject is a young boy whose name is Yshi.

151

Part Two – The Pattern Ages

8

Yshi's Battle

A hot wet wind blew over the plain, rocking the coils, loosening their roots. One stretch had lifted free, and its great weight heaved back and forth like a snake's locomotion, but it was trapped both ends by the roots still bedded deep and held by tough filaments which penetrated tiny fissures in the rocks below the red soil.

The moving stretch, though dangerous, was the best hunting ground. There were parallel drip lines under the coil's scaly sides, where rainwater ran down between the bulges which had been human habitation. Below the drip lines the weed grew tall and thick. When the coil came loose, its roots were dragged backwards and forwards across the weed and hooked whole swathes out of the soil, and tossed them away for the wind to spin into great green balls by tumbling them over the ground. But to catch one was not easy.

The sisters joined hands to form an arc to trap a careering ball. The first to enter bounced out again, and in ducking to avoid being knocked down, one of the women let go and broke the chain. She lost balance and the wind tipped her over, so the others edged backwards to join up with her again. The whistling air slapped their long damp hair around their faces, blinding them and catching in their mouths as they gasped with the effort to repair the human net.

Over and over again they tried to catch one of their prey. Over and over a ball would come near or inside, but with seeming wiliness, escape and bounce away. They knew they had to keep edging sideways to avoid the path of the loose loop, where a sudden whip of the massive coil could crush them to death. But this meant that, without realising it, they were slipping backwards with-wind, and away from the sorory.

Suddenly, with the bizarre predictability of chaos, a ball came which seemed to wish to be caught. It rolled gently inside the arc and traced a slow spiral to the centre and spun quietly around until they closed in around it. The ball was half as high again as they were: a really good catch. Laughing they grabbed the spongy tangle of weed, and collapsed against it to rest. They nibbled a few of the tiny white flowers, deliciously sweet and fresh.

The brother saw the sisters from his perch atop a coil in the sorory. He clung to the green fins and gazed in their direction across the vastness of the plain with his blinking eyes, in order to focus with his evereye. He smiled at their girlish pleasure, a rare respite from their grim existence. In ages gone by they might have been still girls, absorbed in irresponsible fun and playing at love. Boys would have found them desirable, with their full breasts, strong slim limbs, golden brown skin. Their faces, all so alike, had the caste of some ancient race, with broad cheekbones, narrow black eyes, finely chiselled slightly beaked noses and perfectly formed lips. As he watched them, he saw their rush of excited pleasure fade.

They looked around for the nearest refuge from the full force of the wind, and realised how badly positioned they now were. They had to get the ball back to the sorory, in the main local cluster of rooted coil, half daylight into-wind away, but they could not go into-wind with the huge ball. To the east was the path of the loose section. Far over to the west was a rooted section, but an isolated strand, which would hardly soften the wind at all. There was a rooted cluster to the south, with-wind and so easy to get to, but this was far from where they wanted to be.

The brother could hear the sisters with his evereye, as well as see them, over the great distance, half daylight into-wind, and over the cacophony of moving air. He knew what they would decide, but not because his evereye could see the future, eversight probably had never included that gift, but because he could feel the flow of the pattern of their deciding.

'We'll never get it home from here,' a sister said.

'We'll have to plait it up then,' said another.

'That'd take too long, it's such a big one,' said another, 'so there'd be no fresh weed for supper.'

'And we would not be back this day.'

'What do we do then? Let it go and get nearer home and try to catch another one?'

'We could plait up some of it, let the rest go and then see if we can catch a little one nearer home.' And that is what was decided.

The brother nodded to himself. He looked down with his blinking eyes to where the other brother and some sisters were chewing weed, and several little girls, just tottering on their feet, tumbled together in the red mud and occasionally snuggled up to suckle at the women's damply gleaming golden breasts. The clay basin was full of chewed weed pulp and the over-mound was forming. The weed from the last hunt was nearly used up. The rain had filled the basin. Soon they would cover the basin with more clay and leave the pulp for a quarter moon to brew. The water would drain away into the ground, leaving a big round biscuit of nutritious curd. Tomorrow, they would begin again with an empty basin and the new weed pile. At supper there would be plenty of fresh weed to eat.

The brother looked back with his evereye at the hunting party.

Half the group of sisters was holding the ball steady, while the rest plaited, and they would continue until their fingers were tired, and then change over. Each plait was made by forming three continuous hanks by easing in strand after strand. When the three hanks were long enough they were plaited together, and the hanks extended further. When the plait was long enough, it was wound around the waist by turning. The plait was tucked into itself to secure it, and a new plait begun. The sisters ate as they worked, the sweet flowers, the hot little leaves and the crunchy stems.

'That's enough,' thought the brother and, sure enough, the sisters stopped the work, somewhat regretfully, because the big ball was scarcely reduced. But any more and the bulk of the plaits would encumber them too much for another hunt. Pushing into-wind, and keeping clear of the lashing coil, they tramped slowly towards the sorory. They formed their net again when they saw a few balls bouncing their way. They were lucky and caught one small enough to roll into-wind. At last they reached the shelter of the northern cluster of rooted coils. Tired but triumphant they reached the sorory.

The brother got down from his perch, sliding over the side of the coil and down its root, and went to meet them, so that they could share their excitement without disturbing the healing vigil. The little girls left the curd-making group and toddled after him, and were swept up and cuddled by the women. The children wriggled and giggled as their

155

tender skin was rubbed against the weed plaits wound below the women's breasts, pushed high and unusually accessible for suckling and fondling. The squirming little bodies clung on with arms, legs and mouths, resisting being put down. Then the brother helped, and the children hindered, while the sisters unwound the plaits, joined them together, and lashed the ball to the coil root nearest the next empty basin. Then the sisters went to take their turn at the vigil. With solemn, knowing acceptance, the little girls trooped back to the curd-making party.

The sisters who had been on vigil were exhausted, much more tired than the sisters of the hunting party, for all their physical efforts over all daylight. Each sister leaving vigil shared with the sister entering vigil what progress she had made. As her sister sat down beside her at her vigil root, she told of each strand of the severed net that she had touched with her evereye.

The brother listened, knowing he should not, but boys were known to be bad so they could do bad things, and were not told every time.

'There were children putting small trees in holes in the earth,' the sister whispered to her sister. Her voice trembled with the pain of the vision. 'Girls not half way to bleeding, and boys, and elders were present to instruct them. They did these deeds for love and healing because they knew nothing of pattern and the ways of trees. Their elders had told the children of the death of forests far away. They grieved for the animals and painted people who were there. They called their actions for healing "planting trees", not understanding that the way of trees is to make seeds, and for the wind, or climbing or flying animals, to spread the seeds to far enough ground.'

'You know the ways of the trees, my sister,' said the other in ritual reply, 'You are the healing. Share with me the pain.'

'The little trees were hurt; their roots broken and dried up, the patterns of their growing and their place of growing torn apart and lost. Great pits had been torn out of the new place of growing. The patterns of trees in that place were from long ages past and could not be knit.' The sister's voice was scarcely audible. Her eyes poured with tears and her mouth was dry. The other sister wiped her eyes with her hair and moistened her lips with the tear drenched strands.

'You know the ways of the trees, my sister,' the other sister said again, 'You are the healing. Share with me the pain.'

'Those pits dug out for the planting —' she shuddered. 'In them was put dried up residue from the slaughter of slave beasts, and the pain of the beasts' lives and deaths joined with the pain of the soil and the young trees. Stakes made of slaughtered trees were hammered in the pits. The frail little trees were held in the pits, against the stakes, with no care for the lie of the roots or the direction of the sun. Black fibrous stuff was mixed in with the soil from the pits, and the broken mixture piled back in around the poor dried bent roots and the whole mess trodden roughly down. The black stuff had no relation to the soil there and did not know the place of the planting. It came from a distant land where the destruction of forests long before had left a wetness so that plants died and could not be not fully decomposed. The place of the black stuff had made new patterns over the ages, and a new beauty and wholeness had come from its pain. But the new beauty was destroyed for the black stuff for planting. Pain on pain on pain, and those people caused it for love. Such is the pity of the ignorance of pattern.' The sister wept bitterly. The other sister held her close for a long while.

'You know the ways of the trees, my sister,' said the other sister, easing away and then kissing each of her eyes and her forehead. 'You are the healing. Go and rest now, and I will grieve and nurse the hurts in your stead.'

The leaving sister untied the rope of weed by which she was secured to the root against sudden gusts of wind, and the other took her place. The entering sister sat down with legs crossed, put her hands palms upwards on her spread knees, and prepared herself to reach backwards in time with her evereye, back to the times when men blind to the ways of the trees had destroyed the patterns of the earth.

The leaving sister noticed the brother and knew he had been listening. She frowned and waved him away. He watched her squat to urinate, then climb the root which led inside the coil. She and the others from vigil would sleep until supper.

The brother saw that the other brother had completed his work with the curd making. Their eyes met, and the other brother saw his need for comfort. They walked to the coil section they slept in, which was some distance from where the sisters slept. They climbed the root to the opening, walked some way inside to the dark nest they had made of dried weed and made love long and tenderly and then dozed for some while. Then they talked quietly together.

'Yshi,' said the other brother, 'did the sisters scold you?'

'I did wrong. We always do wrong, Han. It is our nature from of

157

old.'

The brothers had secret names for each other. In their travels with their evereyes they had discovered that people of past ages had always had individual names. They had not found a time when this had not been so, even when cultures were close-bonded, and had more together-knowing than alone-knowing. The two boys had invented their names: names that no one they had met in the past had used, which made them feel especially wicked and egocursed. They did not use their names in front of the sisters. Of course, the sisters knew about the secret names, since they knew everything, but boys were expected to be bad.

'I saw you watching the hunt, Yshi.'

'They have not said I should not do that.'

'I suppose you should have helped with the curd.'

'If I do not look out at the plain, and see where loose strands need securing, there will be no more curd. The coils are slowly dying and do not re-root easily. If lengths of coil stay loose, no more weed can grow beneath. And with much coil loose, the wind may take hold and rip out everything. We could be swept to our death, and even if not, there would be no shelter for the sorory and we would all die anyway.'

'The sisters expect that to happen. The coils and the weed were man's evil doing, so the sisters have no concern for them.'

'So I do the bad work that they have need of, and will not acknowledge. That is an old pattern, I think. But the coils bring rain. The dragon's mind may have gone from its coils but the roots draw water and the fins transpire. Surely that makes it easier for the wilderness to come back.'

The brothers deliberately had this exchange often. They were making a pattern of the truth as they saw it. They believed that their pattern would persist and resonate with the becoming. This was their healing vigil, practical and immediate as males' patterns had been in the past. They thought that perhaps men could be part of the healing and make amends. The sisters were fearful of men and men's patterns. Like the other natal groups of sisters, they would kill the brothers as soon as enough girl children had been born. But they had too much humility to deny the boys' truth, and permitted them to practise it.

Yshi went on, 'Other brothers in other sorories are taking up our pattern too. I have met them evereyed and I know.'

Han said, 'But there are so many more sisters than brothers.'

'Pattern has never worked by quantities,' Yshi reminded him.

158

'Anyway, they cannot breed with fewer than two in each sorory. There will always be enough of us.'

'They could have just one boy for breeding.'

'One boy alone would go mad without love,' said Yshi. 'Come here, my brother, my precious lover and friend.' They made love again slowly and tenderly, delighting in each others' shameful maleness.

It was that night that Yshi had the first dream of the battle.

Yshi thrashed madly in his sleep, his arms rained blows, his legs pounded and kicked. Han woke up bruised and scared. He rolled aside. Blind in the darkness he felt his friend's nightmare, heard his groans, but could not get near to wake him. He gathered a ball of weed to cushion the blows and moved towards Yshi hoping for an opportunity to grab hold and shake him to consciousness.

He tried to visualise Yshi's position in order to edge behind, but it was as if the boy was bristling with limbs, all engaged in some desperate fight. Suddenly the struggle ceased, and with a groaning sigh Yshi lay still as death, no sound of breath, no movement against the dry weed.

Han waited a moment and then put out his hand. He encountered Yshi's cheek which was damp and cold. His friend did not move as Han felt his face, discovering eyes and mouth wide open. Han felt for his shoulder and shook him roughly. 'Yshi, Yshi, wake up!' Han panicked. 'Help! Help!' he cried, and ran out of the coil, down the root, and across to the sisters' sleeping place.

They dragged Yshi's inert body out to the coil opening where they could see him by moonlight. The pale gleam was reflected in his unblinking eyes.

'He is dead. My brother is dead,' Han sobbed.

But he was not dead. In a little while he stirred, and moaned softly, shuddered and groaned loudly, and began again to lash about. Han and the sisters held him and shook him awake. They sat him up, then dragged him over to a hollow where rainwater lay and splashed him with cool water. A sister held him against her breast and rocked him gently calling, 'Little brother, it's all right now.'

'Is that you, mother?' were his first words.

'You had a bad dream, little brother,' the sister said, holding him close. 'You will go quietly to sleep now, and tell us of your dream in the morning.'

159

'Yes,' he said.

But in the morning he remembered nothing of the dream. He laughed when the other brother told him of being kicked awake and fetching the sisters to rouse him from his death trance. He would not search for the dream evereyed as the sisters asked him to do. He insisted on going with the other brother to their task of replanting the loose coil.

It was dangerous work, but they had learned from many trials how best to do it. First they walked the length of the loose section, just out of reach of its rippling path, observing its pattern of strong or weak growth. They chose a vigorous green section as near as possible to half way along. They identified the longest root of that section, and stood just clear. They waited patiently for the wind to drop a little and for the root to catch in the lip of the hole it had been dragged out of. Then they both dashed in and threw their bodies around the root, moving with it, helping it to ease back into position instead of rising out again with its swing. With all their strength they resisted the outward tug, digging their feet into the glistening red clay of the root's pit, but pulling them out before they were crushed by the root descending back where it belonged.

If they judged their moment well, the entire root cluster would engage with the set of pits. If not, the bending of some other root would spring the coil section free again. Then the boys would have to dash clear, and wait for an opportunity to try again.

On this occasion, they were successful first time. But the job was not completed then, only the initial stage. What they had to do now was to keep the root in place for some days; the time they had discovered that it took for root fibres to grow down far enough to grip the rock beneath. They had too little strength and weight to resist the full force of the loose coil's former rippling motion, but they were helped. The lengths of coil either side continued to ripple, but with dampened force, as if they were happy to dance to a new tune. All the brothers had to do was to resist the occasional random movement whereby both sides tugged one way, which could happen at any time, and they had to be constantly on the alert.

They could not sleep, but they had brought fresh weed to sustain them. This was weed gathered in handfuls from the plain, which they had plaited as they walked from the sorory and wound around their waists.

Several times on the long wait, the other brother tried to persuade the

160

brother to examine his nightmare. 'The sisters want the knowledge your journey would bring to them,' he said. 'It is there waiting for you to read it.'

'It was my experience, not theirs,' the brother said.

'Well won't you just share it with me then?'

'If I do they'll see it anyway. And I don't think I can get it back, and I don't want to try. I have no feeling about it, but from what you told me of how I was, it was a bad experience. Why should I put myself through that again?'

But he did go through it again. Having been awake and alert for some days they were in need of sleep on their return. They curled up together in their nest of weed and were instantly deeply asleep. Han was rudely awakened by being flung onto his back by a thundering blow from Yshi's fist straight into his chest. He had to wriggle aside to avoid Yshi's thrashing limbs. Yshi was roaring loud and snarling low in a rhythmic beat, and Han felt, rather than heard, the drum which drove him on. Han focused on that drum, seeking to transport himself where Yshi was, and he got a whiff of a pungent odour of exploding chemicals and burning flesh.

Then he was lying in the sun and a sister was stooping over him. He sat up, and the brother was there too, sitting up and looking dazed.

'You must tell us now,' said the sister in a harsh and insistent voice. 'Where have you been? We have to know.'

'Thirsty,' the brother said, and the sister scooped water from a puddle into her hands and brought it carefully to him to suck up.

'I'll try,' he muttered. He rubbed his face and massaged his scalp, walking his fingers through his hair. He settled in vigil position and shut his eyes.

'Too much for telling. Just one thought with so much being and knowing. Have to take fragments, interpret from myself, translate for you here listening. Empty shadow of the thought.'

The whole pattern of men's killing and dying at once. The battle of all battles here and now. Moved by training, fear for, fear of, loyalty, heroism, payment, comradeship. Every blow with every weapon, every wound, every last breath.

Identified with each and all, through ages of men's history. Stone-ager with club. Egyptian, Persian fighting man of infantry, cavalry, archers, charioteers. Greek hoplite in phalanx solid with spears on the plain, weakened on the wooded hill. Roman hastati, principes, triarii in companies disciplined and skilled. Barbarians in brutal hoards scattered, slaughtered, enslaved. Goth, Hun, Mongol, Saracen and Turk. Zulu warrior, Indian brave. Solid formations, lines and columns, sending death. Melee of stabbing and hacking, clash of weapon on armour, penetrating flesh and bone, howls, screams. Plumed warrior's trained muscles so much meat. Frightened lad, malnourished, feeble in body and mind, neck hacked. Shrill whinny of crippled horse, hamstring slashed. Longbowmen, pikemen, arquebusiers, musketeers, horsemen with pistols, infantry, artillery, cannon, howitzers, machine guns. Tanks, trenches, bombs. Choking dust, stinking mud, rotting corpses, poison gas. Severed limbs, spilled guts, exploded flesh, grotesque bodies of friend and foe, discarded lives. Stench of blood and scorched fat. Piss and shit of fear.

Driven by the compulsion of the revolving pattern of killing and dying all the times that are also now. Its function a culling, its hope to be few enough to be at home on earth.

Echoes of the battle. Rugby scrum, whack of racket and bat, bursting lung and straining sinew of athlete. Getting on, staying ahead, exploiting, abusing, discarding. Being the exploited, enslaved, abused, discarded. Succeeding, failing, envying, enduring, gloating, grovelling. The winning and the losing, the killing and the being killed, is the one battle of men.

The function of culling lost in the echoes. Too few die. Earth dies in their stead, guts spilled, skin scraped and burned. Patterns arrested in their becoming —

'That is all I can tell you for now.' He opened his eyes and looked at them.

The sisters leant their heads together and held a whispered sharing.

They looked back at the brother. One said, 'It is as we have said, man is evil and has brought killing and destruction to the world.'

163

'That is true and yet not true,' said the brother. The other brother wondered at his boldness.

'I need to explore the meaning of the dream with my brother,' he went on. 'We will share with you when we have understanding. Come Han.'

'Han?' exclaimed the sister.

'Han is the name of my brother. My name is Yshi. Come Han.' And he led Han to their sleeping place.

The dream of the battle of all battles came over and over again, not every night, and not regularly, but often. Both brothers experienced it now, usually together. Afterwards they talked of it and tried to work out what it meant, beyond the obvious truth of men's history of violence in warfare, which had echoes in the competitiveness and ruthlessness of the culture which, in a later age, had been called necrotech.

One day, when the brothers were guarding a coil they had re-rooted, Yshi said, 'There is a feeling I have that the dream is not condemning men for their violence. Its message seems to be that there is some validity in men killing men which has been denied, and the dream is reminding us, trying to remove a layer of unconsciousness.'

'If that is so, why did the dragon send women only to the outside? The dragon knew all there was to know. If there is a purpose for men's violence, it would have sent men out too, not given women the power of life and death.'

'We do not know that it did that deliberately. Its mind was failing then.'

'The sisters believe it was the dragon's wisdom which gave them the power to keep a few boys only to young manhood for stud, because women are the healers and could bring the wilderness back, whereas men would exploit and so destroy any new life which came.'

The coil on both sides of the root they were guarding suddenly rocked the root one way, threatening to pull it out. They dug their feet in the clay and pushed against the movement with all their strength. It was just enough. They leant against the root breathless and wet with sweat which the damp wind neither washed off nor dried.

Some time later, Yshi picked up the discussion again.

'What you were saying about the dragon's wisdom — The dragon only knew what people knew. Its memory was colossal, but it was only human memory. It would have had the same prejudices as people did — from necrotech mostly, because that's where it all came from.'

164

'But necrotech was very male dominated. Surely it would have made men powerful again.'

'I don't know. There's something in me trying to get out. Let me roll it around for a while.'

It was several hours later, when the sun had gone down and heavy cloud hid the moon and stars, that Yshi spoke again.

'The dragon was a female.'

'What!' said Han.

'The dragon was a world economy, a civilisation. The economy and city culture were built and run by men, but they were female ways made large.'

'I don't understand what you're saying.'

'Well I think I've thought it out in relation to the battle dream. I think I know how to say it to the sisters. You can hear it first of course.'

It is the nature of man to fight. It is the nature of man to kill the beasts of the wilderness and to kill each other. It is the nature of woman to bear children in pain and raise them in gentleness. It is the nature of woman to suffer and to love, and not to hurt and to hate. Woman was stronger than man; out of love the ruin of wilderness began.

Woman raised the orphaned young of the wild beasts and so tamed them for milk and meat and hides, so man no longer needed to hunt. Woman discovered how to tame plants for humans and the tame beasts to eat. Woman loved her mate and her young and for them scratched and plucked and tortured the earth and was deaf to its cries. Woman taught her sons about love and kinship. So man became restrained in his killing. Man killed for land for the women's cultivation, and loved woman and made many children. Man made fortifications to protect his children. Man took up the work of stripping the skin off the earth and was deaf to her agonised cries. Man hid from his own nature behind the walls of his pretended loving kindness, and made temples to worship love and keep it strong, and named the lie 'God' and 'civilisation' and was proud of what he had done. Man was obedient to woman's will and denied his own nature and the culling of man by man was not enough. That is how the wilderness was ruined; by man's power corrupted by woman's love.

Han listened and was amazed. 'Will you tell them this?' he asked.

'I have to,' Yshi said. 'They say they want understanding.'

165

'But this denies all they believe about the wickedness of men, and the hope for new wilderness through women's compassion and healing love.'

'No, I don't believe it does. It is mechanistic thinking which assumes that understanding what went wrong provides solutions. It is impossible to start again when this is what the earth is now.' Yshi swung his arms all around at the bleak, wind-swept plain, now darkened in the night. 'And we cannot retrace the way we have come and rediscover the beginning. The women's healing may not close the wound between the patterns of wilderness present in the past and our hopes and needs for the future, but it is right to try that way. What else could we do? But men could make healing too, why not? And if we succeed, women and men together, there will be a new human culture to bring about. There may be a time when men's nature to kill each other for culling may be needed; if too many infants have been reared for a viable balance with nature.'

'It's the women who do the culling now,' Han observed.

'During the long ages before civilisation, killing was surely known to be part of living. Women and men knew it. And then they would have done their own killing, not left it to others, denying their responsibility.'

'You haven't explained what you meant about the dragon being female,' said Han.

'Haven't I? I thought I had. Don't you see; the economy is when people farm and manufacture for exchange in the market. It sounds benign, a kind of sharing. It provides for the family, the tribe, the nation, or whatever – but it depends on exploitation, disregarding any hurt or damage suffered by any living being or process which is not counted in the economy. It provides an enclosing womb – the city – and an umbilical cord – the systems of provision and the infrastructure. The economy is mother. Do you see?'

'Yes, in a way. But I don't see how men killing each other can be better than that. And there were battles while that was going on. I really am confused now.'

Yshi laughed, 'I know. I'm confusing myself too. But there's important understanding here if we can tease it out.'

They were silent for some time, both minds buzzing with thought. Then Han said, 'It makes sense if you try to imagine the time when people changed from living off the wilderness to taming animals and plants. Before the change, men hunted wild animals, and if there were

166

too many people for the area they were living off, men killed each other until there was balance again. I'm sure it was more complicated than that, but that's roughly it. After the change, more people could be supported on the same area of land, at the expense of the wilderness. If there got to be too many people for the land, the people would destroy more wilderness. It would only be when separate groups grew until the lands they had cleared bordered each other that the old pattern came into play and the men killed each other for each other's land.'

'Yes, that's it!' cried Yshi, relieved and excited. 'Everything that followed is just a complexification of those patterns. If people depend on the wilderness, they love and worship the wilderness, they don't destroy it, they destroy each other to have access to it. With farming, the only natural force which matters is the weather, so the worship of nature is focused on the sky. Love is directed at people and at the sky god. Love and creation, the realm of woman, is dominant. Killing to defend and extend that realm is approved, but is dressed up as heroism and noble sacrifice. Slaughter is hidden, death is denied, destruction is ignored. Evil is invented to justify the distortion.'

'Can we explain all this to the sisters, do you think?' asked Han.

The sisters made a semi-circle around the brothers and listened.

They said nothing for a long time after the brothers had finished.

Then a ripple of gathering attention passed around them and focused on one of the sisters. 'You say that men hunting wild animals and killing other men is good,' she said, 'and women tilling the soil to grow food for the family is bad.'

'Good/bad – that's part of what went wrong,' said Yshi. 'Death, killing, destruction – they are part of life – not bad, but inevitable and necessary. Hiding them, hiding from them, was what was bad, if we have to use that word.'

'So when violence broke out, as it did throughout history, and when men enjoyed violence as part of their entertainment, that was a necessary aspect of human nature trying to get out?' said another sister.

'Women sometimes enjoyed violence too,' Han observed. 'In late necrotech and biotech people seemed to need horror. They probably always have.'

'I'm sure we don't,' a sister said insistently.

Yshi turned to that sister and locked eyes with her. 'Don't you?' he said quietly. 'I watched you when you strangled another sister's male

167

infant for her. I felt that you enjoyed it.'

There was a chorus of hissing in-breath at this.

A sister, grim faced, said, 'You have given us much to think about, our brothers. We will assemble again when we have thoughts to share.'

A month passed, and no more was said about Yshi's battle. Life went on as if the dream had not come, and neither of the brothers dreamt it again.

Then the sisters called a gathering.

One of the sisters spoke. 'Will you tell us what difference this new understanding has made to you, our brothers.'

Yshi spoke: 'Even before the dream we believed we had a role in the healing. We have been tending the little life there is on the plain: the coils and the weed, and the hidden life in the soil which is bound up with the life above. We know you have despised those life forms because they were man's distorted slaves, from the times called bionecrotech and biotech. You seek the patterns destroyed during necrotech, which was wilderness from before there were men on earth. We believe that the life that is here should be nurtured, however it came.'

'We do not hinder you from doing that,' she said.

'But you will kill us when you have had enough children, and our work would cease. Instead, we could leave you at that time, and join with other young men who have completed their fathering with their natal group, and make a new group with any women who may choose to join us.'

'But if we allowed that, men would soon become dominant again.'

'We have tried to tell you that it was not men who were dominant; it only seemed so. But whichever way it was, that is in the past. We understand the influence of pattern, and the tendency of patterns to continue. But we also know that, with understanding, patterns can be changed. Could you not trust us if we promise not to interfere with your way?'

'The time you speak of may be years ahead. Not all our sisters have a girl child, and no boys have been kept as yet. We do not have to decide now. And you ask a great deal.'

Han blurted out, 'You should at least recognise that what we do to save the coils is of value. We are not here just to give you babies.'

The sister responded, 'We do appreciate what you do. But you must

recognise our work too. Our sister has something to share with you.'
She nodded at another sister.

A smile lit the other sister's face. 'Something wonderful has
happened. Come and see.'

She stood up and reached with both hands towards the brothers. They
got to their feet, took her hands and allowed themselves to be led. The
other sisters followed behind. She took them to one of the roots where
the sisters sat at vigil. Standing with her back to the root, she pointed to
another section of coil a short distance away, a section whose life had
left it, its remaining fins grey and stiff. A year before, after a
particularly strong wind, that section had begun to come loose and,
because it was so near the sorory, the brothers had piled clay around the
looseness to hold it steady. There was an opening in it, to a space where
the children sometimes played.

'Go and climb up there,' she said. 'Look at the edge of the opening,
up near the top on that side.'

The boys climbed up and looked. They saw a silvery grey arc, like a
new moon, both hands in length. Its surface was mottled and rough for
the most part, with radiating lines towards the narrowly lobed edges
which turned upwards at their tips. They stared at it in wonder.

'Surely it is living. Have you seen it change and grow?' Yshi asked
the sister below.

'Oh, it is living. I feel it is. I saw it only today, when I was on vigil. I
eversaw something like this pattern, on a tree which was undergoing
corruption. I felt its beauty in the present past, I opened my eyes and,
wonder of wonders, the same pattern was there high above me, on the
dead coil.'

'Has it grown out of the coil?' asked Han. 'It could have been part of
the dragon's patterns, the patterns that were held within it to sustain
human life; there were many such.'

'We have not seen such a growth before, and we have seen much dead
coil,' Yshi said.

'Does it matter how it came?' asked the sister. 'It is life reborn out of
death. It is the herald of regeneration, moonlight gleaming in our
darkness. The patterns of the past have heard our mourning cries. The
wounds men made are healing over and reaching out to us and all will
be well. Blessed sacred life!' And she fell to her knees, and the other
women with her, and the little girls copied them.

Yshi and Han climbed down and stood to one side. As the women bowed in their worship their breasts swayed, heavy with milk. Their wild wet hair blew in the gusts of warm wind, which whistled in and out of the holes in the dragon's dying coils.

Yshi glanced again at the grey arc of new growth. Then he shook his head and marched away. 'You coming, Han,' he said gruffly.

He strode to the edge of the sorory and then stopped, looking into the far distance. Han followed.

Han tried to put his arms around him. 'Yshi, what's the matter? Aren't you pleased about the new life?'

'Yes, I'm pleased, in a way. But why is it taking so long?'

'Why shouldn't it take long? How can we know how long it will take to bring the patterns back?'

'Some pattern has come back in human form. In only a few generations, we have developed the features of the race of people who lived in and revered the forests when necrotech was only cooking fires. The women are very proud of that success. They see it as proof of pattern itself. So why did the forests not come back too with the form of the forest people?'

Han started to respond, but Yshi put his hand up to stop him.

'I know what you'll say: the old human form returned because there are people here for those patterns to resonate with, whereas there is only old biotech coils and bionecrotech weed for the forests to connect to, and those patterns are too foreign and cursed. But I'll tell you stronger reasons why. It's because the women grieve for what they blame men for; they do not repent women's part. But worse than that, they do not celebrate the patterns that are in the past, and so are here now, and which we know through eversight. Only the wound receives their attention, not the healthy body from which the healing would come.'

Han protested, 'They are celebrating now, aren't they? Look at them.' And he gestured towards the sisters, now dancing joyously in front of the arc of new life.'

Yshi turned to look, but the sight seemed suddenly to enrage him.

'Hah! another weird ritual,' he snarled. 'Women are all witches.' Yshi shook his fists towards the sisters and howled aloud, 'Witches!', but the wind muffled his cry and they paid no attention.

Yshi turned back to Han. 'These women – they hunt, they kill, they use us to make their brats. They have all the power. They always have. Mankind is woman. Men just skulk around for a chance to put a cock in. Sometimes they deign to give us some dirty work to do – let us

170

pretend we're top dogs, so we don't even get any gratitude.'

'You've changed since the battle dream, Yshi,' Han said.

'The battle! Yes, that's it! That's man's pattern, man's way of culling and keeping the race strong – not strangling infants, or biting off their balls – that's what the women in some groups are starting to do, I eversaw it – same as domesticated animals in necrotech, bite our balls off. No!'

'What are you going to do?'

'Be a man, instead of their little brother and sperm bank. Raise my sons to be the hunters and warriors of the new world.'

'You can't raise your sons. The sisters would have to bear and suckle them. They would not allow you to have charge of them for a purpose they did not support.'

'Then I will take a wife – a young girl newly bleeding. I eversaw a natal group, not many days from here, with girls about to separate off from their mothers. I will go there, and take a woman to give me sons. Are you coming with me?'

Han felt a tug on his hand. Looking down he saw that one of the little girls had followed him. Out of habit he picked her up. She reached to hold on to his hair, her black eyes staring into his. Her healthy little animal body wriggled strongly against him. Her leg brushed against his cock as he shifted her to straddle his hip.

He looked back at Yshi. 'No, my brother. This is my natal group – and yours. The children here are our children. I cannot leave them and be myself.'

'They will kill you.'

'So be it. That is our way.'

'The women's way, you mean. But not for much longer. The wild beasts will come again, and I shall hunt them with my sons. The battle of men will come again, and I shall fight it with my sons.'

The episode I have just shared

was about the very beginnings of the pattern age. There were great changes in between that time of grief and struggle and the virtually interminable main period of the pattern age.

The women who emerged from the green dragon blamed men for necrotech – with some justification – and they saw their own role as mourners for the earth, and as guides through the tunnel of bereavement to some kind of healing to come. They discovered that the first healing had to be between women and men. They learned that lesson in various ways, and we have seen in the last shift an instance of the painful process of realisation they went through. Their descendants became as completely gender unaware as it is possible to be.

The last episode gave you some idea of how the planet was still in ecological ruins, even after the entire biotech age during which human beings had no further effect on the world outside the green dragon city. The planet had suffered the total extinction of virtually all the natural populations of plants and animals which had evolved before and during humans' time on earth. Although biotech was long in human terms, it was not long enough for evolution to repeat itself.

However, the natural wilderness did eventually return. It may be that during biotech some vital regeneration was taking place beneath the soil and in the oceans. The people of Yshi's time began to see visible signs of the re-emergence of wild plants and animals. Gradually, all the species destroyed during necrotech came back, and their kind lived again. How? The way we understand it is this: although the genetic codes had ceased being passed on by biological reproduction, the patterns of the past had not disappeared; they were still present, and still influential. And the patterns were not completed. So they returned.

I do not expect you to understand and accept this now. I have a shift to recount which should help you. The subject is someone like yourself. He is a necrotech person born into the pattern age. You will understand how he thinks, whereas you would not understand if I took you into the experience of a pattern age person; indeed, I doubt if I could convey in words what it is like to be a person of that time: the kind of being we call 'watersoul', in contrast to your kind, whom we call 'firesoul'.

This was a series of shifts. We are now close enough to my own age for me to travel back there with ease. The subject's name is Roy. You will learn a great deal about the pattern age from his experiences.

9

The New Beginning

'When I was growing up Mother Sage didn't let me play with the slave children.' Roy was surprised at himself for voicing a childish grievance he could not recall ever feeling. What a silly thing to say! he thought. What must the others be thinking of me?

They had been taking turns to tell the stories of their lives from before the trek began. It helped to while away the longer evenings now that winter was approaching, and was relaxing after the lecture sessions when they shared their expertise, and attempted to take notes by the light of crude torches and firelight. They had divided into specialist groups as soon as sufficient people had joined: groups of ten or so huddling over the big books, drawing up contents lists and indexes to pass on to other groups. By the end of the trek they hoped to have collated all the indexes, so that all the ancient knowledge was accessible.

Most of the men's stories were very similar. They simply related accounts of the progress of their education, the compilation of their books, and insights and ambitions that arose from time to time. They had been strictly separated from village life by their Mother Sages, as all the guardians had been called. Roy had hung back from telling his story, increasingly reluctant the more of the others he heard. As he had feared, his story was different, and might appear threatening to the others, and to the realisation of their cherished goal. But it was really too soon to be sure. Taking turns, and telling a little each evening, meant that only early lives had been related, and his story was not very different from theirs at that stage.

He looked around at the listeners. The whitely lit faces, veiled by woodsmoke, appeared friendly enough; no smirks or frowns. He went on.

I do not play with the slave children because, since I am a lord, I have to be grave and studious and not run around laughing or go splashing in the river as the slave children do.

We treat our slaves very well and they are happy and well fed. Mother Sage told me that in the ancient days slaves were made to work until they dropped from exhaustion, and beaten if they disobeyed or tried to run away. Our slaves bring us food and other necessities and they bow smilingly as they back respectfully away. From our hill we can see them working in the village gardens, by the river and over the first firebreak in the nearer forest. They never seem to stop; they are busy all the time at one small task or another, but they giggle and hum little tunes as they go. Mother Sage finds them annoying and silly. I try to follow her example because she is so wise and knowledgeable, but I cannot help seeing their ways as charming.

The slaves understand ancient language, which is the language Mother Sage taught me. But they also have a language of their own which I cannot follow. It consists of signs and facial movements and sing-song sounds; very fluid and complicated, and seems confusing to me, with so much to take in at once. Ancient language, which Mother Sage and I use for speech and writing, is based on everything in the world having a name, and actions and operations on things having names, and then one strings the names and actions together in a single long thread. Mother Sage says that ancient language is logical; it uses the higher functions of the human brain. She says the slaves' language – should one call it a 'language' when it involves more than just the tongue? – is like the grunting and signalling that lower animals do.

I only discovered quite recently that the slaves can write down their language – or perhaps I should say that they have a system for writing, which might, for all I know, have no relation to the miming. It consists of squiggles and little pictures, all over the place on the page, not in an orderly sequence like ancient language has to be. The young ones use scraps of paper to write messages – 'love notes', Mother Sage calls them – to hide in the gardens and forest for others to find.

Mother Sage and I are writing down books of mathematics for the New Beginning which is going to be brought about. I do most of the writing because Mother Sage is very frail and her hands are painful and deformed. She has a wonderful gift which she calls 'eversight' which enables her to see anything and everything that happened in the past in all places in the world. She scans this knowledge and picks out the parts needed for the New Beginning. I wish that I had this gift, but Mother

Sage is proud of the fact that I do not. She says that I am one of the rare people who have the higher kind of mind which is logical, and who have an inward focus of conscious attention so that they can reason. She says that my eversight is there, but is in a dark chamber of my consciousness, so that it does not distract me from my reasoning. She taught me mathematics from my earliest years in order to develop my inward thought and make me forget eversight. She says that eversight is a primitive kind of awareness that even plants and rocks and rivers possess. I asked her if the slaves have it, and she said, 'Of course,' very dismissively.

The slaves bring us paper for the books, and they take away paper with writing on which we have discarded when new information requires changes to be made. They use the other side of our scrap paper for their silly notes. I asked Mother Sage where the paper comes from. She told me that the slaves make it from plants which they grow in the gardens; the same kind of plants as those from which they get fibres to make the fabric for clothing. I was interested to know how this was done but Mother Sage said it was 'just craft work'. She says that I need not know about the slaves' work because it will be superseded by 'technology', which is a word she says with great reverence. When we have technology we will be able to use fire to melt down rocks to make tools and, in due course, we will have machines driven by fire. It is mainly the theory on which technology is based that Mother Sage scans the past for, and I have to write down.

I have had to work very hard recording all these important theories from the past; some are highly complicated, and so obscure that I wonder what use they can possibly be. To encourage me in the work, Mother Sage sometimes describes the technology itself, and the way people lived in those days. Mother Sage is very old and could die at any time. Without her eversight it would seem to me as if the slaves' way of providing for our needs was the only one possible; and the amazing advantages that could be brought about by technology would hardly occur to me in my wildest fancies. For instance, I might imagine how it would be to fly through the sky like a bird, but I would not know that it is possible to build a great container with wings in which hundreds of people are carried through the skies from one side of the world to the other. Indeed, without Mother Sage's knowledge I would not know that the world is a great globe without edges which we could travel round and round endlessly.

It seems to me that one of the greatest wonders of the ancient times was artificial light, whereby the activities of the day can be carried on during the night when the sun is lighting the other side of the world. Mother Sage says that even people as primitive as our slaves used to have artificial light, simply by setting fire to bits of wood or sticks of fat or dishes of oil. In the very beginning of the ancient times people captured fire from the wild, and then discovered how to make sparks of fire by rubbing rough surfaces together until they become hot enough to set dry vegetation alight. I asked Mother Sage why the slaves do not make artificial light in this way, and why we do not have it. She seemed disturbed by my question. She sank deep in thought for a while, and then she said that she would have to tell me more about the slaves' way of life, but not yet because it would distract me from our work on the New Beginning.

Mother Sage says that the New Beginning will bring an even better world than there was at the height of the technological age. This is because we shall be able to choose which technology to employ, whereas before no one knew what would be invented next and so technology was developed step by step as it happened, and some was crude and dirty until it was perfected or superseded. She says that we shall be able to avoid the injustice and suffering there was in the ancient days, which came about as an accidental result of the way the tasks of life were divided between people. Certain small groups of people acquired positions of power over big groups of others, and often these relationships were customary rather than functional. 'Exploitation' is the word she uses for this unfairness. I asked her if our use of the slaves is not exploitation. She was irritated at this, and told me that she had said she would tell me about the slaves later on, and not to concern myself about them.

Mother Sage and I worked on our books of the New Beginning for many years, all through my childhood until I was full grown. Our daily routine was to rise at dawn and, after a little food, Mother Sage was helped by her maidservant or myself to her special place at the top of our hill. She said that the view from there to the far horizon helped her eversight traverse the huge distances into the past. While she was at vigil I did my copying out from the day before. She was brought down at midday. We had our main meal at that time, and then Mother Sage would dictate to me what she had seen in the morning. She had taught me a special script for note-taking called 'shorthand'. At dusk we had

176

our last meal and then we went to bed.

There was much rewriting to do to organise the mathematical knowledge into various subjects, and we devised a complex indexing system so that we could connect the work together in other ways than its main sequence. The working sheets were kept in stiff paper folders, and there were neat little bone clips to hold the sheets together. The final writing out was onto big sheets folded double, which came in bundles of four. These had to be written with great care with newly-made reed pens, in which the tiny inner reed you press on to release the ink is springy, and allows fine lines to be made.

Mother Sage told me about the technology there used to be for the mechanical writing called typing and printing. There were machines which stored what you had written, in such a way that it could be corrected without visible alteration or being copied out again. Many copies could be produced of the same writing for different people to read. There were printed books available to everybody, in brightly coloured covers and with pictures inside. It certainly was a splendid time. Mother Sage is right to want to brings these wonders back. I often wished we could make a start with the writing machines.

We eventually reached a stage at which some of the subjects were sufficiently complete to be considered finished, although Mother Sage said it was not possible to record everything on any subject, although our particular area of knowledge, mathematics, is the easiest from that point of view, because mathematics is not a matter for opinion or selection, it just is, so when we had recorded it, it was done.

Mother Sage had me put all the bundles into a basket for the slaves to take down to the village, where someone would bind them into a volume. I was surprised, because I did not know that the slaves made books. I asked Mother Sage about this and she confirmed that they do not have any books. I thought she would need to explain to the slave how the binding was to be done, but she did not do so. A few days later, a slave I had not seen before brought the volume to us. The bundles had been stitched together into a single block between protective covers of some hard material with animal skin stretched over it. I was very impressed and I asked him how he had done it. He cocked his head on one side and smiled at me. Then he said, slowly and carefully, 'I followed the patterns of the doing of book binding.' Mother Sage then waved him away, and also waved away my question before I could ask it. This too was part of the telling about the slaves which would come in due course.

'I think that is all from my childhood,' Roy said. He rubbed his eyes and peered at the audience for signs of disapproval or suspicion. There were a few slightly puzzled looks, but no one said anything; they all looked ready for sleep. There was a flurry of activity as the fire was closely covered with green wood to keep it smouldering through the night. They lay down where they were, huddled in fur cloaks. Each kept to his personal space. Roy wished he could sneak away and snuggle up with his Fey, but before he had joined the trek it had been decided to segregate the sexes. There was talk of a mass wedding when they reached the new city, and then, he supposed, little houses would be built for couples and their children, just like in the ancient days. Roy's memory flashed back to the little girl in the first sleeping house he had shared in the village, and what she had done to him. There won't be anything like that, he thought, as he drifted off to sleep. His suppressed eversight took over as he dreamed, and gave him a glimpse of the ancient times.

At last I'm at the front of the queue. The uniformed official examines the scrap of paper which is meant to qualify me to get away from this place. He looks dubious. The extra code added by the official at the other desk, obtained from the devices he jabbed and peered at or spoke to, was supposed to be a confirmation of a confirmation of a firm reservation booked in full confidence another lifetime from here.

The official gestures me aside and reaches towards the next person in the queue. After examining his tatty slip meticulously, with a sigh as of disappointment he does some slow motion filling out and stamping, and then hands the person a crisp new slip of card. The recipient gives me a glance of smug commiseration. 'Bin here three days. Camped out there,' he says, gesturing towards the big glass doors beyond the first set of barriers and officials' booths. Outside are vehicles of all sizes, some proud and gleaming, disgorging fat important people, their luggage eagerly grabbed by would-be porters; others dusty wrecks dangling with tinsel and holy pictures. Makeshift habitations clutter the approach, beggars and trinket sellers with faces contorted by doleful or beaming encouragement.

I have been here less than a day, although the clocks go more slowly here than anywhere else in the world. Already encamped inside are heaps of brown people wrapped in copious reddish or dirty white garments, surrounded by skinny big-eyed children and bundles of cloth and string. Will they ever qualify to get out of here? Is this an appropriate route for those kind of people? Should they not be trudging along a dusty track somewhere? I look for the number of my escape route on a great black board currently cranking its information around. I spot it. A flashing indicator tells me it's now or never. I can feel my heart thudding with fear. How will I ever get away?

I can see the means of escape through some enormous windows. A bulging metal canister, sagging, monstrous and ridiculous with its little wings and minuscule wheels, sits in the blazing sun while attendant vehicles and tiny people meander lazily around it. More officials guard a stairway to the canister's bosom.

Looking at the monster my hope sinks deeper. This thing is supposed to fly! to lift into that diaphanous blue nothingness above? Impossible. The Laws of Science will not let it. I shall have to invent a new geometry, with an ideal quadric surface way over there in the hazy distance; so the massive monster can trundle away on its small wheels, reach the surface and be transformed instantly into a zipping mosquito which shoots across the globe until it meets the surface again and materialises massively on the further side. And I get out into the damp cool summer of home.

But not yet. I am on tiptoes, arms bent, fingers spread like a frog, poised for a leap through the glass barrier, if only it would melt away. I feel something on my buttock and look behind me. One of the dark, big-eyed urchins grins up. She pulls at my trousers. I step back automatically, breaking the suction against the glass. More eager hands manoeuvre me over to the heap of people on the floor. I allow myself to be drawn in. Stroking, rubbing, licking and nibbling drown my body in sensation. Innocent sensuality.

Fey's baby drowning in the pool; guiltless neglect. Are the children eating it? natural carnivores, chewing red flesh. Human animals at last; careless, dedicated to pleasure, giggling and burbling.

They were woken up at first light, as on every other morning of the trek, by the giggling and burbling of the people from the nearest village. They had brought a supply of food and a new joiner, with his Fey carrying his basket of books on her head.

The people were busy dividing the meat, herbs and fruit between the

179

groups. Each allocation was left in a basket a short distance away from each campfire. Roy crawled out of his cloak, stood up on stiff legs and stomped awkwardly over to the basket for his group. He mimed his thanks to the nearest villager, who bobbed and smiled back.

A suspicion which had been growing in Roy was confirmed as he lifted the basket. The amount of food being brought to them was not increasing as the numbers on the trek were increasing; if anything it was reducing. Early on, when the travellers were few, it had increased. A rather obvious reality was confronting them: there was a limit to the surplus that a village could supply for the travellers, especially in the winter, when the villagers were barely active in the shorter days, and ate frugally from their meagre stores. The trekkers were going to have to make do with less and less, or find some way of supplementing the donated food. They seemed to regard the provisions as their unquestionable right. He doubted if many of them even knew how to set a trap, let alone be able to tell edible berries or fungus from poisonous ones. Roy decided he should inform someone in authority, even at the risk of giving himself away.

The trekkers had devised a hierarchical leadership structure quite early in the journey; it had seemed the right thing to do. Roy's group of specialists had elected a leader who, so far, had had little to do apart from pass on contents lists and indexes for the collation process, although he was treated with deference and courted as if he had favours to award. Roy presumed that he was the one to approach with his concern over the food.

His name was Alfred, a geometry specialist, with an interest in cartography and astronomy. He was also something of an athlete, one of the few to have trained for the trek. He was a conspicuous figure, often loping ahead, counting his even strides, making detours on either side, and then sitting cross-legged to add to his maps and notes until the rest caught up. Each evening when the sky was clear he spent some time away from the smoky fire, squinting at the heavens and making maps of the most noticeable bodies. His only instrument was a wooden compass. He had already sought out a glass-making technologist, and had handed over his specification for a telescope. He had designed an observatory which he wanted constructed when they got to the city. He was certainly one of the most committed to the New Beginning, whose purpose, he declared, was to bring about the space exploration and colonisation which the ancient technological civilisation had failed to achieve before it collapsed. Roy was nervous of him. But if Alfred wanted all his ambitious plans fulfilled, the travellers had at least to reach their destination, so he should be interested in any problem which came up.

Alfred was exercising when Roy approached him. Roy waited until he was noticed, and then held out the basket.

'Alfred, excuse me disturbing you, but I think we may have a problem with the food,' Roy blurted out.

'What's wrong with the food?' the group leader asked, peering into the basket as he jogged on the spot.

'Oh, there's nothing wrong with it, it's just that they're not bringing more of it as new people join, so we're getting less and less each. Not enough to notice so far. I can tell though by the weight of the basket; and it stands to reason the villages have only so much they can spare us, especially now that winter's coming.'

'Hmm,' said Alfred. 'Looks like enough to me. But if you're right, we'll just have to tell them to bring more.'

'But —' Roy protested tentatively. Just then one of Alfred's cronies jogged up and jerked his thumb to suggest they have a run together, and Alfred went off with him.

Roy was even more worried now. He decided to try the only other way he knew to get something done. After breakfast he went to look for his Fey. He knew where she would be: with the villagers. He found them all, humming and nuzzling together. He drew Fey aside and told her his concern. She shrugged and smiled, then went back to the villagers and a rapid miming discussion took place. She turned around and waved cheerily to him. Roy went back to his group to be ready for the day's journey.

Breaking camp was easy. The men simply decided by the feel and look of the atmosphere whether to wear their cloaks or have them carried. Then, taking nothing but their basketwork water bottles, they formed a column and started walking. The Feys rolled up any cloaks left behind, picked up the books and papers, and packed them into baskets. They cleared away any unburnt wood and food remains and took them off the road into the forest. Then they lifted the baskets onto their heads and formed their own cheerful little mob following on behind.

The route, so far, had been along the cleared passage which Roy still thought of as the second firebreak. It curved gently to skirt a steep forested slope which, in the early morning, cast a deep chilly shade over

181

the grassy track. On the other side of the road was a strip clear felled, with stumps of young trees still visible above the grass, and then young trees standing, scarcely a man's height tall. Beyond that the forest canopy billowed, sunlit grey-green, drifting with morning mist.

The marchers came to a ford over a stream, swollen by recent rain, an opportunity to wash and fill water bottles. The routine, sanctified by many repetitions, was for the women to get into a huddle some distance away while the men undressed, floated their clothes across in baskets to the opposite bank of the stream, and swam or gave themselves a hasty rub down in the chilly water. Afterwards they dressed, filled their water bottles and marched on. Then it was the women's turn: to bathe, pick up the luggage and dash to catch up.

There was a purposefulness about the march which seemed to discourage conversation along the way. As Roy walked he tried to avoid worrying about his own role in the venture, deliberately concentrating on enjoying the experience and the surroundings. He thought about his dream of the night before; its message seemed to be that there is pleasure where you are, and you ought not to strive to be somewhere else. He was feeling relaxed, and happier than he had been since he had joined the march, when someone came up beside him, panting slightly from the effort to catch up.

'Hello there!' the man greeted him. 'I'm Peter from the theology group. We're trying to get to know everybody, and spread the word around.'

Roy would have preferred to continue enjoying his relaxed mood, but he smiled at Peter and said, 'Hello, I'm Roy, classical maths. What's theology? Not one of the branches of knowledge I've heard of.'

'Oh dear, not another one!' Peter's face contorted with surprise and disapproval. 'We study the word of God as revealed in the scriptures. Before we came together for this great journey we recorded the words of the holy Bible itself, and the coincidence of our writings is remarkable.'

'It seems a bit of a waste for you all to have come up with the same knowledge. That's happened with maths too though. It's a pity really there wasn't some coordinated guidance right at the beginning.'

'Of course there was guidance, from God himself,' Peter declaimed.

'Who is God?' Roy felt obliged to ask, inwardly reeling at Peter's disdainful look which suddenly metamorphosed into a smile of glowing beneficence.

182

'There is much saving work to be done,' Peter beamed. 'But do not despair. We will come amongst you and you will hear all that you need to hear.' Then Peter interrupted himself to answer Roy's question. 'God is the Creator of the universe. Has it never occurred to you what a mystery it all is, and to wonder who made it, and for what purpose?'

Roy had his own ideas about what made the universe, but they were in the area he felt he had to keep quiet about. Putting that aside, he thought about what Peter had said. What a strange idea: that some one – *person*, would it be? – had *made* the universe, like you make a basket or a pen. What would this creator make the universe out of? And how would he have created that? And who created the creator? There was no rationality in these ideas. In the end he just shrugged.

Peter looked at him thoughtfully. 'I think I'd like to spend some time with your group,' he said.

'You'd better talk to Alfred, our leader,' Roy replied. 'Do you know him?' Peter shook his head. 'Runs about a lot, makes maps, looks at the stars. You're in luck, there he is, sitting by the side of the road just up ahead.' Peter trotted off. As Roy passed them he saw Alfred nodding up at Peter. Well, it would make a change from maths.

As dusk drew near, the marchers could see a cluster of people on the road ahead. It was the usual group from the next village along the way. Their part in the venture had been so reliable it was now taken for granted. The men apparently assumed that all the villages were, conveniently for the provisioning of the trek, a day's brisk march apart. Roy doubted that, not least because a day's walk was a different distance in the dry of summer from in the winter. Alfred's maps were dotted with village positions, all at some fixed distance perpendicular to the camping locations, but he had not visited even one of them since he had left his own. There were no paths from the road to the villages, but Roy knew that village people took care to take different routes when they came to do any clearing and wood harvesting. The reason was probably to avoid any territorial impact on the wide band of wilderness, whose integrity they respected.

Baskets of provisions were handed out as usual. But then, instead of getting into a sleeping huddle to be there to hand out the morning meal, the villagers melted back into the forest. They left behind them the provisions baskets, and a considerable number of basket traps. None of the men, apart from Roy, seemed to notice. Once they were facing their

183

camp fires the rest of the universe disappeared; everything that mattered was inside their heads. It was time for the lectures and story-telling to resume.

The group leaders were now beginning to organise some cross fertilisation of knowledge between the groups. Their own group was made up of what Alfred called 'classical mathematicians'. Their knowledge was in use during the most extensive period of the ancient times which Alfred now referred to, in the current jargon, as *necrotech*, from the culture's dependence on burning dead organic matter for energy to supplement muscle power. Their expertise was in demand from the technology groups, and two of the group were away giving lectures elsewhere.

Alfred had invited a mathematician called Jasper to talk to the rest of the group about something new to them called 'fractal geometry'. Jasper was an expert in developments in geometry from late necrotech, when the collapse was imminent. He had some meticulous drawings he had made of a shape he called a Sierpinski triangle and the effects of various geometric transformations. Roy noticed how grubby the drawings were getting from being handed around camp fires and being pointed at by sooty fingers. Jasper talked about his plans for having a computer built as soon as they reached the new city, and the patterns he would be able to create with it. As an example, he showed them some ferns he had picked up and showed how fractal-like they were, with individual fronds resembling the whole leaf.

A lively discussion ensued, in which they argued whether nature was *explained* by this geometry or merely imitated, and to what extent useful models could be made of fractal-like forms in the world, such as cloud formations. Could predictions be made from such models? Jasper explained that a distinction had been made between random irregular forms which occurred in nature, and non-random irregular forms which could be produced geometrically. The geometry had been used to make approximations to natural patterns; there was in theory no limit to how closely nature could be modelled, but that there would always be a difference, which could have unpredictable effects.

So far Peter, who Roy noticed had joined their group, had not contributed to the discussion. Probably he was out of his depth, his specialty being nothing to do with maths. But Peter came in at this point.

'What you are saying is that we can never completely penetrate the full mystery of Creation. God's work will always be beyond our understanding.'

Quite a number of the mathematicians were interested in the God ideas, some sympathetic and others highly critical. The discussion became an argument about whether fractal geometry provided insights into how God had created the world, or showed that creation was inherent in the world, so a creator was unnecessary, which was Roy's own view. In fact he had been very excited by Jasper's geometry, as it was consistent with what he had learned of Mother Sage's own theories about patterns in the world.

Roy had meant to keep out of the discussion, in case he said too much and provoked suspicion. But then found himself blurting out, 'Does it matter whether God made the universe or whether it made itself?'

'Of course it matters!' said Peter, in an astonished tone. 'Without God there would be no morality. Holy scripture has given us the Commandments which tell us how to live righteously. They have told us we should love God and our parents, and not kill, or be promiscuous, or steal, or lie. Without the Commandments we would behave like animals.'

'I don't agree,' said Richard, one of those who had argued against the God ideas. 'I know right from wrong without reading the Bible, or listening to theologians.'

Roy had a view on this, and could not resist voicing it. 'What is right or wrong isn't absolute; it depends on the power structures of society. It's only wrong to steal when there is private property. If everybody can help themselves to anything they want, there's no such thing as stealing.'

'You couldn't have a society without property,' said Peter. 'As I said, people would behave like animals: greedy, selfish, uncontrolled. And anyway, the Commandment not to kill must be absolute. Obviously it's always wrong to kill another person,' Peter's voice rang with confidence.

Roy was not going to risk saying what he thought about this; it would not do him any good. No one else said anything, apparently conceding Peter's point.

At this point Alfred thanked Jasper for his fascinating talk. He then declared it was story time, and invited Jasper to stay. He also announced his decision as group leader that they were to reverse the order of

185

telling. Roy, having been the last before, now had to continue his account from where he had left off the previous night. This increased his anxiety. It was a curious decision; Alfred's suspicions must be growing, and Roy's fear returned of the other men's disapproval of what they might regard as his betrayal of the cause. Perhaps he should lie: tell some innocuous story similar to theirs. But he was almost bound to give away the fact that he had actually been a villager – as he probably already had with his concern over the food. So this could be his only chance to influence any of them. He must take it. Even these few men could make a difference if they were persuaded by what he had to tell them. If only his book had not been lost! In any case he might not get as far as what he called his 'realisation' in this part of the telling. Then it would be several nights before his turn came around again. He had no choice but to go on with his story.

10

The Feys

Although the routine of the days did not change over all those years, the pace gradually altered due to Mother Sage becoming more and more frail. When I was a young boy, she needed only someone's arm and her stick to lean on to help her up the hill. In the last years her maidservant and I used to carry her in her basket chair. At that stage the amount of information she brought back for me to note down was much less than it used to be, and I suspected that, since she could not have exhausted all there was to be seen, she was simply sleeping through much of her time of vigil.

Having less to do in the mornings, and Mother Sage never having got around to telling me about the slaves, I suppose it was inevitable that I started taking an interest in the maidservant, who was the one slave I could observe closely, since, with Mother Sage way up the hill, she usually sat near me doing mending or making things. And because I was in the habit of spending my time writing, I took to jotting down notes of what the maidservant said and did. In this way, the writing that I think of as my own book started to build up.

Over the years Mother Sage has had a succession of maidservants. Each of them has been called Fey – every one of them. I was unsure whether Fey was another word for maidservant or a personal name. When it occurred to me to ask her, Mother Sage told me it was a name, but she clearly was not interested in talking about why they all had the same name. I asked the current Fey why all the maidservants have had the same name. She told me that none of them has any name: the slaves do not use personal names; Fey is just the name Mother Sage has given them. I was surprised, and I mentioned to Mother Sage what Fey had said as we ate our afternoon meal together.

She took my question as an opportunity to remind me what primitive people they are: 'Like animals,' she says, not having personal names or naming things around them. They have no regard for individuality, no personal ambitions and no idea of ownership or control. They just mill around doing what their kind has done for countless generations: tend their gardens, make simple things out of some of the materials, keep the firebreaks clear and trap animals. They all sleep together in a heap, fondle each other and giggle all the time. 'They're called "Fey" because they are fated to die young,' she said, and certainly the only old person I've seen is Mother Sage herself.

Next day, I told Fey what Mother Sage had said about her name, and she laughed. Of course, they laugh at everything. But I asked her why she laughed at being given a name which meant she would die young. She said she hoped she would die young, that it was better to 'go to the forest' than to be old and ugly and suffer pain and be weak and useless and lose her teeth and be unable to chew fresh meat. And anyway she would still be here. I think this was the most I had heard her say all at once. She was obviously sincere. Such a strange people; they intrigue me more and more.

Sitting with the Feys, I had observed them engaged at the crafts which Mother Sage despised so much. I had to ask Mother Sage what the tasks and tools were called in the ancient language. When she told me the words, she said yet again that technology would do such work better and faster. But I enjoyed watching the Feys' nimble fingers. They used to spin thread with distaff and spindle, knit parts of garments in multicoloured designs with the wooden needles clicking and jerking, or they would weave or coil baskets of various shapes and sizes.

Beginning to write my own book gave me the incentive to investigate the current Fey's craft work in detail. I felt that, whatever Mother Sage said, these crafts could be part of the New Beginning, along with the technology from the ancient times. So I asked Fey questions about the work she brought with her each day, such as how the fibre she was spinning was extracted from the plants, how the thread was dyed, how she chose the designs for the knitted pieces, or what the sealant was made from that I had seen inside some of the finished baskets. Whatever I asked, and however I phrased the questions, I never got a satisfactory answer. She knew the ancient speech, so she understood each of my words but somehow she did not see what it was I wanted. Willing to please, she would give me whatever I named: the piece of work in her hands, or something fetched from our house or even from the village.

On one occasion my question was about ink. Having tried fetching me a fresh little basket pot of ink, and seeing that this did not satisfy me, she started off for the village, then she stopped and beckoned me to follow her. I had been to the village before – not frequently because Mother Sage had always discouraged it – but I was curious so I followed. When I saw where Fey was taking me, I thought it was a real breakthrough: that she had understood what I wanted to know, because she led me towards a slave who was engaged in making ink. He was mixing various dark-coloured substances with water and filtering the mixture through a fine cloth set inside a basketwork funnel whose spout led into a larger version of the small basket bottles I was used to. I encountered the same problem as I had with Fey when I asked him questions: he could not or would not explain anything. After this episode I went to the village quite often to observe the slaves at their work, and to learn more that way. I then found that the ink makers use the juices crushed out of crinkly brown nuts mixed with a black substance from strange lumps which insects make on a certain tree and a gum obtained from the bark of another tree.

At the time I did not think of this independent activity as any sort of rebellion against Mother Sage. It had never seemed that she ruled my thoughts and actions, although I suppose she did, as anyone bringing up a child must do, even if they do not intend it to be that way.

However, now I was thinking for myself, purposefully with my own book in mind, I began to question certain things. My main question concerned the New Beginning: when was it going to change from information to action? Mother Sage was ancient and frail, and might not live much longer. Without her the ancient memories would vanish. Who besides myself was going to be involved? Of course, I sought a suitable opportunity and asked her. She said that the boys like myself from all the villages would gather for a great march to the place for building the new city. She also said that in due course I would have sons to carry on the work of bringing back civilisation. I asked her whom I would marry, since she had told me of the custom from the ancient days of a man and a woman joining for life for sexual activity and parenting. She said I could marry one of the slave women, which surprised me in view of her low opinion of them. Then she remarked that I would have to pick a very young one because they were so promiscuous that otherwise my chosen bride might be already pregnant with some other man's child and, being a lord, I should have my own sons. Then she became too tired to talk any more, and instructed Fey to help her to bed.

After this conversation I began to look at Fey in a new way. She was young and pretty and smiled a lot, and she seemed to want to please me. I flattered myself that her willingness was more than the eager servitude which the slaves generally showed. It seemed to me that my project of recording the craft skills was a way of pursuing a promising intimacy. She was, I felt, particularly eager to satisfy my curiosity about the crafts now that the episode with the ink had shown her a satisfactory way of responding to my questions: she simply took me to someone who was making whatever I named, so we had many pleasant walks up and down the avenue.

Mainly in order to prolong what I thought was a deepening relationship with Fey, I decided to go through the various types of craft methodically, starting with baskets, which were a major component of the slave people's culture. I brought each type of basket in turn to her, and she duly took me to someone making one, sometimes that day, but more often some days later, presumably because she knew somehow which kinds were going to be made. Interestingly, in view of her lack of comprehension earlier, she never forgot a request, and was able to keep a queue of them in her mind.

Then a new breakthrough in our communication came about. One day, to my surprise and delight, Fey responded differently from before. She took the basket I handed her and mimed the actions of making it, glancing up at me and asking by her expression whether I was following. It seemed that she had at last understood that I had been seeking information from her, when at first she had seemed not to understand the very concept of information. After a while I realised that the miming was, in effect, part of the slave language, and that I understood it. She mimed the actions of making and using the baskets, and she also conveyed something of the experience and consciousness of the people whose way of life involved baskets in so many ways. One important insight was that the slaves do not teach the crafts to their children; they do not need to because the children have eversight, which enables them to copy the actions of all those who have carried out a craft in the past. I remembered then what the book binder had said about following the patterns of the binding of books.

I did not have eversight, but I could record what I had learned. I duly made notes of the basket craft. Those which were containers of liquids and drinking vessels had to be woven finely and close. Some would hold liquid simply by the strands swelling tightly together when wet.

190

Others were sealed: some with river mud first and then some sort of tree sap, wax or other substance produced by insects, sometimes warmed in the sun; others were lined with leather or animal bladder. Looser woven baskets were used to carry and store food from the gardens, as fish and animal traps, and as baby carriers. Fey also explained the construction of the basketwork furniture which we had in our house, and the window lattices and doors and the matting on the floors.

As our mutual understanding grew, I thought about what Mother Sage had said about taking a wife. I knew that in the ancient days marriage arrangements varied between cultures. In some cultures marriage was a liaison between families, in others the partners chose to marry for feelings of sexual attraction and compatibility of personality or interests. I certainly liked Fey's company, and I started thinking about having sexual intercourse with her: something I had no experience of. I remembered Mother Sage telling me that the slaves were promiscuous but this did not cause me to think less of her. I told myself that since she would probably be sexually experienced, I could approach her with sexual overtures and she would know what to do.

So one morning when we were sitting together, I stopped my writing, put my pen down, stood up and walked over to her and, perhaps rather clumsily, bent down and put my arms around her and my cheek next to hers.

To my surprise and dismay, she cried out in alarm and distress; she pushed me away, stood up and ran off up the hill towards Mother Sage's vigil place. I had been brought up to be dignified so I did not run after her, and I waited in some confusion and anxiety to see what would happen next.

While I waited my thoughts were in a turmoil. This seemed to me to be the first time in my life when anyone had denied me something I really wanted. I suppose that my wants had been manipulated. Always having been told I was privileged, I did not see the behaviour that was expected of me as restrictive. I had seen the slave children tumble together in their play, but since I had a life apart, high on the hill in the big house, I did not desire the physical contact they had with each other. I had sometimes seen the behaviour which Mother Sage called 'promiscuous', in which people of all ages fondled each other on the sensitive parts of their bodies, to their obvious mutual enjoyment. But I had been told that civilised people reserved such contact for the marriage bed, so I did not regard it as something I was not allowed, but

191

as something I chose not to indulge in until the proper time and circumstances. Now I saw my situation in another light. Anyone in the village was free to fondle Fey, and I, the great lord from the grand house on the hill, was the only one who was not allowed to.

I waited and fretted all that morning while the sun moved until it reached its greatest height in the sky. This was the time Fey and I usually went to the top of the hill to carry Mother Sage down in her basket chair, so I decided to walk up there. But I found that I was not needed because Fey and another young woman were in attendance and Mother Sage waved me away. I followed them down the hill. When they reached the house and had put the chair down on the veranda, Fey dashed away towards the village, and Mother Sage introduced me to the new Fey.

Suddenly the thoughts of the morning coalesced into a wave of emotions that I had hardly known before; a rush of anger, a flush of embarrassment, but mostly confusion: should I run after Fey; should I demand her return? So I did nothing but stand woodenly, staring in disbelief at Mother Sage; my wise, gentle teacher and guardian, who should not have let this happen.

'Sit down here, Roy,' said Mother Sage gently. 'We need to talk.'

Her words broke my paralysis. 'I don't want to sit down and talk. I want Fey to come back.' I strode towards the avenue which led to the village and shouted out, 'Fey, Fey, come back here! I order you to return.'

'Roy, don't do that. Come here and let me explain.'

I ignored her. I could see Fey still running away. I strode back towards the house where I could see the new Fey disappearing round the back to the servants huts.

'You there! Go after Fey. Fetch her back.'

The new Fey turned and made some miming movements towards Mother Sage. To my astonishment, because I had never in my life seen her use slave language before, Mother Sage mimed a reply. The new Fey turned away and disappeared.

I almost ran down the avenue, but my knees suddenly felt weak. I sank to the ground and began to sob hysterically.

Mother Sage just let me cry. I stopped after a while, got to my feet, and sat down in the chair beside her.

'All right, tell me whatever you have to tell me. I'll listen. But I liked Fey, she was my friend. I didn't mean her any harm. I just wanted —

192

Why can't I have what I want any more? What's happening?' I almost started to cry again.

'Hush, I know,' said Mother Sage soothingly. 'Fey can come back if she wants to, and if you still want her when you understand things better. You may not feel that she is a suitable partner for you – she is expecting a child – I have told you about that problem. But we'll talk about that later. You have to know the truth, and part of it is that you cannot order the people around any longer. I thought you were already beginning to realise that they are not really our slaves – I told you what slavery meant in the ancient times. Making you think they were slaves was part of the environment we provided for you so that you could grow up.

'Sometimes it is necessary to deceive children for their own good; this was often done in the ancient days. I had to encourage you to despise the slaves to convince you that you are superior to the slaves when, in fact, you are just *different*. And of course they have some special powers that you lack, which could make you feel you were inferior to them – and in a way you are.'

She spoke gently, but her words hurt me, made me feel small and pathetic. 'You mean eversight?' I croaked.

'Yes, partly. I told you that eversight is a primitive kind of awareness that all things have, and that is true. I encouraged you to think that your kind of consciousness is superior to eversight. That is not true. Yours is a restricted consciousness, which shuts out eversight. It is a 'handicap', to use the ancient term for something which reduces someone's abilities.'

'Then why did you tell me all those lies?' I burst out. 'Was it some sort of experiment? What about the New Beginning? Is that a lie too?'

Mother Sage shook her head. 'No! But — Yes, maybe it is an experiment - but because we want to help. When you were a little boy, it was decided to try to raise the children like you - for the firesoul completion, which we decided to call the "New Beginning". Very few of your kind are born. They are oddities; they don't fit in. My people are very casual about raising children anyway, so any that need special help usually fade away and die before they are full grown. Shall I tell you how it happened that I became your Mother Sage; would that help? This part is my own story.' She looked at me with what must have been love and concern, but I saw it as pity.

I looked back at her, but my thoughts were directed inwards, warily prowling around what was happening to my identity. I shook my head and shuddered. Trying to escape I looked away: down the hill where Fey had run, then over to the arbour where we had been sitting that morning and her abandoned basketwork, up to my bedroom with its balcony over the veranda where we sat. That was where I needed to be: in my bed, under the covers, where I could make a cocoon for myself for a while, and then see what emerged.

'I just need to think for a bit,' I said huskily. 'Have me some fruit and cordial sent up.' It was the last command I ever issued.

When I woke up from a dream-ridden sleep it was pitch dark night. I must have brooded under my covers, dozed off, and then slept during the entire afternoon and long summer evening. I got up and went out to the balcony. Though I knew the layout of the room intimately, it was strange to trust my memory rather than my sight. It had been a cloudy day, and now no moon and stars were visible. The utter darkness felt appropriate to my still-confused mood. 'Who am I?' I asked the darkness. And it seemed that the darkness answered. 'You are firesoul,' it said. 'You have a burning flame within you which makes everything beyond the moment dark as night, consumed and forgotten.'

'The slave people, the village people, what are they then, how are they different from me?' I asked.

'They are watersoul,' the darkness replied. 'Their soul flows everywhere for all time so that there is no time, other than where patterns grow to completion.'

'I do not understand,' I muttered.

'You will,' it told me.

'I must ask Mother Sage,' I said.

'Mother Sage is dead,' the darkness sighed.

Guilt! Another new emotion assaulting me. I had not let Mother Sage tell me her story. I rushed out of the room, down the stairs, stumbling around the turns of its helix and jarring my ankle as I misjudged the bottom, and then out of the door. I knew somehow that she would still be where I had left her. The basket chair. And in it a little cold figure, like a fallen nestling, so tiny in its aged shrunkenness.

I knelt and put my head in her lap. 'Tell me your story, Mother,' I begged. And my tears began to pour, and shuddering sobs racked my body.

The next morning I woke up in my bed to the sound of heavy rain

194

falling and pouring down off the thatch. The shell chimes outside my door were jingled and the new Fey came in with a tray. I sat up and she put it in front of me and backed away smiling. On it was the usual plate of fruit and meat and a jug of cordial and a mug. I noticed with irritation that the meat was fresh. I had not had the chance to explain that I much preferred the dried meat; it was more tasty because of the herbs and spices which were rubbed in before it was hung up to dry. I did not mind fresh fish, but fresh meat from trapped mammals had a slimy chewiness which made me retch. Mother Sage told me that in the ancient times people used to cook meat on a fire, which softened it and gave it a bitter carbon taste which people liked. I tried this once, not meat from a cooking fire, but charred meat left after a forest fire. I did not really like that much better.

I was hungry because I had missed two meals the day before, so I ate all the food, even the meat, which was worse than I'd remembered from trying it before, as it was tough and stringy.

After I had finished an awful thought came to me. 'They wouldn't, would they!' I said aloud. But I had a feeling that my suspicion was right. My stomach began to heave. And then I thought, 'Well, after all, why not? She's gone from her body. Pity to waste meat that no one needs to catch. Perhaps it's an honour. No, somehow I don't think they know about honour.'

I got up then. On the way to the stream to wash myself I stepped across the veranda. I did not look at the basket chair because I knew she would not be there. But when I got back I sat in it, naked and wet from my bath, and I gazed out through the curtain of rain at the blurred trees and grey sky. Then Mother Sage told me her story.

Roy, my darling little king – the name Roy means 'king', did I ever tell you that? Our life together has been such an adventure. Although I did not give birth to you, I gave you a life you would not have had, and you gave me a second life in return. I am so grateful to you for the sense of wonder you gave me. Curiosity is a delightful feeling. Through you I learned how to peep at the world, and to discover knowledge little by little, and to store it away in secret caches of the mind. I caught a little bit of firesoul from your flame, I think.

I had a full life before as watersoul. Can you imagine how it would be to know yourself as an immortal pattern, as a turn of a cycle, as hugely insignificant, with a universal wisdom awesome in its usualness? Oh dear, I am playing with words, aren't I. More simply, I knew everything just as everything else knows everything. Except for you funny lumps of firesoul nature, that is. You are different. You are arrogant and ignorant, although you don't know it, and you can be so charming. All other beings are all-wise and humble, which could make them seem dull and predictable, I suppose, to people like you anyway. There, I am making judgements every bit as sweeping as if I were firesoul. Watersoul do not assign values; they have no notion of good or bad, or right or wrong, or better or worse; well, perhaps they do in the sense of what is more or less practical or pleasurable, but they have no idea of ethics; they just do as they please. But by becoming partly firesoul, I picked up the habit of judging and evaluating.

In my first life, like all watersoul I was blissfully happy; happy as a fish or a patch of moss or a star. And I was happy when I felt my time had come to an end; that my pattern, this fragment of the human pattern, was completed.

I went to the forest. You have heard the phrase. It is the customary way to death in our village to wander into the deep forest up beyond the second firebreak. It is a reconnection with wilderness. Death then comes, perhaps from a cat or a wolf, perhaps starvation or infection or a poisonous bite or an injury such as a broken limb. It is a last adventure, and eagerly anticipated by all of us.

I awoke knowing that the day had come. I felt the warm bodies of my sleeping companions and we shared some pleasure rubbing. Then I started out on my journey. I walked slowly, weaving a path through the spiral herb beds near our group sleeping-hut, around the orchards, stroking the trees and bushes, taking in the heady scent of blossom, seeing the petals fall and the fruits swell, to be picked and eaten or stored, the leaves falling and the winter sleep coming and the cycle going ever round. Seeing the pattern complete and clear: all the stages present but not confused, was evidence, had I needed it, that my time was almost over.

Then I reached the outer garden, where woody plants for building grow. The pattern is calmer here, generations of young trees slowly growing from seeds spread by their mothers, some carried by birds or buried by small animals. The trees are cut when thumb and finger can just meet around the trunk; sooner than that for those at the edge of the first firebreak, where strips of saplings are cleared whenever it is necessary to re-weave a wall of the storage room beneath a sleeping hut:

196

an important task, since we need provisions for the winter and we must keep raiding animals out. These careful patterns of village life are my soul.

I stepped out of the wood into the wide strip of the firebreak. Here we keep new growth cut close to the ground and grass springs up to cover the earth. Watersoul people have no use for grass. We cannot eat it. We enslave no animals who can. We pick out every blade from the gardens so that valued herbs may thrive. And yet, when we come here, the carpet of grass under our feet rings with the shrill tones of the very beginnings of humanity; co-evolutes of one pattern: hominids, fire, burning forests, grassland, grazing beasts, a tide of transformation echoing down the ages until the fragile uniformity of grass and cattle dragged out the tough tangles of wilderness to fly away in the purging storms which extinguished fire in the souls of men. Cocooned in a worm of life, humanity emerged feminine and watersouled, shunning fire for fear of the pattern returning.

Shuddering at the memory, I walked quickly across the green carpet towards the near forest, eager for the scents and the heady atmosphere of untamed wilderness. I was about to plunge inside, to begin my final adventure, when a strong tug at my clothing jerked me back into the firebreak and my senses back into my lifetime.

A boy had wandered after me, one of the strange lonely little boys who are occasionally born. He had been drawn by an event which I had not noticed, since it was a regular occurrence and part of the patterns. There was a wildfire approaching. Together the boy and I watched the fire sweep across the near forest, its flames licking towards us over the bare firebreak, scorching the green carpet, but finding nothing more substantial to carry it across to our woodland. It might have brought me my death; instead it brought me a new life.

The boy tugged at my skirt, frightened and yet thrilled. Seeing the fire reflected in his excited eyes, I suddenly connected with an ancient human pattern: I found myself looking into a soul quite unlike my own, and I saw why these children are so lost and lonely amongst us. His soul was like the fire which blazes in the moment, its past consumed and black, straining towards its future where there would be fuel for its flames. I felt the heady freedom of an awareness of the potential in the future; the illusion of unrestricted choice and self determination, seemingly unhindered by resonance with patterns already formed. I wondered what the child could become if he were helped to develop his own nature. Could there be a new beginning for his kind? Were these children born because the firesoul pattern is not yet completed?

Soon the fire had passed us, leaving behind smouldering stumps and the bitter stench of woodsmoke. I looked down at the boy. He was staring after the crackling flames and thick curtain of smoke fast disappearing into the distance. I crouched down to his level. 'Wasn't that exciting!' I said. 'What shall we do now?' I had no idea what this meeting, and my glimpse into the boy's soul, was going to mean, but it was clear that my life was not after all to end, but was entering a new phase.

I took his – your – hand, and we went back to the village. That night I took you into my sleeping hut. Later I learned by eversight that what had happened was not an isolated incident, but part of a new pattern of which others were a part. There was a wave of incidents, similar to our meeting at the firebreak, over many villages, perhaps all over the world. Firesoul children were to be raised because their pattern was not completed. Their upbringing was to be modelled on patterns from the past. In particular, the unequal social division which was almost universal in ancient times was to be simulated, by watersoul people acting as slaves so that the firesoul boys could be lords. No authority had dictated what should be done, apart from the need of the firesoul pattern for completion, which is ultimately irresistible, overcoming even watersoul dread of the destructive power of fire in men's hands. We would facilitate, but not participate in, the New Beginning for the firesouls who had not completed.

Through eversight, the guardians discussed how to bring up the firesoul boys. You had to have special houses, village huts would not be suitable for you. Ours would be built half way up the big hill, some way away from the village in the setting sun direction.

Dramatic though the firesoul reawakening was, with its profound effect on our two lives, and on others like us in other villages, once the house was built life soon settled down to a routine little different from before. You will find a record of my part of our task in the big basket in my sleeping room. The experiences and ideas of a watersoul attempting to think like a firesoul may prove to be of value in the great venture ahead of you. My task is done, my foundling child and young lord, and, if the deceit necessary causes you to blame me, my confession is made.

Was it through eversight that Mother Sage told me her story? It all arrived in a flash of time. I was still wet from bathing at the conclusion, still staring at the curtain of rain, my identity and self-worth confirmed but profoundly altered. It seemed that I mattered, but what was I?

I went up to Mother Sage's room and found the basket with her writing in it. The top page was written in very shaky script, unlike her usual neat hand. The first line read, 'I must tell Roy about eversight.' I read the page.

'We invented the ancient language word *eversight* for the watersoul consciousness so that the firesoul boys would think of it as some especially keen sense, like the vision of a bird of prey, perhaps, which you would not envy particularly. But eversight is not a sense, it is a consciousness: a connectedness with the universe, a seamless flowing.

'I allowed you to imagine what I did during my vigils as reading some kind of history book or record of memories, set out in chronological order; but the universe is not as you conceive it. There is no dominant linear order: no time line. The past has no time; it is not really past at all; watersoul know it as all still present, as it was when it happened, although it is hidden from those with firesoul consciousness. The order that is there is pattern, not succession.

'What I had to do to obtain the ancient knowledge needed for your development was to shift my consciousness into that of various people who were alive at that time, and experience their lives in order to share their knowledge and understanding. I had to tune into the patterns of human experience of those ages, but this was difficult because the patterns are weak. The cycles were extenuated by the perpetual change people called *progress*, and then they were interrupted by the collapse, and their immediacy was lost. But for your sake I made myself seek out those patterns, so that you would have a way of being to tune into, and be able to develop your firesoul nature. And gradually I learned to think as you do, and then the search for ancient knowledge became easier. All the other Mother Sages were doing the same, and the pattern grew dense and the path became broad and clear.

'You asked me once why the women who tended me were called Fey. Just as in our time of the watersouls, firesouls are sometimes born, so in the time of firesouls, there were a few people with watersoul and the wisdom it brings. But they were regarded with suspicion by your kind, who were dominant, and many were cruelly persecuted; they were

199

called "witches". By those who were more tolerant, their strangeness was sometimes called "fey", which is why we chose to that as a name for you to use of our kind.

'A few years ago I came across a woman from the end of the ancient period who had something of this strangeness called fey. She was also a mathematician. Without telling you of it, for fear of confusing you, I have been recording her work, which she called "pattern mathematics" – when you thought I was dozing. It is all written down. It may have been a mistake to keep it from you; there may be a special role for you, which will become known to you in due course, for which this knowledge will be useful. But I do not know for sure; I cannot see ahead, and my time has already been overextended.'

Roy paused, knowing that he had said more than enough. Even so he had not arrived at the point in his story when he had experienced the change of heart he called his 'realisation'.

'I think I'll stop there,' he said. 'Does anyone want to ask me anything about what happened?' It was not really a question. Everyone round the campfire had tense, 'I've got something to say', postures.

11

Explaining Pattern

'I've got a question,' said Henry, a number theorist, a dark, slight young man, always quietly spoken and amiable. 'About this *watersoul* and *firesoul* stuff. That's new to me and I don't much like the sound of it.' He looked around. The others visibly relaxed: that was their concern too. Roy felt somewhat relieved that Henry had got in first.

'You seem to have had rather more contact with the slave people than the rest of us, especially during the period you've just been describing. At one point you mentioned incorporating the slaves' so-called "craft skills" into the New Beginning. Personally I can hardly wait for china and glass: clean and elegant things, instead of all that grubby rustic stuff.' His voice was jocular. The others laughed, muttered and murmured in agreement, and Roy felt himself isolated as a person with peculiar ideas.

Henry went on, and his voice rose to a higher pitch. 'In the last part of the story, I got the impression that you have accepted this notion that we – the *firesoul boys*, as you call us – have a mental handicap as compared with the *watersoul*, as you call the slaves.' There was an audible in-breath from the audience, and a corporate rising up as all their spines stiffened. 'Now, taking that just a little bit further, I can see you coming to the conclusion that the New Beginning shouldn't happen at all, that it would be a threat to the lovely life of the watersouls, that we'd devastate the planet all over again. What do you say to that?' His voice had become high and rapid as it built up to the challenge which Roy had been dreading. A loud rumble of agreement rolled round the ring around the campfire.

For a moment Roy's mind went blank, and a lump of fear rose in his throat. 'I have had my doubts,' he said huskily. Their gasp was almost tangible. But uttering the few words triggered some thoughts in his own defence. 'But none of us can be sure what the completion will be,' he said more boldly. 'Each of us is a product of our upbringing. You cannot blame me if I was given the opportunity to learn to respect the village people, and you were taught all along to despise them. But you cannot deny they have special powers; how else would the knowledge we now have have reached us? Could any of you reach it by yourselves?'

Peter, the theologian, immediately rose to his feet and spoke up with his answer to Roy's challenge, 'The knowledge they brought to us came from God. The Mother Sages were merely the channels He used. Through them He has told us many of the laws by which He created the universe.' Peter's voice soared as his words flowed, and his eyes bulged and shone. Short in stature, pale-skinned and plump, yellow curls clustered sparsely on his prematurely balding head, he reminded Roy of an angel on one of the tapestries in his big house on the hill. He raised his little arms. 'This knowledge is the word of the Creator himself, the highest and purest knowledge, sent to us as a sign that we have been chosen to fulfil His holy purpose. That is why the New Beginning was ordained. What you call 'the completion', I call the Covenant.'

Roy took a little comfort from the uneasy shifting, and what he sensed were suppressed sniggers, in response to Peter's declaration. The group's unity was weakened by this second strange person. 'You say that because it's what you were taught that by your Mother Sage,' Roy said. 'Others of us were taught differently. Various stories were told us to convince us of our worth compared with all the other people, who undoubtedly have powers we do not possess.'

'No, you are wrong. I know this from God Himself, my Mother Sage said nothing to me about God. She was a heathen, like all the slaves.'

'You know, what Peter says makes a lot of sense,' said one of Roy's group, named James. 'How could these ignorant peasants bring us all this highly sophisticated knowledge, unless it was through God?' Peter beamed at him approvingly.

'But saying it came from God instead of through the power of eversight doesn't explain anything; it just replaces one mystery with another,' Roy protested.

'Maybe, but the power of God is a mystery recognised during the time of civilisation, which we are here to re-establish,' said James.

'Exactly, it's part of the ancient pattern; it fits in. What we've been taught, and the sort of people we've become, resonate with it. That must

202

be why Peter had those thoughts about God.' Roy turned to Peter. 'They came to you because they were a sub-pattern of the ancient times which resonated with the firesoul pattern. Your unconscious eversight connected you to them and then they surfaced, perhaps in your dreams.'

'What is this nonsense about pattern you keep on about?' said a man named Charles, a theoretical physicist who had joined their group to hear Jasper's lecture. 'You're using a vague word of ordinary conversation as if it were a fundamental concept.'

'Pattern is a model of the world that's like common sense. I think I first picked it up from Mother Sage's story I just told you about. Later on I read the papers about pattern that she picked up from the mathematician from the ancient times. It's just how everything is: patterns in time and space. If you simply accept that the past is still present, which we know, don't we, from the Mother Sages' eversight, you can see how patterns form and change and link together. It's like putting Jasper's fractal geometry in a geometric space which includes time, instead of the space moving through time and changing moment to moment. And you also put consciousness inside the geometric space; then, instead of being outside observers, we're participating in it. If you do that you get pattern.'

The words poured out of Roy's mind, rational thoughts about a way of being that was the opposite of reason. He panicked: he was getting trapped inside his head again, into that seductive realm festooned with logic and filled with ideal constructions, their immutable lines and surfaces extending to infinities and eternities. The soft unfolding beauty of pattern would be corrupted in that realm of absolutes; it belonged outside; he must struggle to keep alive that part of himself which knew the outward world. His senses strained for a glimpse of the moon, the sound of a night bird, but the campfire drew him in. Someone was speaking.

'But you still haven't really said anything,' said Charles. 'Okay, there are patterns, but seeing them doesn't explain why they're there. We're either awe-struck by them, and say God created them, or we think and investigate and come up with scientific explanations.'

'God created the laws of science, remember,' interjected Peter.

'But with pattern you don't need any explanations, apart from noticing the patterns,' Roy said, pleased with himself for saying so much in so few words.

'Look, that's silly! It's just circular what you're saying.' Charles shrugged towards the others, who smirked back their agreement.

'I think it's something you either get or you don't. I can't really justify it logically, without distorting it.'

'Why not! You're supposed to be a mathematician.'

'But maths is just the way we think. It's patterns we create with our brains. All animals use their brains to match patterns they see with patterns they remember. It's how they can tell food and danger and mates from all the irrelevant stuff. What Alfred does with his maps, is similar to what animals do who bury stores of food all over the place, and then have to remember a map so they can go back and dig it up in the winter.'

Alfred himself joined in. 'Yes, I get that. If I make a map of the sky, and join up the stars and measure the distances, that doesn't mean there are triangles and so on in the sky. They're just in my mind and down on the map I draw. And when you identify elliptical orbits: they are just patterns in the mind, like Roy's saying.'

'But saying that doesn't help. I agree there are patterns, of course there are. But saying there are patterns doesn't *explain* the patterns. Roy here seems to be implying that it does. Weren't you?' Charles challenged.

'Yes, I was,' Roy replied, and resisted the warnings of his other self in order to pursue the argument. 'I was trying just now to explain it using the fractal geometry concept of space. If you extend the idea of patterns in space to patterns in space and time and consciousness, you can see that patterns tend to follow on, and copy each other; one moment very like the one before, and then on a larger timescale changes follow lifetimes. Patterns generate, continue for a while and then degenerate. Over even longer periods, they evolve, or complexify. Simple patterns join up to form more complicated ones. And evolution itself has a lifetime. You can see this principle in anything. And when you do, you don't need mechanistic explanations, like science came up with in the ancient times. But you can devise a mathematics for pattern. That's what Mother Sage's fey mathematician did: perhaps she had eversight, or maybe she just realised, I don't know, but she was trying to use the ideas to formulate a rigorous pattern maths.'

He was about to launch into the theory of pattern maths when a vision suddenly appeared to him of a creature part woman, part wild beast, its two heads fused at the back, the four eyes switching from side to side as if straining hopelessly to see the other head, and flashing with love and hostility by turns. Then Roy saw that the creature had no body; the heads had eaten it. He shuddered and clutched at his own head as if to tear off his skull. But the monster and its warning existed in its own time. Outside it had never been; the talking world drew Roy back.

'Wait a minute; before we get on to that,' said Charles. 'Let's go back a bit. Are you suggesting that the laws of science only exist in the human mind, that they do not actually govern the behaviour of entities in the external world?'

The monster flashed its warning, but Roy had to go on. 'Oh, worse than that, I'm afraid.' He gave a nervous little laugh. The argument was alluring, making him forget his fears of being trapped in the mental realm, of dragging pattern there, and of the other men's hostility. 'Pattern means that you can forget about distinct entities or *things*, as such. What we think of as particles and forces and energy fields are all interconnecting patterns. So are plants and animals, their form and perception and memories; so are people, their habits and cultures, their music, art, religion and science. Pattern is everything, everything is pattern.' Why couldn't I just say that? he thought. The fewer words the closer to truth, because there is no truth to discover. But he was compelled to be the part of himself who could play their game.

He went on, 'As an explanation, it is better than anything science has come up with, because it depends on only one axiom, which is that the universe consists entirely of conscious patterns in space and time; hence the patterns of the past are always present. Present patterns are aware of past patterns and of each other; they are influenced by a kind of resonance. All change is growth, evolution and dissolution based on following and complexifying what is already there. The only reason we have a problem with pattern is because we think the past vanishes; we don't have eversight. But that shouldn't be a problem: we've believed in forces we can't see, like gravitational attraction, which we only know about by its effects. And gravitation can be regarded as a geometric phenomenon: so it *is* actually a kind of pattern.' His rational self had quite taken over now.

'Pattern of *what*?' Charles asked. 'There must be some substance these patterns are made of. And that substance would have to have some fundamental properties, so you're back to physics as we know it.'

'That would be true if there were two kinds: the substance and also

205

emptiness, or no-substance. Then you would have to say what the substance is like, compared to emptiness. But according to the single axiom of pattern, everything is pattern. That includes the substance and the no-substance. It's better to conceive it in terms of a single substance, which might just as well be no-substance.'

'That sounds completely weird! Not scientific, is it? You couldn't prove that.'

'I suppose you could call it metaphysics: the basics of existence; the first principles of pattern as a science. All science is based on unprovable metaphysical assumptions deep down, but with classical science many of the assumptions are unstated: like the existence of *things* and *force fields* and their properties, and the idea of *explanation* and the *laws* of science. But the metaphysics of pattern is a much simpler kind, so by what they used to call "the principle of scientific parsimony" pattern is good science.'

'Hmm. But even if we accept all this, what's the point of it? Isn't this concept of pattern so vague it's useless.'

'I think pattern could be useful, but that's not the point. I've said that pattern is the only *explanation*, as such, but that doesn't say we can't use the models of science and maths. As I said, they are patterns, so they are as real as anything else. Pattern does not invalidate the laws of science, because belief in those laws is a pattern in itself. Just because pattern says our particles and forces etc. are in the mind and perhaps not in the *real* world, doesn't mean that the belief in those concepts is not useful and applicable. Indeed, in the ancient times, the models of science were externalised and made real through their application in technology based on science's models. You could say science creates a world in its own image. If it conceives an ideal geometric world it creates architecture based on ideal forms, if it conceives a mechanistic world, it creates machines. At the time of the collapse it was starting to conceive an intelligent organic world, and it created the intos technology which saved humanity from extinction. So you see —'

'Green dragons in space!'

Everyone stared at Alfred, who had stood up and thumped one fist into his palm, a gleeful expression on his face.

'What?' they chorused.

Alfred grinned. 'Sorry. It just took me back to when I was a boy. I've heard lots of you mention the wonders of civilisation and technology your Mother Sages tempted you with to keep you interested in the work. With Roy it was artificial light, aeroplanes and printing. With me it was spaceships. I've been a star gazer all my life. Mother Sage used to say that the intos technology could provide space explorers with artificial worlds to travel around in. The intos used to be called the "green dragon". All the children since the emergence have been told the legend about the black dragon of necrotech and the green dragon of biotech. So: "green dragons in space"! I loved it. That's the point of all this for me.'

'Didn't the dragon depend on solar energy, like a plant? How would it survive away from the sun?' asked Charles. Everyone laughed at him treating Alfred's boyhood dream as part of the serious discussion. But Alfred was happy to play.

'Oh, it would milk some other source of energy. There's energy everywhere,' he replied confidently. 'It's intelligent organic, so it would work it out, like we would, only better because it's not limited biologically to one configuration. What's interesting from what Roy's been saying is that the people who invented the intos didn't use science or maths, in any conventional sense. They called what they did "intuitive innovation". What they achieved, or rather what the intos turned itself into as it learned, was impossible by the laws of science. It only happened because science was discredited at that time: it didn't contribute directly to the economy, my Mother Sage told me. So the technologists were allowed to try the impossible. Perhaps intuitive innovation was based on pattern: pattern mathematics even.'

'Rubbish! Dangerous rubbish!' Peter rose to his feet, his red juicy lips wobbling wetly with passionate fury. 'The intos was a manifestation of evil; it was not based on scientific principles, which are the laws of God. It was dreamt up by power crazy technicians who denied science's truths, tried to play God and created a monster they had no control over. The people who sought refuge inside the intos were corrupted; they became idle parasites in a Hell of disgusting fantasies. No men emerged at the end of that period, just a few pregnant women who practised male infanticide, keeping just a few young men for stud. Their descendants are these tribes of dirty peasant people who live like animals. They are totally uncivilised, have no religious faith, and absolutely no sense of purpose. They are the lowest grovelling savages, and Roy here thinks they've got super-human powers. He is a heretic, and a threat to the New Beginning, and we should deal with him accordingly!'

Roy had forgotten his fears when his rational self had taken over. In desperation he tried to treat Peter's outburst as a contribution to the discussion.

'But we wouldn't have been born if it were not for the intos. Through the intos humanity left behind the awfulness it had perpetrated: all the wars, the poverty, the disease, the deserts and the storms. It made the New Beginning possible.' But Roy's reply only emphasised the doubts he had admitted having, by reminding the group of the dark history of civilisation. Peter said nothing more; he did not need to.

There was a long silence. They could hear the crackling of the fire. A wolf howled. A feeling of vulnerability arose as a collective shiver. They had forgotten the world around as they faced the campfire and each other and the reassuring power of the rational mind. Only Roy knew that this was the pattern which had given Man his original identity and, with the tamed fire itself, his dominion over nature.

At last Alfred cleared his throat, to signal he was going to speak in his capacity of leader. 'This has been an interesting evening. I don't think there's time for anyone else to go on with his story, even if —' He paused. 'What I suggest is we hear the rest of Roy's story tomorrow. I know we're all feeling a bit uneasy about Roy's – er, unusual ideas, but I don't want us to rush into condemning anyone before we know the whole thing. What do you say?'

There was a sigh of relief and a murmur of assent. Roy had to join in, although he would have preferred his next turn to be after everyone else's because he dreaded everyone's reaction – not just Peter's – to what he had done after Mother Sage's death. With the system of reversing the sequence, and with twelve in the group and probably time for one or two stories each evening, it would have been half a moon's cycle before it was his turn again. And who knows, some of the others' stories might turn out to have similar experiences and insights to his own, which might then have to be taken seriously – and that was the reason he had joined the march, after all. But Alfred was right; they had to hear the rest of his story as soon as possible.

With the threat of what tomorrow's revelations would bring, Roy longed for some comfort; he was strongly tempted to disregard the convention and go to find his Fey. He lay down, but the thought of her kept him awake long after the other men had gone to sleep. The moon was full and bright above the smoke. At last he crawled slowly and carefully away.

No one woke up, so Roy got to his feet and walked back the way the march had come. When he was well clear of the fires he came to the first sleeping huddle. The moon was full, and bright enough for him to see the women. He lifted a curtain of hair gently and peeped at the moonlit face of one of the fey's. No, that was not her. He tried another, and then another. None of them awoke, but each stirred and cuddled up closer to a nearby body. Roy's Fey was not in this huddle. He walked further, and skirted the next mound of bodies, drawing aside more hair. Not there either. At the next huddle, as he lifted a mass of dark curly locks to reveal a stranger's face, the fey opened her eyes. She turned and reached up for him with both thin arms. Oh well! he sighed. Getting onto his hands and knees and wriggling his way in, he enfolded the fey's warm back in his front. The huddle of women's bodies closed in around him.

The morning was strangely quiet. To the astonishment of all the men, apart from Roy, there were no chattering villagers bustling around, and no tasty food arranged in baskets for each group. Roy came back from his cosy night with the feys to an uproar of complaint and anger. He could not help being conspicuous because he was with the women, and because he was carrying two basket traps, each with most of its compartments occupied with small birds and animals flapping or scuttling around. His Fey, whom he had found when morning came, walked beside him with more baskets on her head. Other feys followed with similar burdens.

'Breakfast!' Roy announced, putting down his baskets. He reached into a compartment, grabbed its occupant and dispatched it neatly with a blow from a stone on the back of its head. He held it up towards Alfred, who had walked over to see what was going on.

Roy could see Alfred struggling to decide how to react. Anger showed in his face.

He squatted down to Roy's level and hissed, 'What do you think you're playing at? I tried to be fair to you last night and this is all the thanks I get!'

'It's nothing to do with last night. Not directly anyway,' Roy said. 'It's just that I know more about the village life than the rest of you. I tried to warn you yesterday morning. The villagers haven't enough surplus food to feed us as winter draws in. The people who came last

209

night left traps and the feys set them. There's quite a good catch. We can cook the meat. Look, they're quite easy to skin.' He demonstrated, cutting a hole in the animal's belly with a bone knife, he pulled out its guts, then he separated the skin from the flesh and pulled the little pink body out.

Alfred made a disgusted face. 'I don't think the men will want to do that,' he said.

'They will if you leaders tell them to. Anyway, it's either that or go without breakfast.'

'Why can't the feys do it?'

'They'll do some, but it'll be quicker if everyone joins in, and the feys won't do the cooking, or go near the fires.' Roy resisted asking why the feys should do all the work, but Alfred probably received that message too.

'All right. I'll see what I can do just this once. But I want to talk to you as we're marching. We'll have to find some way of sorting this out.'

Roy continued to kill and skin the animals as Alfred gathered together a leaders' meeting to discuss the emergency.

When Alfred had gone, Jasper came up to Roy to ask what was going on. Roy explained. Jasper nodded and reached for one of the animals. 'Show me,' he said. Charles and two others joined them. Roy noticed Alfred glance over in their direction. After a while Alfred led the leaders to his group's fire, where several animals were now skewered close together on a stick over the refuelled fire, the flames grilling them nicely. Roy explained the technique, and gave them a taste each.

Then the leaders withdrew again for further discussion. They were near enough to Roy's group for the grumbling mood to be audible. But at last they dispersed, and Alfred returned and ordered Roy and the men he had coached to go to the other camp fires and pass on what had to be done.

The sun was higher than usual when they were ready to resume the journey. Roy took his place in the column as usual. As he strode along he realised he was feeling happy and relaxed. Nothing dreadful was going to happen during the day. His night with the feys had somehow reassured him that he was not getting stuck inside his head again. He was going to have to tell the rest of his story this evening. He would just do that when the time came, and then whatever the consequences would be would be. Until then he was not going to worry.

Then Alfred came up beside him. 'You're looking pleased with yourself this morning,' he said.

'I had a good night,' Roy smiled.

Alfred looked embarrassed. 'Yes, well, we couldn't all — Be a shambles wouldn't it? We have to have discipline, and maintain our integrity. Well, they are villagers, the feys. Not good to mix, in the present circumstances. When we get there we can make suitable arrangements. Anyway,' Alfred said firmly, drawing himself into his leader's role, 'Roy, we need to talk. Now, tell me why there's a problem with the food supplies. I really don't see why there should be. I know you think it's this "thinking they're our slaves" business, and we can just exploit them. Well that isn't my attitude. The way I look at it is this: they must want to help us, they decided to bring us all up, didn't they? Presumably they'll benefit from civilisation in the end. "Development" was what they called it in the ancient days.' He looked at Roy, who frowned and opened his mouth to reply, but Alfred went on.

'Anyway, never mind all that, let's just work out the sums. There are currently about a thousand of us on the march. There are more people than that in each village who are fed all right on a regular basis. Isn't that right?' Roy nodded, and Alfred warmed to his argument. 'All they have to provide for us is two meals, and then we move on. When we were living in the villages there was plenty of food for us: there's no actual increase in numbers. There are massive food stores under the houses, filled up every winter with nuts, dried meat, dried fruit, seeds, honey, cordial – you name it. And yet you say it's winter coming on that makes the problem.'

For a moment Roy had doubts. Was he nursing a moral position which did not stand up? Did he really know what the village people wanted? Was he trying to protect their culture because he found it attractive, from changes they actually looked forward to? But he pushed those considerations aside; they were not the point. What about the practicalities?

'I haven't worked it out logistically; I just noticed that the baskets seemed to weigh the same each day – had done for more than a moon's cycle, I think – and during that time twenty to thirty men would have joined us. Perhaps I jumped to the conclusion I did about the surpluses. But I think, in a way, it's that they don't really have any surpluses as such: only supplies to cater for accidental losses such as pest or disease

211

damage, or spring coming late. And they practically hibernate in winter, so each person eats very little, whereas we're marching during the day and expending energy in the evenings: mental work uses energy you know.'

'Okay, I see that. But let's work it out,' Alfred said. 'We need to estimate how many days' supplies we're depriving a village of, at hibernation levels of consumption. How much less do they eat through the winter, would you say?'

'I don't know really. Let's say a quarter.'

'A quarter less, or a quarter of?' Alfred asked.

'Of,' said Roy.

'That's a huge reduction. Don't they need energy to keep warm?'

'Well they sleep huddled together – you've seen the feys, and in the winter they doze through most of the day and night. And they put on a lot of weight during the autumn harvest-time feasting, so some of their stores are in their bodies. It may even be less than a quarter, I don't know. I'm sure it's not more. I lived with them for more than a season cycle, so I think my impression is reliable, but they don't actually measure or count anything; it's all done by patterns.'

Alfred frowned. 'Let's leave all that stuff 'til this evening,' he muttered. 'Okay, let's assume it's a quarter. So what's the population of a village?'

'I don't know if they're all the same – I doubt it. But I did once work out the size of *our* village. There are about three hundred sleeping huts with six or seven in each during the summer; in winter they double up. Anyway, that works out to about two thousand. Quite a few people go to the forest after the autumn feasts. Most of the babies are born in the autumn, but they don't eat anything, they just add to the nursing women's consumption a bit – living off their fat really. The numbers are least in the winter, but only by fifty or so I should think. We may as well assume two thousand.'

'They do live like animals!' Alfred exclaimed, obviously referring to Peter's outburst the previous evening.

'Yes, they *do* live like animals. Their life is in ecological balance so that the human animal isn't being disruptive.'

'But they change the ecology. The gardens are highly artificial.'

'All living things affect the ecology. That's fine, as long as the overall balance is sustained. The people don't disturb the soil: it's wild underneath the gardens; and they don't use fire, so energy is conserved within the living system. Using fire and digging the soil for farming and mineral extraction were fundamental to human culture in the ancient times. From that point of view, the village people are not behaving like humans, but more like animals. But that doesn't make their way inferior.'

Alfred seemed interested. 'So is fire technology why they call us "firesoul"?'

'Yes, that's the basis,' Roy replied. 'Last night you mentioned the legend about the dragons. According to that, people made the black dragon of fire at the very beginning. The way I've worked it out is that fire is what made us human. We came from primates who had already domesticated wildfire: using fire to drive out game and later encouraging grassland for grazing animals, deliberately or accidentally, I don't know. Be interesting to know if anyone's looked that far back by eversight. The "soul" part refers to our minds: it was presumably gathering around the campfire which turned our consciousness inwards, hence "firesoul". We live in our minds; it's as if there's another world in there, which we like better than the one outside. It's not like that for the watersoul people. They're not enclosed in their minds and separate from each other, they're all rolled up together, and with the others in the past whose pattern they continue. I think that's the way all animals are – plants too – perhaps everything. So the reason humans were so destructive was that we were not part of it all, at least, we believed we weren't. And our lot on this march have been brought up to pick up that pattern. The Mother Sages did a good job, but they couldn't have done it without the need for completion.'

'Hmm,' said Alfred, dubiously. 'I suppose you have to get into the pattern way of thinking for that to make sense. Anyway, we're getting off the subject, which was the winter stores. If we assume two thousand people in a village, that's twice as many as we are. We need an active day's supply each, that's four times a hibernation day's supply. So that only deprives them of two days' reserves. Doesn't seem too bad, does it?'

Roy felt confused. He had been so sure he was right about the food. Then the people from the next village had only brought enough food for one meal, leaving the traps, just as if they had picked up his concern and made it true.

'I'm not so sure any more,' he said, 'but perhaps we needed this to happen: it shows we don't have to rely on the villages. That's probably a good thing to realise because we can't be sure there'll be a village nearby all the way to the city. Which reminds me, I was going to ask you, where are we headed for? Where is the new city?'

'I don't know that I can answer that really,' said Alfred. 'I think it's just assumed we'll know in some way, or that we'll choose the best situation we come across, probably on a big river, most likely at an estuary, somewhere to build a harbour and be able to use boats for transport and trade and so on. But to start with we're just following the road, to see where it ends up.'

'But this isn't a road!' exclaimed Roy. 'It may not end anywhere.'

'What do you mean? Of course it's a road, and we're going along it. We'll get somewhere.'

'When I lived in my village this "road", as you call it, was just the second firebreak. The sections of the firebreak are maintained by different villages, and they join up, otherwise they'd be useless for stopping fire. But no one travels from one section to another; that's not what they're for. Just because you can go along something doesn't mean it's going anywhere. Perhaps the sections go all around this range of hills and join up in a great loop.'

Alfred looked stunned. 'But I've been plotting the direction,' he said, 'and, allowing for skirting the contours, we're going almost directly south.'

'It could be a very big loop,' said Roy. 'But I suppose the firebreak could stretch from one part of a coast to another. Anyway, perhaps we'll be able to see the sea from some point, and we can leave the firebreak and make a new path through the forest. Then we'll be glad we can set traps and prepare our own meat.'

Alfred's face brightened. 'We could hunt – you know, properly.' And he mimed throwing a spear and then aiming a bow. He looked at Roy. 'There are big animals in the forest; those with horns or tusks. Why don't they hunt those? Why just traps?'

'They don't have reasons for why they do things.'

'I know: it's just pattern; hunting's not part of their patterns. But why not? There must *be* a reason, even if they don't think that way. They could make the weapons surely? After all they make tools.' He paused. 'I know, weapons are aggressive; tools aren't – but the trapped animals still die, so it's just as aggressive really.'

214

'Trapping doesn't *feel* aggressive,' Roy said. 'It's as if the animals give themselves. We put a little feast in each trap for the animal, and it gives in return. If you look at the traps, there's nothing to stop the animal getting out after it's had the food. I mean, there's no wide open door, and it's easier to get in than out, but an intelligent creature could find its way. But they choose not to. Anyway, that's how I see it, although I hadn't worked it out before you asked. But I could be quite wrong; it was just the track you were following.'

Alfred had been looking uneasy, but then he brightened. 'Talking of tracks! I've been neglecting my mapping work discussing this food business. I'd really better get on. See you later!'

Roy watched him bound off, but carried on thinking about watersoul ways. It might simply be that running around hunting wastes energy and trapping is less effort. On the other hand, it might be fear of picking up firesoul patterns – hunting big grazing animals and later on enslaving them. The people leave them for the hunting beasts, like wolves, whose pattern has always been to control the grazers' numbers.

Roy's musings were interrupted by someone hurrying from behind to join him. It was Jasper, who clearly had something urgent on his mind. 'Roy, can I ask you something about what you were saying last night?' he asked.

Roy would rather have walked alone but he was grateful for Jasper's support over the breakfast crisis. 'Yes Jasper, what do you want to know?' he asked.

'The papers you told us your Mother Sage wrote for you, the pattern maths stuff, could I have a look at them?'

'I'm really sorry to disappoint you, but we didn't bring them with us,' Roy replied.

'But why not? I would really have liked to see what pattern maths was all about,' Jasper said wistfully.

'Yes, I'm really sorry. I'd have been glad to let you have it. The actual theory was your sort of stuff: something like an extension of Klein's geometry groups, but going beyond topology to a completely comprehensive geometric space – like I was saying last night, including time – multi-dimensional time actually – and discontinuous space as a result – and universal consciousness. In such a geometric space, no properties are absolutely preserved, but there's a set of soft properties and relationships; what were they now? — Oh, yes: self- and other-

215

similarity, lifecycle, evolution and dissolution, and completion. I think I could remember most of it, given a few weeks of peace and quiet somewhere. Not much chance of me getting that, I suppose.'

'Could we, could some of us, go back and pick the papers up, perhaps?' asked Jasper.

'I don't think they'd be much use if you did. They got in a mess – that was why we didn't bring them. I don't think you could make any sense of them now.'

'What do you mean: they got in a mess? How?' Jasper's voice was husky with anxiety.

'They got torn up for messages and love notes; you know, the sort of thing the youngsters do in the mating games. Village people are pretty careless about property. They found the basket of paper in my room in the big house. I would have told you about that in the next part of my story.'

'But that's dreadful!' Jasper almost wailed. 'You heard what Alfred said: this stuff may have been the basis of the intos. I have a hunch that the New Beginning has to progress rapidly to where we left off technologically – if we're to avoid the disasters of the ancient times.' He said this pointedly, the implication being that if Roy's knowledge were valuable for building a new kind of New Beginning, Roy himself would no longer be seen as a threat – except perhaps by Peter.

It was a bizarre situation for Roy: being the only doubter, and perhaps the only one to know about a new kind of mathematics which could be crucial to the success of what he dreaded. It had not occurred to him that any maths would be that important. The mathematicians were the least necessary for the initial stages. The technologists: those who knew how to extract metal from rocks, make glass, fire clay, make tools, construct buildings, lay roads, pipe water, dispose of waste; they would build the city, and civilisation would grow and progress from there – only then would it be possible to consider sophisticated developments like the intos, and by then it could be too late. There were agronomists amongst the marchers, and those who could make agricultural chemicals and machinery, probably biotechnologists too, of the pre-intos variety, so there would be forest clearance for necrotech agriculture. There did not seem to be any gardeners on the march, apart from the feys, who did not count. The village people were all excellent gardeners, but they did not need a New Beginning; they needed protecting from it.

Roy suddenly felt his earlier sense of well-being fade; he was tired of

216

all the words and ideas and arguments which threatened to drive him back inside his head. He was reminded of the crisis he'd been through in the village when he'd stuck his head on the rocks as if to smash it to pieces to get free, to get outside his head into the real world. How was he going to be able to get them to see what he had been through? He was aware of Jasper saying something else, but he could not listen.

'Sorry, Jasper, would you leave me alone now. I've got to think – about tonight you know,' he managed to say. He saw Jasper's hurt look, and felt for him. He seemed to have his own doubts to wrestle with and perhaps the others would see those as a threat too.

'I shouldn't say anything to anyone else about your interest in pattern maths,' he warned, 'and about the New Beginning depending on something that might not be available. They don't like doubters – you could be in trouble too.'

Jasper looked as if he might protest; probably insist on his firm commitment to building the new city – he was no doubter, certainly not! But to Roy's relief, he said nothing and soon fell behind to join his usual group.

Roy took the few steps off the road into the forest and squatted to empty his bowels. The stress he had been going through had upset his guts, and the liquid shit left a burning sensation. He tore up some moist moss to wipe himself. He stepped back and waited, still and quiet, to see the first response to his addition to the ecology. Some tiny flies darted down, a small frog hopped up, the flies scattered, the frog waited for their return. In time, as the stuff soaked down to the soil, creatures too small to see would take an interest. You do not have to be a scientist to know when you are joining in the processes and when you are disrupting them, Roy thought to himself. If you do not try to understand, you know all that matters.

He willed his mind to hush. Living with rational thinkers bent on an important project, he easily reverted to that way of being. The brief escape he had enjoyed in the village seemed another lifetime away. Roy shut his eyes and concentrated on the rattling whisper of the trees at the forest edge. The sound was diffuse enough for time to linger uninterrupted by the moment. But a bird's sudden burst of piping song broke through. Roy remembered Mother Sage telling him about the myth of naming: the belief that singling out some thing, say a bird, and giving it a name, a name for its kind, gave a human being power over what was named. But the price of that power was the fragmentation, the separation, the instant and the location, which left man lonely and, if he would admit it to himself, afraid.

Perhaps, Roy thought, describing to the others how he had been changed would take him back to that blissful state, as near as one like himself could become to being watersoul, a ripple in the unending pattern.

12

Habitation

'I don't know if you can imagine how I felt after my Mother Sage died. All your Mother Sages were with you right up to the day you left for the march. They waved you on your way – I saw some of them. Then they would have gone to the forest, I am sure, since their task was done and they were old. But I expect you imagine them still alive, don't you?'

Roy saw pain in some of their faces, but he did not wait for anyone to comment.

That time was very terrible for me. My grief and hurt were overwhelming. Not only had Mother Sage left me, but my identity had been shattered. I had no one to talk to about my suffering, having lost the very person I would have been able to share my thoughts and feelings with. I had been trained not to show strong emotions, even to deny I had any, which must have contributed to the trauma I went through.

The loneliness of losing my companion and guardian was emphasised because, without her, the environment she had surrounded me with began to disintegrate. Most of the servants rolled up their bedding and went down the hill. Village people don't have any sense of responsibility; it was only Mother Sage's influence that kept them from going off to do what they pleased. The new Fey stayed for a while. She brought me food twice a day for several days, and then she too went, and I was left to fend for myself. It is pointless now to wrap all that happened to me during that period in descriptions of loneliness and woe. I did recover myself, and I learned a great deal.

I had a look at the papers in Mother Sage's basket. None of it had been bound, but most of the loose sheets were in groups enclosed in folders. Several of these containing the journal she had told me about, dated by the calendar system she had devised for my benefit: days within moon cycles within season cycles numbered from when the project of bringing me up was begun. It was all written in tiny script, the lines close together and on both sides of each page. So many words! I started reading it, but I found it disturbing, not so much because it brought my loss vividly to my consciousness, but because I discovered in it another person besides the Mother Sage I had known for most of my life. This person was the one I had had a poignant glimpse of when she told her story just after she died: the watersoul woman drawn back from her going to the forest to be my guardian. The interplay between the two personalities was clearly apparent, but manifested in unexpected ways. I would have thought it would have troubled the watersoul woman to put on a pretence of despising her own people; but not so; she had the careless innocence which I later found was typical of her people. It was the personality coloured by firesoul values who was troubled by the deception.

Putting the journal aside, I looked to see what else there was and found a small bundle of pink-dyed folders labelled 'Pattern Mathematics – Bony Bailey'. I could not read that either because the identity I had lost was as an important New Beginning mathematician, and I wanted nothing more to do with mathematical ideas.

There was another collection of papers which were notes about the project of bringing me up as firesoul. I certainly did not want to know any more about that terrible deception.

While I was trying to make up my mind what to do next I took to wandering around the empty house. The drawing room and dining room had many embroidered wall hangings showing scenes from the ancient days. Some of the pictures showed what Mother Sage had called 'classical scenes', of gods and nymphs and mythical creatures or charming young couples tending flocks of animals amongst flowery meadows and little hills. Other pictures Mother Sage had called 'religious'; they were less jolly. Some had been taken down. They had shown cruel torture, and had given me bad dreams. Mother Sage had been explaining the religious stories to me, but then she stopped. There were violent scenes in other pictures: plumed generals on horseback and armies engaged in battle, and huntsmen slaughtering wild beasts. They hadn't bothered me that much, I think because they were not meant to affect you like the religious ones were.

There was quite a different kind of picture, which had always fascinated me, hanging in my old schoolroom. It showed a city with towering buildings, wide streets teeming with vehicles, and skies streaked with gleaming aeroplanes. I remembered, when I was a boy, going to the tapestry workroom when that picture was being stitched. I suppose that at first the 'slaves' had 'followed the patterns of tapestry making', and so created close copies of tapestries they saw in the past. Only later did they make one to Mother Sage's design.

When I was little I used to enjoy crawling around on the floor of the drawing room tracing the pattern in the fur carpet. The village people only kill small wild animals and so the carpet was made up from hundreds of little pelts stitched together in a complex geometric design.

The drawing room had more furniture than Mother Sage and I could ever use. There were leather-covered chairs and couches, and others of fine basketwork, with fringed and embroidered cushions. Other items were purely decorative. Displayed on basketwork tables were sculptures of wood and bone: several women in coyly erotic poses, a few fearful beasts leaping to the kill, a warrior in a plumed helmet plunging his sword into a fantastic monster. There were basketwork vases, once always full of fresh flowers, now holding dead stalks and surrounded by shrivelled petals.

Compared with the simple dwellings of the village people my house was a palace. Like a wealthy man from the ancient times I had many possessions. I had been told as a child that these things showed how important I was, and how the 'slaves' had laboured long hours to make them for me, and the latter was surely true. I was to discover later that the village people make things as much for the fun of making them as for their usefulness. They were perpetually discarding and remaking, using materials which grow abundantly and are decomposed to good mulch when discarded. But nothing they make is anyone's personal possession. And there is no ownership of houses, land or produce from the gardens. Children do not belong to anyone in particular, love and lovers belong to anyone or no one. Curiously, judged by firesoul values, the absence of property is as much carelessness as sharing; one could not say for sure that it is good or bad, it could be seen as a kind of selfishness, even cruelty, in spite of the people having no sense of the separate self to benefit from any selfish behaviour.

But I am getting ahead of my story; my understanding of watersoul ways was meagre and uncertain before I went to live with the people. Having been reminded of crawling on the fur carpet and watching the tapestry-making when I was much younger, I thought perhaps it would help me come to terms with what had happened if I read the papers about how my upbringing was decided upon. I read through the first folder. In it were records of eversight discussions with other Mother Sages, in which they agreed on what aspects of the ancient pattern they could and should replicate for the boys.

The most difficult issue was the use of fire. In principle, fire technology was an essential component. At first many of the Mother Sages, including my own, had expressed willingness to use fire; but they could not find ways of using it that were satisfactory. The main problem was that they could not get the other village people who were supposed to be servants to cooperate, not in lighting or using fires, or in moving big stones to make fireplaces, or in digging up clay for bricks. The Mother Sages could have had fires on the ground in the open which they lit and used themselves, but that would have distracted them from the education work, and lowered their status, which they felt ought to be between the firesoul 'lords' and the 'servants or slaves'. Fire inside a house made entirely of wood was only possible with a centre fireplace on an earth floor and a smoke hole in the roof. A single great hall was a possibility, but the Mother Sages decided on a house design with several elegantly furnished rooms. So there would be no fire.

Another important topic was whether to bring the boys up singly or to bring groups of them together at an early stage into schools. It was the problem with fire that decided this. Fire was linked to the pattern of inturned consciousness, and the isolated self. There would be no fire to reinforce and confirm this essential personality component, therefore it would be confirmed by keeping the boys physically isolated instead, apart from the mother figures, who would carefully avoid being too affectionate and physically close to their charges.

I could not go on reading about these deliberations. It reminded me of what Mother Sage had told me about artificial environments for wild animals called 'zoos', which they had in the ancient times. This was in response to questions I asked about the hunting scenes on the tapestries. It seems some people were sorry that the wild animals had been killed and the wild places they had lived in destroyed, so they collected the last few animals and kept them in zoos. In order for the animals to exhibit their natural behaviour and, most importantly when there were few or none left in the wild, to mate and reproduce their kind, they had to be provided with surroundings sufficiently like their natural habitat. That was what the Mother Sages had been doing for us firesoul boys.

Mother Sage had told me that the firesoul boys before us had faded away and died because the watersoul village was not a suitable environment for them; even so the discussions about us made me feel uncomfortable. It was as if it was us they were constructing, rather than the environment, and I suppose that was what was done to children in the ancient times. Later, when I began to think in a pattern way, I realised that what the Mother Sages were doing was tuning in to an old pattern, which was present, although its links with ongoing human behaviour had been almost entirely broken. We were the only fragments of its continuing manifestation.

There was an account in the folder about the building of our house. The house was to be large and rectangular in shape, and durable, which required a great deal of timber. So a swathe of forest trees from the village to half way up the hill was cut down. To make the foundation of the house a number of tree trunks were cut to form piles and driven into the ground using rocks. A sturdy frame was constructed and filled in and roofed with shingle. The upper floor was rigidly boarded.

Stone axes with long wooden handles had been made for cutting down the big trees. I had seen the axes because, after the house was finished, they were arranged on a table in a special little room which was never to be used. Mother Sage said that this symbolised that the pattern of felling and construction was completed. The episode had been disturbing for the people, who naturally followed old patterns and disliked anything new. When it was all over a healing process began. When the people wandered up or down the cleared avenue they brought pocketfuls of fruit to munch on the way. Then they pushed into the earth some of the small fruit seeds, and any of the stones they did not crack open to eat. When the house was first built the avenue must have looked like a grand drive, such as big houses used to have in the ancient times. But over the years the hillside and the area around the house became an orchard garden, which matured to harmonious balance.

I went outside then to look at the house. I had not noticed what a bad state it was in. It was covered with moss, many of the shingles on the walls and roof were soft and rotten, loose or missing. It occurred to me what a lot of wood would be needed to keep the house in good repair. Those axes would have been kept busy felling forest trees. Supposing the whole village lived in houses like this, there would surely be hardly any forest left. I began to wonder what effect the New Beginning would have. Not only would vast amounts of timber be needed, but mountains

223

would be demolished for rock and minerals.

I went back into the house and into the little room where the axes were. I pulled at the handle of one of them and the whole arrangement fell down. The axe was heavy. I lugged it out and went around the back to the servants' huts. There were six huts, sleeping six or seven people each. There were several big forest trees in amongst the huts. I took a swipe at one of them with the axe. The sharp stone blade bit in deeply, but I could see that it would take me some time to make the V-shaped holes necessary for the tree to fall. I had never tried to do it, but I guessed I could do it in an hour. I found myself talking to the tree.

'I could cut you down in an hour. How long has it taken you to grow? Fifty season cycles? So the new houses have to last that long. Mine didn't, but we'll have technology – chemicals or something – to stop the wood from rotting.'

I imagined the tree lying at my feet. 'Now what?' I asked it. 'I'd have to cut you up. Branches off first, then into lengths, then into thin slices for floor boards and shingles. I suppose when they built my house they propped the sections up and then split them with blows from above.' I mimed the actions. 'My word, they must have worked hard! But of course, for the New Beginning there'll be people who know how to get metals to make better tools, and even machinery. Then it'll be easier: we'd have you in nice pieces in no time.

'Now, how many of you will it need to house properly all the people who lived here? There were six or seven people to each of the six two-roomed huts, which is about forty people. The two of us had ten rooms between us in the big house. So we'll need twenty houses with ten rooms. Each house needs the timber from a strip of ground the size of the avenue. My goodness, we'd have to clear the whole hillside. So what about the village?'

I climbed up the ladder of one of the huts and onto the roof, then onto a branch of my tree, and as high as I could get. I parted the branches to look down at the village. Mentally I sectioned off the village into groups of ten huts, and grouped these in threes.

'If there are six or seven people to a hut, each of those sections would house two hundred people. There are about ten such groups, so this is a village of about two thousand people. We'd have to clear the forest at least to the second firebreak,' I told the tree. 'I suppose there'd be other materials: stone, blocks of baked clay, perhaps even metal sections, I don't know. But they'd have to be dug out of the ground, so the forest

224

would be cleared anyway, perhaps just as fuel for the fire technology.' I climbed down thoughtfully.

Picking up the axe, I went back to the big house. I took a swipe at a section of the side wall, severing a supporting pole. A cascade of shingles slithered down to leave a gaping hole.

'Much easier to destroy than to build,' I muttered.

I no longer wanted to be in the big, empty, rotting house that had been my childhood cage. I decided to move into one of the servants' huts, which are very small; really more like nests. I had watched when the first one was being built, much to Mother Sage's annoyance. There were plenty of rooms in the house for the servants, but they did not like them, they were too hard and square apparently. They had tolerated them for a few years, but then Mother Sage reluctantly agreed that they could make their own sleeping huts, as long as they were tucked away in the forest at the back, out of my view. But I insisted on watching the construction, and Mother Sage, grudgingly at first, explained the principles and techniques which were used.

Down in the village there is a long slow cycle of hut-building. Oval rings of fruit or nut trees are grown from seed, so that many season cycles hence they can be used for hut frames. As they grow they are pruned so that there are branches only where they would be needed. They bear fruit meanwhile, and some never become huts.

When the trees in one of the rings are tall and strong enough, a hut can be built onto them. Lengths of bamboo from the bamboo island, or small roundwood coppice or saplings from the outer garden, or wood from old huts are used for the rest of the frame. The thickest poles are hung from bands over the 'V' formed by the first branching and lashed together at first floor level. On these are built the supports for the upper floor and the roof. The walls are filled in with lightly framed woven mats. The roof is thatched with reeds. The upper floor, which is the communal sleeping area is made of tough webbing, attached to the poles at the sides and forming a bouncy floor on which are piled fur blankets and feather quilts. The lower floor is enclosed in secure panels to make a food storeroom.

Each hut lasts about the same number of season cycles as a human lifespan which, for these people, is intentionally short. During that time, the hut would have its walls replaced and its thatch renewed as often as necessary to keep it neat, and secure against predators and vermin.

When the supporting trees grow too big, the hut is abandoned and another one made on another tree ring.

When the servants built their huts behind the house on the hill, they picked out a number of naturally occurring collections of young trees in the forest behind us. Some of the smallest trees were cut down to leave suitable rings, and the huts were built in the usual fashion, using the felled trees as poles instead of bringing bamboo or wood from elsewhere. At the time, my attitudes coached by Mother Sage, I shared her distaste at the idea of sleeping curled up with several others on a bouncy platform. I retired to my four poster bed in my own chamber, and Mother Sage to hers, but I fancy the house echoed with emptiness after the servants moved out.

Now, years later, I was moving out of the big house into a sleeping hut. I collected some bedding, rolled it into a bundle for putting over my shoulder to climb the ladder, and made a cosy nest in one of the sleeping huts. I slept very soundly that night, and felt ready for anything in the morning, as if my mind had been cleansed of anxiety. I climbed out into the sunlit garden, and went to the stream to wash my body. Approaching the massive shape of the big house on my return, a thought that seemed to have come from a forgotten dream came to me, and I spoke it aloud to the house:

'I wonder if we should make the New Beginning of civilisation. The village way is easy, and the people are happy. They have everything they want round about them, and they can tell what effect they are having: all living things have an effect; that's all right as long as it all cycles. But shut inside a city with everything brought in from outside we wouldn't know if all the forests were cut down and the land turned to deserts. Perhaps the wonders of technology would only make the destruction worse. How would we know? Could it be that busy garden villages are better than lonely cities?'

Though the words I uttered were calmly rational, the implications for my life were shattering. The words echoed through my head, sending reverberations of such force they crushed my soul, my whole reason for being. I shuddered, screwed my eyes shut and crossed my arms around my body as if to defend myself against physical attack.

But nothing happened. I was still there. Mother Sage had raised me for the New Beginning, and fed me with knowledge. I was approaching manhood with a life to live. I relaxed and opened my eyes. The decaying house confronted me.

'How can she have been wrong?' I asked the house. 'And all the others like her who decided to raise firesoul boys? They were convinced the boys were being born because there was a pattern which had to be completed. Of course they assumed that it was the catastrophe brought about by firesoul technology that had to be healed and continued in a better way. But if there is no better way: if firesoul technology would always be destructive and could only be available to a very few people, with the rest miserable slaves, and with constant wars over land and what had to be stripped off the land and taken out of it —

'But perhaps civilisation is worth even such a price, which must be paid again and again. And cities, and grand buildings, are merely the shell. Within the shell, the embryo grows: human creativity – art, literature, philosophy, science, mathematics – that is worth any price, surely?'

13

Pattern Mathematics

So that was how it was that at last I turned to the pattern mathematics folders Mother Sage had left for me. In it she had recorded the work of Bony Bailey, a mathematician from the ancient times. The first part was not so much mathematics as what I understood to be philosophy, since it concerned two views of how people could think. As I read it, I could sense – as if with eversight – the woman from necrotech thinking as she wrote.

Pattern is an alternative conceptual model to the 'reason model' of contemporary science and mathematics.

The reason model evolved with the first human societies and civilisations. It was first of all practical and then became abstract and intellectual. Basic ideas such as number and measurement arose out of the need to assess quantities, in order to administer property, to engage in trade and to construct buildings and machinery. The large brain of Homo sapiens helped him to accumulate information: originally about the location of sources of food and other useful materials; later on about how to make things and about how to engage in co-operative activities.

When social organisation gave rise to societies divided by class, there were people who were not engaged in the day to day practicalities of survival since their needs were taken care of by servants and slaves. They had spare mental capacity, which, for some of them, came to be employed in further study of the once purely practical ideas of number, measurement and shape. The abstract study of these ideas came to be associated with the concept of 'explanation': the ideas were used to conceive models of what underlay the universe, and how its divine creator had made it, assuming that the God had a mind similar to their own.

Economy has always been a guiding principle of conceptual thought.

228

In the case of the reason model, economy manifested as the thinkers' search for the simplest possible ideas to form their basis for comprehension; and then combining the simple ideas, as necessary, to explain more complicated situations. The rightness of this approach was never questioned, since the goal of formulating explanations was so eagerly pursued. It did not occur to them that the result was an extreme lack of economy in the world as they saw it.

For example, take a straight line of some arbitrary length: either a real rod of a thin material, say a precisely straight wooden stick; or a mental image of a rod. In the concrete world or in the abstract world, the rod is limited in size: we could agree that to see it that way is an economical view of the rod. But looked at from the reason model, it contains an abundance of infinities. It can be divided up endlessly to make an infinity of rational numbers. In amongst the rational numbers is another infinity of irrational numbers. The rod could be repeated endlessly to extend through an infinity of one dimensional space. It could be used to delimit an endless number of two- or three-dimensional spaces, and an endless variety of shapes and sizes. The concept of number: that purest and simplest of ideas is hugely and absurdly uneconomical in the mental world where it resides.

If reason's economical models and its uneconomical world had stayed inside the brains of thinkers, they would have been impotent and harmless. However, they have been externalised, made manifest in the world, leading eventually to such monstrosities as financial worlds of huge numbers and uncontrollable power and influence, computer technology and mass production, simplistic models of how crop plants grow and, in general, uniformity, repetition, loss of diversity, homogenisation of human culture and the degradation and disruption of many of the processes of life on earth.

What then is the pattern model? Crudely speaking, it is the reverse of reason's model. It resides in the world, rather than in the mind. It is economical in repetition: there are no identical patterns; the universe and everything in it is finite and contained within their lifetimes; no thing includes or measures, as that rod did, infinities or eternities. On the other hand, pattern accepts complexity and does not require simple explanations, or reduction into simple components. I imagine it existing in the environment of an alternative human society as intricately patterned, consciously designed, productive gardens.

Describing the pattern model as a conceptual model is purely a device:

an understanding bridge. As far as I am aware, no culture has yet come into being which employs pattern as a model. I think of pattern as the opposite of reason, and a philosophical outlook yet to be adopted. As the opposite of reason, pattern would not be the subject of intellectual exploration; it would be the unstated basis for a way of life. One cannot take the pattern model any further as an alternative conceptual model to reason's model without accepting some form of hybrid between the two. Such a hybrid model could make the case for pattern, when no one living by pattern would bother to do such a thing. A hybrid model requires a hybrid thinker. I propose to take that role. I shall say more about reason's model than about pattern's because the first step is always to question your own certainties, or they will be a barrier to alternative ideas.

One objection someone might make to the pattern model is that to be a model it must reside in the human brain. But I have said that pattern is not a model, but a way of living. So what would the pattern living people use their brains for? To see: the brain is an organ of sight. People do what all animals do with their brains: observe interesting connections in time and space: let's call this vision in time as well as space 'eversight'.

A further difference between reason's model and pattern is that rational thinkers believe themselves to be detached from the world they conceptualise about or observe in their experiments. But this detachment is always a pretence. Pattern people would have a focus of consciousness directed outwards, rather than inwards like rational thinkers. They would be curious about each other's patterns, which would be shared rather than possessed, and they would be intimately involved in their human companions and in their surroundings. They would not be interested in a serious, moralistic, selfish, possessive or even altruistic way, but casually and for fun. Pattern consciousness would be about interconnectedness – a form of spirituality. But it would be quite different from the spirituality that is discovered through meditation, the spirituality that is called 'the inward light', which one could call 'firesoul'. The pattern kind of outward spirituality could be called 'watersoul', to reflect a flow of transient mingling and merging.

I like to think that I am watersoul. I feel that I am beginning a new human pattern which others may follow in the future. It was thinking about this possibility that led me to conceiving a pattern geometry.

230

I was intrigued that Bony Bailey used the terms 'eversight' and 'watersoul'. Perhaps this was where Mother Sage had got them from, there being no words – in the ancient language sense – in the watersoul village people's language for anything, let alone for their own nature. It was interesting too that Bony lacked the detachment of all the other mathematicians Mother Sage had contacted for the New Beginning. She wrote as a real person, which made me wonder how she looked. Mother Sage had experienced her through eversight, which meant from inside her skin, so she would not have seen her face – unless she saw her in a mirror, of course. Firesoul people had to have mirrors to develop their individual selfhood. In every room of the big house, there were shallow bowls of water to serve as mirrors for me to see myself in. I remember Mother Sage showing me myself when I was a boy: 'See, there's Roy in the mirror.'

Bony called herself watersoul, so perhaps she looked like the village feys: lithe and slender with long thick hair. But Mother Sage had said that people usually cut their hair short in the ancient times. A servant has always cut mine. Men used to cut the hair on their faces close to the skin too, which village men do not do, but have long beards. I have too little facial hair as yet for that to be necessary. Mother Sage has very long hair, but she has it plaited and twisted around her head. That was a practice for older women in the ancient times, I believe.

Perhaps Bony had permanent layers of fat – as Mother Sage told me many had in the ancient times – even more than the deposits the village people accumulate before the winter in preparation for hibernation. This was due to their unhealthy diet, consisting mainly of grass seeds and the infant milk from large animals they had tamed. And it was such hard work to get food that way that the people in cities had to employ many slaves to labour on the land, and to carry out food preparation. That is another reason not to cut down the forests when the New Beginning comes: so that there is lovely food from the gardens and forests.

After a break for these speculations, I returned to reading about pattern mathematics.

The reason model includes the study of Euclidean geometry. The main characteristic of this geometry is that rigid bodies are preserved in all their properties as transformations are performed on them. So if a shape in a Euclidean plane, a triangle, say, is rotated about a point, translated from one position to another or reflected in a line, its shape, the lengths

231

of its sides, the angles between its sides, and its area are not altered.

Euclidean geometry is a firesoul pattern. As a pattern it persists. It is taken up readily by those educated in firesoul science, or the reason model as I have been calling it. But it also becomes part of the 'common sense' of all firesoul people. Of course, they say, a triangle stays the same shape and size if you turn it over or throw it across the room; unless it gets broken of course.

But firesoul science, physics in particular, produces various ideas which suggest a reality full of bodies which are far from rigid and invariant. There are tiny charged particles spinning in a void, waves of electromagnetic energy, quantum fields which are particles and waves, bodies shrinking and getting heavier when they travel very fast, matter turning into energy. Surprisingly, none of these ideas caused Euclidean geometry to be abandoned; and rigid bodies are still common sense. Various other geometries have been devised: projective and non-Euclidean geometry, topology, fractal geometry, but only for specialists. Curiously, Euclidean geometry is generally thought of as two-dimensional, in spite of people believing they inhabit a three dimensional universe. No one really expects geometry to be like the real world, or vice versa, and yet they still think Euclidean geometry is 'true'.

A pattern-living person would need no conceptual model, but I need to understand pattern conceptually. Because I am a mathematician by training, I need to describe pattern mathematically. I know that Euclidean geometry will be useless to describe it. In the pattern world things are far from rigid, solid or invariant. Not even time behaves as the reason model assumes. In fact time is the very notion that has to be tackled first.

Scientists are used to showing time as if it were space: draw an axis and label it 't'. Draw another axis at right angles and label it 'p' for position in all the space dimensions: lovely, just like the Euclidean plane. I do the same, but I use the whole of the plane for the present time, as if I am looking down on it.

Now here comes the neat trick: what I see is not a solid time plane, it is discontinuous, full of holes. Through the holes I see other time planes, also discontinuous. They are stacked up, not an infinite number – pattern has no infinities – but there are plenty of them. Just to complicate matters, because pattern willingly accepts complexity in its models in order to let the world be economical, when I look through lots of the holes I am not seeing corresponding lots of locations in the planes below, but far far fewer.

Of course I could, if I wished, draw a single line through my stack of time planes and call that the time line as the reason model represents it. That line has a tiny bit of validity as the direction of evolution or complexification, but it is not very useful, so I do not bother.

I come next to what is in the holey time planes. I have used up three dimensions to represent my 'plenty of' time planes; there is no room for any geometric shapes in space dimensions. Fortunately, this is not a problem. I simply use my own intuitive model of how the world is and was, and put it 'over there', separate from the time block.

I am making a big assumption in taking my own intuitive understanding of the world as how it 'really' is. But I am being economical with the world in doing so. Why invent an underlying real world, say one of particles, waves and forces, or an overarching ideal world, when what I know best is the world I live in.

It may seem as if having the set of time planes and the world as it is and was is breaking the pattern principle of keeping the world simple. But reason's model multiplies the world extravagantly by its model of time, in which the entire universe is thrown away with every infinitesimal instant of time that passes. Some versions of reason's model, while struggling with a probabilistic quantum theory, even postulate multiple universes, representing each and every possibility, being thrown away every instant. In addition, reason's model has an extra realm of existence: the one containing the transcendent laws of nature or science.

But, you may argue, if my spatial universe includes what is and what was, I must have a universe for every instant too. But this is where the holes in the time planes come in. Each different pattern – leaving aside what precisely a pattern is – exists only once. Take a pattern completed in a particular time plane: that pattern exists in the time planes which span its lifetime, and nowhere else; but it shines like a sun into all succeeding time planes so that viewed 'from above', which means 'as in the present' for that plane, many many exact duplicates can be seen.

An example will help. About three quarters of the way through the evolution of life on earth the eukaryotic cell emerged. This is a nucleated cell, which could reproduce sexually, and which made possible the explosion of variety and complexity of multi-cellular life forms which followed. By pattern theory, there is just one eukaryotic

233

cell, complete in its eukaryotic-ness. Later eukaryotes include this one, not as copies or variants of it, but by holes in the time plane showing it as if copied, exactly or with variations. Any variations over and above the original exist in the time planes of the completion of each variation, and shine through subsequent holes to give rise to apparent copies. The billions, trillions, zillions of various eukaryotes in living beings in any present time result from the shining through time of the unique completed patterns existing in their own time.

The pattern model described is not meant to suggest that one cell, of the many once existing, is 'kept', in memory as it were, to act as a model, and the rest pass away with the passage of time. The model asserts that there is and ever was only one – of each new level of differentness. Thus the pattern model is as economical with the world as possible.

A pattern can be anything: an electron, an atom, a molecule, a simple cell, an organelle, an eukaryote, a multicellular organism, the behaviour of an organism, the relationships in an ecosystem, a planetary process, a human culture, a set of beliefs and so on. Every different pattern is based on patterns in the past, only what is different about it existing in its own time.

Pattern theory does not include any mechanisms which make it work. All that is needed is the recognition that every pattern is aware: of itself in the present and during its lifetime, of the earlier patterns shining into it, of other patterns resembling it, of other patterns of which it is a part. Awareness includes the tendency for new variations to be slight. Most pattern, when viewed 'from above its timeplane' in its present, is past pattern, unchanged. New variations which do occur are not spontaneous and instantaneous differences, they arise from local circumstances and they occupy time, each has a lifetime and is compelled to complete itself.

There was a great deal more pattern mathematics, which I worked through gradually, and which often threatened to burst my mind, so different was it from what I had learned before. At the very end was some additional writing from Mother Sage herself. It seems that Mother Sage believed that part of her own self was identical with Bony Bailey: part of her was Bony Bailey shining through the holes in the pattern geometry. She called that 'soul-sharing'. It seems that everyone shares soul: we are all composites, with very little uniqueness in each of us.

234

Mother Sage shared the tiny part of Bony Bailey's nature which was watersoul, but not the larger part which was firesoul. Since I am firesoul, I share that larger part, I suppose. And this is part of a common pattern of all firesoul humanity. I am all of them, and hardly at all myself. That is a hard idea for a firesoul individual to accept.

Awareness of pattern – not in an intellectual, inwardly conscious way but in an outwardly conscious way – is a watersoul attribute. At Bony's time, and earlier in necrotech, the only watersouls were those few people Mother Sage had told me about called fairies and witches. Were they mathematicians? I came to regard our feys as mathematicians. Twice each day I went outside the house with my gathering basket. Even with my limited vision, I could see that the productive gardens depended on an intricate and fluid geometry for their partnership with nature. Imagine being able to create designs in geometric spaces in multi-dimensional time! But Bony's insights had approached such a vision – so it could be understood by a firesoul person sympathetic to watersoul ways. Surely that is what I was becoming. Perhaps then, there was a special role for me in the New Beginning. I could explain my concerns about big houses, and other destructive things which people had built in the ancient times. I could stop the village ways being destroyed, and help firesouls and watersouls to live together.

I needed to test these ideas against real life. There was only one thing to do. I had to go to the village and see if, now that I was full grown, I might survive and be accepted amongst the watersoul people.

But not yet. First I had to read carefully through every word of Mother Sage's journal to prepare me for the role I would have in reverse of hers. She had had to sublimate her watersoul nature to live with me; now I would make adjustments to fit in with the watersouls. Hence it was several moon cycles from Mother Sage's death before I ventured down the avenue to the village.

14

The Village

Roy could hardly believe how dreadful life in the village had become since the night he had done the wrong thing. Less than a moon cycle earlier, when he had come down from the big house to the village to live, he had been welcomed like everybody's long lost brother, or lover. He had been hugged and kissed, fondled and fussed, fed delicacies, had flowers put in his hair, and everyone wanted to sleep with him. Now he had to sleep alone; and in spite of having slept alone for as long as he could remember, he now hated it, because it meant he was shunned.

On the night it happened he had been thrown down the ladder of the sleeping hut he had been in, and discovered that, by the strange collective sense they all possessed, everyone knew about it, and he was pushed out of every hut he tried to climb into. At last, exhausted from emotional trauma, rejected in all his approaches, bruised from being repeatedly thrown down ladders, he had stumbled around in the dark and had come upon an abandoned sleeping hut. Climbing its ladder and crawling in he found some mouldy-smelling bedding: a rotting quilt, its filling flattened and leaking out, and a fur blanket split down the middle. After tossing about for what seemed like half the night, no sooner had he fallen asleep than he plummeted down through a hole which had opened in the webbing of the chamber floor. He fell into the storeroom beneath and smashed through the spikes of broken baskets to the earth floor and the stench of rotten nuts and vermin droppings. He was too wretched to do more than push baskets aside to make a space on the earth floor and wrap the bedding that had fallen with him around his trembling body and wait for the dawn.

In the morning his punishment continued. The boys ridiculed him by turning their backs, bending over, pulling up their tunics to display their bare bottoms and making suggestive wiggles at him. The girls shrieked and ran for protection, dodging behind another person, a tree or a hut.

Everyone else, children and older people, ignored him. He begged and pleaded for them to explain what he had done to deserve this treatment, but they would not talk to him in his language. A few boys responded in mime-song jingles whose crude meaning was obvious enough.

In a way, he knew what his offence had been. He had tried to copulate with another boy who had enthusiastically engaged with him in mutual fondling, and who seemed to be offering his responsive arsehole to provide for Roy's aroused sexual interest. What he did not understand was why, when every other sensual stimulation was indulged in with ecstatic abandon, what he had tried to do was bad enough to cause the whole community to subject him to this cruel rejection.

The shunning went on day after day, although the mockery diminished as the boys apparently lost interest in it. Roy began to feel invisible, and more lonely in the densely populated village than he had felt when he was alone in the big house. He helped himself to food and ate apart from the rest of them. He cleaned out the hut he had found and took a good fur blanket and a new quilt from one of the other huts. It was uncomfortable on the bare earth, but the webbing of the upper chamber floor was rotten and beyond repair, even if he had had the skill to mend it. Before that awful night he had been interested in learning all he could about village life and finding a useful role for himself. Now that did not seem possible, and he wandered around purposelessly.

When it first happened Roy had been deeply emotionally upset by the incident and its outcome, but a few days later he told himself that he was just shocked at the sudden change of treatment. He had been raised as a thinking creature rather than a feeling one, and as an independent person rather than part of a community. He told himself that he had not felt altogether comfortable with all the cuddling and contact, so perhaps what had happened was not so very terrible. He was certainly aggrieved at their behaviour: after all, he was perfectly willing to accept any rules and taboos there might be; there was no need for the exaggerated reaction to what he had done simply from ignorance of their ways.

The best thing to do would be to remove himself from the situation for a while and to think out what to do next. No one paid any attention when he took two large gathering baskets and collected some provisions from the storerooms which were being stuffed full ready for winter hibernation. He tied up his bedding into a roll and slung it over his back. Thus provided for he walked back up the hill to the big house.

Roy made himself comfortable in his old room, rather than in the

237

sleeping hut around the back. He felt quite relieved to be back in familiar surroundings. He told himself he had plenty to occupy himself with because he had to think through what he knew of the village way of life before he attempted to try it out again, as he supposed he would have to do. He was sure there would be some useful information in Mother Sage's writings, particular amongst the papers on how the firesoul boys were to be brought up.

The first thing he had to know was why his sexual needs were incompatible with the village practices. This was not difficult to discover. There was a paper in the upbringing folder on that very subject, headed 'Pleasure and Sex'. What it told him was that in ancient times, in necrotech, the awarding or denying of pleasure was an important part of wielding power, which was a major factor in firesoul culture. Sensual pleasure was regarded as a preliminary to sexual mating, which was a form of possession, and resulted in children, who were a form of property and the inheritors of property. So sensual pleasure and copulation was restricted to the courtship and marriage situation, and strictly limited or disapproved of towards children and old people, and forbidden between close relatives and between people of the same gender. This had the effect of rendering the males either dominant, competitive and aggressive, or resigned to such attitudes and behaviours in other men, as required by the economic relations of the necrotech culture.

The firesoul sexual behaviour could be traced back to human evolutionary origins. Humans are unusual in the animal kingdom in that they do not have a mating season, but are sexually active throughout every year of adult life. Presumably this gave them a survival advantage by helping to create social bonding, but it meant that their population could, and often did, soar up to and beyond the limits of natural resources. Watersoul had continued human evolution and removed the earlier weakness by separating the lifelong human and animal need for affection and sensual pleasure from the occasional necessity for mating and reproduction.

Watersoul people indulge in 'pleasure rubbing', which includes all forms of gentle, affectionate, mutually acceptable, sensual play (except actual copulation), very freely, night and day, and all through their lives. Since pleasure is not restricted in their childhood, the urgent and aggressive desire for it suffered particularly by the males of the ancient culture is never seen amongst watersoul people.

The sensual preferences of the two human types are quite different. Watersoul like to prolong feelings of ecstasy indefinitely, whereas the firesoul pattern was to seek an intense climax, like the fatal blow of a conquest. It is as if watersoul and firesoul are contrasting patterns of nature: water cascading endlessly over the rocks; fire burning itself out in a devastating roar.

Copulation between watersoul is reserved for the young couples who are responsible for breeding. They engage in a preliminary selection ritual consisting of coy, flirtatious games. Sexual intercourse is carried out very hurriedly in the middle of winter, and regarded as a duty, not a pleasure.

Penetration of the vagina by the penis is not otherwise practised because it can cause pain and damage to small girls. Similarly, there is no anal penetration by the penis, because that can be painful, and damage the sphincter muscle. The vagina and the anus are, nevertheless, enjoyed as pleasure centres, and are fondled, nibbled and licked without restraint. The main reason for this otherwise free and easy culture having a strict rule is to avoid the firesoul pattern whereby inflicting, or even suffering, pain was enjoyed, and for some was essential to sexual arousal. It is easy for the watersoul to follow a pattern of no penetration by the penis for pleasure for anyone, and every other pleasure permitted for everyone. They are too lazy to keep to a more complex set of rules for particular groups.

That explained the incident in the village. Roy would have picked up the firesoul pattern of pleasure involving thrusting in his penis, so when he was sensually stimulated by that boy in the intense fashion which watersoul enjoyed, he sought a sexual climax by penetrating the orifice which seemed to be offered. He had no idea he was offending against the one watersoul rule that ensured the greatest heights of sensual delight for every pleasure partner and never any risk of pain or discomfort.

There had been an incident on his very first night which could have ended similarly badly, Roy thought. During the day a little girl had attached herself to him, and it was she who led him to a sleeping hut when it got dark. It was strange after having slept alone for as long as he could remember to be surrounded by other bodies. And the stroking he had been greeted with on his arrival continued and intensified. He was unsure whether he liked being with bodies which seemed to be trying to merge with his. His clothes were taken off. He was kissed and nibbled and licked. The little girl clung on to him with her arms and legs. She was a lovely creature, so smooth, warm and lithe. He was disturbed that his contact with her made his penis stiffen, and even more bothered when she discovered this and began to play with it, sucking the tip, caressing it all the way down to his testicles, and then squeezing its length between her thighs. At last he gently prised her off and went out through the curtain, down the ladder and then into the gardens to finish off his aroused desire in private. He climbed back in and the child found him again, cuddled up to him contentedly and went to sleep, as he did too very soon afterwards. Suppose he had been carried away then, and had hurt the little girl?

Roy still did not understand the incident that occurred just before Mother Sage died, when his embrace was rejected so emphatically by Fey. He read on, and that too was explained.

The Mother Sages had to raise their charges to pick up the ancient firesoul patterns. They decided that, for a firesoul boy to grow up to be a firesoul man, with a strong sex and power drive, he had to be deprived of affection and sensual contact in childhood. Accordingly each Mother Sage was careful to maintain a stiffly deferential distance from her 'young lord'. In addition, the 'slaves' had to be prevented from indulging in pleasure rubbing with the firesoul boy, or with each other when he was around. This was a rule which the Mother Sages had applied most strictly; anyone who broke it would be guilty of hindering their charges' development, and the firesoul completion. Being strict with the villagers was difficult since the very idea of discipline was so foreign to their nature, so the Mother Sages would have to break into storms of rage if anyone so much as touched the boys. That was why Fey shrieked and ran off when Roy tried to embrace her.

On reading this, Roy was somewhat reassured about his own feelings and needs, but he was, if anything, even more angry. The Mother Sages' stratagem had worked well on him. He had scarcely realised this before, because he was unused to introspection about personal matters, but he had developed into a typical firesoul man: frustrated and lustful, with an urgent need for sexual intercourse with a woman of child-bearing age. He had also probably picked up the associated firesoul pattern of falling in love, which was supposed to lead to wooing and winning and mating for life. But the woman he had begun to love and desire, had already been pregnant. In firesoul terms this meant she was unsuitable as a wife since she 'belonged' to someone else, and was

240

spoilt or soiled as far as any other man was concerned.

But now he knew why he was so different from them, would he be sure to behave in an acceptable way when he went back? The fact that he had not hurt the little girl was surely encouraging, and it had been quite some time before he had done anything to hurt or abuse anyone else. Would they give him another chance: welcome him, or shun him still? He had no way of knowing how long it would be that he had to depend on the village; how long before he could join the other firesoul boys who would, presumably, be like himself. If only Mother Sage had not died before that time came. Could he even be sure that it would come? If only there was someone he could talk to, but even in the happy days he had enjoyed before he did wrong, no one would talk to him in his language. He had found he could follow the mime-song, but it seemed only to be suitable for immediate practical communication, not for sharing your thoughts with. But of course watersoul shared thoughts – if they could be described as having thoughts – through eversight, and they did not need language for that. And their thoughts were not like his, inward and self-aware, but were shared soul resonating through the patterns of the past.

Then a wave of satisfaction suddenly came over Roy: was it not wonderful that he had acquired some inkling of this other way of being? His words might be inadequate to describe it, but he had some sense of what watersoul was. He had respected village people and their ways all his life, in spite of Mother Sage discouraging his interest. He may have gone along with the 'slaves and servants' charade, but he had known deep down that the people were different, rather than inferior. He had begun his own book to set down what he found out about them. He had made a detailed study of the baskets with Fey.

Fey! She could be the answer to his immediate problem. He had seen her around the village, but she had not approached him and he was a little shy of her. She was very big with child, which was no surprise. Perhaps he could persuade her to talk to him, and she might be willing to plead with the others that he be given another chance, tell them how he regretted his mistake and would not repeat it.

Roy slept well that night. In the morning he went to the basket he stored his own writing in and read it through again. It was good enough, he thought, to explain the crafts to someone who knew nothing of them. So, when he joined the other firesouls, if he discovered they lacked respect for the villagers' skills, he could show them this writing.

241

He also had the material on pattern mathematics, which helped to explain what watersoul was in theoretical terms. But he had little besides the upbringing folders to describe what watersoul people were like and how they lived. He had decided to stay for a while in the house, so this would be a potentially useful occupation. He got out paper, pens and ink and began. As the words flowed from his mind onto the paper he was surprised at how much he knew about these mysterious people.

'The first thing to understand and accept is that watersoul people do not think. They use their brains to see, not to reason. They know but they do not comprehend. This only makes sense by contrast with ourselves. We have a limited vision of the world: we perceive through our senses only our immediate surroundings and the present moment. We use our brains to store impressions, and to relate those impressions to each other in order to anticipate what is likely to occur in the future and hence make decisions. We retain in our minds selected patterns and regularities which fit in with a culturally agreed conceptual model of what the world is like which has been put there by early socialisation and teaching. We externalise our inner world through technology, thus validating the model, but disrupting the patterns we have overlooked.

'The watersoul, on the other hand, use their brains as receivers, capable of seeing, but not usually storing, any part of the pattern universe in time and space. Their actions are not determined by choice and free will but by resonance with those past patterns which constitute their extended self, or shared soul. Because their brains are open receivers they cannot simultaneously be closed receptacles for self-consciousness. The watersoul, in particular those of a particular village, are one collective being, not many individuals. And they are one in conjunction with their gardens. Their gardens are part of their shared soul.'

'That's good,' Fey said. 'You could call us the fey, instead of putting "watersoul" all the time.'

'I thought "fey" was a word for the women.'

'Well it shouldn't be, whatever Mother Sage may have meant by it. We're genderless in the villages. Anyone who behaves in an obviously male or female way would be driven out.'

'I thought you were gentle people.'

'They weren't gentle with you, were they?'

'Well they were nasty, but they didn't exactly drive me out.'

'Oh, I think they did. Anyway, let's get on with this. You haven't included the forests; after "their gardens" you should put "and local forests".'

'And they are one in conjunction with their gardens and local forests. Their gardens and forests are part of the fey shared soul.' Roy read out. 'Is that right?' She nodded and smiled. 'I don't really see *why*, though,' he said. 'You create the *gardens*, so I can see *them* as part of your collective extended self. But the forests are just there, part of nature but not part of you, surely?'

Roy's life had changed again, this time very much for the better. Two days after he had retreated back to the big house, Fey had turned up, with more baskets of provisions and a roll of bedding over her back; clearly having come to stay.

'Can I come in?' she said in mime-song.

He replied with gestures he hoped would convey something like, 'Of course. I'm delighted to see you,' which he was, although he found her huge belly disconcerting, so that he had to fix his eyes on her face.

'You need someone to talk to,' she said in the ancient language.

'Oh, yes!' Roy replied feelingly.

'Dialogue. Firesoul minds need it, isn't that so?'

'Well, yes, I suppose we do – sharing ideas and so on. But just to talk and not be alone —'

'I'll talk with you – you can have some dialogue – for three days.'

'Why just three days?' he asked, puzzled. 'And what happens after that?'

'Too much firesoul talking is disagreeable for us. But you can have three days. Then maybe you can come out of your head just a little way. It would be a lovely change for you to get out of that prison, and all the words buzzing around in there.'

'Are you going to stay with me then, up here? Longer than three days?' he asked eagerly.

'Only until the courtship and feasting is over. After that the people will begin to get sleepy for the winter, so they won't mind if you are there. It is too cold in the winter for only two bodies to keep each other warm.'

'Mother Sage and I slept alone in the winter, and we didn't hibernate,' Roy remarked.

'That was part of your regime, but I expect a couple of the "servants" got into Mother Sage's bed, poor old thing. And some of us used to warm your bed up before you got into it.'

'You used to warm my bed? And you're going to sleep with me here?'

'If you don't try to put your penis inside me.'

Roy looked away from her, embarrassed. 'I understand: only cuddles – pleasure rubbing.' He looked back at her. 'And then we both go to hibernate in the village?' She nodded. 'But what will happen afterwards? Will they shun me again when spring comes? And how long will it be before I can join the other firesouls?'

'You really are a proper firesoul, aren't you? So bothered about the future, and you have to have plans all worked out in your head. I think three days of this may be too much for me.'

Roy looked at her perfect face distorted in a scowl, and could not help bursting into laughter.

'Oh, sorry,' he managed to say. 'You just look so funny all screwed up and cross.'

Her scowl turned to a smile and then giggles. She reached out to him, and they clung together, laughing uncontrollably.

At last Roy pushed her away. The contact had reinforced his awareness of her pregnancy. 'What about the child?' he blurted out. 'Surely it's coming soon. Will it be born here or down there? Won't you need help?'

She shrugged. 'Oh, never mind about that. This baby is not coming to stay. It will go back to the patterns.'

'I don't understand,' he said.

'That's because you don't understand our ways,' she said.

'I am trying to. I've been writing down what I know about you. Would you like to see? You could help me get it right. It could be our project for these three days. I want to be sure that the firesouls respect you. I want to be sure the New Beginning doesn't interfere with the watersoul villages. I think that might be my special role and purpose.'
She scowled again, this time in fun, and they both burst out laughing again.

So that was how Roy came to be reading his account of watersoul ways to Fey. She explained to him about the fey relationship with forests, and he was amazed at how fluent she was in a language she had hardly used before. If he asked how she did it, probably she would say, 'By following the patterns of speaking the ancient language.' He listened carefully, and recorded her words in the shorthand Mother Sage had taught him.

'Necrotech people did not understand life,' Fey said. 'They did not know themselves as engaged in the flow of life, but as individual flames of self-consciousness. They consumed what nature provided as if feeding their fires with dead fuel. In the beginning there were primitive peoples who necessarily had some understanding of interacting with nature, but their cultures were all destroyed by those who had compounded their isolation by enclosing themselves in buildings inside cities.

'By the end of necrotech all the wild forests had been cut down because the people did not know that wild forests are the source of the life patterns of the land. They saw them only as places to take wood from. During the period of breakdown which led to bionecrotech, they began to see the forests as an important source of what they called "genetic resources" from which they could extract codes that enabled them to manipulate living creatures. So they sent experts to collect the genetic material to store it away so that it could be used to make monstrous distorted plants and animals for their machines to make into fuel for human bodies. From those monsters came the green dragon which saved the people from their own folly, and kept the records of their history so they could re-live their past for entertainment and not die from boredom. A few of the people came to understand what necrotech had done because so much knowledge of the past gave them eversight, and they knew the patterns of the past directly, and they were ashamed.

'After the green dragon, the women made a pledge that they would not use fire, and they vowed they would not destroy the natural patterns when they returned. There were many pledges which followed: not to dig the earth or tear out rocks, not to hunt or enslave animals. When the wild forests came back, the people respected them, and knew they were the source of the patterns of life, and that the plants we select for our gardens are only borrowed from the forests, and that we ourselves are borrowed from the forests, to which we will return.'

'How did the forests come back?' asked Roy.

'Their patterns had only been interrupted. No patterns are ever destroyed. They are present in the past where all the patterns are, almost in their entirety; only at the surface of change and evolution do slight differences emerge. The patterns of the forests are very strong, so they

245

found their way over the hacking and burning and back to the surface of evolution.'

'But how could that be, when the species had become extinct, and their genetic codes gone?'

'The genetic codes are merely echoes of the patterns of the past. Bionecrotech technologists thought the codes determined living form because they found that by manipulating the codes they could make new forms. But this is because pattern influence can pass either way, so fragile new patterns of distorted life echo the manipulated codes by resonance. But it is the patterns of the past which bring about the on-going forms of life, not the codes. So what was extinct can come back, as used to occur occasionally even in necrotech when the destructive forces left nature alone for a while.'

'If I were describing the village way of life to firesoul people, could I explain it as a system consisting of people within garden within forest? The village people's needs for food, clothing and shelter are met from the immediate surrounding area which they have modified by selecting for useful plants, and thus creating a garden. Then there are cycles of interaction and renewal between the garden and the forest.'

'I don't like the word "system": it sounds too regular, almost mechanical. What's wrong with the word "pattern"? Isn't that what you mean?'

'Well, yes, but I know the firesoul boys have been taught the old science. "Pattern" would be too vague a word for them.'

'It's universal, not vague. You'll have to tell them about pattern mathematics.'

'Did Mother Sage tell you about that? Did you know I'd been working on it?'

She laughed. 'Your mind was bursting with the effort to get round those ideas, and it sent out a beacon that any fey would pick up.'

'I thought they were brilliant ideas,' Roy joked, 'but I didn't know their light was actually visible!'

'Fire metaphor,' she said solemnly, 'it's unavoidable with firesoul language.' Then she smiled. 'But it wasn't the ideas that shone out, but your efforts to stuff them into your brain.'

'Do you understand the ideas? Mother Sage did, I think – she didn't just copy them down.'

'I didn't try. Horrible stuff! We don't like to use our minds in that way. Mother Sage, well — Anyway, tell me what you have written

246

next. After the bit about sharing soul with the gardens and forests.'

He read, 'Firesoul science inclines us to look for uniform elements making up any more complex whole. But our science has never really understood living systems where emergent properties arise over and above the properties of the constituent parts, and how diversity is essential to unity, and uniformity is not sustainable. Individual fey are far from being identical cells of their collective being, they are very varied. They are highly curious about the patterns manifested in each fey person, and in the past patterns being shared and variously combined and refined in each other.'

'That's a clever little bit. Did you see that from what Mother Sage wrote about her fey mathematician from necrotech?'

'Do you know about everything I do?'

'I can know; it's there to be known.'

'Isn't that rather confusing? How do you decide what to focus on?'

'It's the same kind of process as when you shift focus with your vision: you can be vaguely aware of things that you're not concentrating on, can't you, and shift from one area to another? But what's wrong with confusion? It means flowing together, which is what watersoul do.'

'I just can't imagine what it would be like. I'm sure that in necrotech someone with such powers would be revered as a wizard or high priest.'

'Or burned as a witch.'

He stared at her, as if seeing her for the first time. She has a witchy look, he thought. It's those black eyes. And her fine-boned face and sharply-bowed sensual mouth, and her floating mess of purple hair: the fascinating kind of witch, rather than the crone. How did he know how a witch might look? It no longer surprised him to have knowledge he had never been taught. He knew and accepted the process whereby he had been given enough of the firesoul pattern to connect him to all the rest. He liked to think of it as the unconscious eversight Mother Sage had told him he had: a shared firesoul eversight.

'Is it possible for someone to be both watersoul and firesoul?' he found himself asking.

'No more possible than someone being both a frog and a tree; they're different patterns.'

'Couldn't they change though? Mother Sage had a firesoul life after her watersoul one.'

'No, Mother Sage was always watersoul.'

'But she told me she had caught a little firesoul from my flame.'

247

Fey visibly shuddered. 'I don't like the idea of a pattern emerging whereby watersoul and firesoul are mixed.'

'Wouldn't it be more confusion?' Roy teased.

'No. Patterns – like fire and water – that are incompatible can't flow together. But firesoul has a long history, and it was the first human pattern, and it's still there in the past. We all fear its return; you know what pain and destruction it caused.'

'Why did you agree to the firesoul boys being raised, then?'

'We thought that the firesoul pattern kept trying to come back because it needed completion, and if we helped the completion – whatever that might be – come about, firesoul would go away and leave us alone.'

'Perhaps the completion is a synthesis between us,' Roy persisted.

'No, it can't be that.'

'Why not?'

'How could firesoul need a synthesis with something it didn't even know was possible?'

'But Mother Sage told me that everything in the universe has eversight, even us, though we don't know it consciously.'

'Yes. So?'

'Isn't having eversight the same as being watersoul?'

'No, not really. Eversight is a way of knowing, like a universal science. But every creature has to have a way of doing – a technology, if you like – as well as a way of knowing. The firesoul way of doing was necrotech.'

'And the watersoul way of doing is gardening?'

'Yes.'

'Well then, perhaps the completion is about firesoul learning how to be gardeners. Perhaps if we become gardeners our eversight would become conscious, and we'd become watersoul.'

'Well one thing I am sure of is you won't get to be watersoul by trying to think it out. We'll do an experiment if you like, to see if you can get out of your head.'

'You said that before: getting out of my head.'

'Well that's where you think your "self" is, isn't it?'

'And you don't.'

'You know we don't: you've written about that. Although speaking firesoul language brings that sense with it. Language is a very powerful pattern.'

'Is that why they wouldn't talk to me in my language in the village?'

She nodded and frowned, putting her hand to her forehead. 'We are always fearful about firesoul coming back in here. We'd all get trapped in our heads, not knowing the patterns of the past and afraid of not having a future. That would be terrible.'

Terrible to be the way I am! Roy thought. And I can't be any other way. He felt a pain somewhere in his chest, and said huskily, 'All right, I understand: you getting like me would be terrible; me getting like you is impossible. I don't mind going along with that.'

Fey looked at him apologetic and sympathetic. 'You are quite a sweet boy really,' she said and stroked his face. 'I don't know about *impossible* – we can try.'

He smiled wanly. 'You mean that experiment to get me out of my head,' he said. 'Can you explain?'

'Er, let me see, you'll want to know: the axioms, the hypothesis, the empirical approach, the recording of data and calculations, and all that. But I can keep to myself how I'll make sure I get to be proved right.'

'You're a cruel tease! You know I think all that's rubbish.' She opened her mouth to interrupt, he reached out to cover her lips. 'No, please, Fey, just tell me what I have to do.'

'You go outside and look around, and come back and tell me what you've seen.'

'Is that all?'

'Yes! Go on, do as you're told.'

'It's getting dark.'

'Well be quick then.'

'Can't I just look out of the window?'

Roy went down the winding stairs and out through the door of the house. He looked around at the gloom. He saw tree silhouettes against the greenish-blue luminosity of the sky. Below the sky line he could see suspended circular spots of the same shade of blue, shining with reflected light against the dark vanishing shapes of bare branches. Fruits, left on the trees unharvested while he was wrestling with ideas and then absent in the village. What a waste! But he had been too preoccupied to think of saving any produce for the winter.

He went back inside and upstairs and told Fey what he had seen.

She smiled and nodded. 'What sort of fruits?'

He looked at her puzzled. 'I thought watersoul didn't use names?'

'We don't. But you do. You have to build your bridge with the material you have. What kind of fruit?'

'Apples,' he said.

She smiled and nodded.

'Is that it?'

'For now. Let's go to bed.'

The 'experiment' continued the following day, in intervals between the work with the account of the watersoul and village ways. At dawn the next morning she sent him out.

There was more to hear than to see. There was a strong wind moving the trees, and the sound was as if all their branches were rubbing and grinding together, and crying out hoarsely in complaint. On top of that was the rustling of dry leaves still attached to young trees lower down, and above all the eerie hoot as of a horn, its impure note emerging from the roar of the air. A few birds tweeted nervously. Even the light seemed reluctant to come, and brought no shadows. Roy saw a few tiny white daisy flowers, incongruous in the damp deadness on the ground.

He went back to bed and told Fey and she smiled and nodded. 'Thank you,' she said. 'I've brought up some food for breakfast, then we'll get on with the project.' They ate, snuggled under the covers, and then dashed out for a quick bathe in the chilly stream and rubbed each other dry. Roy had never been so happy.

'Where did we get to?' Roy asked.

'The bit about us being different and interested in each others' patterns.'

He read, 'But they do not evaluate these characteristics, nor do they have any preference or possessiveness for likeness, or dislike of unlikeness.' He looked at her, 'I don't know why I wrote that. I just had a feeling it was true. But they didn't like me, did they? I suppose because I am firesoul.'

'It is true. We don't like or dislike others. But we are wary of firesoul patterns emerging, which they do sometimes, not just in boys like you, but a less obvious version which doesn't develop until adolescence. It could be called "father bent" in ancient language. Males who are father bent are inclined to take charge, to instruct, to impose their preferences, to protect and have favourites, and to be sexual rather than sensual in their physical contact with others – they want to put their penis inside.' She looked at Roy and he grimaced. 'Anyone who begins to show these characteristics is shunned by others; he might even be chased into the forest and not come back.'

'I see. I suppose there isn't a female equivalent – a "mother bent", wouldn't it be?'

'Yes, there is mother bent. It's a tendency in a woman to prefer, and be protective towards, infants born to herself over those born of other women.'

'That's a bit difficult to deal with. What do you do, take her baby away?'

'Something like that. Go on, tell me the next part.'

Roy could tell that 'mother bent' was not something Fey wanted to talk about, perhaps because of her baby that was coming. Probably he would find out then.

'Well it's all got a bit out of sequence, but I had a bit about death that linked up with the part about shared soul and extended self.'

'Yes. What did you put?'

'The shared soul or extended self extends to those whom we should regard as no longer living. The watersoul do not have any notion of death as oblivion. Because their seeing and knowing includes the past, no one can cease to be, or no longer be involved with the ongoing patterns. Watersoul have no fear of death, no reluctance to die, or any regret at any individual's death. They are, if anything, least concerned about babies' and young children's deaths. This is due to their knowledge that there is no new pattern in a very young child: to the fey a child is a copy of earlier patterns.'

Roy looked up. 'I remembered Mother Sage saying something about you being careless about your children, and I worked out for myself why that might be from the pattern maths stuff.'

'Clever,' she said. 'You're allowing your pattern understanding to grow. But we would put it more strongly than you did: a baby is *identical* to earlier patterns.'

'Yes, I know, I shouldn't have said *copy*; I do understand that, it's in the next bit.' He continued reading, 'In the child, earlier patterns shine through; there is nothing in the child's present which was not there before in the past. So if it dies, nothing is lost. In any case, the fey do not have a sense of individual self awareness to lose: their minds are receptive and open, outward directed, not enclosed.'

'Yes, that's very good. Difficult for those firesouls to accept though. Don't you have a problem with it?'

He frowned as he considered. 'Well, I don't have any problem with it

251

as just ideas. What actually happens could be more difficult.'

'It might help if you made the firesouls look at their own attitudes to death. You could make some comment about how strange it was in necrotech the fuss they made about people's dead bodies: funeral ceremonies, tombs and all that,' said Fey. 'It's an important part of the pattern: firesoul don't know they'll always have their past so they're afraid of having no future. *Always have.*' She tutted with annoyance. "That's got meaning in it I don't want. The past is timeless, not eternal, and no one can *possess* it, even his own bit of past. That's the trouble with firesoul language, it includes all the basic firesoul assumptions, and it's hopeless using it for pattern ideas. Didn't you find that with the mathematics?'

But Roy was not paying attention. He was still thinking of what she had said just before. 'What do *you* do with dead bodies?' he asked, trying to make it sound like a casual question.

She looked hard at him. 'Why do you ask?'

He blurted out, 'When Mother Sage died, I had this feeling the servants cut her body up and gave me some to eat.'

She laughed. 'I doubt that, we don't eat large creatures. It's a consequence of the pledges: no domestic animals, no hunting with weapons, so we don't have the tools to do butchering, and it would make a big mess. Usually people go to the forest and part of the body is eaten by wild creatures and the rest rots away. The servants would have taken Mother Sage's body to the forest.'

'Oh, thank you,' Roy sighed with relief. 'I didn't like the idea of you being cannibals. I agree with you about funerals and tombs, but somehow cannibalism is too much the other way. And the thought of eating Mother Sage, even if her living pattern was over, and the body wasn't her — It's good to have you put me right on these things, even if it's only for three days. The next section is where I tried to describe how you live. I expect it's wrong and incomplete in places. But I've got you to tell me.'

'I think we need a break,' Fey said. 'Why don't you go and do some more of our experiment.'

Roy went outside. The wind had dropped and it was raining. In the even light from the grey sky there were no shadows. It was quite still, except in the pond where raindrops caused circles to ripple outwards, one here, one there, spaced out when he first looked. A few moments later there were so many drops the circles were muddled up: confused, he thought with a smile. He preferred the clear patterns of the separate circles. A few brown leaves drifted down as if from the sky to join others lying delicately on the evergreen herbs, the newly fallen ones poised like boats with high prows, or the backs of brown creatures snuffling around; you could see all sorts of shapes in them. The leaves from previous days were sodden and flattened. A squirrel spiralled a tree, and spun back down with rippling tail, and sat attentive on the ground for a moment before bending down to make a hole for a nut and then leaping away on its powerful back legs.

'Good,' was all Fey said when he described it to her.

They shared some food, then went to bed for a cuddle and a doze. Roy found himself resenting the waste of talking time, when the daylight was so short anyway, but it was she who decided how they spent the precious days, and she would not fill all the time with work on Roy's project.

But there was still light and time left for more work when she decided they should get up.

'Now, tell me what you have put on how we live,' Fey said. 'That's important if you want the firesoul boys to respect us.'

Roy read out, 'I shall now describe how the fey live. You may judge it primitive, but remember that they know all about firesoul and necrotech, and they have chosen their way of life in full knowledge of what is possible. The fey are gardeners. Perhaps the human animal is naturally a gardener, and if our species had not domesticated fire, enslaved certain plants and animals for farming, and developed in the necrotech direction, we would have been gardeners. So, when we had tried the necrotech route, and destroyed or disrupted all the necessary natural resources, and made ourselves wretchedly unhappy, and perhaps rather surprisingly survived to try again, we turned at last to gardening.

'Mother Sage once told me that some firesoul people were gardeners, but that most of their gardening was directed at creating pleasant environments they could occasionally escape to from the stresses of necrotech. I should think the gardeners were probably the most contented of the firesoul, even if they could not avoid entirely the obligation to pay through their labour for anything they were allowed to enjoy.

'Gardening for the fey is the primary occupation and the main source of pleasure as well as of bodily nourishment. Watching them garden has

253

reminded me of ants or bees constantly engaged in the process of creating and tending their world. The fey garden is a work of art: intricately patterned, lovingly coaxed into conformity with the evolving design. Every fey knows without any instruction which tiny seedlings are desired in any little niche and which ones gently to tease out. I could not do such work because I have no eversight to show me the past pattern of a seedling which appears in its present exactly like another. I did learn the flavours and uses of a few herbs which I could recognise in their mature form. Even that was difficult for me since fey do not give names to species of plants. The little knowledge I had enabled me to do some gathering when I lived in the village. There is no other gardening work that I can do, since crude work that someone unskilled could have carried out, such as digging, is never done. Indeed, one can never see the soil in a fey garden, let alone disturb it, which they don't do because it is one of the pledges.'

Fey interrupted him. 'Where did you get that part about seedlings from? Obviously not from your last visit.'

'I went to the village many times with you, didn't I? It was springtime then, and I watched people kneeling on mats picking out tiny seedlings, and I wondered how they knew which ones to take and which to leave. I worked out later how eversight would help.'

'I shouldn't really have done that you know: talk to you and take you to the village,' Fey said. 'It was against Mother Sage's rules: we were supposed to keep a respectful distance. She used to be very strict with us, but she slackened off when she discovered her soul friend from necrotech. That shows she was still watersoul: she pleased herself rather than do her duty. Pleasure is what matters most to us. But she had worked very hard before that to keep you away from the village. Your house had been built too close to the village – Mother Sage knew that. It would have been better over the other side of the hill, out of sight, but the villagers wouldn't do it – too much effort. And she'd have liked a more permanent staff of servants. Most of the other Mother Sages got their way, but not yours. So, with the house being so close, we kept swapping over, and wandering up and down. Poor Mother Sage, she did have such a struggle. And you, poor thing, now you don't know what you are.'

'Don't worry about me, I'm working it out. I'm sure it was meant for me to be different.'

'There's no such thing as *meant*.'

'There's completion.'

'That's not the same as *meant*. That word suggests there's some power, like a god, with a purpose we're involved in. Completion's not like that. Oh dear, you've almost got me arguing. If you've found purpose and meaning in your life, and I'm helping you, we'd better keep on with it. Go on, what've you got next?'

'The fey only work during the daylight hours, and not for all that time if they do not wish to. There is other work besides gardening: making baskets and clothing, setting and collecting traps, gathering food from the gardens or from the forest, preparing food for the day or for storage (no cooking is done, of course, since fire is not used at all), keeping the firebreaks clear, repairing or occasionally constructing sleeping huts. The fey find all work enjoyable. The materials used grow in the gardens or in the forest or by the river. Fresh things are made for the pleasure of creating. Everything they make: the clothes, the baskets, the little thatched sleeping huts, is beautiful. Some artefacts are plain, others are elaborately decorated for no particular reason. Everything that is made is shared and passed around freely. Private possessions are unknown.

'After dark the fey go to the sleeping huts, each of which has one sleeping chamber for several people, who all sleep cuddled up together. The groups often change about from one night to the next, and there is no regular pattern to who sleeps with whom, such as mating pairs, close relatives, or those of the same age or gender.

'The group does more than just sleep during the hours of dark. The other activity is what is translated into the ancient language as "pleasure rubbing". The same kind of activity goes on in the daytime too, but the sleeping arrangements lend themselves to plenty of this sensual contact during the night.'

Roy looked up. 'I've got a paper about pleasure that Mother Sage left; I can put that in there. Shall I read it to you?'

'No, I know what it says. Go on with what you wrote.'

'Depending on how you look and your expectations, you could see little variation in the villagers' activities from day to day or else much change. For much of a season cycle, the daily routine only varies due to the weather and the days being long or short. On the other hand, the gardens follow cycles through the seasons, which are reflected in the gardening activities. There is one major seasonal change: the fey hibernate through the winter dormancy and, in the autumn, well before winter really sets in, there is what we could see as a festive period, in which there is feasting and particularly intense merriment. This is also the time for courtship, in which selection is made for the sexual coupling which takes place in a little interlude in the hibernation, the timing being chosen so that babies are born during the autumn, and taken into winter dormancy as tiny infants needing only breast milk. The close of the feasting is also the time older people "go to the forest".'

'That's all fine. You've described our way of life well. But you can't read any more, it's too dark. Time for bed.'

Roy went outside to urinate, and found himself continuing the experiment. It was indeed dark, and he could see very little on the ground. He looked up. The wind had returned and driven away the clouds, leaving the sky clear and thick with stars. He stared up at the stars. He had been taught that they were so far away that the light he was seeing had left them millions of years before. He was looking at the past. Was this like eversight? he wondered. No, he was still seeing only an instant, not timeless patterns. Suddenly he felt very small and mortal. His life was so brief compared to the lives of the stars up there. And then oblivion, forever. He all but fainted with the sheer awfulness of the realisation. He shuddered, and ran inside and up the twisting stairs, and into the bed which was already warm from Fey's body. He wriggled out of his clothes and wrapped his naked body close around hers. Don't ever leave me! he begged her silently.

In the morning when he awoke Fey was not there. He waited for her to return, with some breakfast perhaps. But after quite a while she had not come, and there was no sound of her moving around.

At last he got up, dressed quickly and went outside. There was no sign of her. Then he heard a muffled cry over in the direction of the stream. He went towards it.

She was sitting on the bank of the stream, a shawl over her shoulders, but naked below. Her feet were in the water and she was bending over and moaning.

Of course, he thought, the baby is coming, she's in labour. He ran down the slope to her.

'Fey, are you all right? Why didn't you wake me? What can I do to help? Shall I fetch someone from the village?'

She looked up at him, with a vague expression. He started to repeat what he had just said. She interrupted with a gesture and said something in mime-song. He could tell the general sense was, 'Go away, leave me alone, I don't want any help.'

Reluctantly he left her. For most of the day her labour continued. He went part of the way to her several times, but she had not moved – nothing appeared to have changed. After a while he began to occupy himself copying out his shorthand notes of Fey's contributions to his project. What a wise and clever women she is, he thought. What a good team we are. He allowed himself to imagine the two of them being a couple, a family with the coming child. He did not care that some other man had mated with her, so the child was not his own; he was not firesoul to that extent. He would not want to own Fey, or their children. He became more and more sure that a synthesis was possible between watersoul and firesoul, and that his, and Fey's, role was to help bring that about.

At midday, Roy went all the way down the path to the stream. She was just the same. He wondered why she had her feet in the cold water; perhaps it distracts her from the pain, he thought. He asked her again if she needed help, or if he could get her something to eat, or something warmer to put around her. Again she dismissed him. He was worried: how long would this go on? Were she and the baby going to be all right? Should he perhaps disobey her and fetch help? Was she in too much pain to tell what she needed?

At dusk he decided he must do something, she couldn't stay there all night. He got a basket and put in it her tunic, her boots and a fur cloak, and some food. The sky was streaked with red as he walked down the path again. Now she was standing on the bank, naked, spreading the shawl on the ground.

At first he thought the red in the water was reflection from the sunset. Then he saw the child. It was lying in a pool of water, which was red with blood. The water was over its face and it was still. Something in his chest went into spasm. Oh, how dreadful! and it was all his fault, he should have fetched help.

He knelt down. It was a perfect little boy, still attached to the afterbirth in the water beside it. Gently he lifted the baby up.

He looked up at her. 'Oh my poor Fey, I'm so sorry, I should have helped you, but you —'

She said nothing and her face was expressionless. She bent down to take the child and afterbirth from him, and laid them on the shawl.

Looking at her he suddenly realised his misunderstanding. He knew, without doubt. She had killed the baby; drowned it, or prevented it from starting to breathe.

'Why?' he cried. He stood up and grabbed hold of her as she was about to draw the shawl together. 'Tell me why!' he demanded. She looked at him with her deep black eyes, and shrugged.

He snatched at an explanation. 'To show you're not mother bent, is that it?' She shrugged again. He tried another possibility, 'Is it because the child could be tainted by contact with me?' No response. 'Are there too many babies this time – the gardens haven't the capacity for extra mouths to feed?' She shrugged free of his hands on her arms. She saw the basket he had brought with her clothes in. She looked at him and nodded her thanks with a faint smile before putting them on. Then she finished drawing the shawl together, lifted it over her shoulder and started to walk down the hill towards the village.

'What are you going to do with that?' His earlier squeamish fear of cannibalism came back. It was only a dead body, a small tender animal, so why wouldn't they? 'Are you going to eat it?' he called after her disappearing back.

As Roy watched her go it occurred to him that this should have been their third day of talking. Fey had said they would be together in the house until the end of the feasting, and then go down for the hibernation. In the spring he would be accepted in the village and learn more about it. After some time the other firesouls would come, and Fey would have gone with him, wouldn't she? But now?

Roy cried himself to sleep that night. When he woke up he momentarily forgot what had happened. He reached out for Fey and remembered. He cried some more, then he felt angry, and kicked and screamed and thumped the pillows. But there was no one there to receive his feelings. He felt his rational self beginning to take charge.

'What am I doing making judgements?' he said to himself out loud. 'I know perfectly well they're different. Mother Sage said they don't have any sense of right or wrong like firesoul do, because they don't have social inequalities to maintain. I've got to work this thing out, and then we'll see.'

So he got up, went out for a wash, going some way upstream from the place where Fey had given birth. He had some breakfast and then set to to resume his writing. He'd start with looking at his own attitudes and firesoul patterns, especially the matter of making judgements. As he put pen to paper he felt better, and in control.

'Much of the fey way of living and being I have found utterly delightful, which is not surprising because delight and pleasure are eagerly sought by them and readily available: to be fey is to please and be pleased. But because I am firesoul I judge and evaluate. I don't approve of all their ways. For example, I didn't think it was right to have what I think of as sexual intercourse – never mind whether or not it involves penetration – with a little girl, even if she likes it. So I ask myself: is this good pleasure or bad pleasure? I have learned to seek for answers to such questions in my own attitudes and the patterns I was brought up to resonate with.

'The general reason for making judgements I understand well enough. Firesoul attitudes derive from necrotech, which was an exploitative society based on fire and destruction technology. Using destructive technology is wasteful, and its benefits transient and so necessarily restricted to a privileged few. Hence what is "good" is behaviour which is in the interests of those few; what is "bad" is what does not suit them.

'If one is brought up as firesoul, one automatically makes judgements, and also one wants to interfere with and rectify what is found "not good". But this can be a mistake. To illustrate the point, it would be consistent with firesoul thinking to admire the form and graceful movement of a wild animal, such as a lion, but judge its hunting and killing as cruel, and even to wish to "improve" the lion by making it a "compassionate" vegetarian, which might lie down peacefully beside its erstwhile prey. But then it would not be a lion. Alter any part of the creature's nature and you have destroyed its nature. The pathetic monsters which resulted from the domestication of certain species of wild animals is evidence of that.

'I have wondered what would happen to the watersoul people if firesoul men were to carry out an investigation of the watersoul way of living. The firesouls might approve of the watersouls' skills at crafts and gardening, and perhaps their sense of fun and play, but they would want to "correct" what they perceived as unacceptable population control, in particular infanticide and carelessness towards young children. They would want to teach the watersoul "proper" sexual practices, improve their technological base by, for example, introducing lamps or materials produced by melting, smelting or firing, extend their life expectation, cure their illnesses, stop them "going to the forest", and so on. If that were even attempted, the way of watersoul would be destroyed. I can see that. I fear that other firesoul men would not.'

'I'm not so sure that I wouldn't wish to reform them myself,' Roy said to himself when he had finished. 'Look at all that stuff I was dreaming about me, Fey and the baby. I think she's right: trying to combine watersoul and firesoul would probably be disastrous for the watersoul. That's an old pattern too: city cultures destroying rural ones to exploit their land and labour, and making out they were helping. "Development", they called it. I suppose the New Beginning could be different. Mother Sage seemed to think so. Oh, I don't know what I think any more!'

After this there did not seem to be anything more to write about. Roy hung around outside the house much of the time for several days, hoping Fey would come back.

One morning it was raining heavily so he did not venture out. He decided to tidy up his writing so that it was a proper book in a sensible sequence, with contents list, numbered pages and an index. He decided to incorporate some of Mother Sage's writing, including the pattern mathematics. Some of it would have to be rewritten. He got absorbed in the task. Soon it was as if he had never left the house to go to the village. Fey and the baby were just two other ghosts besides Mother Sage and Bony, and he forgot about Fey's experiment to see if he could get outside his head.

Roy stayed enclosed in his head, within his cell, in the house and its grounds until the resources of his environment were obviously dwindling. The supplies he and Fey had brought from the village were soon used up and he lived off dried fruit and nuts from the basement stores. It was produce from the previous year's harvest, but some was still edible.

It was the depletion of paper Roy noticed first. The schoolroom cupboard was empty. A hunt in the basement stores found two baskets of new paper, but also a damaged basket, its contents a mess of paper ribbons where some animal had made a nest. Only then did he realise that he must have left the basement door ajar, and allowed in small animals which had raided the remaining supplies of dried fruits and nuts. He had not thought to set traps for the pests, although he knew that the servants used to do so in case any gnawed their way in.

After that disaster, Roy had to gather food from outside, nipping out into the gardens for a few green herbs and withered apples. The need to provide for himself broke his inward concentration, and he began to take stock, not only of the food situation, but of how he was living, and how long he could continue that way.

He was suddenly achingly lonely. The ghosts in his cell, whom he talked to when he was thinking out what to write, had seemed sufficient companionship when he was deep in his studies. He became aware of his body, hunched, thin, pale and grubby from its period of confinement. He went to the garden pond, knelt at its edge and peered at his reflection in the water.

His cheeks and upper lip had fluffy tufts of beard hair interspersed with adolescent spottiness made worse from his recent lack of fresh food. His hair had grown over his ears and was dirty and matted. When was the last time someone had combed it? His body servant used to do that, and it had not occurred to him to do it himself. The villagers had groomed him until that awful night, and Fey had done so too.

'What am I going to do?' he said aloud to the reflection, to the image of the boy-man body containing his mind and his self, the eyes staring back at him. The sight and sound of his own person shook Roy's self-pity and pitched him into the world.

He stood up and turned slowly around, scanning the familiar but forgotten place he had lived in for as long as he could remember. The garden had a neglected look. It was still garden, but well on its way to merging with the neighbouring forest. How quickly that had happened! how powerful wild nature must be to have made its mark after less than one season cycle.

'What am I going to do?' he asked himself again, strangely scared but fascinated by the sound of his own voice breaking the hush. 'I can't stay here any more, I can't go to the village, the other firesouls may never come, and I'm a mixed up firesoul anyway.' It occurred to him to go and get some of his dirty linen tunics to wash in the stream, and a comb to see if he could sort out his hair, when the thought came to him, 'Perhaps what I should do is go to the forest.'

As soon as the thought had voiced itself, the idea became strangely attractive. He remembered Mother Sage saying the watersoul looked forward to it as an adventure. Well, he could treat it like that. And something might happen; he might even meet up with the firesoul men: if it was 'meant'. And even oblivion was better than being thrown up and down by the cruel tricks life played.

He sorted out a few things from the house to take with him: a water bottle which he filled from the stream, a shoulder basket with some extra clothing in it, his strongest boots, a fur cloak with a hood. He set off in the opposite direction from the village, up the hill on the path Mother Sage used to use. He reached her vigil place, where there was a rocky outcrop, and sat there for a while as nostalgic thoughts washed over him. He fancied he could feel Mother Sage still present through the years of drawing in the distant past from wherever it lay.

He wandered on, making detours off the path to pick nuts and berries and mushrooms. He decided it did not matter whether what he ate was poisonous or not. It might be a better way to go than waiting for a wolf or a bear or some accident to get him. He found some little brown mushrooms and a bright red kind which he was sure he should not eat, but he did not care. He came across a stream and refilled his water bottle, then he spread his cloak, sat down and tucked into his wild feast sitting on the rocks with his feet dangling in a little waterfall.

Something strange is happening in my head. There is someone inside my skull walking about. Now I am in there too, also walking. My whole body is in the place where only my brain should be. The person walking beside me is Mother Sage, and we are discussing my book which she is carrying, tucked under her arm.

'This is a good firesoul way to get outside your head,' Mother Sage is saying approvingly, tapping the book. 'Now anyone can tell what was in your mind, and they can build a world to match it, and then the world in your head is outside where you are. That's the way to do it. And it's a lovely index, so people can find each of your thoughts directly, and time isn't a problem any more.

'Fey's experiment is not suitable for a firesoul,' she says dismissively. 'Much too difficult for you. You could try getting out of your head by getting inside it. According to the ancient mystics, the way to enlightenment is inwards. Of course, it is impossible to be sure what is in and what is out. It may be that the problem with firesoul is that they are turned inside out. So perhaps inwards is really outwards, if you see what I mean. The light inside could be the sun outside, which has to be the source of all light on earth. Or maybe what firesoul see as fire is really the reflection of the sun, which might bounce about in the inside of their skulls, like in a cave of shadows. It would do that, don't you think. Have you considered that possibility at all?

'But going inside must restrict the flow. So watersoul generally prefer the outwards perspective. The higher vantage point is advantageous, like my hill, you know. I could see everything from there. Then you don't need all these books.' And she drops the bundle under her arm, and a crowd of village youngsters run up and catch the pages as they fall, and eagerly show each other that the paper is blank on one side. As they run about I can feel their feet thundering in my head. I chase after then to retrieve my precious book, and my feet are so cold in the damp dark of the cave and I turn to ask Mother Sage the way to the hill, but she has turned into a blood-red stream and is flowing away.

I wade into her stream. The water bubbles merrily over the rocks and makes room for my legs as I wade in. I sink down slowly into the chilliness and rub my belly and chest and my upper arms. Submerged up to my neck I float and can twist about. Taking a breath I roll over, duck my hair in the water to get it clean. My hair is long and green. I watch the green tendrils waving and little fish darting through them. There are curving channels in the muddy bottom, which part at each stone leaving it isolated and washed clean.

I say to Mother Sage, who is the stream, 'I am fire and molten rock which wants to be water and mud like you. The fire makes the stone; the water wears down the stone into mud. Then there is life in the earth. And fire destroys life, as firesoul had destroyed life before. So, what was the pattern that had to be completed?'

'You can see it for yourself,' says Mother Sage. 'You don't need me any more.'

And I look up at the stars and I see they are the firesoul people, billions and billions of souls. I stare up and the lights go out one by one, each little pattern disappears, and at last the pattern of patterns is gone, so how can it be completed? And I see that they did it to themselves. Each of the patterns was incomplete because its entire being was annihilated by its own certainty that its own past pattern does not exist, so even what had been never was.

To believe that the past only exists in memories stored in the cells of a brain which rots away at death means that death destroys everything. Their only hope of escape from oblivion was the belief, that some of the people clung to, that they have immortal souls separate from their bodies which would survive death and continue living in future lives, to be reborn on earth or to go to some other world. And they keep all the dead bodies safely in case they are needed again.

But time ceases when a pattern ends; there is no future, only the

263

timeless past, which firesoul does not know. So all the firesouls met oblivion at death, and ceased to know that they had ever been: a state of ultimate incompleteness, which would have to be resolved else the human pattern in its entirety would never reach completion. Is that what Mother Sage says I know?

So maybe ... just possibly ... could it be that ... my task is to make the transition from firesoul to watersoul so that all those uncompleted firesoul patterns would follow me and wake up to their immortality?

But can it be done, changing one's deepest nature like that? The village people are so strange. How can I become like them? Even for the high purpose I had been shown.

But had I been shown any purpose? Maybe it was just a notion. It sounded too huge a purpose anyhow.

But then, watersoul seem to have no purpose. They prefer nothing to change from the patterns of the village in the past. So for me to become watersoul I have to have no purpose. If this is the purpose, I have to forget it.

So when I go to the village it is best to go for no reason, but just because it is there. Or because I need pleasure and company and something to do. If being part of the busyness down there takes the blinkers of my mind away and lets my watersoul free, perhaps that in itself will begin a pattern for the other firesoul boys to follow. That is the best I can hope to achieve. No, forget about achieving. I must get back to the village.

Roy woke up in the village. He was in a sleeping hut with the curtain drawn back to let in the light. Fey was leaning over him.

'I got back to the village,' he smiled.

Fey turned to someone standing on the ladder looking in. 'I think you could fetch him some food now,' she said in mime-song.

He felt his stomach heaving, and he leaned over the bowl she held and brought up a vile bitter taste and little else.

Fey wiped his mouth and held a cup of water for him to sip.

'Life's thrown me up again,' Roy joked. 'I went to the forest, you know, to escape the ups and downs. How did I get back?'

'You went to the forest and ate some poisonous mushrooms,' she said. 'You had such a dream we all heard it and knew where to find you. You're lucky they only gave you bad dreams.'

'I thought it was a lovely dream; perhaps I'll go back to it,' Roy said, feeling his mind drifting. 'I'm going to save all the firesoul: billions and billions of them, like the stars in the sky,' and he waved his arms about.

'Silly firesoul boy, such big ideas!' she said. 'Now you must try to stay awake. You've been very sick.'

'You're speaking my language, is this our third day?' Roy asked. 'What happened to the baby? No, no, it's all right, I'm not going to make judgements. I know about judgements. I finished my book, you know, with an index and everything. Where is my book? There was something in the dream. Oh, never mind. What's going to happen now?'

Someone came with a bowl of fruit puree. Fey fed it to him with a little bone spoon. He felt his stomach heave, but he kept the food down. After a while gurgling noises came from his insides.

'That's a good sign,' said Fey.

Roy's dreams were soon to resume. The village was settling down for hibernation and Roy was to be included. He was sharing a sleeping hut with a lot of other people, including Fey. People changed huts and companions less frequently than he remembered from before, and there were about twice as many to each hut: twelve one time when he managed to count them.

At first he was sure he would not be able to hibernate. He would be getting up and out while there was daylight. He did so for a few days, but it was very still and quiet and empty outside, with a haunted feel to it which reminded him of being in the old house and garden. So he went back inside, snuggled up for a bit of pleasure rubbing, and dozed.

'What are you making?' she asks. 'It looks like a shoe. You're making a shoe out of river mud.'

I look up and smile. 'You'll see what it is when I've finished. Look, I've done all these different ones, to see which works best. Careful! they're quite soft,' I warn her, as she goes to pick one up. I was going to smooth out her finger prints, but I decide to leave them there.

Carefully I carry the wicker tray the objects are standing on and I look around for the place where the sun shines hottest. A rock island in the river looks ideal. There is nothing to shade it and it will stay sunny all day. But how can I get there with my burden? I put the tray down on the grassy bank. Then I sit on the edge and swing my legs over until my feet are dangling in the water. How deep is it? I strip off my tunic. Edging myself further down I feel the side of the bank smooth against my heels. The water is waist high when I feel the stones of the river bed. I wade gingerly in the direction of the sunny island. Some boys have gathered to watch.

'Don't touch those things on the tray,' I warn them.

'What are they?' one of them asks.

'I think they're clay shoes,' Fey tells them, and they laugh. 'What are you doing, Roy? Can't you swim?' she calls to me.

'I want to put the tray on this island so the clay will bake in the sun.'

'We'll help,' a boy says. He organises the others into a chain from the river's edge to the island. Then they pass the tray from one hand to the next.

All day long the objects stand in the hot summer sun. In the evening I gather the boys together again and we retrieve the tray. Gently I thread a piece of linen cord through the narrow hole in the 'toe' of one of the clay 'shoes', and carefully pour nut oil into the larger opening. I rub two sticks together under a pile of dry grass and strips of bark until I have a spark, and the grass catches fire. I wait for the ends of the bark to catch fire and I take a burning strip and put it to the wick. The oil burns with a bright steady flame. Success, first time. I hold up the lamp. 'Look, boys, we have light!'

Roy was pleased with this dream and decided to record it. He crawled out of the sleeping huddle, slowly and carefully so as not to disturb anyone. He untied the rope to let down the basket with his clothes in and dressed. He drew aside the thick curtain and squeezed through, lifted the flap door and wriggled his legs out onto the ladder. The light was dazzling. When he emerged he saw that everywhere was brilliant white. It had snowed in the night.

Coming down the ladder he found that the snow was not very deep, but it had drifted against the store door, so he cleared it away. He opened the door and helped himself to a handful of nuts and an apple, shut the door and secured the catch. He walked a few paces and then urinated, making a yellow stain in the whiteness.

To record the dream he had to go up the hill to the house. It was not possible to keep any personal belongings in the village because anything could happen to them. Children might play with his papers and mess them up as happened in his dream. As he walked he composed what he would write.

The dream was the latest in a series on the same theme. There had

266

been a progression. In the earliest ones he had failed to make the lamps: he could not find suitable clay, could not get the shape right, the objects collapsed or crumbled to dust when they dried. Then he could not make fire: could not find suitable sticks, or dry grass, or get the bark taper to burn. Then the lamps did not work: the wick would not light, or it went out, or the oil burned too fast, or made dense choking smoke. So this last dream was a triumph. 'Let there be light!' he proclaimed out loud.

He hands the lamp to a boy, who looks at it in wonder. 'What is it for?' he asks.

'To light the darkness,' I tell him.

'But why?' says the boy.

'So that you do not have to sleep as soon as night comes.'

'We don't have to sleep when night comes now. It is a time for pleasure.'

'Yes, but now you can stay up and see to make things in the evenings and have more time in the daylight for gardening.'

'But we have enough time now to make all we want.'

'You could exchange mime-song with each other and tell stories.'

'We don't need stories, we have eversight. And it is too cold at night to sit up and talk; it is better to snuggle up together for pleasure rubbing.'

'Now you have fire you can make stoves to keep warm. Perhaps I should make a stove next out of clay.'

I struggle and struggle to make a stove. And last I succeed. I fetch dry wood from the forest and assemble it in the stove. I light the fire.

Fey sees my fire. She rushes to it. She throws herself onto the stove and smashes it. The fire sets light to her clothes and she burns. I scream and scream.

'Hush, hush, you'll wake everyone,' said Fey, putting her hand over Roy's mouth.

I am in the between-forest: between the first and second firebreaks. I am hunting the flightless birds that live here. I have shot several with my catapult and put them in the bag over my shoulder. The last bird I shot at I lost. I was sure I had hit it, but it shuffled off into the undergrowth, and I am trying to follow it.

I fancy there is a movement over there, but mouldy leaves muffle sound. The dappled shade makes ghostly patterns which could be anything or nothing. Even the bright red-brown of the bird is camouflaged here.

I feel something behind me. I sense, but cannot see or hear, whatever it is skirting around me in a wide arc. It is ahead of me now. Is that it there? The grey shape. Some large animal. The tiny muscles on my skin tingle with fear.

The grey shape approaches, a creeping forward and a crouching. I freeze. Closer and closer it comes. Suddenly it darts forward. Something drops at my feet. The grey shape leaps away in two twisted bounds. I look down. There is the red bird, still living but wounded. I despatch it with a sharp stone I carry with me for this purpose, and put the warm body in my bag.

I look up to where my helper leapt away. I see it now, sitting, back legs crouched down, forelegs straight. It's head is tilted to one side, mouth agape and panting. It regards me as if puzzled, as much with itself as at me. I sense it remembers a bond between us. I remember it too. I move towards it but it dashes away. 'Goodbye, old friend,' I call softly after it. See you again soon.

I have another friend now besides Fey. He is a boy, younger than I am. I call him Amadeus, after a famous musician, but only to myself. He is watersoul so he does not want an individual name. But he likes me and we spend much time together at the old house.

I am teaching Amadeus mathematics. He is an able pupil, and is happy to use his mind this way, unlike Fey, who won't talk to me in my language any more. Amadeus likes the books Mother Sage and I had bound in covers. He likes to turn the pages, and he will read aloud when I ask him to, and he listens when I explain the ideas, and he seems to grasp them straight away.

In return, Amadeus is instructing me about music. The villagers do not have any music, unless you count their mime-song as music, but it is more like the tweeting of birds, as Mother Sage used to say. But Amadeus is using his eversight, like Mother Sage used to do, to shift to the lives of musicians in necrotech and tell me how they experienced music.

I learned a little of the theory of harmony when I was a boy. Mother Sage and I used to sing together, sometimes exercises, but also lovely tunes she had experienced on her shifts. She had someone make a bamboo pipe for me, but I never learned to play it very well, so she allowed me to drop that part of my studies. I found the pipe and gave it to Amadeus to play, which he was able to do when he came back from the shifts. Now he is teaching me to play. I am struggling, but I am determined to master this art.

I have plans to introduce firesoul music to the village. I believe they are too wary of anything firesoul, but music cannot be bad. Mother Sâge used to say that music was the best part of firesoul culture. When I understand it well enough Amadeus and I will have more instruments made. With village materials various wind and string and percussion instruments can be made. We shall have an orchestra, and a choir. It will be wonderful!

When spring came and the village came out of hibernation, Roy was eager to tell Fey about his dreams. She was willing to listen, but she made it clear she did not intend to speak to him in his language; she would only respond in mime-song. She also conveyed the suggestion that Roy should resume the experiment.

Roy related to Fey all his dreams, and his interpretation and elaboration of them, which consisted of various aspects of Roy's two realisations: the synthesis between watersoul and firesoul; and the awakening of the firesoul to their immortality. She listened attentively, and made no attempt to criticise or argue.

While Fey was busy with life in the village, Roy was engaged in his personal projects: getting out of his head through Fey's experiment and what he thought of as Mother Sage's alternatives of further writing and inward meditation; and finding himself ways of contributing to village life and learning some skills. He became fluent at mime-song, managed to make some functionally adequate gathering baskets and learned to recognise more herbs. What he enjoyed most was firebreak clearing work because it required little skill and plenty of hard work, and it meant going through the forest, which he loved.

Following on from the music dream, Roy brought down from the house the bamboo pipe which he found still hanging by its decorative tassels on a peg on the schoolroom wall. He tried to interest the children in playing the pipe. They humoured him, but did not seem at all thrilled by being able to make tunes.

After several attempts Roy became quite frustrated, and told Fey about it and asked for her help. When he had finished she sat in silence for a while. Then she indicated she had something important to tell him, that she would tell it in mime-song, and that they would work on this until he understood.

The communication required them to invent gestures and sounds for some ideas not usually conveyed in this language. At first Roy was pleased with the task. But as he began to see what it was she had to tell him, he became overwhelmed with disappointment.

Watersoul had nothing to gain from firesoul music. They were attuned to the experience and knowledge of the patterns, in which were melodies and harmonies more fascinating, delightful and wonderful than any music could be. Music had been the nearest firesoul could come to knowing the patterns, to transcending the handicap of being aware only of the present and losing the timeless past. Music allowed them to trap in their minds crude copies of partial patterns, and grasp faint echoes of the sonorous intricacies of the patterns, which are the essence and spirit of all that has ever been.

'But Mother Sage said that everything has eversight,' Roy said imploringly. She nodded, her black eyes glistening with sympathetic tears. He continued to the unavoidable conclusion, 'So every creature, plant, animal, rock, water, air, star, everything knows the more-than-music of the patterns. Only firesoul has shut himself away with the less-than-pattern of music as consolation.' She drew him close and he sobbed brokenly in her arms.

He mumbled into her hair, 'And I suppose it's the same with art and poetry and dancing. All we can do is make echoes and shadows in our heads and tell ourselves we're the most advanced creatures that ever evolved, and all the time we're the lowest and deafest and blindest and stupidest.'

At last he calmed down a little and pulled away from her.

'Thank you for telling me,' he said. 'It's always best to know. I knew before, but there's knowing and really knowing. I'll just have to work harder to get outside my head. I'll go and write it all this down; that usually helps.'

She smiled and nodded and gave him a squeeze, and gestured, 'Go along then, I'll see you later.'

Roy trudged up the hill, deep in despair. 'I was so happy,' he moaned to himself, 'I'd got everything worked out, and then: smash! life knocks me down again. That seems to be my pattern since Mother Sage died. They should have left me in the forest.'

Part way up the hill Roy left the path to go to the place where Fey had given birth. He did his meditation there. The place humbled him. It helped to remind him of how much he did not understand about the fey and the village. In spite of all the ups and downs, he still had the habit of thinking of himself as the person he was brought up to be: the young lord, with a good mind, whose ideas mattered, with an important role in the New Beginning for civilisation. That self-confident personality bobbed up again whatever happened, and the lessons he had been learning about his own inadequacy never quite got home. So he came to the place where his fondest dreams had been shattered, to remind himself not to hope.

He pulled off his boots and his tunic and sat where Fey had sat. He looked at the pool where her baby had died, now clear and clean. He had taught himself not to pity the baby. It was a small step now to pity himself. Even that baby knew the patterns, was part of the patterns still.

'I've got to get out of my head!' Roy cried out, and he thought he heard the sound reverberate somewhere in the hills above him, perhaps from Mother Sage's vigil place, perhaps from where he had that dream after eating the mushrooms. But to hear himself in the huge space which was outside his head was frightening. He would be safer back inside himself.

'I can't get out,' he moaned, 'I won't let myself.'

He felt so wretched he was desperate. He threw himself off the bank into the stream and its jagged rocks. He banged his head down onto the rocks as if to smash a way out, and banged and banged again, and blood spurted out and dyed the pool red once more.

He came to, and found himself cradled in Fey's lap, with an excruciating pain on his forehead. He put a hand up to touch it and felt the cut ends of threads sticking up. Someone had put stitches in his head, which was swollen tight and hot.

'Don't touch. I've mended you,' Fey said in his language. 'You didn't come back for supper, so I went to look for you.'

'I wanted to get out of my head,' Roy whispered.

'You can't do it like this, silly boy. The others wanted to take you to the forest. We don't usually mend people.'

'No, I suppose you wouldn't,' he almost nodded, but it hurt.

'What are we going to do with you until the firesouls come?'

'Are they coming?'

'Oh yes, the trek has started.'

271

'When will it get here?'

'A little before next hibernation, I think.'

'Why so long?'

'Firesouls are joining the trek one each day from each village they pass. They are approaching a place on the second firebreak a moon cycle from here where several threads of the trek will join up, but each of the threads has a long way still to go before they get to the joining place.'

'Will you come with me?'

'Yes, I will come with you. But that is enough talking. Try to sleep now.'

Roy had a quiet summer. Now he had something to look forward to he was more settled in his mind, although that event seemed far off, and full of its own uncertainties. He decided to enjoy the warm weather and the lovely village gardens, then it would be harvest and feasting time. After that his new life would begin.

He was still hopeful that the two cultures would be able to coexist, and have gifts to offer each other. The mushroom dream of leading the firesoul to immortality was now an embarrassing memory. He knew he had been out of his mind with madness rather than with enlightened consciousness.

At last summer was past, and the season came for the harvest and feasting which Roy had missed the previous year. Everyone ate as they picked and prepared food for storage. They stuffed themselves with fruit and nuts, which Roy enjoyed, and fresh-killed raw meat, which he left to them. There was much giggling and silly antics associated with baskets of fungus which were hallucinogenic, but mildly so, and not poisonous, so he had a little and felt and acted silly too. It was wonderful to let his mind have a holiday.

There was even more pleasure rubbing than usual, but any girl around his own age whom he approached darted away giggling. He was not to be included in the courting going on between boys and girls, who were, he judged, barely past puberty. The boys wooed the girls by enticing them to places in the gardens and forest by leaving trails of presents, linked together by picture clues drawn on scraps of material. Roy remembered Mother Sage talking about these games, and how the youngsters had taken to using their leftover paper for this purpose. He picked up some of the scraps to study later.

He followed one of the girls to see what the couple would do when

272

she reached her wooer, but as he knew from the paper Mother Sage had written, they did not have sex together, did not even engage in the usual pleasure rubbing. They mime-sang and flirted. They returned to the village hand in hand. At night they went to separate sleeping houses and the next day had little to do with each other, their courtship apparently done. In the middle of winter they would emerge from hibernation, pair up as decided by the courtship and engage in hasty sexual intercourse. The courtship itself was a silly, apparently pointless performance. But it occurred to him that other animals had silly, apparently pointless mating rituals too.

Roy looked at the bundle of love notes he had picked up.

'That's funny,' he said to himself, 'It looks as if they've still got some scrap paper left from when Mother Sage was alive. That's her writing on the back.'

He looked more closely and realised to his horror that the writing was part of the pattern mathematics. What had happened?

There was only one way to find out. He went up the hill at a run. He reached the house panting with effort and anxiety. He dashed up to his old room.

His writing basket was open, and empty, so the precious papers of his book of the watersoul village ways were destroyed too. There were signs that the youngsters had been writing their love notes and clues in his room, and had used his pens and ink. A snowy layer of scraps littered the floor.

In a panic he dashed to Mother Sage's room. Her basket was closed. He looked inside. At least the books of mathematics for the New Beginning were safe.

He went back to his room and collected the scraps together and put them back in the baskets. They were quite full, so perhaps there was not much missing. 'Perhaps I could find all the pieces and fit them together again. It's not as if they've been burnt. Every piece is around somewhere. But what a task to fit it back together!'

He ran back to the village. He found Fey and told her what had happened. She rounded up some of the courting boys and girls, and explained in mime-song that Roy wanted back the pieces of paper they had used. She showed no sign of being displeased with them, but he should not have expected her to.

They engaged in this hunt as if it were another game, dashing around the favourite trysts, rummaging around in the scented ramblers trailing up the trellis walls of thatched bowers, peering under garden seats, poking under lavender bushes and sage plants in the herb spirals, seeking in every cosy nook and cranny and flowery bank in the orchards and the near forest.

They brought back baskets full of scraps. Inwardly groaning, and full of frustrated anger, Roy had to smile his thanks. He packed all the pieces into one basket with an arching handle for easy carrying. He filled a similar basket with provisions. He heaved a bedding roll over his shoulder, picked up the baskets and made his way back up the hill. He collapsed exhausted on his bed.

In the morning Fey arrived at the house with a someone Roy did not recognise. 'This is the messenger,' she said. 'We've got to go now.

'Go where?'

'To join the trek.' she said. 'We'll go from here.'

'I'll fetch the mathematics books. It's a pity about the others – the ones which really mattered.'

'Less for me to carry, though.'

'We'll only need one basket. Why should you carry it?'

'They'll expect that. I'm your slave wife, remember!'

15

The Completion

So, dear reader from necrotech,
we have almost reached the end of the
story: the story of humanity. You have arrived at the completion time
where my life is, and there is little more to tell. At the beginning of my
story for you, I promised I would tell you why the people of my time
are taking journeys into our past, which is your future.

My story for you has been my thesis for the Completion Archive.
When I have finished it, I shall return to my village. We do not know if
anyone will read these books. Perhaps no one will, but in case the last
cycle of the ages has not yet come, we are leaving a record of our
understanding for those who follow. We set these records down in
writing, not to be preserved in physical form, but to go to the patterns
as writing to be picked up as such, and set down again. I have chosen to
write my book for the troubled time at the end of necrotech.

I have not put anything about myself in until now, because I felt that it
would confuse you, my reader, who had so far to come and so much to
take in. So I shall say just a little now.

I am now doing the final copying out from the records I made of my
shifts. At dawn this morning I climbed barefoot all the way up the hill
above our village, up the natural stairway of stones beside the stream to
the tree I call the fire tree. It is past harvest season now and the tree is
laden with glowing berries. Its scarlet and orange leaves within leaves
make tongues of flame against the sky. Opposite the fire tree, is a great
flat rock, overhung by another, and thatched from above with a thick
grass mat. It is cosy and sheltered here. I am sitting with my legs
crossed, tucking my cold feet under my thick knitted gown.

I made this gown while awaiting my baby. Others from my village
went on the journey to where the fibre plants grow, which was too tiring

for me with my great belly. They gathered the stems, and soaked them to remove the threads. With juice from crushed berries, I dyed some of the rolls of fibre a soft blue. I spun the thread myself using a distaff and spindle. Then I knitted the garment slowly. We prefer to work slowly, and interweave our working rhythms with our wanderings in the paths of time. The patterns in the wood of the tree from which the needles were made added their immortal nature to each stitch, and the patterns of the lifetimes of my baby were reflected in the fabric.

My baby came late in my bleeding years. Other girls conceived when they were twelve, thirteen, or fourteen summers. I was sixteen, and thought myself infertile, like so many others in this twilight of our kind. For two years I suckled him. Then he went for his raising to those who had done their completion task. Now my work is nearly finished, and it was decided that this should be the last. We are expecting the call for the last journey to reach us very soon.

I am writing in the book which I made. The paper itself I made from fibre plant pulp, pressed and dried. I stitched the bundles of sheets together, over tapes, and glued the bundles to webbing with boiled animal glue. I made thick card and treated some skins and formed these into a cover. I glued the first and last pages and the tapes to the inside of the cover, and the book was done. The squareness of the book frightens me, and my name, whose letters I pressed onto its spine. They are firesoul patterns.

We had a naming before the book making. Before the naming I had no name: it is not our way. My name is Pool. They gave me this name for my blue eyes and calm round face and wavy hair. I like the name but I shall forget it when the task is done. Not long now; the birth of my book is near, the last stage of labour almost over.

Before the book-making were the shifts: journeys through the patterns of the present past, which we remembered and recorded. Then we had to select the ones which made up a journey a reader could follow, and reach coherent understanding of the patterns of humankind. Then if there is another cycle, we hope it will be less painful than the one before.

Before the shift we learnt the language of words, so that we could understand the thinking of the subject of the shift. When we knew the language of words we explored the Completion Library, smoothing threads of puzzlement by picking through the thesis books of past completion tasks, until we felt ready.

The completion age has been the age of reconciliation and letting go. The watersoul at last gave up their fear of firesoul. The firesoul learned to recognise what the watersoul had achieved, and gave up their futile ambitions and pride.

My people are the last embers of the firesoul, although we are scarcely firesoul at all, having absorbed much of watersoul nature. As you know, we have eversight. We also live almost in the watersoul way in that we do not use fire or disturb the ground. But we have the firesoul conception of time, and so we expect there to be an end to any journey or story. We see the completion as the end, and hence as the death and extinction of humankind. We fear annihilation and oblivion in the time following that final death.

We have the firesoul need to understand before we can let go the lofty human aspirations which were never realised. There will be no brave journeys through outer space to the stars. There will be no colonisation of galaxies. We shall never know if there are firesoul people on other planets, but we hope that if there are, they draw on the lessons we have learnt, rather than carrying our pain and suffering into the future.

The process we have engaged in during the completion age – and a long age it has been, of many generations – has taught us what the completion is not. The completion is not the working out to reach understanding. It is not the death, the end or the letting go. What the completion is can be stated very simply: it is the stage in the life cycle of a pattern when all its potential has been experienced. At that stage, time has no meaning because there is no further change. The completion of the human pattern would be humanity's complete fulfilment.

The irony is that human fulfilment has already been attained: by the watersoul in the pattern age. What more could there be to achieve than a life of communal pleasure, harmony and security in the immortal past? The watersoul enjoyed complete happiness: the satisfaction of gardening and craft work and indulgence in indiscriminate sensual delight. They were wise, passionate, brutal yet wholly innocent. The population of watersoul individuals grew to be greater than that of necrotech at its most populous, since their gardens were highly productive and caused no destruction. Wilderness beyond human influence flourished and evolved undisturbed. New life forms spread into the forests bordering the watersoul gardens, introducing fresh variation for the designs. The pattern age rolled on as if interminably, while the watersoul continued to intermingle with nature in their gardens and nearby forests. At times

277

and places, natural events destroyed some villages or moved them on. Ice Ages, in particular, drove a slow human tide away from or towards the poles, onto and off coastal land. Still the watersoul thrived.

There were occasional New Beginnings of firesoul during the pattern age. Cities were built, large areas of wild forest were destroyed. Once their resources were exhausted, the cities failed, and the forests recovered again from the perpetual patterns. As the cycle repeated, the firesoul grew sometimes nearer and sometimes further away from the realisation that to take any more from nature than food, clothing, a few utensils and shelter for sleeping destroys the wild forest and makes shortages and conflict, and begins a vicious spiral of destruction and suffering: the cultural pattern of firesoul. The watersoul suffered enslavement and displacement at firesoul hands. They grew sometimes less and sometimes more afraid of firesoul patterns destroying their ways and inturning their minds.

You may wonder what happened to Roy's New Beginning, but that is not important. I doubt whether the firesoul men would have been deterred by Roy's insights. The burning desire to keep going is a strong firesoul pattern, and unless many others had become close enough to the watersoul to question their own nature, the march would have pressed on regardless.

Roy did come to understand what completion is. On another shift, I became Roy, still on the march, in conversation with Alfred.

'I still don't see what the completion of the human pattern would be,' Alfred was saying.

'I'm not sure, but I think it's when we're just going round and round the same cycle, and the tiny bit of difference each time round just vanishes, and the cycles of time cease, but we're all still there: complete and unchanging.'

'Could our pattern "shine through the holes", like in the pattern mathematics, and be part of further patterns elsewhere in the universe?' suggested Alfred, his eyes sparkling.

'Maybe,' said Roy, 'but wouldn't thinking that just be firesoul ambition and arrogance?'

'That's a bit hard! Surely, there has to be intelligent life on other planets, in other star systems, in the past or in the future, and wouldn't we influence each other – completed or not?' Alfred persisted.

'We can't *know* there are other stars,' Roy remarked.

'Of course there are – we can see them.'

'Perhaps we're seeing the same star repeated in space and time. The watersoul villagers don't see any stars. They make love and sleep at night, and don't worship any gods they might look for in the heavens.'

'I wouldn't want such a limited vision of the cosmos!'

'The watersoul see depths of complexity and change around about them. To them, what is near is unlimited, what is beyond the horizon or above the sky has no appeal or reality, and so it doesn't exist for them. It is our vision that is limited – tiny sparks of life isolated in eternities and infinities of space and time, and eventual oblivion for everything.'

We do not expect there to be any further New Beginnings: we few remaining firesoul have lost any desire for civilisation. To us it seems that the watersoul people have already gone from the earth, having dwindled away in their villages, untroubled by their end coming upon them since they know they cannot cease to be present and aware in the timeless patterns.

We remain, awaiting our end, doing whatever it occurs to us to do before we are able, at last, to face the final letting go.

In my time humanity has been waning. In all the villages the courtship time narrowed. Fewer babies were born to younger and younger mothers. Some failed to mature sexually and were sterile.

What little is still to come I can tell you now.

Epilogue

As their numbers dwindled they merged their little bands into larger, until at last there came a time when no more children matured sexually. Their bodies stayed childlike though full grown.

Then they called each other to gather together into one last group – in the land once called Africa where humanity had been born.

They picked up their gathering baskets, their traps, their bedding and their few implements, and set out on the long last trek. From all directions they came. From the vast cold and temperate reaches, from the warm band around the equator. Those who had oceans in their direct path veered polewards until they reached a land or ice bridge.

It was many season cycles before all were assembled. Most died on the journey. Those who gathered in their final home would scarcely have populated a small village; old children with calm all-wise faces and innocent bodies.

They discarded their traps and lived on the fruits of the forest.

Each new-moon-rise they gathered in a great wheel and drowned in the pale light, sending their wordless, soundless song to the universe, as if to say: 'The human story is completed, this is the end.'

One by one the forest took them. Until there were – no more.